Zephrum Gates
&
The Belly
of The Beast

By Tricia Riel

This book is a work of fiction. People, places, events, and situations are the product of the author's imagination. Any resemblance to actual persons, living or dead, or historical events, is purely coincidental.

Zephrum Gates & The Belly of The Beast

Kindle Direct Publishing, Seattle, Washington

Special Thanks

Big Thanks to my amazing literary editor (Susan Sernau). Susan helped me bring every page to life with specific feedback on rhythm & pacing, she reminded me to "show" & not "tell"... & she helped me to craft an incredible synopsis. She always believed in the story & she says that I'm her favorite author to work with. ☺

Big thanks to my first love (Ed Rossi, "Eddie Spaghetti") for reading the entire manuscript & giving me valuable insight on the writing & the characters, to my niece (Julianne Saunders) who read the early chapters & gave me junior editorial perspectives, to good friend Beth Brown (for reading the early chapters & giving me clever advice on the direction of the story), to (Brandy Whisenant) for the imaginative Zephrum Gates cover art, to our incredibly sweet photographer (Sarah Meyer) for taking photos of the chapter sketches, to my birthday sister (Kelly Karaba/"Kelly Compost") for invaluable computer graphics help on the cover, to BFF Sheyda Gomez (for her enthusiastic support), to Jet Markov (for creating the Audible Book Covers & for being very "punny"), to Darienne Highsmith (for saving the day with formatting help), to all of the Zephrum Gates characters (for helping me feel a little less alone in the world), to my super community, to my supportive family, and to the amazing Nakita (for being an anchor for my heart & soul for so many years).

This book is dedicated to Nakita, one of the greatest loves of my life. To some, she was just a dog. To me, she was the best friend a girl could have ever asked for. My peaceful warrior & furry Zen master playmate. Here's to keeping her spirit alive, as we do with all of those that live in our hearts.

Dedicated to Nakita

Zephrum Gates & The Belly of The Beast

Table of Contents

Tricia Riel

--Chapter 1--

"The Mountain Cave"

It was a dark and stormy night. The winds howled and rain came down in sheets. Droplets like arrows inundated the sky with a downpour of endless wetness. Lightning cracked the heavens and thunder rumbled in the distance.

With each bursting blue fire bolt from the storm, a painful moan sighed from the darkest part of a high mountain hollow. "AAhhhoooahh…"

Simmering atop an abandoned fire pit in the den, a sizzling cauldron oozed with sludge and slime. A strange hissing sound emanated from the pewter pot. "Sssssss…."

The vessel shook and quivered. Gnarled fingers reached over the edges of the cauldron and clutched the rim.

A slight tremor shook the pot. Contorted hands wrapped around the cauldron's margins. Finally, a shriveled body emerged from the slimy goo. It looked part goblin and part horror. The gooey monster slithered out of the giant basin and flopped onto the stone slab beneath.

The creature gasped for breath. Its eyelids fluttered, revealing glowing yellow eyes with jet black slits in the center. Then, as one last lightning bolt fractured the upper atmosphere, the creature screeched again.

"Aaaarrrghhh…"

Writhing, its body stretched and stood upright. The being trembled as it lumbered to the cave's entrance. It was dripping with green mucus. Hunchbacked and shivering in its own gunk at the edge of the world, the monster howled. The roar pierced the storm into an instant silence.

"Raaaarrrr…AHHH!"

"TWO Voices!?!?" screamed the creature.

Long twiggy fingers wrapped around its head and pulled at its pointy ears. "WHY must I hear TWO voices?"

The mutated beast hit its head with its gooey fists. "This is TORTURE!"

Another voice spoke from within the creature. "It is I, Master. Your faithful goblin servant, Virgil."

The creature looked down at its hands in disbelief.

"How can this be?" said the stronger voice. "Virgil? How is it that I can hear YOU within my OWN mind?"

"Master, I was plunged into your vat of sludge. I cannot say for how long I was in there. But now, it appears we are ONE."

"Aaarrrr…"

The creature slammed its body into the rock wall, "Get OUT! Get out of my head! LEAVE me!"

"I cannot," sniveled the goblin voice.

"But you MUST!" The creature banged its body up against the rock wall with greater force.

"Strasidous. Sire. I cannot. You are within me now. I know not how, but I hear you as though you are myself."

The creature flailed itself around the cave, falling over boulders and stumbling over thick stalagmites from the floor.

Finally, breathless and bloody… it stopped.

"And what of Zephrum Gates? Is she no longer?"

The goblin voice shivered from within. "I know not, sire. I believe she be f..f..fr..free. I was plunged into your cauldron in her place."

"Aaarrr…" The creature arched its body upward and screamed, "But it is SHE that we must capture, not YOU!"

"Yes, Sire. We must capture Zephrum Gates… together."

"TOGETHER?!?" The creature cocked its head and snarled.

"Yes, Sire. We are now ONE. Your aims are MY aims, YOUR wishes are MY desires. MY body is YOURS to use as YOU see fit."

"But… This is madness." The creature banged itself upon the head.

"Yes, Sire… And yet, it appears to be truth. We are Strasidious and Virgil together. You are more powerful than you were before, more able. You are more than a mere wisp of ether in a vat of sludge. You have a body again, a body that you can now use."

The eyes rolled back inside its head, "Virgil and Strasidous? Together as ONE?"

"Yes, Sire. Although it defies all logic, it appears to be so."

"We are… Aaaaargh….." "VIRGIDOUS!!"

Lightning struck and crackled, splitting the very fabric of the sky. The rock floor shook beneath their feet.

"Yes, Sire. Whatever you say. Virgidous, we are."

Looking at his slimy arms, a slow grin spread across the monster's face. "Now that I have a body, I can capture Zephrum Gates. I can stop her power from growing. I can block her from defeating me. I can absorb her before she is able to do any more in the name of 'good' in the world!"

"Yes, Sire. As is your wish, you may do what you like."

At that, the new "Virgidous" grabbed a random piece of burlap material from the empty dragon's nest on the rock floor and wrapped it around himself. He snatched a sack of coins and jewels from the mound of plenty in this dragon's den and started scaling down the mountain.

"It's now or never."

"Yes, sire… Now or never."

"SHUT UP, Virgil!" said the voice, grabbing himself roughly by the arm.

"Yes, sire… Whatever you say."

"As we journey, I will unveil my plan. We are going to be VERY busy, my strange friend. Very busy indeed."

The slithering figure of "Virgidous" slunk down the mountain in the dark of the night until he disappeared as a mere speck in the blackening darkness.

--Chapter 2--

"The Cabin"

The evening storm left a wet freshness all over the plants of the forest. The sun sparkled upon leaves and ferns as though the violent squall from the night before had never happened.

Deep within the glistening woods outside of Haversville was a quaint little cabin, tucked into a clearing amongst the trees. It was a snug house, thickly surrounded by herbs and flowers. The wooden porch of the humble home was the stage for a couple of rocking chairs and a number of potted plants. Hummingbirds chirped and fluttered around the cottage. Sunbeams tunneled through the forest, lighting up the small log house.

Through the kitchen window, came the sharp sound of someone hammering on a steel pipe.

A muffled voice came from under the sink, "Zephrum… Can you pass me that 'thing-a-ma-jig' on the kitchen countertop?"
Zephrum's Great Aunt Gussie was tinkering with the plumbing under her kitchen basin. She moved her shoulders under the sink, then banged her head on a pipe. "Ouch… I can't make head nor tails out of things down here."
"Huh? What?" said Zephrum, shaking off her daydream. She looked up sheepishly from her bowl of breakfast mush.

"Get me that 'doo-hickey' on the counter, will you?" Great Aunt Gussie's voice was muted.

Zephrum looked over at the tools that were spread out on the counter. "Which one is the 'doo-hickey'?"

"You know… The one with the rubber 'whosie-what's it' for a handle. It's red."

"Sometimes, understanding Great Aunt Gussie is about as easy as stapling water to a tree," muttered Zephrum as she rose from the table.

"Hurry up, Zephrum. It smells like a turd-supermarket under here."

Zephrum giggled as she grabbed the tool with the red handle, and handed it down to Great Aunt Gussie.

"What took you so long?" Aunt Gussie gripped the tool. "Oh…my favorite wrench. This tool is the best thing since sliced bread."

There was more clanging and banging from under the sink. Then Aunt Gussie said, "I think this will fix it. Turn that faucet on up there, will you? Give it a whirl."

Zephrum turned the water faucet on. "Ahhh…" bellowed Aunt Gussie from below. "Turn that darned thing off!"

Zephrum quickly twisted the tap in the other direction. Aunt Gussie emerged from under the counters. Water dripped from the curlers in her hair. "Well… everything's just coming up goose eggs down there. I guess we'll need to make a visit to the hardware store to get some new parts. That leak will turn into a little lake under the sink if we don't do something about it soon. Water, water, everywhere."

Aunt Gussie put a small bucket under the leak. "When we go into town, we should get you some new notebooks and visit the bookstore too. We just got a letter about your new classes at Fiddlesticks. Looks like you'll need a good number of books this year. Your head is likely to explode with all the new information you'll learn."

"Explode?!?" cried Zephrum.

"Oh… Don't have a cow! Classes at Fiddlesticks will be challenging this year, but the teachers are planning some fascinating subjects for you."

Zephrum sighed. If this year was going to be as wild and dangerous as last year, Zephrum had mixed feelings about returning.

"I hear that Dr. Malvin Moot will be teaching TWO new classes," continued Aunt Gussie, grabbing for a dishtowel. "One is on 'Scientific Inventions to Change the World' and the other is an 'Oceanography' class that will involve a number of field trips."

Aunt Gussie took a paper out of an envelope. "Here, take a look at the list of new academic courses that will be offered to second year students this term."

Zephrum took the paper from her aunt and skimmed the page.

- Circus Arts and Daily Warm-ups with Magenta Scorcher, Teele Bender, and Scrap
- Meditation and Aikido with Carmen Brownie
- Forecasting the Future Through Mathematical Trends with Waldo Vestor
- How to Really See in Art with Autumn Visage
- Writing the Truth with Dexter Droudy
- Mythical Sea Creatures in Literature with Mrs. Raxapod
- Scientific Inventions to Change the World with Dr. Malvin Moot
- And… Oceanography with Dr. Malvin Moot

The Oceanography class will require a signed permission slip for regular field trips and planned outings.

Regular Circus Classes, Electives, and Independent studies will resume each afternoon.

As Zephrum finished reading the list, Aunt Gussie said, "Oh, I wish I had been able to go to a school like Fiddlesticks when I was a young whipper-snapper like you. What a fabulous life you have, Zephrum. Truly."

Zephrum nodded vaguely. She was deep in thought.
Last year had been her first year at Fiddlesticks School for
Alternative Thinkers with Unusual Abilities. Her heart fluttered
as she thought about seeing the cute Gai Holmes, but
thudded apprehensively as she remembered her run-in with
the evil Strasidous Rowpe.

Aunt Gussie peered at Zephrum's face. "Your forehead
looks as wrinkled as a lizard's elbow. What's all that about?"
"I don't know," said Zephrum as she shrugged her
shoulders.
"You can't pull the wool over my eyes, Zephrum. I
know you too well for that. You think I was born yesterday?"

"Well… it's just… the dreams of Strasidous Rowpe
have not stopped, even though we think we saw him sizzle to
nothing with that goblin friend of his in that cauldron of muck
last year. I thought I'd be done with him, but his presence in
my dreams is even stronger than it was before. With that
storm last night, my dreams were crazy nightmare-ish."

"Well… it was one heck of a storm," said Aunt Gussie
as she dried off her curlers with her dishtowel.
"I don't get it," said Zephrum. "I thought Strasidous was
gone. Why am I still dreaming about him? I don't want to
endanger everybody at Fiddlesticks again. I just feel we
haven't seen the last of him… and I guess I just can't stop
thinking about it. Plus, my wind powers feel kookier than ever.
Being part wind fairy can be so unpredictable."
A sudden wind blew into the kitchen windows, rippling
the curtains around like bright billowing parachutes.

"Mmm… I see," said Aunt Gussie, eyeing the moving
curtains as she started to put her work tools back into her
toolbox. "Well… What are you going to do about it?"
"I don't know," said Zephrum, putting her hand to her
forehead. "How should I know? I'm just a kid. Don't YOU
have any ideas?"

"You know me, Zephrum. I'm always full of ideas," said Aunt Gussie, snapping her toolbox shut.

"It sounds like you have some things to sort out inside. Maybe these dreams are just feelings you didn't completely understand last year? Maybe you'll create a whole new wind invention in one of Dr. Malvin Moot's new classes? I really couldn't say. But it's up to you to take the bull by the horns and direct yourself in the ways you'd most like to grow. Teachers can help you along the way, but ultimately, it's YOU who will forge your way in the world… so it's YOU who must decide what's best."

Zephrum looked dully at her shoes.

"All I know," continued Aunt Gussie, "is that faith is a house with many rooms. You must find a way to believe in yourself…and then, move forward from there."

She put her arm around Zephrum. "We should just go into town and get all of your school supplies. Don't you worry your little head about Strasidous Rowpe. There's no way he could have survived after all of this time. Really."

Just then, a strange scent permeated through the cabin, accompanied by a mist of vile vapor. Zephrum's black doggie, Nomad, started barking at the nebulous mist floating throughout the kitchen.

Aunt Gussie wrinkled her face as though somebody had just held a small poop under her nose, "What is that disgusting smell?"

Zephrum's stomach churned. It was a smell she could never forget. Her thoughts trembled past the words in her throat. "It's…It's…the vapor of…Strasidous Rowpe."

--Chapter 3--
"Grizalda the Great"

The journey down the mountain was arduous for Virgidous. A sickening vapor rose from his body as he moved. His harsh breathing sounded like blacksmith bellows by the time he reached the bottom of the mountain. "Not much further, Sire."

"I know, Virgil. I can smell the scent of our goblin kin in the air."

Once at the bottom of the mountain, it was just a short trek to the goblin hovel under the center of Haversville. Virgidous could smell the ocean mist, coming from the nearby boat docks.

News of the return of their illustrious leader, Strasidous Rowpe, spread fast amongst the masses. As soon as Virgidous set foot into the underground tunnels, a ruddy cart screeched and scooped him up. One of the rolling trollies brought him directly to the goblin elders under the city center of Haversville. He grinned when he heard the familiar sound of goblins at work.

"Count those coins!"

"Sort those jewels!"

"Gather that gold!"

From the forever forests to the great ocean, shrieking orders echoed from damp holes and huge subterranean caves.

"But why are we doing all this?" asked a young goblin.

"No questions!!" bellowed a craggy older goblin. "We are doing what we must. We are amassing power and strength for The Great One. Now, shut up and keep counting."

The young goblin looked down at his mound of plenty and continued sorting and calculating.

In a small cave under The Haversville Bank in the center of town, a quiet meeting with Virgidous and the goblin elders was taking place. Virgidous sat on a large flat rock in their midst with musty green vapor rising from his body.

"Virgidous. Sire. What would you like us to do next, my lord?"

"SILENCE!" roared Virgidous. "All of these voices are making my head pound."

"We repent, Sire." The goblin bowed until its jewel studded necklaces clattered against the floor.

"Grrr..." growled Virgidous. "Fine. I'll tell you what I want. I want to see the likes of Zephrum Gates at my mercy. What we need now is the all-knowing foretelling abilities of... Grizalda the Great."

The goblins screamed in horror.

"But Sire," said the eldest. "Grizalda is the most cantankerous of all goblins. Even the grouchiest of goblin folk would rather give up a fortune than meet up with her delirium."

"Yes, Sire," another elder chimed in. "Grizalda is the most crusty of oracles. Can we not use one of our stolen crystal balls for your purposes?"

"SILENCE!!" bellowed Virgidous. "This is mindless chatter!"

The circle of elder goblins fell to their knees and bowed to the ground with their hindsides in the air.

Glaring at the small goblin group, Virgidous asked, "Am I your esteemed leader or not?"

The elder goblins were too frightened to respond.

"Will you do my bidding or not?" Peering into the souls of every goblin in the cavern, Virgidous continued. "Am I not your guide to all that is prosperous and powerful? Have I ever failed you in days past?"

"Of course, Sire," said the goblins, falling to the floor to grovel for forgiveness. "We will do anything you ask." "You are wise and corrupt and we value you more than all others."

Virgidous hollered, bellowing louder than before. "Then BRING ME GRIZALDA!! And do it NOW!!"

"Yes, Sire." "Of course, Master." "We will gather her at once." The elders bowed and apologized and shrunk from the underground cave.

Virgidous tried to avoid the goblins' mournful eyes as they respectfully backed out of the room. He squatted down to the dirt floor and wrapped his gangly green fingers around his forehead. "Why must this ache plague my head so?"

Virgil's voice emerged. "Sire, in time, we will be linked together with greater ease. I am sure of it."

Virgidous slapped himself across the cheek, "HOW can you know such things?"

Virgil recovered himself. "It is simply my hope, Sire," he said humbly. "Nothing more."

Just then, one of the elder goblins returned with a smaller goblin wearing a tiny jeweled turban. "Sire, Grizalda resides with The Creeper Clan close to our great ocean. Our relations with this clan are somewhat, eh… strained, Sire." He shoved the little goblin forward. "If you wish to know your next plan of action, I'm sure that our in-house Goblin Fortune-Teller can assist."

"This is Rubbish!" screamed Virgidous. "When I ask for Grizalda the Great, I do not expect a mere imitation. If you are too afraid to speak with Grizalda's clan, I will go myself. Bring me your best swordsman. I will take your warrior with me and undertake the journey myself."

"Yes, Sire. At once."

Within moments, the elder goblin returned with a muscular goblin dressed in warrior garb. She wore body armor and a round shield. "Sire, this is Zultr Zeki, our finest swordswoman."

Zultr Zeki bowed her head. "Sire… It is an honor to be of service. I pledge to klomp any who get in our way."

"Then let us depart without delay," said Virgidous.

"Yes, sire," said Zultr Zeki.

Virgidous and Zultr Zeki shoved their way out of the chamber, as the eldest goblin scampered aside.

Virgidous and Zeki marched quickly to the main nexus of the Goblin Conveyor Cart system. Zeki motioned towards an empty cart on the tracks. "After you, Sire."

Virgidous got into the cart. His gnarly knees folded up to his nose in the rickety old wagon, while Zeki gave it a push from behind. Zeki ran to catch up and then flung herself into the cart. They scooted and swerved along the underground tracks through tunnels of dank dark, ducking their heads to avoid stalactites as they moved. Eventually, they approached a massive dark chamber in the dingy underbelly of the caverns. With a final scream of the brakes, the cart rattled to a stop.

"Sire. We must change our mode of transport here… as this point begins Creeper Clan territory." Zultr Zeki helped Virgidous out of the cart and pointed towards a number of hanging vines along the dark dank wall. The light of day shone through from a circular water well up above. "We must travel by Creeper Vine now."

Virgidous and Zeki grabbed a couple of vines and were immediately roped upward through a vertical tunnel that reached to the light of day. Once they reached the top of the cavern, the two crawled over the stones of an old water well and plunked their feet upon the ground.

Zeki squinted in the sunlight. "Too bright up here if you ask me."

Scrunching up his eyes, Virgidous said, "Yes, too bright indeed."

Zeki pointed her sword in the direction of an old lighthouse in the distance. It was a haunting site, all alone on the rocky peninsula. Shredded curtains floated from the dark stone window holes like spider legs trying to escape. "Sire, it is there that Grizalda The Great resides."

Tricia Riel

Pink flamingo lawn ornaments surrounded the lighthouse, along with a group of stone markers jetting up from the ground. "Zeki... It is a strange site indeed. What are those rocks for?"

"Sire... It is Grizalda's graveyard of Gathering Squee."
"Squee?" asked Virgidous.
"Yes, Sire. Because Gathering Squee are expendable, they are great protectors. They are goblin folk from the realm of the undead. The thing about Squee is that they are nearly impossible to get rid of. The Squee can be a nuisance, but are certain to alarm Grizalda if danger is afoot."
"I see," said Virgidous as they walked. "Have you conquered a Squee before?"
"Yes, Sire," bragged Zultr Zeki. "Many-a-time. It is not through strength that we conquer them, but through cunning."

"Cunning...Yes." Virgidous' lips curled in a sinister smile.
"Sire, I recommend a trap for these Squee. We must bait them if we are to overcome them."
"What do you suggest?" asked Virgidous.
"Squee cannot resist the temptation of enchanted feathers, Sire. We should gather some seagull feathers and be armed with them as we approach."

"Feathers?!?" cried Virgidous. "You expect us to protect ourselves with feathers?"
"Yes, Sire. The feathers will be a most certain distraction. Once the Squee are enthralled by our enchanted feathers, they will leave us an open path to Grizalda's Lantern Room at the top of her lighthouse."
"And then?" asked Virgidous.
"Once there, Sire... We will have unfettered access to Grizalda and all of her foretellings."
"So it is," said Virgidous.

As they made their way to the lighthouse at the edge of the sea, Virgidous and Zeki picked up as many stray seagull feathers as they could find. Finally, Zultr Zeki snapped her fingers to enchant the quills.

Traipsing through the sand with a waddle, Zeki and Virgidous approached the lighthouse. They were loaded with a full arsenal as they pushed forward, ready to defend themselves.

As expected, the Gathering Squee started to move toward them. With whispered moans, a half dozen Squee rose from the sand, moving like mindless zombies; single-minded with arms outstretched.

Once Virgidous and Zeki got closer, they revealed their feathers from beneath their cloaks. The Squee made a high-pitched squeal that pierced their ears. Virdgidous recoiled from the sound, while Zeki grimaced and closed her eyes tight.

They dropped a couple of feathers a few feet from where they stood. The Squee gravitated to the feathers like moths to a flame, as if they had no will of their own.

Virgidous and Zeki smiled poisonous grins to each other. They continued placing feathers on the ground. They moved closer and closer to the lighthouse entrance, unobstructed by the Gathering Squee.

"They look like simple goblin kin now, don't they?" said Zeki.

"Yes," said Virgidous with a sinister smirk.

Zultr Zeki opened the creaky door to the stone lighthouse. She eyed the bones that were hung above the entryway. "We should go to the stairs and make our way to the lantern room above."

The toilsome journey up the narrow stone staircase was a strenuous pilgrimage for Virgidous. He wheezed heavily as he reached the top of the winding stairs.

"Sire, Be you alright?" asked Zeki.

Virgidous gasped for breath until he was able to speak. "Uh…Yes. All is well. Let us complete our task here."

And at that, the goblin swordswoman used a martial arts kick to the wooden entrance of the lantern room and bravely broke the door down. She entered the glassed-in housing at the top of the lighthouse, with Virgidous following close behind.

There, sitting on a large cushion of seaweed was Grizalda. The green warts on her large face were cracked and dried, very much like the rest of her. She wore a jeweled turban that was bedecked with small snake-head skeletons and one "all-seeing eye" in the center of a triangle. Burlap clothes hung over her large frame and were decorated with rubies and bones. She was smoking a cigar and gazing at the rune stones on her table. As Zeki and Virgidous approached, she gave a yellow-toothed smile. "I was expecting you."

She motioned to them. "What are you waiting for? You've come a long way to hear what my hearthstones will reveal. Are you certain that you are prepared for what I have to say?"

Virgidous moved towards Grizalda's table as his faithful goblin swordswoman guarded the door.

Virgidous sniffed the smell of the lantern room and commented on the strange stench that oozed from a dark vat of simmering sludge. "What is that smell?"

"Did you come to ask me about my decorating?" Grizalda snapped. "Or do you want to hear me speak about things of greater importance?"

Virgidous dropped a large sack of coins on Grizalda's divining table. "You know why I'm here."

"Yes," said Grizalda. She closed her eyes and nodded. "The girl. Your power. Your plan. You want to know it all."

"Yes," said Virgidous as he moved closer to Grizalda's table.

"Let us see what my great Roks will say." Grizalda gathered her goblin rune stones into a sack and mixed them up. She took out five of the Roks in sequence, counting in ancient goblin as she placed each one onto her table. "Ash... Dub... Gahk... Futh... Haa."

For a moment, she stared upon the hearthstones. Then, she spoke. "Ash. You will need to move forward with stealth or else your strength could be used against you."

Taking another look at the stones, she continued, "Dub. And you must commission the help of creatures that are much stronger than yourself."

Peering into the stones further, she said, "Gahk. For it is only with the help of these other creatures that you can achieve your aims of gaining ultimate power over all things."

She continued, "Futh. In regard to the girl, your only hope of thwarting her powers is to diminish them with the help of ancient magic residing in our great ocean."

"Haa. And finally, you must know that your demise is imminent. You cannot remain as you are and continue for long. You must build a great ship and seek out... the... the Leviathan." Her terror-filled eyes practically bulged out of her head.

Grizalda threw her head back and screamed like a peacock. Her body shook like a jack-hammer. Her eyelids flitted and her body flinched. Suddenly, she began talking in ancient Goblinese.

"You will be a slave to potions. Give many thanks... for the time you have. Your quest is long, indeed. An epic battle within is certain. Build a ship. Go out to sea. Cast spells where you must. Sift through what humans cannot. The only creature besides a Leviathan that can help you now is the most ancient of... of... Globsters."

With that, Grizalda The Great fell face first onto her rune table, sending up a poof of dust.

Virgidous dashed over to Grizalda's side. "Grizalda… Are you still with us? Is that it?"

Grizalda bolted upright and blurted out, "Garbage Guts! Barnacles! Trash of doom! YOUR salvation!"

And then she plunked back down upon the table.

Virgidous shook Grizlada's shoulders, but she did not stir.

Zeki peered out of the windows at the Squee down below. "Sire, I believe we are running out of time. The enchantment on the feathers is wearing off and the Squee are beginning to lose interest in them. If we do not depart now, the Squee may never allow us to leave."

"Fine," said Virgidous. He paused, hoping for one last bit of prophecy, but Grizalda simply began to snore. "Let us slip away while we still can."

Zeki and Virgidous raced out of the lantern room, scampered down the lighthouse steps, and scurried past the Squee outside.

The Squee were nibbling and munching on bits of downy barbs and then spitting them to the ground. They gagged on the feathers and simply dropped them wherever they stood. The feathers were clearly losing their fascination.

Before long, Zeki and Virgidous were back at the Creeper Clan's vine hole. Once they were holding onto vines growing over an old water well, the snake-like vines activated and moved them downward to the underground conveyor cart tracks that had brought them there. They climbed into a waiting cart. The cart leapt to life with a magical squeal. It swerved and turned through the darkness, grinding a slow path back to the main nexus where their journey began.

Zeki helped Virgidous out of the cart. "Is there anything else, Sire?"

"I believe your task is nearly done," said Virgidous as he stabilized himself on the rocky floor. "You can accompany me back to the elder chamber and I will reward you most handsomely for your bravery."

"Of course, Sire. As you please."

An elder goblin's face broke into a toothy grin when they returned. "Welcome back," he rasped. "What news?"

"Gather the elders and I will reveal our plan," said Virgidous with a wheeze.

The elders arrived at the cave's entrance within moments.

"What news, Sire?" "Yes, Master. What did you find out?"

"We will need to construct a great ship, one that can sail at sea," Virgidous announced. "And we must do it in secret. Once it is finished, I will reveal the rest of our plan to you. For now, building a ship is our greatest priority."

"A ship?" Chortled an elder goblin, so stooped over that his unkept beard almost touched the ground. "Where shall we build this great ship, sire?"

"I don't know and I don't care," snapped Virgidous. "Just find us a secret hideaway for the construction of our great vessel and do it quickly."

The goblins in the chamber tittered with glee. Hiding things of great importance was a thrill to them, but to hide something HUGE was a most welcome challenge.

"We will need a human warehouse near the shipyards of our great ocean," said Virgidous.

Virgil's voice surfaced from within, "Yes, sire. But once we have built our great vessel near the shipyard, how will we ever find what we seek?"

The Virgidous creature slapped himself upside the head. "Virgil... What did I tell you about speaking in front of others?"

Virgil's voice quivered. "Yes, sire. I forgot."

"Virgil... SHUT UP!" thundered Strasidous.

Two elder goblins eyed one another with perplexed looks as Virgidous regained his composure. "It's an adjustment, this new body."

The goblins all fell to the floor, sputtering and talking over one another.

"Yes, sire."

"Of course."

"We understand."

"No word of it beyond these walls."

"Good." Virgidous held up a bony greenish hand, clenching the fingers into a tight fist. "I am in control," he declared. "I have everything in hand."

The small group of yellow-eyed goblins howled with sniggers and cackles.

Virgidous clasped his gnarled goblin hands over his pointy ears at the ruckus. He gave a wide sinister smile. "I think I will retire now. Give me notice once our plans are all in place."

His minions bowed their bald heads. "Of course, Sire," said the hunchback with the wart on his nose.

"Yes," said his swarthy companion.

"As you wish," said the third, who was the ugliest one of all.

Virgidous bowed to the elder goblins as he departed. He shuffled through the underground tunnels until he reached a small alcove.

"Ahh… Here, I can think," said Virgidous. He tilted his head back and closed his eyes. After a moment, he pushed on a door and entered his sleeping chamber. Virgidous sat down on the sleeping mat on the dirt floor, grabbed his head, and pulled at his ears.

"Sire?" said Virgil's voice.

"What is it now, Virgil?"

"How will these creatures help us defeat Zephrum Gates? HOW will we ever find… a Leviathan? And a Globster? You know… out there?"

"Good questions, Virgil."

For a moment, there was no chatter.

Then, the stronger Strasidous voice said, "We will have to lure the creatures out of hiding. We will need to give them what they each desire above all else. We will have to offer them something they can't resist."

Virgil's voice tentatively asked, "And what is that, Sire?"

"The globster feasts on barnacles and trash, trash of all kinds," said Strasidous. "For the Leviathan… only time will tell."

"And Zephrum Gates, Sire. What of her?"

"Zephrum Gates? She is doomed. She is surely doomed. Bwa.. ha.. ha.. ha.. ha…" his wicked voice echoing off the cavern walls.

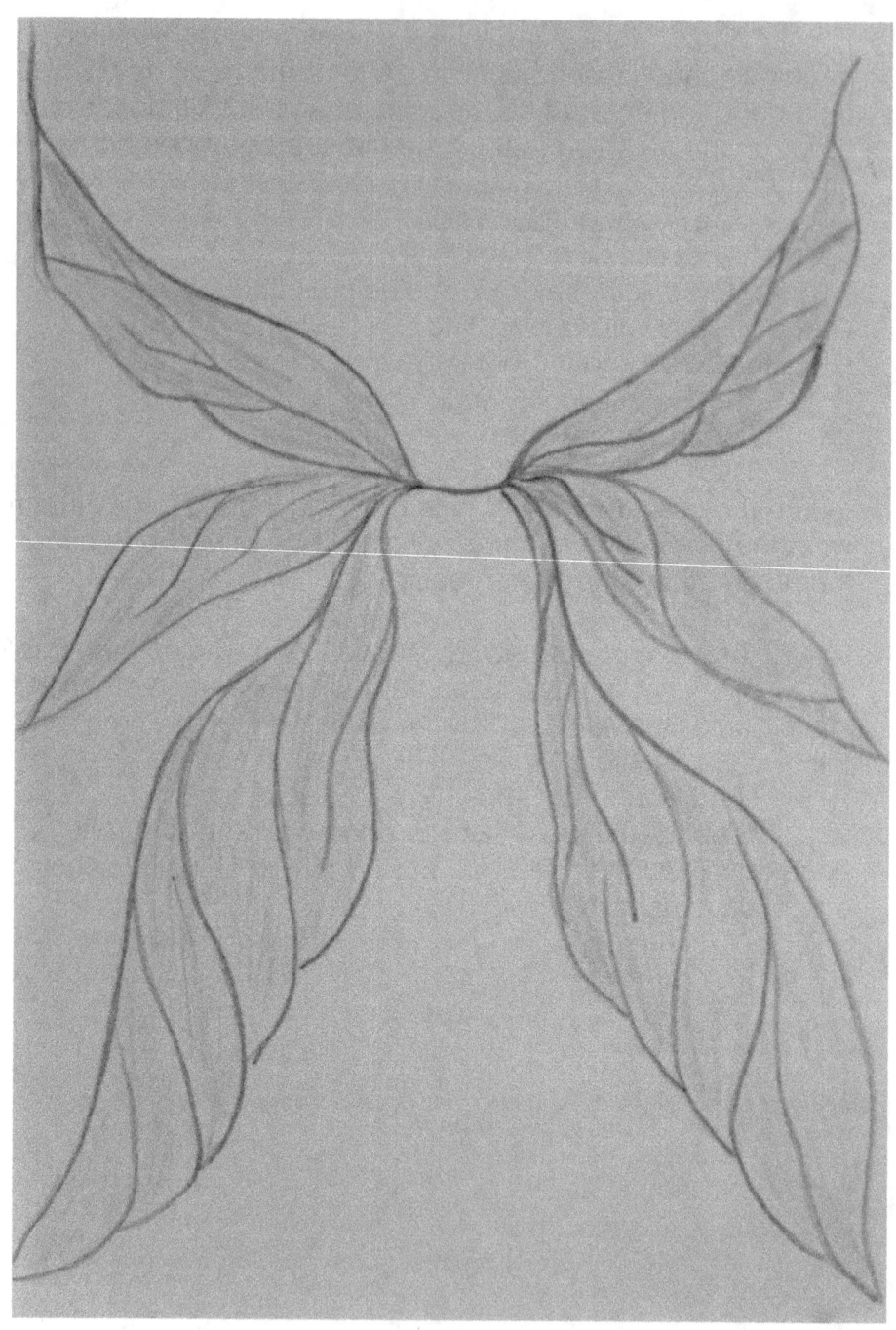

~~Chapter 4~~

"Aynia's Telling"

By the time Zephrum and Great Aunt Gussie returned from town, there was only a hint of the noxious gas they had smelled before.

Aunt Gussie breathlessly put her packages down on the kitchen counter and pulled out some new sink parts. "These new gaskets and pipes should spruce up our sink in a jiffy. You know, I didn't want to make the trip to that silly hardware store, but the job that never gets started takes the longest to finish."

Aunt Gussie fiddled with the sink parts. "I'll tell you. That man from the plumbing department was as beef-witted as a slab of salami."

Zephrum giggled. "Yeah, He probably wouldn't know that a pampered cow gives you really spoiled milk."

"Exactly," said Aunt Gussie. "Really, most people wouldn't know reason if it came up and shook their hand."

Suddenly, the air filled with swirling sparkles. A sweet tinkling floated in on the breeze.

Zephrum squeaked. She jumped so high that it looked as though her spine sneezed.

Before their very eyes, a diminutive fairy hovered over near the kitchen sink. The fluttering of her wings made her long blondish locks blow gently over her greenish shoulders.

Aunt Gussie greeted the tiny fairy. "Oh Aynia...You look lovely. You've got eyelashes like a national forest."

The beautiful fairy's wings beat more softly as she tried to settle. When the sparkles cleared, the fairy struggled to stand gracefully in one place.

"Oh Aynia," cried Aunt Gussie. "I've got eyes in the back of my head, but I didn't even see you coming. How are things in Fairyland?"

Aynia put her hands on her hips and wobbled.
"I come for some telling
From those that we know
The news gives me fright
From my wings to my toe

The Master of Darkness
Has returned from the dead
He has re-joined with Goblins
And all of those he led

"Are you talking about Strasidous Rowpe?" cried Zephrum. "I knew that stench wasn't an accident."

Aynia nodded. She fluttered to a new spot on the counters, nearly banging into a coffee mug.
"He wields a strange body
He walks with us now
He is both split and whole
I can't tell you how

He commands those in the shadows
Giving strength to his cause
It defies Every Logic
And All Natural Laws"

"Now Aynia," said Aunt Gussie. "My trust in you is marrow-deep, but split in two? Really?"
Aynia scowled. She fluttered over to the packages and disappeared into an open bag. Her voice twittered from inside.
"He has received advice
From a powerful Teller
Revealing many things
That are less than stellar

He will seek the help
of a Monster from the Sea
Thwarting his efforts
Is the only way to be

Befriending water monsters
Is our only real hope

For without their assistance
We surely cannot cope."

"Water Monsters?!?" blurted Zephrum.

Peeking her head inside the kitchen faucet and out again, Aynia popped out a "Yes."
"His power will grow
In his direction, it will tip
For he and his followers
Will build a great ship

They will set sail
On an epic search
They will find their monster
From their sailing perch

He will inspire others
With mindlessness that is rash
He will gather garbage
An overload of Trash

If we cannot block him
All will surely be lost
You must stop this madness
And really, at any cost

He is fearless in his search
And cares not what awaits
The Leviathan will help him
And deal us the worst of fates."

Zephrum stood with her mouth agape. Even Aunt Gussie was stunned into silence.
To fix the drip, Aynia swished her fairy's wand over the spout of the kitchen faucet and clumsily slipped on the air where she stood. The sink glowed as the dripping from the sink stopped. Aynia composed herself.

"We of Fairyland
are affected by his return
We are not as graceful
It seems we can barely turn."

She mindfully tried to stabilize her fairy body as she finished with fairy finality.

"I cannot fix all things
As easily as this sink
But now I must go
As fast as you can blink."

In an instant, she zoomed out of the kitchen window, leaving a trail of glittery fairy dust in her wake.

Aunt Gussie and Zephrum stared at the spot where Aynia last hovered.

"Oh no," Zephrum finally said. "She's left us before she even got to tell us where Strasidous is."

"Mmm… Well, it sure sounds like we are treading on thin ice, doesn't it?"

"Yes, it does. This is horrible." Zephrum grabbed at her untidy braids and pulled hard. "Strasidous Rowpe has somehow returned with more power than he had before?! We're doomed!"

"I admit that Strasidous Rowpe is really beginning to grind my gears," said Aunt Gussie. "That Strasidous was always up to no good. Getting mixed up with him again would not be wise. You know he just wants to rain on our parade."

"And suck the living force out of ME," said Zephrum.

Doggie Nomad sidled up next to Zephrum. Her light brown eyes gazed deeply into Zephrum's eyes as she leaned her soft calm body up against her, an anchor of support.

"It sounds as though we should leave well enough alone, Zephrum," added Aunt Gussie as she grabbed the handle of her toolbox.

"But what about what Aynia said?" asked Zephrum.

"I know. She did seem all in a tizzy. But ya' know Aynia has always been a bit grim. I think you should take her message with a grain of salt."

"But what if Strasidous comes after me again?" Zephrum started pacing near the kitchen table.

"There's not really much we can do about a rumor," said Aunt Gussie as she brought her toolbox to her storage closet. "I wish he could just bury the hatchet and move on."

"And what did Aynia mean about befriending Sea Monsters?!" asked Zephrum.

"It is a bit of an oddball message, isn't it?" said Aunt Gussie. "I think you should just get all your ducks in a row and forget about it."

"What? Forget about it?" asked Zephrum.

"Well…with all of the troubles we've had with Strasidous Rowpe in the past, it's easy to expect the other shoe to drop any moment. Rather than getting ourselves all worked up about this news, maybe it's best to just be practical and focus on things that we actually have control over. For you, that would be doing well in school this year."

"You mean…just act NORMAL?!?" interjected Zeprhum. "After all of that news Aynia just told us?"

"Well… It's good to look before you leap, of course," said Aunt Gussie. "But just remember that the mightiest works do start with the smallest steps."

"Sure," said Zephrum. "When you're baking a cake or planting a garden, but we have just been warned about Sea Monsters!"

"True," added Aunt Gussie as she finished unpacking the last of her supplies from her shopping bag. "It does seem like we just got walloped with quite a message, doesn't it?"

"Walloped, yes. We were told of our impending doom," said Zephrum.

"Oh Zephrum…You sure seem like you've got a glitch in your hiccup."

"You heard the same stuff I heard. Aren't you concerned?" asked Zephrum.

"Oh, of course I am," said Aunt Gussie. "But you've got to wake up and smell the coffee. I'm pretty sure that Strasidous Rowpe is history. You were just given a warning, as well as some very helpful advice. I'd say that could all be very valuable if we end up being faced with any real danger in the near future."

"What are we supposed to do now?" asked Zephrum.

"Well…" said Aunt Gussie. "Don't let Aynia's words give you the gollywobbles. When your own imagination can't find a solution to your problems, you must seek a greater Imagination."

"That's not a real answer, Aunt Gussie."

"Mmm… Well… Seeking the perspectives of your friends and searching your heart will help you see through this jumble of information, I think. Life is full of twists and turns you never see coming. This situation is just a turn, Zephrum. Having fair warning about things we might encounter is a great gift indeed. It gives you an edge and helps you imagine what you can do if you're actually faced with a dire situation. For now, I think you should just let it all settle inside you for a bit. You can't respond to a future that has not even arrived yet. You can only prepare yourself for possibilities."

"True," said Zephrum as she took a deep breath in. "But Aynia was acting really strange, don't you think?"

"Yes. She did seem to be bumping into things quite a bit, didn't she?" said Aunt Gussie. She turned on the kitchen faucet. "Seems like she was able to help us out with this big leak, but yes…Aynia was acting a bit kooky."

Zephrum's eyes narrowed under her furrowed brows.

"Let's get all packed for Fiddlesticks and then bring you over to start the new school year," said Aunt Gussie. "Seeing all of your old friends and starting classes again will make you as happy as a clam in the mud. Really."

--Chapter 5--

"The Leviathan"

Deep beneath the sea, a mammoth creature swam, arrowing itself and flying through the underwater currents as though the water itself was part of his body. His long, wide wings, decorated with powerful spikes, propelled him forward as he swerved with unimaginable speed.

"Mmm…" said his deep rumbling. "I hunger for a giant."

His full round chest as strong as a shell of steel, parted the waters as he glided where he wished. With his long twisting neck, he veered right and left as he searched. Finally, through the extreme darkness of the deep, he spotted a large fish and spoke to his inner mind. "Yes. My dinner."

With lightning speed, his curving tail and flapping wings made the depths churn like a boiling cauldron. He darted towards the unsuspecting creature and stirred up the sea like a pot of ointment. The strength and graceful form of this creature was immense.

He angled around to catch his dinner by surprise and then, dashed forward with stealth. In an instant, he chomped the large fish and gobbled it up.

"Num..num..num…grrrr…"

"That was just a mere snack." He chewed the last of the bones and flesh. "Me want something bigger. Much bigger. My huntings have been slim since the sea has become so dark in spots. Beneath floating islands of strange, large stretches of territory seem almost dead with darkness. Mmm…I wonder where the light that helps our sea life flourish has gone to?"

He looked around to assess where the greatest light was seeping through the waters above. The Leviathan said, "No matter. My connection to my spirit ancestors will guide me to where I must go."

With that, he moved swiftly, his giant form disappearing into the ocean depths.

--Chapter 6--

"Back at Fiddlesticks"

At Fiddlesticks School for Alternative Thinkers with Unusual Abilities, the staff was getting ready to welcome all of the students back for the new school year. Director Dexter Droudy was running around with a nervousness that made him look as anxious as a junebug in a henhouse. His thick eyeglasses barely hung onto his face as he raced around the property taking care of smatterings of this and that. He wanted everything to be just right for the returning students.

The large octagonal Sun Lodge was being swept and readied for a big group orientation circle. Splintered sunshine streamed in from the broad windows and warmed the wide wood floorboards.

There was quite a bit of hubbub going on all over the property. Head Cook Mrs. Fliffle had prepared little finger foods and snacks for the arriving students. Psychic Intuitive, Carmen Brownie, was cleansing the energy of the room with a smoking smudge stick of sage, and Art Teacher Autumn Visage was hanging a few paintings in the common space.

General handyman, Rock-o Pounder, was tinkering with all the major equipment that helped things run smoothly. He was clearing out the heating system, checking vents, and swiping handfuls of snacks when Mrs. Fliffle wasn't looking. "Mmm...Dat's yummier than I imagined. I might have ta' get me some more of dat," he said to himself as he tried to hide the fact that he was chewing.

The investment banker and math teacher, Waldo Vestor, was just sitting in one place like a grumpy cat turd on a holiday. He was looking at a spreadsheet and calculating the future operating budget for Fiddlesticks.

Music teacher Adolfo Hemming was working out a tune on the piano, while Teele Bender, Magenta Scorcher, and "Scrap" (the main circus teachers) were in the Circus Tent setting up gymnastic mats and making sure the rigging lines were secure.

Dr. Malvin Moot, the science teacher was excitedly preparing a slide show presentation to help generate enthusiasm for the new classes he planned to teach this year. Almost lost in his white lab coat, notes spilled out from his pockets. He plugged equipment cords into electric outlets and stacked his index cards in a specific order on a podium, practically bubbling over with uncontainable joy.

Great Aunt Gussie, Zephrum, her loyal doggie companion Nomad, and their neighbor Mrs. Raxapod caught a ride to Fiddlesticks together with the environmental activist, Francine Muller. Mrs. Raxapod would be teaching a class on "Mythical Creatures in Literature." Her problematic son, Razebir, was also in the car, whining about things that didn't really matter. "Zephrum is bothering me."

Zephrum's jaw dropped. "I'm not even doing anything."

"Did too," said Razebir.

"Did not," retorted Zephrum.

"Did too." "Did not." "Did too."

"Alright now, you two" Aunt Gussie interrupted. "Settle down. Now, it's just noise coming out of your face."

Zephrum and Razebir both crossed their arms in front of their own chests and "harrumpffed" in their seats.

Francine had picked them all up in her car, which was fueled by pollution-free vegetable oil. As they drove onto the turnoff for Fiddlesticks, the dirt road wound before them like a string.

Once they arrived, Zephrum and Razebir brought their luggage to their assigned cabins. Students were staying in cabins, yurts, and straw bale houses. Once everybody dropped off their stuff, they trickled into the Sun Lodge for their first orientation meeting.

There were a number of new students this year, each one had been invited to Fiddlesticks in mysterious and unique ways. Some kids had received invitation letters via homing pigeon, others via mysterious notes delivered under their pillows in the night, and some via message bottles (Zephrum had experienced this when she was younger).

Since Zephrum was now 14 years old, she wasn't one of the youngest kids anymore. Uncertain looks covered the faces of the newer kids, while returning students greeted each other with warm smiles and high fives. Zephrum's whole body went a flutter when she saw the tall figure of Gai Holmes entering the Sun Lodge. She could barely believe it. He looked even taller than last year.

Mr. Waldo Vestor looked up from his papers when he saw Gai's long hair swoosh in the door. "Well…if it isn't our resident skyscraper!" Gai smiled and shook Mr. Vestor's hand warmly.

"Why does Gai have to be soooo charming?" Zephrum rolled her eyes with a smile.

Finally, some of Zephrum's girlfriends arrived. Haversville County's distinguished science fair winner, Sarah Bellum, had to un-fog her eyeglasses before she could see anybody inside the Sun Lodge. Right behind her was Misty Falls (who had abilities akin to water fairies). Finally, Zephrum's best friend (Daphne Gumption) came in. Daphne and Misty both came into the Sun Lodge at the same time and started screaming with high-pitched enthusiasm when they saw Zephrum. Running up to her, they jumped up and down. Then, they huddled around her with hugs so tight that Zephrum could barely breathe.

Gai spied this scene from a distance and just took a deep breath in. "Whoa… Zephrum is way more popular than I remembered," he whispered to himself. "Even though me and Zephrum had so many wild and scary adventures last year, this frenzy of girly enthusiasm feels somehow intimidating."

Just at that moment, one of Gai's juggler friends, Red Raspini, whacked Gai hard on the back as a greeting. Gai flashed him a big smile and punched him in the arm. They cracked up laughing.

After everyone had arrived and checked in, Rock-o Pounder stood next to Dexter Droudy in the center of the room. Rock-o firmly planted his snowshoe-sized feet and let out a loud whistle. Rock-o grabbed the school's rubber chicken as a "talking stick" and began. "All right...All of youz just calm down and clear the ear wax out of those cabbage heads you call your brains."

Giggles and muttered sounds emanated from the group. Rock-o continued, "Get yourselves all situated in a circle for your orientation, alright then?"

Within moments, people found friends to be next to and were all grabbing places to sit on the floor. Once Rock-o saw everyone had basically settled, he let out a loud, "Hoo-wee..."

"Hoo-wee..." The crowd roared back.

Rock-o passed the rubber chicken on to Dexter. "Without further a do, I present to you...Mr. Dexter Droudy," he bellowed.

The crowd clapped and cheered.

"Welcome back Fiddlesticks students," Dexter said in his typical jittery manner. And welcome to our new students as well. This is going to be a fabulous year with academic challenges. It will be fun and full of lots of on-hand experiential learning. I know you've all had a chance to take a look at your course schedules, so I'm sure that you are all as excited as we are. So...without getting too distracted by the details, I'd like to have our music teacher, Mr. Adolfo Hemming, welcome you with a new piece of music he has composed for the occasion."

Dexter brought the rubber chicken over to Mr. Hemming, who directed the students to sing a song in different parts and sections. Then, he played the piano and pointed to the groups as it was their turn to sing. The song cycled around in rounds until the Sun Lodge brimmed with new life.

After the song came to an end, Great Aunt Gussie said, "Oh, I'd give my right arm to be able to play piano like that."

Students laughed at the thought.

Dexter walked over to the piano and picked up the rubber chicken. "You see how easy it is for us to work together as a group? It's this kind of harmony and ease that will make our new school year together a great one. Tomorrow, we'll start our day off with our daily warm-up in the Circus Tent. Then, we'll get right into our regular class schedule. For now... Dr. Malvin Moot has put together a preliminary presentation about his science classes, which I think you will enjoy quite a bit."

Dexter brought the rubber chicken over to Dr. Malvin Moot, who messed up his hair with his hands as he stood up. "This is a little slideshow to get you excited about our oceanography classes this term." Dr. Moot pushed a remote and started showing photos of our ocean and some beautiful sea creatures that live there.

Zephrum knew that danger was lurking in the nearby ocean. Watching the images made Zephrum feel very uneasy. She hoped that Aunt Gussie had a chance to tell the other teachers about the warning? Thinking about it, Zephrum wondered if Dr. Malvin Moot would consider changing his course of study to keep kids away from the dangers of the sea.

"I must say," bounced Malvin, distracting Zephrum from her thoughts. "The oceanography classes I've created are the best idea for academic classes I've had so far. I'm particularly excited about the field trips we've planned. Really...I think I might be looking forward to this more than ANY of the other classes I've led before."

"Well...that answers that," thought Zephrum. "I'm pretty sure we are all destined for total disaster."

After further orientation about Fiddlesticks, as well as a basic introduction circle, kids were able to dig into the snacks that Mrs. Fliffle had made for everybody. There was a bit of informal socializing and a tour of the Circus Tent. Over near the aerial equipment, Magenta Scorcher explained the circus tent safety rules. While talking, she glared at Zephrum as though to burn her apart with her piercing laser eyes.

The trampoline and partner acrobatics coach, Teele Bender, greeted his returning students by squeezing them with his giant muscular arms.

The resident clown teacher, "Scrap," was sporting a red clown nose and a bow tie that was bigger than her head. As she introduced herself, she spoke to everybody in "kazoo language" through a miniature kazoo that seemed to be permanently attached to her lips. Then, everybody was set free to unpack and set themselves up for the duration of their stay.

As soon as they got to their cabin, Zephrum told Daphne all about the visit from Aynia…and the news about Strasidous Rowpe still being alive.

"What?!? Really? How could that be? We saw his goblin servant being plunged into Strasidous' vat of sludge and ether last year. Nothing could have survived in THAT."

"I don't know," said Zephrum. "This is just the news from Aynia."

"And we're supposed to watch out for sea monsters now?" said Daphne. "Is there no end to how weird it gets? I mean, seriously. What are we supposed to do with information like that?"

"I guess we're supposed to befriend creatures in the sea," said Zephrum. "But I have no idea what a 'Leviathan' is. Do you?"

"No," replied Daphne, "but with all this focus on the oceans in our classes this year, I'll bet we can convince Mrs. Raxapod to help us study up about them in her Mythical Creatures in Literature Class."

"According to Aynia, there's some issue with an overload of trash…and a Leviathan can deal us the worst of fates, so we had better learn something about it," added Zephrum.

"However it goes," said Daphne, "I can't wait to draw one."

"Speaking of drawing," said Zephrum. "Did you create anything interesting over the summer break? Were you able to tell the future with your art much?"

"Oh yeah," said Daphne nonchalantly. "I'm always foretelling the future with my art, as usual. Nothing major. It's just my parents have a really hard time springing surprises on me."

Both girls giggled.

"There was one interesting thing that I kept on drawing throughout the summer, though," said Daphne. "It was an 'all-seeing eye' in a triangle. Every time I would sketch it, I felt it looking back at me somehow. Really weird and powerful."

"Did you ever faint after sketching it?" asked Zephrum.

"No, actually. I would have expected that I would faint, like I normally do when I sketch something that has to do with the future. Who knows? Maybe my artistic future-telling skills are getting more developed?" commented Daphne.

"Who knows?" said Zephrum. "Weird that you felt it was looking back at you. Can art usually do that?"

Daphne jumped up and tickled Zephrum in the side. "Only if it's a sketch of the Boogie Man. Ha! Ha!"

The girls set off to brush their teeth in the outside bathroom near their cabin. Then, they snuggled into their own beds for the night. Finally, Zephrum's black dog Nomad curled up on a dog blanket on Zephrum's bed, and began dreaming wiser beside her.

--Chapter 7--

"Potions"

Meanwhile, deep within the Goblin caverns, a nebulous mist formed around the new Virgidous. He was weak and confused. He could not keep focused and was slipping in and out of arguments with himself. Often, he'd speak in gibberish that didn't make sense to anybody else. "Grinsty Burgle Barger! Gatesy Zergumstigger! Eeeg Woggie! Grrr…"

Whenever he'd drift off to sleep, he'd scream as though he was living in a nightmare. "Get out of my mind!" "Aaarrghhh… Trouble beyond troubles! Zgrrr…"

Not knowing exactly what to do, the elder goblins brought in their expert goblin healer as a consultant. Hovering over Virgidous, a caped goblin with an odd cross-eyed expression took a good hard look at his newest patient. Licking Virgidous' arm with a long tongue, the healer finally declared his recommended treatment. "I say he needs a potion of ToadFlax in order to regain his clear and corrupt faculties."

The elder goblins whispered and grumbled. Virgidous was losing his energy and could barely stay coherent. His head bobbled upon his neck like a bubble meandering down a stream.

"But ToadFlax?" protested one of the elder goblins.

"Can't we find something less potent?" said the goblin holding his gold satin pants up with one hand.

"Yes…Something without so many unusual, um, side effects?" said the craggiest goblin.

"Who knows how long this will allow him to stay with us?" said the most wrinkly one.

The strange goblin healer's eyes wandered in opposite directions as he spoke. "If we want him to remain with us at all, he will need the help of this special potion. ToadFlax comes from the milky juice of the skin glands of the poisonous brown cane toad…and it is the ONLY way to bring our cherished leader back to us."

A rustle of wind whistled through the darkness of the goblin's underground cavities. The news of their leader's condition had spread quickly amongst the followers. Whispers littered the threads between all of their goblin ears.

"Alright already!" said the goblin wearing the cowboy hat studded with green sequins. "We will administer the ToadFlax to Virgidous and hope that he will regain his powers before losing his mind…or worse."

Healer Groikz (as he was known) set out to his underground laboratory where he stored all manner of vile things. Once there, he made a fresh batch of ToadFlax from the poisonous skin glands of their toad brethren, the brown cane toad. The healer goblin added some herbs to the milky liquid and warmed the mixture under a flame to activate the ingredients. Without waiting for the formula to fully cool, he grabbed the vial. His flabby feet slapped against the rock floor with such a speedy wet scamper that he was practically a blur.

The air was still and stiff as the healer entered the dank chambers where Virgidous tossed and turned.

"Sire, you will need this to regain your strength," said Healer Groikz.

Virgidous was not responsive.

"Sire… If you will allow me to assist, I will."

Silence.

With his long gangly fingers, the goblin pried open the mouth of Virgidous and poured the entire contents of the dark vial down his throat. Immediately, Virgidous sat bolt upright, smoke puffing from his ears. His eyes bugged out so far that they looked like they were headed for outer space. He gagged and coughed and gagged again.

The elder goblins watched in wonder. The healer bowed his head to Virgidous. "And now, Sire. You are well."

Virgidous gave the goblin healer a shifty gaze and said, "Is it YOU that revived me?"

Shrinking back, Healer Groikz's eyes moved in crosswise directions. Finally, he whispered, "Yes Sire."

The elder goblins froze. The tense silence stretched into eternity.

"Healer!" Virgidous proclaimed at last. "You will be rewarded most handsomely for this service."

"Yes, Sire," said the healer as he bowed. "But Sire, you will need this treatment on a regular basis."

"Fine," stated Virgidous. "Make me as much as I will need."

"Yes, Sire. Of course," said the goblin obediently. "But you should know that the side effects can be quite strange, Sire."

"Strange?" questioned Virgidous.

"Yes. You might start seeing things that are not in our midst. You could be convinced that these things are real, that they are signs of things to come...but it would all be just mere imaginings, Sire."

"Well, it worked," said Virgidous rising to his feet to show off his vim and vigor. "Now, It will be up to YOU to make sure my dosage is just right."

"Yes, Sire," said Healer Groikz.

"Be sure to stock me up with at least three days of this potion on a regular basis, so that I may travel. We are ALL going to be VERY busy."

"Yes, Sire," said the healer goblin.

The elder goblins all finally melted an exhale of relief.

Virgidous stood up and opened his arms wide to the room. He pumped up his chest. "We are going to gain secret access to infinite realms of power, power beyond your wildest dreams."

"Yes, Sire."

"Of course, Sire"

"As you command, Sire."

In practically no time at all, Virgidous was overseeing their mammoth ship-building project in a large human warehouse near the ocean.

The elder goblins had commissioned "worker goblins" to execute the construction.

It took a number of days for these worker goblins to start the epic task of building their vessel.

First, they assembled the boat ribs. Then, they screwed together simple lap joints. They put them on a strong back jig to position them correctly and stabilized the structure.

They even got to the point of placing the main keel down the center, inside the notches of the ribs.

"This is no ordinary ship," said Virgidous. "You will have to infuse a magic binding spell into every part as you go."

From that point forward, the worker goblins spoke magical incantations as they worked.

"Muuuchh Better," sighed Virgidous during his first visit to the construction site.

The second time Virgidous made his way to the warehouse, he watched the worker goblins notching the frames and constructing the longitudinal elements.

"This is taking MUCH too long," exclaimed Virgidous. "We must speed up the process at once." He left the site in a huff.

The third time he made it to the ship's construction site, he started barking out orders again. "You must construct each section of this ship with perfection!" he insisted. "This is not a mere boat. It is the vessel that will lead us to our greatest glory. It will lead us to unlimited power. It will be our crowning achievement. Do not skimp on any detail. Do you HEAR me?"

Virgidous stopped short. He peered into the deepest part of the boat's skeleton. "Ah...My friend...Of course we have time for you. What can we do for you?"

The nearby goblins looked in the direction that Virgidous was speaking. Nothing was there.

"I know," said Virgidous. "I've been telling these goblin fools to speed it up all day. Why don't they see the urgency as WE do?"

The goblins all looked at one another with perplexed glances.

Virgidous' eyes widened. He nodded. "Yes...For capturing Zephrum Gates will grow our power to such an immense level. Nothing will stop us from gaining ultimate control over all things...not wind...not rain...and surely not the little pipsqueak that SHE is."

The befuddled goblins shrugged their shoulders in wonder.

"Yes...my thoughts exactly. I will tell them to double the number of goblins working on this boat...and we will set sail within no time at all. Good bye, old friend."

Virgidous looked up and glared at the goblins standing closest to him. "Well...You heard him. Get to it! Double the work force on this project...and do it NOW!"

"Yes, Sire," said one of the grimy goblins, scurrying away.

"But Sire, we saw nobody else here," stammered another goblin. "WHO were you talking to?"

"Oh..." said Virgidous. "That was my good old friend from childhood, Gordon. Didn't you see him?" Virgidous pointed into the skeleton of the boat. "He was standing right there!"

"Sire..." confessed the goblin. "Are you feeling alright? Is it possible that your ToadFlax potion was a bit too potent today? You are the only one who saw your friend."

"Rubbish!" protested Virgidous. "I am as clear thinking as...as... as that large bug flying by in the clear air above us."

"Ok, Sire." His sideways eyes met those of another goblin in waiting, who shook his head.

"Fine," said the head goblin. "Perhaps it is time for your check-up with our goblin healer. He wanted to see you daily in the beginning, yes?"

Virgidous waved his hands around as he said, "Oh, whatever. I tell you, I've never felt better. Never been more on top of my game. The visit from my friend has fueled my wish to capture Zephrum Gates. You know, that's what friends are for. To inspire you...to inspire you to live your life path...your path of gaining ultimate power over all things...as you know it's meant to be."

"Yes, Sire," said the goblin agreeably. "But to us, your friend was a mere apparition. None of us actually saw him, besides you."

"Goblins have the worst eyesight! You should all have that checked. Maybe it's too bright in here for all of you? We should find a way to make it darker. Maybe shade the windows of the warehouse better? Do it at once!"

"Yes, sire," said the goblin as he ushered Virgidous by the arm. "In the meantime, let us get you to our goblin healer, for your check-up."

"Fine. Fine," said Virgidous. He headed away from the structure of the boat. "But I tell you…I feel VERY clear headed. I'm better than fine. Really."

--Chapter 8--

"The Whimpus"

Back at Fiddlesticks, Zephrum and her friends were settling into their new school schedule. Circus Warm-ups in the morning were energizing, "Forecasting the Future with Mathematical Trends" with Waldo Vestor was a fun way to learn about the wonder of numbers, and "How to Really See in Art" with Autumn Visage gave students much more artistic perspective than they had experienced before.

The brainy Sarah Bellum was really excited to take Dr. Malvin Moot's class on "Scientific Inventions to Change the World" because each student would be able to create one of their own inventions as a final project. Zephrum figured that Sarah probably already had an idea for an invention, even though it was just their first week of classes.

"Mythical Sea Creatures in Literature" with Mrs. Raxapod seemed like it was going to be a fun and imaginative class, but it looked like they were going to have to do a lot of memorizing.

It was Dr. Malvin Moot's oceanography class that Zephrum was REALLY dreading. She knew that something horrible was waiting for her in the nearby ocean, but what? And how was she ever going to get out of the field trips?

One late afternoon during this first week of the school session while Zephrum was doing her independent study time with the Fiddlesticks horses, she took a little break to think about how she could possibly stay out of trouble this year. She lay down on a stack of hay bales with her black doggie, Nomad. They were outside of the horse's corral, relaxing together. Nomad smelled the breeze, while Zephrum just day dreamed, looking up into the mashed potato clouds in the sky. Drinking in the light, she suddenly got an idea. "I know. I'll go horseback riding on Majestic. That always helps clear my mind."

But because so many strange things happened in the surrounding woods last year, Fiddlesticks still had a pretty strict rule that students had to be accompanied by a buddy if they were going to venture onto the nearby trails. So early in the school year, she wondered who she could ask to go with her? It had to be somebody who already knew how to ride. Daphne was busy in an Artist's tutorial with Autumn Visage…and Misty Falls was busy "clowning around" in the Circus tent. "I guess I'll have to ask Gai. Oh…but I haven't even had a real conversation with him yet. Is my stomach going to get all full of butterflies when I talk to him?"

She admired the horse's beautiful wings that had grown from them last year. Despite their beauty, Zephrum was troubling herself about Gai when he rolled up with Red Raspini in a wheel barrel. Gai made a large braking sound. "This is as far as this taxi will take you, sir."

He tilted the wheelbarrow until Red dumped out on the ground.

Red laughed and then ran off in the direction of the Circus Tent.

"Hey," said Gai. "What are you up to? Want to go on a horseback ride or something?"

Zephrum kind of stumbled over her tongue. "Uh..ga..ahh… Yes." "Funny, I was just thinking how great that would be."

"OK," said Gai. "Let's get the horses ready and go."

They walked all bouncy into the barn, got horse tack for Majestic…and some for Starstruck (the stocky horse that Gai was going to ride). The horses' saddles didn't quite fit them – and hadn't since they all grew wings last year, so Gai and Zephrum decided to ride bareback with simple saddle pads on the horses' backs. They quickly secured the saddle pads with a strap, and then put on the reins.

Once the horses were all ready to go, Zephrum and Gai walked them out to the nearby Fire Road, with doggie Nomad prancing behind. The river was babbling by and there was a light breeze in the air.

They mounted in silence. Gai finally spoke. "So…Have you been worrying about Strasidous Rowpe? Or is that all behind us now?"

The hairs on her body stood on end and some of the color left her face.

Majestic shivered and Zephrum felt a chill run through her spine at the mere mention of Strasidous' name.

Sinking a little in her seat on Majestic's back, she confessed, "Well…the truth is… I've still been having weird dreams about him. And Aynia of Fairyland came to warn me and Aunt Gussie that he's still alive and has more power than before."

"What?!?!"

"I know," said Zephrum. "I could barely believe it myself, but I guess he's re-joined with goblins and is going to seek the help of some monster from the sea."

"Seriously?!?" said Gai. "How could he have survived? The last we saw of him, he was just a mere wisp of nothing in a bubbling slime of sludge."

"I know," said Zephrum. "It sounds unbelievable, but Aynia says he's building a great ship and that our only real hope is to befriend Water Monsters…and stay clear of a Leviathan creature."

"What?!?" said Gai. "What's a Leviathan?"

"I don't know," said Zephrum. "Sounds scary, whatever it is. Anyway, somehow, the return of Strasidous is affecting Aynia's ability to fly straight. She bumps into things every few seconds."

"Ha! Really?!?" Gai grinned.

Seeing Zephrum's serious expression, he frowned. "Uh…I mean, whoa… That sounds serious."

"Well," said Zephrum. "I know it can't be good. I just want to find a way to stay out of his way. How about we just ride?"

"Alright, let's go," said Gai. "How about east?"

"Yes…Sounds good," said Zephrum.

Gai and Zephrum started at a trot. They cantered up inclines…and made the horses slow to a walk when they came to hills going downward. They rode almost as far as Donald Snodgrass's Corn Farm when they decided they should turn around.

"Have you taken the horses on any flights ever since they grew wings at the end of last year?" asked Gai.

"No. I guess they need some magical orders from our rowan branch to fly…which is actually pretty good," said Zephrum. "I mean, at least we don't have to worry about them flying off from their corral."

"Ha! Right," said Gai.

Being with Gai was as fun as Zephrum remembered. This ride on the Fire Road was just what she needed. She felt lighter and happier and much less worried about things.

As they drew closer to Fiddlesticks, the thick of the woods pressed upon the path. Suddenly, Gai pointed and said, "Uh, Zephrum… uh… What's that?"

A spinning torrent of leaves and brush blocked the bend in the Fire Road, less than twenty feet ahead of them. At first, they heard it only like a gentle noise on the edge of hearing, but it turned into a low droning sound that soon surrounded them like a phantom of the woods. Zephrum nudged Majestic to a nearby tree and snapped a thick dry branch off the tree. She threw it at the tempest on the path in front of her. The stick looked like an airborn ax as it spun towards the twister.

The moment it struck, the whirling leaves wobbled to a slow blur to reveal a bloodthirsty gorilla-like animal. It looked like it was 7 feet tall. It had a stocky black body and was scarcely covered with fur. Its lower legs stood on hooves. The creature looked as stunned as Zephrum and Gai.

"Grrr…" it growled. "I wanted to turn you into molasses or maple syrup! I was meant to surprise you into submission! I knew I should have waited until the sun went down further. Why must nature present me with such trickery?"

The monster looked up at Zephrum and Gai and let out a screeching howl. "Ahwooo…. And who are YOU that should stop my whirlwind of wonder?"

Zephrum and Gai sat stupefied upon their horses.

The large creature banged its over-large fists onto the forest floor and protested. "No words?!? Can you not explain how a whimpus as powerful as me…has been stopped in the middle of my spiraling splendor? Are you part of the conspiracy to control all magical things? Are you in league with the goblins' treacherous leader that we have heard so much about? Speak! Before I smash you to bits with my club-like arms. Speak!!"

"The goblins' treacherous leader?" blurted Zephrum. "What? What do you know about him?"

The whimpus spun closer to Zephrum. "Ahh… So you ARE part of his evil plan to control all magical creatures? I knew it."

"No, no," said Zephrum. "He's after me too. Strasidous Rowpe. What do you know of him? Where is he now?"

Clomping closer to Zephrum, the whimpus bellowed, "Ah… Strasidous Rowpe is no longer. He is now called, Virgidous. He looks part goblin and part horror. His evil vapor is affecting us all on land, but it is his thirst for power within the ocean that will surely be the end of life as we know it."

"The Ocean?" said Gai. "What is he doing there?"

"I know not of his evil plans. Just that if he is able to infect our ocean with his misery, all life as we know it will be in great peril…even for us magical beings. He lusts for secret access to infinite realms of power and believes he will find it there…in our great waters."

The monster glared at them, a hungry look in his eyes. "Now tell me why I should not spin you into a tasty liquid as a treat."

"Uh…ah…" commented Zephrum.

"My power grows at sundown, when I will rotate into such a speedy gyration that you will never see me coming. Be forewarned, I will not mistake earth's timing again. So long as I possess my powers, I will be the most wondrous whimpus in all of these woods."

The whimpus turned around and built up a speedy spin.

"Uh, Zephrum," said Gai. "We had better get out of here."

"Agreed," said Zephrum. She called for Nomad, kicked her heels into Majestic's sides, and they rode for Fiddlesticks like a bolt of thunder.

By the time they reached Fiddlesticks, the red sun was setting. They dismounted and walked their horses as they approached the corral. "It looks like protecting our oceans is more important than we thought. We had better tell the others about this," said Zephrum.

"For sure," said Gai. "And we should be sure to warn everybody about going into the woods around sundown too. I don't think that whimpus will be stopped so easily the next time he sees one of us."

--Chapter 9--

"The Banshee"

Zephrum and Gai ran towards the Sun Lodge. Many of the teachers from the staff had gathered in there before the dinner cowbell rang. Great Aunt Gussie was standing near a drawing easel with Autumn Visage. Both of them were admiring a sketch that Daphne had drawn that afternoon. Magenta Scorcher stood nearby, glaring at the sketch as though she might spit flames at it, while Teele Bender spoke proudly, "I don't know what eet is, but I would say that eet is very eemaginative."

"I agree," said Aunt Gussie. "It does seem to be a bit of a whirlwind, whatever it is."

Zephrum and Gai raced up to the clump of teachers.

"Aunt Gussie!" Zephrum cried. "We just met a strange creature in the woods."

"Yeah," added Gai, gasping for air. "It was a whirling whimpus."

"Yes," said Zephrum. "That's what it said it was."

"A whimpus?" asked Aunt Gussie. "Ohhh, we haven't seen any whimpus in these woods for years."

"You know what a whimpus is?" asked Gai.

"Oh yes," said Aunt Gussie knowledgeably. "But witnessing one coming out of the blue like this is not something that most people live to tell about. Are you sure it was a whimpus?"

"Yes. Positive," said Zephrum. "First, we thought it was just a strange swirl of leaves and forest duff on the path ahead of us."

"But then, we heard a low droning sound," said Gai.

"And I don't know," said Zephrum. "I just threw a stick in the direction of the spiraling mass of leaves, out of instinct."

"Yea," said Gai. "And the stick interrupted the whimpus. That's when he stopped spinning. That's when we saw him."

"Yes," said Zephrum, sounding more winded than before. "Once he stopped whirling, he told us who he was and wondered if we were part of the treacherous plan of Strasidous Rowpe."

"But he called him…uh…Virgidous," added Gai.

"Yeah, that's what he said," panted Zephrum breathlessly. "He said that Strasidous' evil vapor is affecting us all on land and all of the magical creatures too…but that it's Strasidous' thirst for power within the ocean that will surely be the end of life as we know it."

"What else did it say?" asked Aunt Gussie. "You two have got me on the edge of my seat."

"Uh…" added Zephrum. "He said that if Strasidous or Virgidous or whatever he's calling himself…is able to infect our ocean with his misery, all life as we know it will be in great peril."

Gai cleared his throat. "He says that this Virgidous lusts for secret access to infinite realms of power and believes he will find it in our great waters."

Zephrum bounced on her toes. "He also said that a whimpus' power grows at sundown…and he seemed intent on spinning us into a tasty liquid as a treat."

"Yeah," said Gai. "I think we had all better stay away from the woods around sundown, just to be safe."

"Well…" said Aunt Gussie finally, "That sure does sound like a whimpus to me. They are like a bull in a china shop, aren't they?" She shook her head. "So destructive with their whirling madness."

"What are we going to do now?" asked Zephrum.

"Zees is nonsense," said Magenta, still looking at everyone with her simmering smolder. "Why is eet that this leetle girl is always creating such stories?"

Zephrum's attention snapped in the direction of Magenta's brilliant red hair.

"Zees is just ze first week of classes and she is already claiming a ridiculous monster exists in ze woods. What is wrong weeth thees girl?"

"Well," said Aunt Gussie. "I don't know if you've ever seen a whimpus, Magenta, but it is quite a frightening sight."

"If it was real, I'm sure eet would be very scary. But thees girl makes up stories just like my leetle sister did. And I can tell you zat indulging her leetle fantasies will come to no good."

"How much experience do you have with magical creatures?" asked Autumn Visage.

"Ssss…" hissed Magenta. "I know nothing of thees things. I just theenk thees little girl is a disturbance to life here at Feedlesticks and that we should not entertain her needless fictions."

"Mmm..hmm…" said Aunt Gussie. "Well, you admitted yourself that you know as much about magical creatures…as…as an ant knows about spaceship navigation."

Practically blistering to a boil, Magenta hissed, "Mark my words. Thees girl and her leettle myths will send us all down a path of regret if we continue to listen to her madness."

"Cheese and rice," swore Aunt Gussie. "If you can't be kind, at least have the decency to be vague."

"What?" seared Magenta.

"I've just heard death threats more sensitive than your blathering," said Aunt Gussie.

"Me?!? Not sensiteev?" shriveled Magenta. "Really, thees girl's story is simply foolishness."

A shriek suddenly came from outside. The teaching staff rushed outside the French doors of the Sun Lodge.

Just overhead, a winged female figure screeched over the roof of the Sun Lodge. It was a ghostly white part-spirit. The speed at which she flew made her hair whip in the wind behind her.

Putting her hand to her face, Autumn Visage said, "Oh my word! What is that?"

"Oh…That looks like a Banshee to me," said Aunt Gussie with her hand on her hip. "They scream like that when a family member's death is imminent. If that whimpus actually got one of her Banshee kin, she's likely to wail like that for weeks."

Zephrum and Gai watched wide-eyed as the Banshee sped out of sight.

Aunt Gussie looked at Magenta and said, "Now, was that just our 'foolish imagination'…or something we all actually saw?"

Magenta took off in a huff. She arrowed out of the Sun Lodge, slamming one of the French doors behind her.

"In her next life, I'm quite sure she'll be coming back as a toilet brush," said Gussie, eliciting an uncomfortable chuckle from the crowd.

Mrs. Fliffle then rang the dinner cowbell and the Fiddlesticks students streamed into the Sun Lodge for their supper.

Aunt Gussie and Autumn Visage encouraged Zephrum and Gai to join the other kids. "We'll talk about all of this later," whispered Autumn.

Zephrum and Gai found Daphne and sat with her at one of the low dining tables. They told her all about what happened with the whimpus and the Banshee.

"I still can't believe that the teachers seemed so unconcerned about it," said Zephrum as she played with the food on her plate.

"Yeah," said Gai. "If they had been faced with a whimpus like we were, they'd probably be feeling as intense as we are. I won't lie. That thing was scary."

"That Banshee was pretty scary too," said Zephrum.

"It looks like we're going to have another interesting year at Fiddlesticks, huh?" said Daphne with a smile.

Zephrum put her hand to her forehead, obviously troubled.

"Don't worry, Zephrum," said Gai as he reached his hand onto her shoulder. "Hey…maybe we'll even have a chance to get the horses flying again. That would be fun, right?"

Zephrum grinned at Gai. Her smile was not convincing.

Daphne took a small notebook out of her bag and set it next to her dinner plate. She started sketching. In practically no time, she had drawn a rough sketch of the whimpus and the Banshee.

"Wow!" said Gai. "How did you know they looked like this?"

"Yeah," said Zephrum. "It looks exactly like the whimpus we came across in the woods."

"And just like the Banshee that flew over the Sun Lodge afterwards," said Gai, impressed.

Daphne looked at the sketch and shrugged her shoulders, "I guess you guys were just really good at describing."

Zephrum noticed a smaller doodle in the corner of the drawing and said, "What's this with the eyeball inside a triangle?"

"Oh...I don't know," said Daphne. "Remember how I told you that I kept on drawing this image? It feels like some kind of 'all-seeing eye' or something."

Zephrum nodded, "I wonder what it means."

Gai took a look at the sketch. "Yeah...I wonder."

"It's a question for me too," said Daphne. "With all of these magical sightings happening so soon in our school year, it makes me really wonder what will happen next."

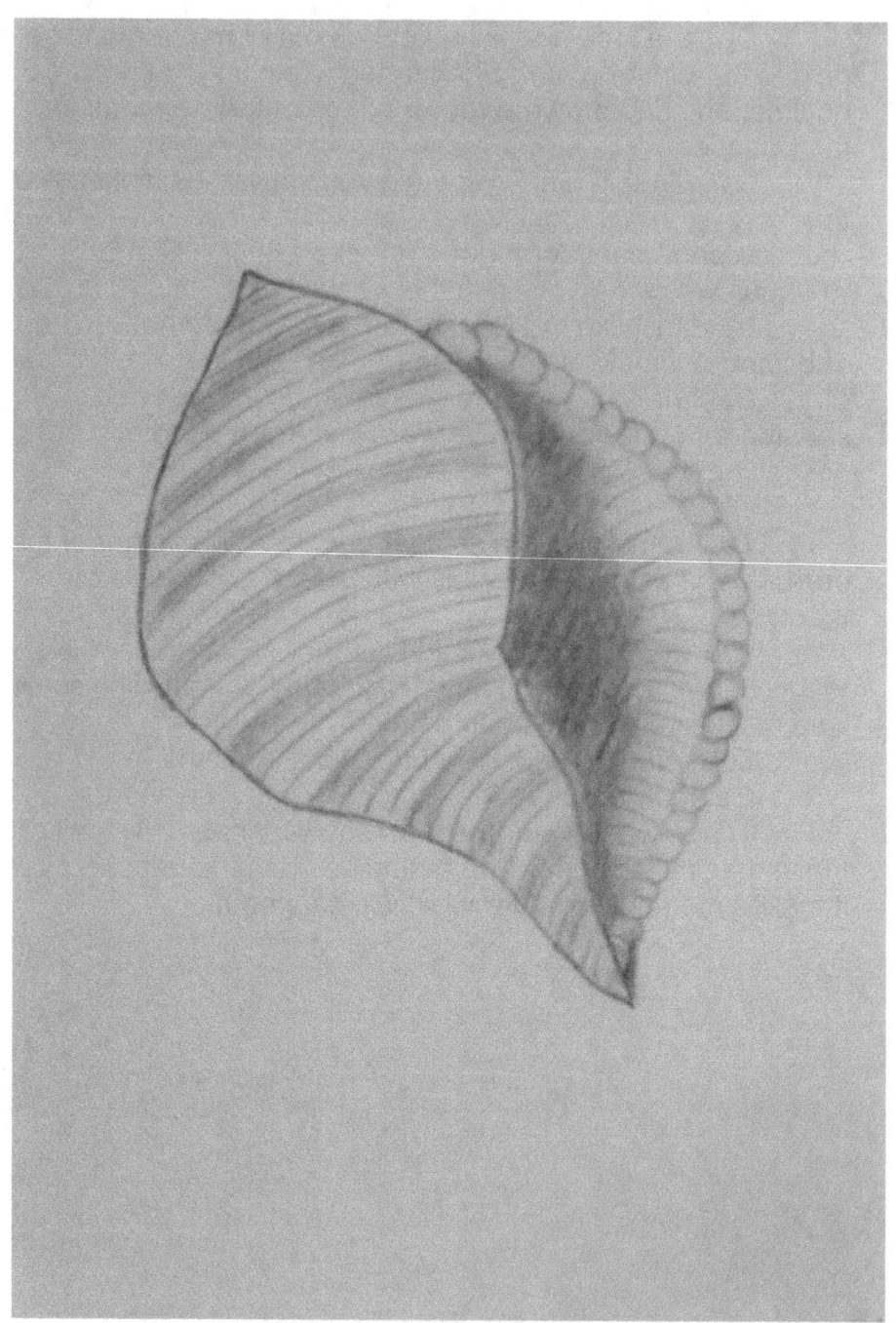

--Chapter 10--

"Song of The Sea"

Despite the sightings of strange magical creatures, the Fiddlesticks staff tried their best to keep student life on course. The day after Zephrum and Gai saw the whimpus, Dr. Malvin Moot surprised his oceanography class with an impromptu field trip. A shuttle van was hired to bring all of the students to the sandy shore of the Haversville Town Beach. Zephrum and Daphne sat next to each other in the large van on the way there.

Once everyone was at the beach, Dr. Malvin Moot instructed the students to pick up things that interested them.

"The treasures we find along the ocean's shore are just a mere fraction of what lives inside these vast waters, but it will give us an idea of what life is like beneath the sea."

Zephrum and Daphne walked together at the edge of the water, picking up stray shells and rocks. They looked at a pretty blue jellyfish that lurked just beneath the surface of the water and they explored mounds of seaweed. They noticed stray bits of trash washing up onto the shore, picked the objects up, and put them in a bag that Zephrum found in her backpack.

"It's crazy how much garbage ends up in the sea," said Zephrum.

"Totally," commented Daphne as she picked up an old plastic bottle. "It's so easy to recycle these things. It's nuts that people don't try to care a little more."

"I've heard that there's a huge 'garbage island' floating around in the ocean…and that it spans miles and miles," said Zephrum.

"I heard about that too," said Daphne. "I guess that fish are getting stuck in nets…and whales are eating garbage and getting sick from stuff stuck inside them."

"So sad, especially when it's so easy to prevent," said Zephrum with a frown.

"And super stupid too," Daphne agreed.

Zephrum tripped on something and saw a beautiful large empty shell. "What's that?" She picked it up and put it near her ear.

Her mouth opened wide.

"What is it?" asked Daphne.

Zephrum's eyes grew wider as she listened. At first, it was like an echo chamber blowing the sound of the waves into her ear. Then, it turned into a kind of hum hum humming that eventually became words. "The Sea Needs You. Help the Sea."

"What is it, Zephrum?" Daphne asked again.

Zephrum put her hand up and said. "Shhh…"

The haunting tune continued.

"Calling to you…
The spirit of the sea."

Hum..hum..hmmm…

The song trailed off.

Zephrum held the shell out and looked up at Daphne. "This seashell just sang a song to me."

"No?!? Really?"

"Yes. A song about the spirit of the sea," said Zephrum.

"Wow. Cool. Let me listen." Daphne put the shell up to her ear. At first, she heard a similar echo of waves, a humming. And then,

"All we wish
Is to simply be
Taking Care
Is the key.
Hmmm…"

Daphne took the shell away from her ear. "Whoa…I heard it too."

"What did you hear?" asked Zephrum.

"Waves, a hum, and then something about taking care being the key," reported Daphne.

"Cool," said Zephrum. "We should bring this shell back to Dr. Moot's class."

"For sure," said Daphne.

"I guess this oceanography class is going to be alright afterall," said Zephrum.

"Yes," said Daphne. "Hey, let's catch up with the others and show them this shell."

Daphne and Zephrum met up with their friends a few moments later.

"Hey," said Daphne. "Check out what we found. This shell. It sings in your ear."

"Well, all shells do that," said Sarah Bellum. "The rushing sounds that we hear are actually the noise of the surrounding environment, resonating within the cavity of the shell."

"But this is different," said Zephrum. "It actually sings words."

"Let me hear," said Gai. He reached out his hand for the shell.

When Gai put the shell up to his ear, he expected to hear the echo of the open waves.

"Ocean spirits
Come through me."

"Cool!" cried Gai.

"I want to listen," said Misty.

When Misty put the shell up to her ear, her eyes grew as wide as saucers. There was the sound of a torrent of churning water. Suddenly, a gush of water came pouring out of the shell...with a force so strong that everyone jumped back. Misty fell to the sand, drenched from the vast wave of water coming out of the shell.

She dropped the shell to the ground. The torrent of water stopped.

A mammoth amount of trash and a strange vapor that reeked of a rancid smell spewed from the empty shell.

"It smells like the vapor of Strasidous Rowpe," cried Zephrum as the children jumped back from the sudden surge of trash and water.

Gai and Daphne rushed over to Misty and helped her up.

"Whoa…" said Misty. "I can't believe all of that water and trash came out of that shell. How was it able to do that?"

Zephrum suddenly grabbed her head. Her brain was pounding. She moaned with pain.

Gusts of wind wisped the nearby sand into the air.

A deep and scary voice grated Zephrum's nerves and chilled her blood.

"My Globster needs trash…and LOTS of it. I will end you, Miss Gates. You and all of your little friends. Bwa..ha..ha..ha…"

"Stop! Stoooppp!" cried Zephrum, putting her hands over her ears. She screamed as the vapor swirled away in a powerful gust that blew the plastics and trash all around them in a chaotic flurry.

--Chapter 11--

"Sarah Bellum's Idea"

When Dr. Malvin Moot heard about the shell, he herded the students back to Fiddlesticks immediately.

"Misty and Zephrum, I insist that you check in with Nurse Asa, so she can take a look at you."

Daphne, Gai, and Sarah Bellum waited for them in the Healing Dome's entryway while Dexter went to retrieve some dry clothes for Misty.

Nurse Asa looked Zephrum in the eyes. "How are you feeling?"

"I'm fine," said Zephrum. "Really, I'm OK now."

"Just to be sure, we're going to take a record of your vital signs," said Nurse Asa. She bustled off to get a thermometer, her stethoscope, and a blood pressure cuff.

"Hey Misty, has anything like that ever happened to you before? I mean, at the beach?" asked Zephrum.

"No," said Misty in a daze. "I've never seen a sea shell spew out so much water and stuff. Pretty weird, huh?"

"Yeah," said Zephrum. "Clearly, it's not a typical seashell."

"And what about you?" said Misty. "Have you ever heard the voice of Strasidous Rowpe when his vapor has been around?"

"No," said Zephrum gloomily. "He must be gaining in strength somehow."

Dexter rushed into the healing dome with some fresh clothes. "Oh, Misty, Here you go. Put these on right away. Sitting in wet clothes can't be good for you."

Misty slipped behind a partition and changed her clothes while Dexter paced in a line. After a few minutes, Misty finally emerged in her dry garb and sat back down next to Zephrum.

"How do you girls feel?" asked Dexter.

"Fine." "OK now," they said at the same time.

Nurse Asa returned with her supplies. "I think I've got it from here, Dexter."

"Alright," he said. "But be sure to notify me if there's anything unusual about them. I'll be in my office, writing up an incident report."

"Of course," said Nurse Asa.

The girls couldn't talk while their lips were closed around the thermometers. Nurse Asa tracked the seconds on her wristwatch as the girls just looked at each other. Finally, Nurse Asa took the thermometers out to check their temperature readings. "Well, everything's normal there."

She proceeded to check their blood pressure, their eyes, their ears, their bones, and their reflexes. Finally, she said, "As far as I can tell, you're both perfectly normal. Please come by the Healing Dome if you notice anything out of the ordinary in the next day or two, alright?"

"OK," chimed the girls.

"What did Nurse Asa say?" asked Daphne when the girls emerged from the healing dome.

"She thinks we're fine," said Zephrum.

"What have they done with that seashell?" asked Misty.

"I guess that Dr. Moot is going to be inspecting it in his lab, for now," said Gai.

"I couldn't believe all the trash that came out of it," said Misty.

"I know," said Sarah. "It gave me an idea. I think we should construct an invention that will rid our oceans of trash."

"It does seem like a good idea, but the whole ocean?" said Daphne. "Obviously, trash is a major problem, but wow."

"I wonder how we could do it," said Gai.

"Well…I had been thinking about it before our field trip to the beach," said Sarah. "And I think we could create a kind of filtration machine that would attract trash and be able to filter out organic matter."

"I'll have to talk with Dr. Moot about it," Sarah continued. "But I think we could surround one of those garbage islands with a series of long floating booms, connected to the filters."

"Cool idea!" said Zephrum.

"Yes," said Sarah. "The floating booms would contain the garbage islands while the filtration machines do their work."

"It would be cool if something like that could actually help," said Zephrum

"It sure would," said Daphne. "But what about the vapor of Strasidous Rowpe? If it comes back, will Zephrum start screaming her head off again?"

Nobody knew what to say.

Daphne continued, "I mean, Zephrum. None of us heard what you heard."

"Well…" said Gai. "I felt a similar kind of headache around the same time that Zephrum put her hands to her head, but I definitely didn't hear anything."

"Obviously, Strasidous Rowpe's power is growing," said Zephrum. "We should probably figure out ways to be more prepared the next time we go on one of our oceanography field trips."

"Yeah," said Gai. "We should always bring our rowan branch with us. You know, just in case we all need to get away quick."

"It worked for us last year," said Zephrum.

"Yes," added Misty. "But remember how it works. You have to be SUPER specific with your words while you're connected to it, or else we would risk getting separated again."

Zephrum's memory flashed back to being stuck alone in underground goblin caves last year. "Definitely," she said. "We'll have to be really careful."

Just as they reached the horse corral, Aunt Gussie came rushing up to the group with Nomad prancing alongside. Great Aunt Gussie's curlers were dangling and bobbing up and down as she approached. "Oh Zephrum! Misty! I heard what happened at the beach! That seashell must have given you two the heebie-jeebies. What a fright! Are you alright?"

"Yes," said Zephrum, "except Misty got pretty wet."

Zephrum leaned down to Nomad and gave her a warm hug.

"You know," said Aunt Gussie, "sea shells like that are one-in-a-million."

"You've heard of shells like this before?" asked Misty.

"Oh yes," said Aunt Gussie. "Some old Sea Witches used to use shells like this to give them messages from the past or future. But all of that water and trash coming out of it is something I simply cannot explain."

"Yeah, it was pretty wild," said Gai.

"And there was this vapor too," added Zephrum. "It smelled like the vapor of Strasidous Rowpe."

"Oh…I figured you'd be spinning your wheels about this, Zephrum," said Aunt Gussie. She fiddled with one of her curlers.

"It's just I've never heard him in my head like that before," said Zephrum. "I mean, while being awake. What if he tries to capture me like he tried to do before?"

"It's true that the past can feel like a wilderness of terrors," said Aunt Gussie.

"His voice said that the globster needs lots of trash and that he would end me and all of my friends," said Zephrum. "What are we supposed to do?"

Aunt Gussie scooped Zephrum into a hug. "Well…you've got to anchor yourself in the land of the living. Strasidous Rowpe is not quite a man anymore. He is a mere apparition. What could he accomplish as a vapor?"

There was no sound on the still air. Zephrum's eyes met with Gai's.

Aunt Gussie added, "Don't let fear turn you away from your playful heart, kids. Keep your eye on your own true north and things will turn out fine."

Sarah piped up. "Well…we were thinking of creating an invention that could collect all of the trash in the oceans."

"Now you're talking," said Aunt Gussie. "Imagination is its own form of courage."

Sarah's eyes lit up. "I think we could surround one of those garbage islands in the ocean with a series of long floating booms, connected to filters…kind of like an array."

"You're not just a hat rack, are you?" said Aunt Gussie.

Sarah blushed a little. "But we'd have to figure a lot of things out."

"Now, don't throw in the towel before you even begin," said Aunt Gussie.

Zephrum sighed. "It seems like getting rid of the huge amount of trash in the oceans would be a good idea, especially if Strasidous Rowpe's globster feeds off of it."

"Normally, I think that concern over our waters is something of a dry subject," chuckled Aunt Gussie, "but being that our ocean is just a stone's throw away from us, we might actually be able to make things better out there."

"You think we could really make a difference?" asked Daphne.

"Well…" said Aunt Gussie. "No army can hold back a good thought. Just keep on doing little things and expect big results and you'll surely be on the right track."

The sun was escaping from the broken clouds.

"But what about that vapor of Strasidous Rowpe?" asked Zephrum. "It feels like he must be gaining in power if I can hear him in my head whenever the vapor comes around."

There was an uncomfortable silence. "Well…I might be all washed up now that I'm getting on in years, but I've learned that almost everything we want is on the other side of fear," said Aunt Gussie.

Zephrum shrugged her shoulders. "I guess."

"Remember your power, Zephrum," said Aunt Gussie. "You've done amazing and miraculous things before. A little vapor couldn't possibly hurt you. Don't trouble your head about it, especially when you have so many other fascinating things to focus on in school this year."

"Do you think Dr. Moot could help us construct my invention?" asked Sarah.

"Do you think getting rid of the trash in the ocean will prevent Strasidous from gaining more power?" asked Zephrum.

"Well...it might," said Aunt Gussie. "The main thing is that you're putting energy into whatever floats your boat....and that's bound to help unlock your passion for life, right?"

"Alright then," said Aunt Gussie. She looked at her wristwatch. "Oh...I've lost my head. It's almost time for dinner. Goodness, if my memory was any worse, I could plan my own surprise party."

--Chapter 12--
"Pirates"

Back at the goblins' secret warehouse at the docks, goblins were almost done constructing their great ship.

They attached the plywood and trim to meet the frames, put the bottom planking on, and adhered brackets and cleats where needed. The worker goblins faired the main structure by sanding it until it was smooth. They hoisted the mast and secured the boom for the mainsail. The last thing they had to do was saturate the outside of the boat with a magical sealant.

A circlet of enthusiastic goblins surrounded the boat. They chanted an incantation in ancient Goblinese. "Yark Yark Doum! Durbuluk! Yark Yark Doum! Durbuluk! Guul'dar! We dominate the seas." It was a devious spell of protection, giving them strength and ensuring the surrender of all in their path. As with most goblin spells, this one invoked sly trickery as a pathway to their good fortune. "Yark Yark Doum! Durbuluk! Yark Yark Doum! Durbuluk! Guul'dar! We dominate the seas." After the spell was cast, their crooked ways would naturally assist them, no matter what obstacles they faced.

The spell concluded with the goblins howling and whooping like a pack of demented wolves.

"The NOISE!" protested Virgidous. "Stop the NOISE!"

"I need to THINK," said Virgidous. "This is a wonderfully wily vessel, but it is too bright on the deck for most of our goblin kin to captain. What will we do?"

Virgil's voice suddenly surfaced. "Sire…goblins could remain below deck, in the dark dank of the ship's under-quarters."

"Yes, Virgil. We would all delight in the shadowless dark of the bowels of the ship, but WHO will pilot the vessel?"

"Sire," continued Virgil's voice. "We could easily bribe… Pirates!"

"PIRATES?!?" exclaimed the stronger voice of Strasidous from within.

Virgil forged ahead. "Yes, sire. We still have plenty of gold and treasure in the dragon's abandoned den from whence we came. It would not take much to entice pirates, as their greed is matched only by our own."

"True," said the Strasidous voice.

"And sire," continued Virgil's voice, "We could also deceive them by giving them much less than they deserve."

Virgidous exploded, "Bwa..ha..ha..ha..ha...."

After a short pause, the Strasidous voice said, "Yes...and we could confuse them with one of our perceptual spells, so they will accept even the most meager treasure and do our bidding, while thinking it is THEIRS. We will let them believe they have scored the greatest treasure of their lousy miserable pirate lives...for the short-lived glory of captaining our ship."

"And..." added Strasidous. "They will be so distracted by the fleeting euphoria of sailing our ship that they will never know what is coming to them. Once we are finished with them, we will FEED the pirates to the Globster as a tasty treat."

A deep silence followed this devious thought.

"Yes, sire! Yes. Brilliant," said the Virgil voice. "We will attain a tango of pirates right away."

"Yes," said Strasidous with a sneer. "And then, our plan will unfold with duplicitous ease."
"Bwa..ha..ha..ha..ha..."

Virgidous called on Warrior Zultr Zeki to go with him to Buccaneer's Barnacle, which was the nearest pirate tavern in town.

The aroma of fish guts filled the air as they ambled down the alley to the heavy gate of the bar. The door creaked as they opened it.

The smell of a thousand sweaty socks wafted up their noses, piercing their sinuses like a rancid dagger. Ropes, netting, and anchors decorated the darkened walls. Behind the bar was an old man with a long gray beard. He was placing large tankards in front of three scraggly pirates in front of him. "One last drink for all of you before this old geezer hits the hay for the night."

"Aaarrghh…" said the few scallywags.

"I think we're in the right place," whispered Zultr Zeki.

The biggest man at the bar was a black-bearded pirate, the infamous Captain Muttonchops. The other two pirates were slamming shot glasses down onto the bar and screaming in an enthusiastic manner, "Yaarrrr…"

"Geezer…Give us another!" demanded the one pirate with a peg leg.

"No can do," said the old man in a raspy voice. "This Geezer's got to get my ship ready for me morning fishin' voyage."

"Aaarrrgh…" protested the pirates at an even higher decibel.

Strasidous flinched as he took in the racket. "Virgil, you might need to handle this. Their NOISE is already putting me beyond my edge."

"Yes, Sire," said Virgil's voice.

Zultr Zeki gave a sideways glance at Virgidous when she heard Virgil's voice surface.

Captain Muttonchops turned on his barstool, suddenly noting the strange pair of goblins at the door. "Ahhh… Look what the bilge rats dragged in."

The pirates whooped even louder than before. The smaller scraggly pirate next to Muttonchops laughed so loud that his mouth opened wide enough to reveal his missing front teeth.

"Blimey!" Captain Muttonchops continued. "If it isn't our old friend, Bucko Virgil." He raised his mug. "Are you here for grog? Or is it a proper flogging you've come for?"

"Ha! Ha! Ha! Ha! Ha!" screeched his pirate sidekicks, more boisterous than before.

Muttonchops snapped a frayed leather hand whip in the air and Virgil recoiled.

Zultr Zeki pushed forward, her chest pumped up behind her warrior's shield.

"Oh…Now don't get your peg leg in a hole," said Muttonchops, looking at her. "We're just having a little fun. Isn't that right, boys?"

"Yaarrr…" echoed the other two pirates in chorus.

The peg leg pirate spit nut shells to the ground and the littler one swaggered off his stool.

Muttonchops stood up. He took three very slow steps towards Virgil. He peered into Virgil's face. "I know you as a lying blaggard. What do you want? Why are you here? I know you must have some sort of conniving plan."

Vapor rose off of his body as he spoke.

Virgil threw a sack of coins on the bar and said, "I have a job for you, and booty treasure for you and your whole crew."

"Look me in the deadlights and tell me you speak truth," said Muttonchops.

"Yes, Muttonchops! It's true," responded Virgil. "And the opportunity to captain your own state-of-the-art vessel as well."

"Sink me?!?"

"Nooo…?!?"

"Shiver me Timbers?!?"

"Yes," said Virgil with a sly look. "We are searching for a Globster. We will thwart the efforts of a mere child, who impedes our path to the success we so deserve. Then, we will gain ultimate power over all things with the help of… of… a Leviathan."

"Begad? You think me foolish and addled?"

"No, Muttonchops," responded Virgil in his way. "It is our deep respect for you and your fiendish ways that has brought me here."

"But a Leviathan?!? It's a thing of myth."

"Yes. And also the creature that will elevate us beyond our wildest dreams," said Virgil.

The three pirates looked into the empty air clearly imagining the riches they could obtain. "Aaahhh…"

"Will the ship have a crow's nest as a lookout point at the top of the highest mast?" asked Muttonchops.

"For you," said Virgil. "Anything."

"Can we fly our Jolly Roger flag and watch the skull and crossbones be our telltale in the wind?"

"Of course," reassured Virgil. "Like I said, our ship is your ship."

"Mmm…" said Muttonchops, scratching at his beard. "Is this a Man-of-War ship? Will we at least have a small monkey cannon?"

"If it is your wish, we will provide."

The pirates exploded into howling.

"Aaarrgh…"

"Aye…"

"Yaarrrr…"

Muttonchops gave Virgil a sideways glance, "You're not trying to hornswaggle us, are ya'?"

"No. No cheating here," said Virgil, crossing his fingers behind his back.

Muttonchops looked dreamily into the far distant nowhere, "Cap'n Muttonchops. Ahhh… I like the sound of that."

The other two pirates clinked their tankards and drank.

"Me matey," said Muttonchops. "Me hearties here seem to be very enthusiastic about this idea. We'll weigh anchor and be ready to set sail whenever you are."

This was the kind of opportunity that Muttonchops just couldn't refuse.

"A voyage out at sea with me and me crew is just the kind of profitable adventure we need," said Muttonchops. "We should splice the mainbrace together, goblin."

"Yes. Splice the mainbrace. Uh? What do you mean?" asked an admittedly confused Virgil.

"Drink on it," said Muttonchops. "All fortuitous deals begin with a ceremonial toast. I be one of the best seadogs on this side of Jewel Island. I'll bring my crew of buccaneers. We'll all help rid yourself of your little problems AND bring in some booty at the same time."

"Yes," said the Virgil voice. "I'm sure we will all benefit greatly. I can bring you to our grand ship at once."

The raucous crew of pirates left the tavern with the two odd goblins.

Cleaning a glass with a white dishtowel, Geezer watched their backs as they departed. "Mmm..." he commented. "Pirates and goblins workin' together. This can't be good. Definitely not good at all."

--Chapter 13--

"First Voyage"

Eventually, the pirates reached the docks and set their eyes on the new boat.

"Blimey! It's a prize of a ship!" exclaimed Muttonchops as he looked upon the goblin's new sailing vessel.

He opened his arms wide and motioned to his entourage of pirates and said, "Avast ye all. This is our new ship."

"Aarrgh…" chimed his tango of pirates.

"Get your duffles packed, for we're soon to set sail," announced Muttonchops. "First, we'll inspect this ship from bow to stern."

"Aye, aye, Cap'n…" said the pirate with the peg leg. "We'll check it from the crow's nest to the poop deck."

"Yarrgh…" said the littlest pirate. "We'll check it from fore to aft."

"Get to it," said Muttonchops. "These goblins are landlubbers. That's why they need us. Scallywags, I tell ya'."

As his pirate minions hobbled along the deck, looking at all aspects of the rigging and woodwork, Muttonchops paused. Virgidous had an odd look on his face. "Be you afeard to be out at sea with me and me crew?"

"No," exclaimed Virgil in his slimy way. "Remember…we have invited you to sail our ship."

"Mmm…" Muttonchops gave the goblin a sideways glance. "Whatever you say, goblin."

"Be there a HOLD for our prisoners down below? And where be the Head?" He examined the rigging and looked around the ship.

"Yes," said Virgil. "There is an iron-gated cell down below, as well as a bathroom. We have thought of everything."

The Captain's pirate minions finally returned, smiling toothy grins.

"Me hearties. What do you think? Will it sail?" asked Muttonchops.

"Yaarrgh…" exclaimed the pirate with the scraggly beard.

"Aye!" affirmed the pirate with the peg leg.

Muttonchops swaggered up to the telescope and peered inside. He swiveled the telescope all around its full radius, looking out to sea. "Ah…Me Captain's Spyglass…" He spoke as though he was drinking the finest rum. "The red dusk bodes well for the next day's sail."

"Yaarrgh…" exclaimed the pirates at his side.

And so, it was settled. The ship was acceptable for the pirates and they would set sail the next day. They would search for the trash-eating Globster…and hope to find the mythical Leviathan as well.

Back at the underground goblin caverns, it was a sleepless night for Virgidous. Both voices were battling each other within. "Am I Virgil?" "No, I am Strasidous Rowpe! I am the most powerful of all. I am in control, as always!"

The goblin could not know if his "normal goblin self" would surface…or if Strasidous would be able to continue to steer them clearly. It was probably due to the stress of the imminent sailing journey, but it felt as though the veil between their two personalities was becoming thinner and thinner as more responsibility toppled upon him.

Virgidous finally drifted off to sleep and began dreaming about the mythical Leviathan….AND Grizalda the Great.

In his slumber, Grizalda's craggy spirit shook him by the shoulders and said, "Be forewarned, my evil friend. For if you anger the Leviathan you seek, it can send forth from its mouth a heat so great as to make all the waters of the deep boil."

Virgidous tossed and turned, sweating in his sleep.

"No living creature can endure the odor of the Leviathan if he puts his head into paradise," continued Grizalda. Shrouded in a mist of fog, she added, "BUT…his eyes…like eyelids of the morning…possess an illuminating power which can assist you in your quest for ultimate control over all things. Just one glance into the Leviathan's eyes and you could become more powerful than you have ever imagined."

"OR worse!" Grizalda's spirit took a puff of her cigar. She continued, "But be forewarned. For this power could come at a VERY high price."

"What? What is the price?" asked Strasidous in his dream. "I will do whatever it takes. Just tell me."

Grizalda's ethereal craggy form was beginning to dissipate. "You won't like it, Dark One. For you will need help. You will need the help of…the infamous… Zephrum Gates!"

And then, without warning, Virgidous sat bolt upright, eyes glowing with greed…and AWAKE!

The early morning did not come soon enough for Virgidous. "My wish to gain control over all things is imminent. I can taste it. Since a Leviathan can eat a whole whale each week, finding a larger globster will be the ultimate lure for this creature." He rubbed his hands together in a greedy way as he thought about it. "I will find the Leviathan without that pesky Zephrum Gates."

"But Sire," asked Virgil's voice from within. "What if we do need her help?"

"Rubbish," screamed the stronger Strasidous voice. "Zephrum Gates is a mere pipsqueak."

"Of course, Sire," responded Virgil's voice. "But if we must seek her out, how will we get her to help us?"

"Virgil," said the Strasidous voice. "We will cross that bridge IF we get to it."

Suddenly there was a loud knock on the thick door. "Sire…It is I. Zultr Zeki. I am here to escort you to the ship for our first great sailing journey."

Despite the challenges of his sleepless night, Virgidous sprang up from his bed. He grabbed a small shoulder bag, opened the door, and was apparently quite ready to go. "Yes, Zeki," said Virgidous in a single-minded tone. "I have been looking forward to this since the middle of the night. Let's go!"

They dashed through the Goblin caverns, then traveled via the subterranean cart system. They swerved as they rolled upon the tracks. Finally, Zultr Zeki pulled on the lever to bring them to a stop. They got out of the cart and walked up through a narrow tunnel of dirt stairs that opened up to the docks where their fine ship was anchored.

The scraggly gang of pirates swaggered up to the boat at the same time. Captain Muttonchops was already there. He pointed to the vessel and screamed, "All hands ahoy! The last one on the boat will be kicked in the dungbie."

The tango of pirates all scrambled to get onto the ship before the others. The pirate with the peg leg was unusually fast.

Muttonchops gave a sideways glance to Virgidous. "Nobody likes to get kicked in the keester."

"Yes," said Virgidous. "A boot to one's rear end is not the best way to start the day."

"Ha..Ha..Ha," laughed Muttonchops. "I can see this is going to be quite a journey. You see the humor of us Freebooters! Aarrgh!" He slapped Virgidous on the back and said, "We are able seamen, but we also enjoy our fun."

Virgidous hacked up a dry cough. He was not as enthusiastic about the "fun" as the pirates.

Muttonchops stepped onto the deck of the boat and started barking out orders. "Hoist the sails aloft!" he cried. "Bosun! Get up in the Crow's Nest and be our eyes."

"Aye Aye, Cap'n," said the small bosun.

"You deck hands…Free the Lines!"

"Weigh anchor…and get ready to set sail!"

"Fair winds to us all…"

With that, the ship floated into the bay and glided out to sea. The sea wind blew, making the pirate's messy hair swirl about their faces.

They started to sing a shanty.

"Yo Ho Ho…and a bottle of Rum.

Out on the Seas…For the Globster we come.

Yo Ho Ho…And the loveliest wench…

We'll find this Creature…by sniffing his stench."

When the song finally wound down, Muttonchops finally went into his Captain's cabin and returned to the main deck with a box. He opened it up. "A snack of boiled cackle fruit for all of ye old seadogs!"

Three nearby pirates scrambled towards the box, which was filled with boiled chicken eggs. They threw the eggs to pirates that couldn't move from their posts. They cracked the shells off, threw the bits of shell overboard, and gobbled up the eggs. "Aaargh…"

Every day, the pirates worked hard. Muttonchops had a different special food stashed away for his crew each day. Every night, they let the sails down for a number of hours (so they could rest and float upon the ocean waves).

Finally, after three days of sailing, they reached one of the garbage islands out at sea. "Circle around this mass…and keep an eye out for the infamous Globster," said Muttonchops.

Soon enough, a super large fish surfaced. It was blob-like and going slow. "Ah," sneered Virgidous. "The Globster."

He walked up to the Captain's telescope to get a closer look at the vile thing. "As you see," he said to Zultr Zeki, "this large creature loves to be around bits of trash. We will have to create an incantation that will inspire all humans to be MORE careless than ever. If we can get them to throw more and more trash into the oceans, they will actually help us execute their own demise. Bwa..ha..ha..ha…"

"Yes Sire," agreed Zultr Zeki.

They surveyed the sea for quite some time, but there was no sight of the Leviathan. "Mmm…" said Virgidous, finally. "I had a clairvoyant dream with Grizalda The Great. I was led to believe that finding the Leviathan would be quite possible." He rubbed his chin. "Although…she did suggest that we might actually need to commission the help of Zephrum Gates to make it so."

"Zephrum Gates?!?" asked Zultr Zeki in alarm.

"I know," said Virgidous in a detestable way. "Getting the help of that little twerp could prove to be our biggest challenge, but I have my ways. We'll have to seek her out after we return to dry land. I will travel to her forest via our underground caverns and I will 'convince' her."

"Yes, Sire," said Zeki. "As you wish."

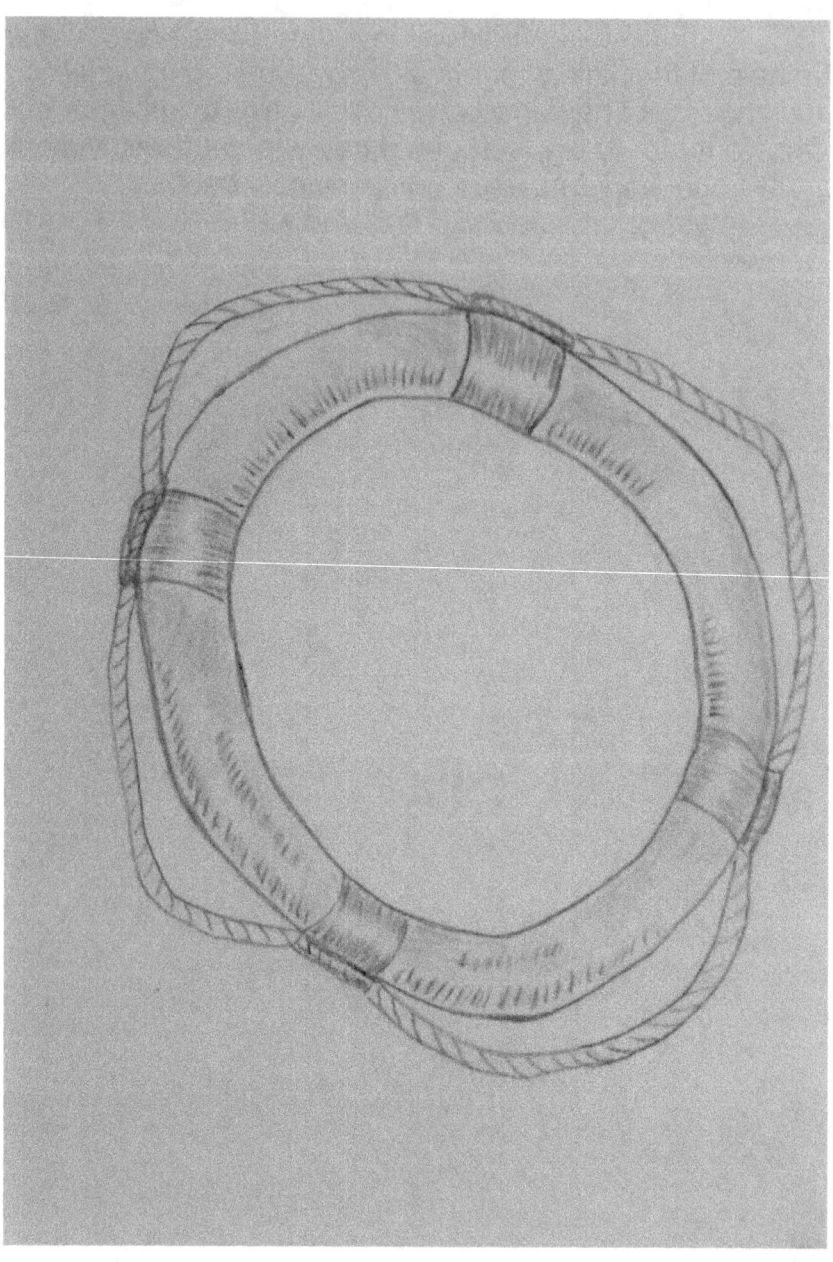

--Chapter 14--

"The Big Splash"

Meanwhile, back at Fiddlesticks, the students got more deeply involved in all of their school projects. Dr. Moot was quite enthusiastic about Sarah Bellum's idea for ridding our oceans of trash. He suggested that the new invention become a team project that the whole class could work on.

"Firstly, we'll analyze how large our filters must be," he said. "And then, we'll start construction."

"In our oceanography class, we'll study the kinds of creatures that appear to be the most affected by garbage in the sea. We'll look at which kinds of sea creatures tend to travel together…and which just naturally gravitate towards the garbage islands in the water. We'll take all of this data into account as we construct our 'array'."

A new field trip was scheduled as well. "We want you all to get up close and personal with the sea life living in our nearby ocean."

Aunt Gussie volunteered to be a chaperone for this field trip, as she also wanted students to learn about the healing properties of seaweeds. "Oh…The vitamins and minerals in seaweeds are beneficial as a garden mulch," she told the children, "but it's also a tasty dietary supplement in the foods we eat."

Waldo Vestor had acquired the use of a boat that was owned and operated by a local fisherman, named Geezer Fraggle.

As the students arrived at the docks with Dr. Moot and Great Aunt Gussie, Geezer was organizing ropes and hoisting sails to ready the boat for their ocean trip.

Gussie took one look at this gray bearded man with his yellow raincoat and rubber boots...and she had to stabilize herself by grabbing onto Zephrum's shoulder. "Have you ever seen a man more fetching than this?" Aunt Gussie whispered into her ear. "What a head turner! Oh, my heart's gone all a flutter." She waved her hand like a fan in front of her face. "I'm losing my head." She was a bit flushed in the face.

Daphne covered her mouth with her hand and tried to hide her giggles. Oblivious, Aunt Gussie kept staring at Geezer as though hypnotized.

At that moment, Geezer looked up from his ropes and caught Aunt Gussie's eye. "What a woman!" he muttered to himself. "She's a real traffic stopper!"

The two looked at each other as though they had never seen anything more beautiful.

Aunt Gussie finally remembered her head and continued guiding the group of students toward the boat.

The kids walked onto the ship via a wide wood plank that connected the dock to the boat. Their eyes widened as they took in all the wonder of this real sailing ship. There were all sorts of questions and comments. "How does it sail?" "What's that big pole for?" "What do these ropes do?"

After everyone was ushered onto the vessel, Geezer called for their attention. "OK, now. Everybody should sit down on the seats bordering the edges of the boat here." Once the kids were seated and looking towards him, Geezer began. "The front of the boat is called the bow, while the back is referred to as the stern, or aft. The right side of the boat is the starboard side, while the left is the port side. This big central pole is the mast. It holds the mainsail. And this here long metal piece that guides the bottom of the mainsail is the boom. Whenever we change our direction...or our tack, the boom will help move the sail to the other side of the boat. That's when we'll all have to be careful and keep our heads out of the way. Or else...you guessed it, it will go 'boom' ...right on your noggins."

Gai raised his hand. "How will we know when the sail is going to move to the other side?"

"As Captain," said Geezer. "I'll shout out some old sailor terms. I'll say 'Ready About.' Then, I'll wait for you all to say 'Ready!' Finally, as the boom moves across to the other side of the boat, I'll say 'Hard a lee!' Trust me, you won't miss it."

Geezer pointed out the rigging lines and the telltales. He said, "We've got to be sure that these ropes always remain free. And if you look up at those stringy pieces of yarn at the front of the boat…the telltales, we'll know which way the wind is blowing and we'll be able to adjust the sails and our heading…in order to get the maximum boost from the wind."

The students all stood open mouthed.

Geezer continued, "Once we're underway, I trust that you'll all be careful. The deck can sometimes get a bit slippery when water splashes on it." He paused for a moment. "Are we all ready for our first sailing voyage?"

"Aye, Aye, Captain!"

"Yes!"

"Totally!"

"Now, everybody has got to get geared up with their life jackets," he said. "Safety first!"

The Fiddlesticks students enthusiastically grabbed life jackets from a pile on the deck.

Dr. Moot and Aunt Gussie assisted the students by clipping their life jackets and making sure their straps were snug.

After everybody was ready, Dr. Moot approached Geezer, who was sailing the boat out of the marina where it had been docked. "Geezer…We are here to survey the garbage island that has been approaching our coast. Is it possible to get close to it? Do you have an idea of where it is?"

"Well," said Geezer. "As you know, it moves all the time. Usually, I try to stay as far away from it as possible. But yes, I have an idea of where one of those garbage islands in the sea might be, as I know where I saw a big floating mass of it last."

Geezer set the sailboat on a trajectory that was sure to bring them to the pile of yuck that had accumulated in the nearby waters.

Once the boat was on a stable course, he looked to Gussie, who was standing nearby him, admiring his skill and knowledge.

Aunt Gussie said, "I must say, I'm quite impressed with you and all of your natural skills."

"Oh, it's nothing for an old sea dog like me," said Geezer.

"Usually, I like to say that a woman without a man is like a fish without a bicycle," said Aunt Gussie.

Geezer cocked his head to one angle, a confused look on his face.

"What I mean to say," said Aunt Gussie, "is you make me feel differently." She eyed Geezer up and down and said, "You are quite an inspiration, Mr. Fraggle."

"Oh...Call me Geezer."

"Of course," said Gussie. "Geezer it is."

As they made their way to the floating garbage island, the two chatted on as though they were the only two people in the world. They completely ignored the students. They were obviously smitten with each other. Zephrum had never seen Aunt Gussie giggle so much.

Geezer put his arm around Gussie as he pointed out landmarks and explained about all the aspects of sailing his great ship. "The islands in this part of the ocean have changed a bit due to melting glacial ice, but our sea is still mesmerizing. It's full of life and new surprises every day."

"Oh..." said Gussie. "That's fascinating. You are like the flame to my fire with all of this talk."

"Having someone be as interested as you just lifts my heart. You're like the water to my ocean. And what a beauty you are."

"Oh…it's been so long since somebody has appreciated me like this, Geezer. You're like the bee to my bonnet," said Aunt Gussie. "So complimentary."

"Oh…" said Geezer. "You're like the wind to my breath."

Aunt Gussie blushed and looked at her toes. "Really?"

"Oh yes," said Geezer. "To find a woman like you is a dream come true. You're like the bark to my tree."

Swooning, Aunt Gussie added, "And you're like the hoot to my owl."

Zephrum could have sworn she saw Aunt Gussie blushing.

All of this talk was a bit much…and it didn't seem to be losing steam.

Zephrum thought, "Wow…These two are almost as lovey-dovey as Daphne Gumption's parents."

Finally, Zephrum decided to go up to the bow of the boat and get some distance from all of the old-person flirting. She looked out at the lonely ocean waves until she spotted the garbage island in the distance. They were coming upon it fairly fast. She stood there, wondering how so much trash could have collected in the sea and why it all seemed to congregate in one place.

Because she was so lost in thought, Zephrum didn't even notice Razebir (her annoying neighbor from up river). He was sneaking up behind her with a wooden paddle. Clearly, he had gotten it into his head that it would be funny to smack Zephrum on her behind with the oar.

Sneaking up behind her on tip toe, he was stepping as quietly as he could. Then, "BAM!"

As she got hit on the butt, Zephrum lost her balance on the slippery bow and actually tripped OVERBOARD. Splash!!!

"What was THAT?!?"

"Hey, what happened at the front of the boat?"

"What was that big splash?"

Razebir was as surprised as everybody else. Talking to himself, he said, "I didn't know she'd just flip over like that! Ha!"

Meanwhile, Zephrum was splashing around and spraying water from her lips. She began swimming along the starboard side of the boat. She tried to find a place to grab onto, but the slippery sides were too smooth and the boat was moving too fast.

"Oh my Goodness!" cried Aunt Gussie. The love trance was broken.

"What's all the commotion about?" said Geezer.

"Zephrum fell overboard," screamed Razebir. "She was swimming along side to find a way back up, but we sailed right past her." He pointed behind the boat to where Zephrum was splashing about in their wake.

Geezer immediately adjusted the mainsail and the rudder to alter the boat's course. As the vessel turned back and got closer to Zephrum, Geezer adjusted the sails again. He said, "It looks like it's time for us to put this ship in irons." He looked up at the flapping sail, which was no longer catching the wind.

"Don't you worry about a thing." Aunt Gussie screamed down to Zephrum. "We'll get you back up here in a jiffy."

"I'll bring the rope ladder up from down below," said Geezer.

He yelled out at Zephrum, "For now, hold onto this flotation donut." He tossed a flotation device out to her and Zephrum grabbed it.

"Hold on, Zephrum," screamed Aunt Gussie. "Geezer is getting his thing-a-ma-bob from down below."

Suddenly, a great wave swelled the water near the boat. Before their very eyes, a large blob-shaped fish the size of a giant whale began to surface.

Zephrum held on tight to the floaty circle and tried to swim away from the mysterious creature, which was headed her way. A humongous mouth opened to a small trash pile not too far away from Zephrum. The giant mouth glided closer to her.

"Oh, no!" said Zephrum.

Large razor sharp teeth arrowed toward her. The creature had such stinky buzzard breath that it smelled like day-old road kill.

A swirl of wind formed around Zephrum and made the sails of the ship flutter madly about. Her power was emerging.

The squail of the ocean waves suddenly became a rough torrent. "This wind feels like it's going to blow my curlers into sawdust," said Aunt Gussie.

Geezer climbed back up on deck and screamed over the wind, "Yes. It just shakes your rear molars, doesn't it?"

Finally, he managed to secure the rope ladder to some cleats on the edge of the boat and dropped it overboard. To bring her closer to the boat, Geezer pulled on a ropey tether attached to Zephrum's floaty donut.

The open-mouthed creature altered its course in the choppy waves JUST before it reached Zephrum's splashing figure.

Zephrum eventually pulled herself closer to the hanging rope ladder. She climbed up the ladder as all of the kids from her class looked into the water.

Zephrum finally pulled herself onto the ship. Geezer helped her back aboard. "Little Lady, this isn't quite the place for an afternoon swim."

"You're telling ME! What WAS that creature?" said Zephrum.

"Oh," said Geezer. "That giant globster feeds on trash of all kinds. It's been showing up more and more often, as the seas fill with this mindless mess. I can't believe it hasn't gotten sick on it all, but it seems to love the stuff...along with jellyfish and barnacles and other bits of ick from the ocean."

"You see," said Geezer as he put a wool blanket around Zephrum's shoulders, "Salps and ick also gravitate towards these garbage islands, linked up like chains. I think it's the jellyfish and barnacles that the creature is <u>really</u> going for, but it's just generally indiscriminate with the stuff that goes into its mouth. You were lucky, Miss Zephrum. It probably would have swallowed you whole if it got to you."

Zephrum shivered. "Yeah…I guess. I felt something hit my butt. What was it? How did I actually slip overboard?"

Daphne nodded toward Razebir, who was staring down at his feet. He was holding an oar in his hands.

Aunt Gussie wrapped the wool blanket around Zephrum a little more tightly. "Oh my heavens, Zephrum. You sure do find a way into trouble, don't you?"

"Things just keep happening to me!" said Zephrum.

"Well…" said Dr. Moot, "Now that we've seen that a Globster could be near the garbage islands out here, we know we'll have to be extra careful while setting up our invention."

"Totally!" Zephrum agreed.

--Chapter 15--

"Leviathan Ponderings"

Further out in the ocean, the Leviathan was searching. His churning stirred a glistening white wake as wild as a unicorn's mane behind him.

Snorts through his nose threw out flashes of light as he soared through the tumultuous waters. "Ever since my great ocean has started to sicken, I have begun to tire of the effort I must exert to look for prey. Must I travel to warmer waters southward? Why must there be such toil? What is the root cause of this problem?"

And then, as was usual when he asked deep pondering questions, his spirit ancestors responded. "Strasidous Rowpe...an evil so great...has cast a spell upon humanity."

"Huh?" asked the Leviathan's inner mind. "What is a Strasidous Rowpe?"

"He was once a man, but now he is part horror."

"Grrr..." growled the Leviathan. "Tell me more."

"Humanity, inspired by Strasidous Rowpe...has become unconscious. Through their lack of care, they spoil the waters."

"How can one species create such havoc?" asked the Leviathan in his mind.

"It is through matter they call 'plas-teek'...and through oil they dredge from the ground and the seas...and through a strange vapor of 'rrr-diation' that kills."

"A perplexing creature...Umans." And then, the Leviathan asked, "But what is 'rrr-diation'."

"It is a waste of ether we cannot explain."

Just then, his eyes, like rays of the dawn, spotted something...something very large.

Ahead was the most giant sort of whale he had ever seen. "Mmm..." he grumbled. "Eating a creature this large will satiate my hunger for quite some time. I wonder how it has grown to be so huge?"

"It is a Globster from ancient times. It has grown over an aeon, like yourself," whispered his ancestors.

"Mmm…" thought the great sea monster. "I will watch this creature and learn its ways. Then, I will surmise my best method of attack."

The Leviathan swerved and glided closer to the globster, but remained hidden and out of view. Through the aeons of time that he had lived, he discovered ways to blend in with the sea. That way, his prey was always caught by surprise.

"Quick deaths are the best deaths," he said to his own mind as he considered his skills.

"It is the most compassionate way to kill." Forming a snarling smile, he revealed jagged sharp teeth on the side of his large mouth. "AND…the most efficient way as well."

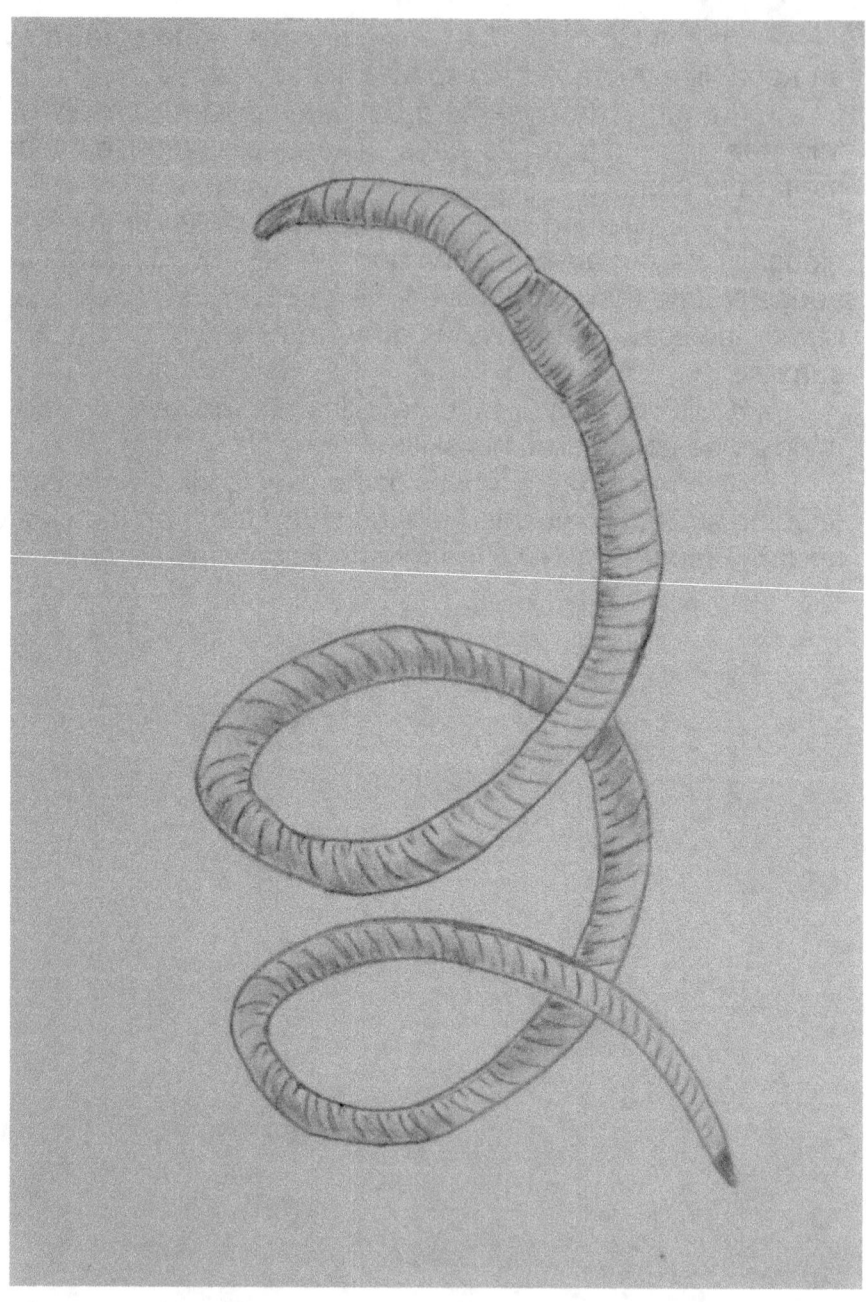

--Chapter 16--
"What's a Kilbit?"

The Fiddlesticks staff was concerned. Both field trips to the ocean had now ended with emergencies of quite the unusual nature. What were they going to do to ensure the safety of the students? Reinforcing the importance of the buddy system (even when on Geezer's boat) might help, but it looked like students were going to need to be MUCH more careful. "We'll have to think of a more proactive plan," said Dexter, definitively.

Meanwhile, after falling into the ocean and facing the giant mouth of a Globster, Zephrum was feeling very much on edge. She tossed and turned throughout the night. Her dreams were filled with images of razor sharp teeth threatening her. She couldn't sleep, so she snuggled with her doggie Nomad, hoping it would help to calm her mind.

"You and Majestic have been such good friends to me," she whispered into Nomad's floppy ear. "You are always there for me, always fun to be with, and always loyal."

"You'd never hit me in the rear end with a paddle or play tricks on me. You are probably the truest friend I've ever had."

Nomad nuzzled her nose up against Zephrum's shoulder. A teardrop formed in Zephrum's eye. Nomad licked her cheek to scoop it away. Zephrum's heart felt warm and protected when she was with her dog. It was such a great gift that the Fiddlesticks staff allowed Zephrum to have Nomad with her, as her doggie presence really helped Zephrum cope with all of her many mixed up feelings. After a little more whispering into Nomad's ear, Zephrum eventually drifted back to sleep.

"Wow, Zephrum," said Daphne when she woke the next morning. "I had some wild dreams last night. What about you?"

Zephrum shrugged her shoulders. "I wish you hadn't reminded me. I kept on dreaming about that Globster."

"Well..." said Daphne. "That was pretty scary. It makes sense that you'd dream about it."

"What were you dreaming about?" asked Zephrum.

"It's kind of hard to explain," admitted Daphne. "I think I'm going to have to draw it out on my sketchpad. But, I dreamt of that eye inside the triangle again. But now, it was attached to a huge turban and a really ugly head."

"Eeuuwww..." said Zeprhum.

"I know," added Daphne. "The head was smoking a large cigar and the face was cracked and filled with warts and stuff."

"The weirdest part is that I could 'hear' the voice. It was a rough smoker's voice."

"What did it say?" asked Zephrum.

Trying to imitate the rough scratchy voice the best she could, Daphne said, "It said, 'Danger is Imminent.' Something about dog spirits as protection...and...another bit about...well...a worm."

"A worm?"

"Yeah," said Daphne. "It said the only thing that could help protect us from some kind of Sea Monster...is a worm."

"Whoa..." said Zephrum.

"I know. Super weird. I'm going to go sketch it all out, while it's still fresh in my mind. I want to get to it before classes start today." Daphne got up, changed out of her pajamas super fast, and ran over to the large drawing easel in the Sun Lodge.

Zephrum got up slowly, let Nomad out of the cabin for a morning tinkle, and gave her some breakfast kibble when she came back in. While Nomad was eating, Zephrum went to their nearby outhouse bathroom to brush her teeth and get ready for the day.

She returned to the cabin and changed into her day clothes. Then she went over to the horse's corral as Nomad happily pranced behind. Zephrum put half a flake of alfalfa and half a flake of dry hay into each horse feeder. While the horses were chomping away at their morning feed, she shoveled up their horse poo from the night and put it all into a wheel barrel. She rolled the wheel barrel over to the Fiddlesticks Community Garden and dumped it in a pile next to the garden's fence. Nomad followed Zephrum wherever she went, as usual. "Helping the horses is helping me take my mind off of the razor sharp globster teeth from my dream." Her body shook, just thinking about it.

The breakfast cowbell bonged. When Zephrum entered the Sun Lodge, she found Daphne standing in front of the easel and looking at the sketch from her dream.

There on the sketchpad was a drawing of Nomad. Next to Nomad was an ugly face, smoking a large cigar and wearing a giant turban. The turban had all kinds of bones and strange artifacts on it. An eye inside a triangle was positioned at the very center of the turban, as Daphne had described.

Next to this ugly creature was a SUPER large Sea Monster. It was breathing fire, shaking in apparent fright, and glaring at a dangling little worm. At the bottom of the page, Daphne had written the letters, "KILBIT."

"What's a 'Kilbit'?" asked Zephrum.

Daphne shrugged her shoulders and said, "I don't know. It was something the ugly faced turban woman said in my dream last night. I don't know if the letters stand for something…or if it's an actual word."

"Mmm…" said Zephrum. She cocked her head to one side. "I guess we'll have to research it."

"Whoo…weeee…" screamed Rock-o Pounder suddenly.

"Whoo…weee… Whoo…weee…" the students screamed back.

"OK…" screamed Rock-o. "Now that we alls got yur' attentions, we'd like yous to listen to Dexter, as he has a few morning announcements."

Dexter began in his typical nervous manner. "Fiddlesticks Students...As you know, we've had a number of incidents on our most recent field trips. Because of this, we'd like to impress upon all of you...that you must always have a buddy with you, whether you are here at Fiddlesticks...or out on a field trip. We'd like to make sure you all stay safe. Understood?"

Unenthusiastic mumbles came from the students. "Understood." "OK." "Understood."

"OK," said Rocko. "Now yous can all go get your breakfast. We'll start classes at the usual time, after yous all finish up, alright?"

There was a bit of clamor as students got their breakfast from the kitchen island counter. Mrs. Fliffle had prepared scrambled eggs, buttered toast, and warm muffins. There was always cereal, yogurt, coconut milk, and fresh fruit for students who preferred something else. Daphne brought her new sketch over to their breakfast table so that she and Zephrum could look at it while they ate their morning meal.

Gai, Red Raspini, Misty Falls, and Sarah Bellum sat at the same table as Zephrum and Daphne. When Daphne showed the sketch, everybody had a lot to say.

"Wow...That ugly turban person is kind of scary looking."

"Is that a Sea Monster?"

"Why is Nomad in the sketch?"

"What's that little squiggly thing?"

"Well," said Daphne, "I guess that Nomad is some kind of protector. And yes, I think it's a Sea Monster. The squiggly thing is a worm."

"A worm?" asked Gai. "Why is it there?"

"I don't know," said Daphne. "I guess a worm can help us somehow, but I don't know how."

"Yeah," added Zephrum. "And we don't know what a 'Kilbit' is either."

"I've seen that word before," said Sarah. She dug around in her school bag and pulled out a battered copy of 'Mythical Creatures in Literature.'

As she flipped through the pages, everybody else commented on how ugly the turban creature was.

Daphne said, "In my dream last night, she kind of sounded like a craggy old smoker. Imitating the voice as best she could, she said, 'Danger is imminent'."

Everybody cracked up.

"I found it. Look!" said Sarah. "A Kilbit is actually a WORM!"

Sarah started reading from her book, "A Kilbit is a small worm that actually clings to the gills of large fish and kills them. Although it is very small, even the largest of creatures fear it."

"Cool," interjected Gai.

"There's more," continued Sarah. "There's a whole list of sea creatures that try to avoid this little worm." She showed the long listing to everybody and then, started reading it. "The Hafgufa, a Makara, a Namazu Catfish, an Ogopogo, a Sisiutl …mmm…" She scanned to the bottom of the list and back up again. "And The Leviathan."

"The what?!?" roared Zephrum. "The Leviathan?!?"

"Yes…That's one of the creatures on the list," said Sarah, matter-of-factly.

Zephrum, Daphne, and Gai just looked at each other.

"What is it?" asked Misty.

"Well…" said Zephrum. "Before school began this term, Aynia came to me and Aunt Gussie with all kinds of cryptic warnings about the new year. She actually said that 'befriending sea monsters is our only real hope…and that a 'Leviathan' could deal us the worst of fates."

"Befriending Sea Monsters?" asked Sarah. "Seriously?!?" She closed her book. "You realize that this book is mostly about MYTHICAL creatures, right?"

"Of course," said Zephrum. "But after dealing with a dragon last year…and a whimpus and a singing sea shell this year, I figure that anything could happen."

"We could ask Geezer if he knows anything about a Kilbit the next time we have a field trip out on his boat," said Misty.

"True," said Sarah. "I think that Daphne must have just been a little scared after seeing Zephrum fall overboard yesterday, though. All of these images are probably just your subconscious…working out your fears."

"Maaaybe…" said Daphne, trailing off.

"Super imaginative, though" commented Sarah. "I wish I could draw like that."

After they finished eating, everyone brought their dishes over to the group of students washing dishes that morning, then left the Sun Lodge to get ready for another day of classes.

Gai ran up to Zephrum and Daphne just outside the Sun Lodge. He touched them both by the shoulders and said, "You know, after seeing all of the future telling sketches that Daphne did last year, I'm pretty sure this most recent sketch is probably more than just 'mere imagination'. Don't let Sarah's comment get to you. I know she didn't mean to put you down. We'll figure out what it all means. I know we will."

"Well, that was an exciting boat trip yesterday, wasn't it?" said Dr. Malvin Moot when he started his oceanography class.

"Because of the globster sighting, I thought we'd all be curious about whale anatomy."

He pulled out a large poster with labels of external whale parts. Looking at the poster, he pointed to fins and eyes and blowholes. "All this makes sense, yes?"

Then, he pulled out another large flat poster and hung it up. "This image shows more of the inside of a whale. You see how a whale is very much like us. That's because they are mammals as well. The bones are impressive, as are the muscles. Here's the mouth, teeth, and stomach. Obviously MUCH bigger than our own digestive system."

"Yeah," said Razebir. "Big enough for a whole person. I definitely wouldn't want to be swallowed up by one of them."

"Let's hope you won't," said Dr. Moot.

Zephrum glared over at Razebir.

Later on, in their "Inventions to Change the World" class, Dr. Moot asked students to brainstorm new ideas. This was a very lively class, as students were broken up into small groups to discuss the possibilities.

Ideas that were proposed were varied. There was a soccer ball that could store kinetic energy from kicking it…and be able to power a light bulb later. Somebody thought of bicycle-powered blenders…a teleporter…etc…

Zephrum's mind was swimming with all of the new ideas.

During Partner Acrobatics class in the afternoon, she started to think that partner-acro was like its own kind of "invention." She was the flyer for a 3-person trick, called a "Ninja Star."

Gai and Red Raspini laid on the floor mats, side by side. Then, they put their feet up in the air.

The partner acrobatics teacher, Mr. Teele Bender said, "Remembah…Bases…Keep your legs strong like bulls, so you can support your flyers as they cartwheel their hips onto your flat feet."

Zephrum started to really get the hang of it. She'd lift her upper body to allow the guys to move their feet to her torso. Then, she'd put her legs into a wide straddle position to cartwheel back over their feet again. They were getting so good at the circuit that they started to be able to do it faster and faster. Zephrum's legs began to look like spinning windmills and the guys were beginning to have a hard time keeping up.

"Zephrum…You're going too fast. Slow down," said Gai.

Zephrum was having such a great time that she didn't want to stop. "Don't worry. I've got this!" she cried.

Suddenly, Zephrum floated above Gai and Red. She was still doing the "Ninja Star" pattern, but was completely levitated above the ground. Her legs, like helicopter blades…were spinning so fast that it created a buoyant wind that spun her towards the ceiling of the circus tent.

"Whoa…" said Teele Bender.

All of the other kids gawked as they watched Zephrum fly higher and higher.

"OK," said Teele as his giant arm muscles tensed up. "That's enough, Zephrum. Try to slow it down and come back to us now, alright?"

Zephrum wanted to do as he said, but she wasn't quite sure how to control her speed. She was all the way at the cupola...in the very tippy top of the circus tent.

"Zephrum!!" screamed Gai. "Remember how you were able to help us safely land when we were on that flying carpet ride last year? I know you can do it."

Gai's confidence in Zephrum helped. As she thought of all of the zooming and swerving she and Gai and Daphne did on their unexpected carpet ride last year, the spinning of Zephrum's legs slowed. Her body changed into the shape of an arrow and she flew down to where Gai stood. Then, at the last moment, she swerved and flew out into the open air!

--Chapter 17--
"Flight"

Never before had Zephrum flown by her own wind power. She had created wind before...and flown on horses and a carpet. She had even cushioned her high plunge into the water with a swirling wind. But THIS was a whole new kind of flying.

"Wow! How am I doing this?" said Zephrum as she soared over the trees. "I could probably travel ANYwhere like this." She zoomed around in a zig-zagging fashion, maneuvering in the sky with her mere thoughts.

Suddenly, she realized she had flown quite a distance from Fiddlesticks. "Oh, no! What am I thinking? I'm getting pretty far away from school...and without a buddy." Her momentary lapse in confidence made her body start to dip down slightly. "Whoa... I had better be careful. I almost just hit a couple of pointy treetops."

She veered back towards Fiddlesticks and swooped down towards the open area just outside of The Sun Lodge. Finally, she glided down to the ground, drifting to an easy stop on the grass near the circus tent. Students from the Partner Acrobatics class had rushed outside when she first took off into the air. A group of them rushed towards her as her feet touched the earth.

"Wow! How did you do that?"

"Where did you go?"

"Can you do it again?"

Zephrum was in a bit of a shock. She had never done that kind of thing before and didn't know if she could do it again.

Teele Bender rushed through the circle of kids surrounding Zephrum. "Alright already. De show ist ova. Everybody get back into de Circus Tent and back to class."

He looked at Gai and Red and asked, "Would you two escort Zephrum ova to the Healing Dome, so that Nurse Asa can take a look at her?"

"But I feel fine," protested Zephrum.

"I'm sure you do, Zephrum, but I'd like Nurse Asa to take a look at you, either way."

"OK," said Zephrum.

"Zephrum, have you ever flown like that before?" asked Gai as they made their way to the Healing Dome.

"No," said Zephrum. "I can't explain it. And I don't know if I could do it again."

"Why don't you just try it?" said Red.

"What about our Buddy System?" asked Zephrum. "I'd be breaking the school rules if I go off by myself like that again."

"I'll be your buddy," offered Gai. "Just jump on my back like I'm giving you a piggy back ride and see if you can fly both of us."

Zephrum thought about it for a moment and finally said, "Well, I guess it couldn't hurt to try."

She jumped onto Gai's back and held on tight.

"I'll just start running to get us going," said Gai.

He started jogging forward and then said, "OK, Zephrum! Go for it!"

Zephrum shut her eyes and wished to be flying back in the air. Within moments, Gai's feet were running above the ground. Without warning, they both took off…whizzing into the sky at an unbelievable speed. Gai and Zephrum's eyes opened wide as their hair flapped wildly around in the wind. "Wow!" screamed Gai. "This is wild!"

"I know," said Zephrum.

They swerved and swooped along, drifting just above the fire road that led to the town of Haversville.

Suddenly, Zephrum saw a strange vapor ahead of her. "Oh, no," said Zephrum. "It looks like the vapor of Strasidous Rowpe."

"Could he actually be around?" asked Gai.

"I don't know," cried Zephrum. "I don't see him anywhere. She dipped down lower and lower all the same.

Noticing their decent, Gai said, "Um, Zephrum… Are we landing?"

"It seems like it," said Zephrum.

Within moments, Gai's feet touched back down to the ground. He ran a little bit as they landed.

Zephrum jumped off his back. "I guess I just got a little scared, ya' know?"

"Yeah," said Gai. "Understandably."

Just then, a strange goblin appeared from a burned out stump of a tree. "Well, Miss Gates," said the familiar voice. "I thought I was going to have to find my way to you, but it seems you have found ME!"

Zephrum stood dumbfounded.

"Don't you recognize me?" said Virgidous.

Zephrum cocked her head to one angle.

"It's your old friend, Strasidous Rowpe."

Shivers ran through Zephrum's spine. Gai stood up straighter.

"I am within the body of my loyal goblin servant, Virgil. I am now called Virgidous!" He smirked at Zephrum and said, "A clever new name, don't you think?"

"Uh..." said Zephrum, not knowing how to respond.

"Of course, it's brilliant!" screamed Virgidous.

"Why were you looking for me?" snapped Zephrum.

"You want to get straight to business, I see," commented Virgidous. "I like that, Miss Wind Fairy." He put his hand to his chin. "Well, you see, Miss Gates. I have been advised that getting you involved in my cause...will help me execute my grand plans."

"And what plans are those?" asked Zephrum bravely.

"In all good time, Miss Gates. In all good time."

"Why should I help you?" asked Zephrum.

"Tisk, Tisk. Don't tell me you are still harboring ill will towards me," said Virgidous. He opened his arms wide to display his form. "As you can see, I've changed."

"Sure," said Zephrum squinting her eyes at him. "So what do you have in mind?"

"Well..." said Virgidous. "I am on a great search and I am under the impression that you can help me find the creature I seek."

"You mean, a sea monster?" asked Zephrum.

Virgidous rubbed his hands together. "I can see you've been doing your homework, Miss Gates. Very good. Very good indeed."

"How can a sea monster help you?" asked Zephrum.

"Oh…" said Virgidous, leaning backwards slightly. "That is for me to know and for you to experience…after we find it."

"No deal," said Zephrum. "I don't want to help you. You're responsible for my parents going missing when I was a baby. You tried to squish me into a hole and extinguish me out of existence when I was 12. And you manipulated a dragon creature to snatch me up last year. You tried to suck the life force out of my bloody finger too. You are a very bad man."

"Oh…" said Virgidous, pretending to be offended. "That was the old me. I was desperate. I have a new vision now. And it includes you, Miss Gates."

"Me? Why? Why don't you find some other kid to help you?" asked Zephrum.

"But it must be you, Miss Gates," continued Virgidous. "You will have riches beyond your wildest dreams. And power beyond power."

"I don't care," cried Zephrum. "I don't want to have anything to do with you. I don't trust you."

"Yes, yes," said Virgidous, becoming slightly more agitated. "I can see how you might have that little problem, but I don't need your trust. Just your help."

"Listen," interjected Gai. "She said she doesn't want to help you, so just beat it."

With a wave of the goblin's fingers, Gai's body flew up into the air and got thrown smack into the trunk of a tree.

Zephrum ran over to Gai. "Gai, are you alright?"

Stunned, Gai sat up slowly. "Yeah, I'm Ok, Zephrum. Don't worry."

"You come here to ask me for help and then you throw one of my friends up against a tree?!? What is wrong with you?" Her eyes narrowed as she fiercely stared Virgidous down.

"True," said Virgidous, nodding his head. "I sometimes forget my own power. This is something I know you can relate to, Miss Gates."

"I am NEVER going to help you with ANYTHING!" screamed Zephrum.

"Bwa..ha..ha..ha..ha.." laughed Virgidous. "Oh, but you will, Miss Gates. You will, whether you want to or not."

"I will NOT!"

"We could go on like this for an eternity, Little Miss Wind Fairy," said Virgidous. "I will give you until sundown to come to my aid."

He threw a thick gold coin at her. "Blow on this coin to let me know that you will join me. If you do not agree to assist me, you will lose something very near and dear to you. And then, Miss Gates…you will never forgive yourself."

He laughed maniacally, "Bwa..ha..ha..ha..ha…" Then, he disappeared, leaving only a dark purple vapor where he last stood.

Gai got up from the ground and brushed himself off. "Wow, Zephrum. I can't believe you stood up to him like that."

"Me neither." She looked down at the ground, picked up the coin, and stuffed it into her pocket. "But I have a feeling we haven't seen the last of him."

"Yeah," said Gai. "Maybe we should go back to Fiddlesticks to ask the others what we should do next."

"I don't think I'm going to be able to fly us back there," said Zephrum, discouragingly.

"It's OK," said Gai. "I like walking with you too."

Zephrum blushed slightly as she and Gai started to walk back towards the school.

"I wonder what he could mean about losing something near and dear to me?" asked Zephrum.

"I don't know," said Gai. "But I'll bet your Aunt Gussie can help us figure it out."

"I hope so," said Zephrum. "I really do."

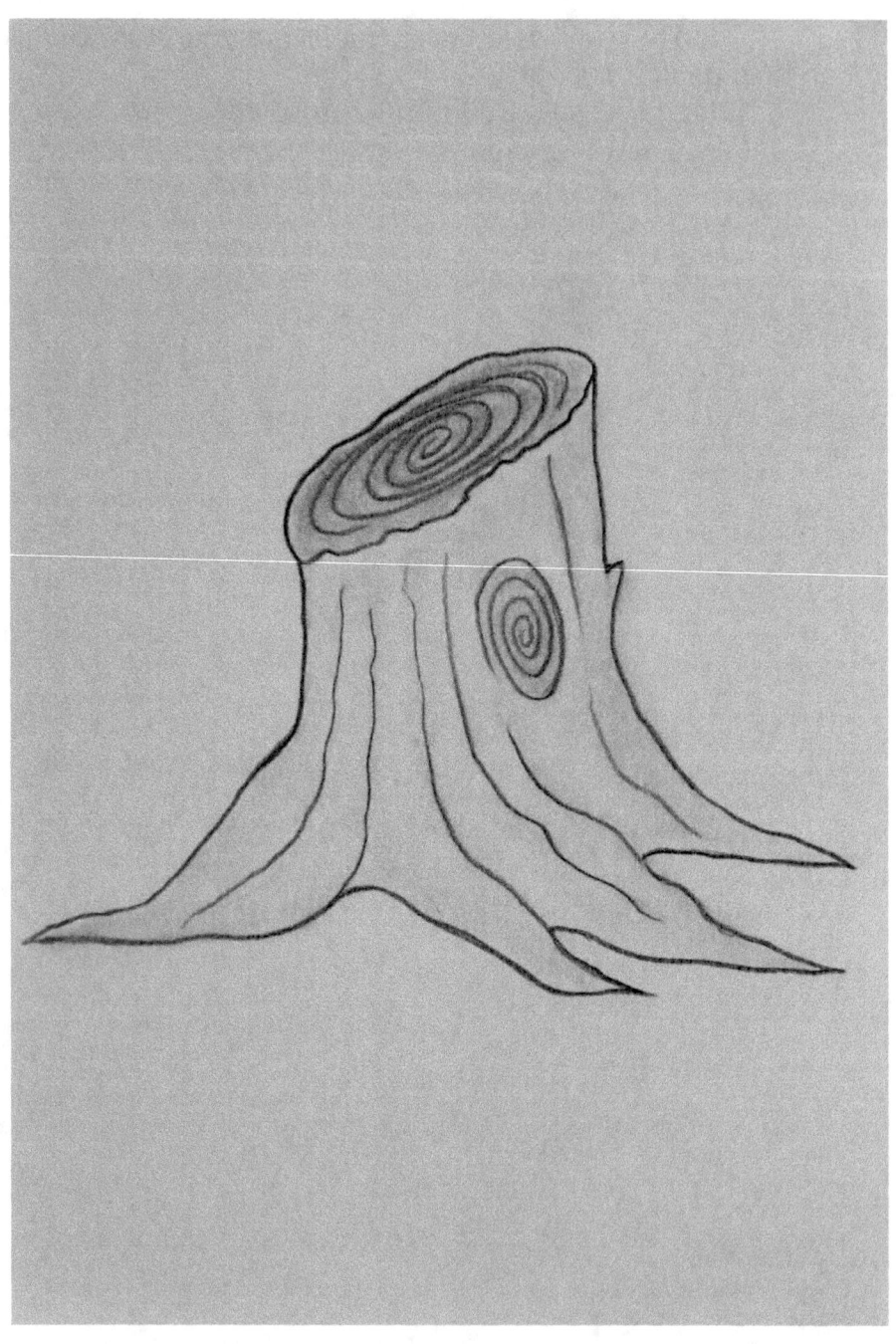

--Chapter 18--

"Nomad"

Within the goblin tunnels beneath the town center of Haversville, Virgidous then collected a number of his goblin brethren. "We must increase our spell against humanity now, while I am feeling so wicked and strong."

"Yes, Sire," responded a wrinkly elder goblin.

"As you say," said the goblin wearing the most ornate robes.

"We must circle up and cast a spell that will increase the stupidity of humanity. They must become more unconscious of the impact of their actions, so they will continue to pollute and destroy themselves."

Cackles uttered from the group of goblins surrounding Virgidous.

"Let us chant our spell together now. We must put our plan in motion while I am feeling extra iniquitous."

The small circlet of goblins gathered around him. "Repeat after me," said Virgidous.

"Molkac rhaan drol. Humans be dumb," they repeated.

"Molkac rhaan drol. Humans be dumb."

"Molkakekhec rhaan tokhel. Humanity be stupid," Virgidous chanted in ancient Goblinese.

The circlet of goblins chanted, "Molkakekhec rhaan tokhel. Humans be stupid."

Virgidous continued, "Duul dan ac or olaac. Throw trash into your oceans."

"Duul dan ac or olaac. Throw trash into your oceans," echoed the goblins.

Virgidous narrowed his eyes as he uttered one last order. "Druun ar khruul! Do it now!"

"And now together!" cried Virgidous.

"Molkac rhaan drol.
Molkakekhec rhaan tokhel.
Duul dan ac or olaac.

Druun ar khruul! "

With that, Virgidous snapped his fingers to activate the spell. Instantly, an odd blue light emanated from their circle and Virgidous laughed maniacally, "Bwa..ha..ha..ha…" Virgidous' laughter echoed down the corridors of the caves.

Meanwhile, Zephrum and Gai walked back through the woods to Fiddlesticks. Dark gray clouds gathered in the sky above them.

Zephrum glanced over her shoulder and said, "Did you feel that? I keep on feeling like somebody is walking behind us or something."

"Yeah, me too," said Gai. "But whenever I turn around, nobody else is there."

"I guess we're just kind of freaked out by Strasidous Rowpe… or Virgidous… or whatever he's calling himself," said Zephrum.

"Yeah," said Gai. "I can't believe he threw me up against a tree with just a small lift of his fingers."

"I wonder what he has in mind now? I know he wants me to help him find a sea monster, but why?" asked Zephrum.

"I'm worried about those threats he made to you," said Gai.

Zephrum nodded. "What could he mean about me losing something near and dear to me?"

Zephrum put her hand to her head and said, "We're probably going to be in a lot of trouble for flying off… especially after Mr. Bender told us to go to the Healing Dome."

"Yeah," said Gai. "But flying in the air like that was totally worth it."

Zephrum smiled. "Yeah. It really was pretty cool, wasn't it?"

"At least we didn't break the rule about being without a buddy," said Gai.

"Ha..Ha!" Zephrum laughed.

As they walked, Gai pointed out aspects of the river that help the surrounding trees to grow. He said, "See how certain plants help maintain the river's border? Like this skunk cabbage here." He pointed to a large green leafy plant.

"Oh, and beavers are especially helpful because they help create more diversity in the spots where they build damns. They take down trees and help water to stay in an area when the river is low. This helps create marshes, which helps create meadows, which helps create forests," Gai continued.

"Hey…why don't we play a game of 'Eye Spy' for a bit."

Zephrum eagerly said, "Yeah. It will help us stay alert and give us something fun to do as we walk".

"I see something green," said Zephrum.

"I see something pointy," said Gai.

This game went on for quite a while until Zephrum looked at Gai and said, "I see something Tall."

"Do you mean ME?" asked Gai.

They both cracked up.

After Zephrum and Gai disappeared, Red had to admit that he had seen Gai and Zephrum fly off together, going west. Speaking to Teele Bender, he said, "But I don't think they'll be gone long."

"Didn't I ask you and Gai to escort Zephrum to the Healing Dome?" asked Teele.

"Uh… yeah," said Red. He looked down at his feet.

"For your sake, I hope those two are back soon," said Teele. "Stay out here und wait for dem. And let me know when dey get back, alright?"

"OK," said Red, obediently. He looked at his watch, shook his head, and mumbled to himself, "Those guys are going to be in sooo much trouble when they get back."

When Zephrum and Gai finally walked back up to Fiddlesticks from the fire road, Daphne and Red were waiting for them.

"Whoa…What happened to you guys?" asked Daphne.

"We bumped into Strasidous Rowpe," said Zephrum.

"What?!?" cried Daphne.

"He threw me up against a tree trunk with a wave of his fingers," said Gai.

"And was full of strange threats towards me if I didn't agree to help him find a Sea Monster," added Zephrum.

"That's nuts," said Red.

Zephrum and Gai told Daphne and Red everything that had happened. "You better go to the Healing Dome to check in with Nurse Asa," Red said when they finished. "She's been expecting you."

Zephrum turned to go, then frowned. "I really need to check in with Great Aunt Gussie to ask her what we should do now," said Zephrum. "Daphne, can you go find her and bring her over to the Healing Dome to talk to me?"

"Sure," said Daphne. She ran off in the direction of the Sun Lodge.

"I'd better stay with you guys this time," said Red. "Or else I'll get in double trouble with Mr. Bender."

The three of them walked into the Healing Dome and Nurse Asa gave Zephrum and Gai a thorough checkup. After she took temperatures, blood pressure, listened to their hearts, and checked their bodies for aches and pains, she said, "Once again, it's miraculous, but it seems that you are completely normal."

Just then, Aunt Gussie burst into the Healing Dome. "Oh my Heavens! Zephrum, What kind of trouble did you get yourself into now? You're flying all over heck and back now? Gosh Diddly Darn! Have you lost your marbles?!?"

"Well…" Zephrum tried to explain. "It was kind of an accident. I didn't even know I could do a thing like that."

"What in the chicken head do you mean?" asked Aunt Gussie. "You're part wind fairy! You've flown before. You've got to be careful. You can't just go off on joy rides like this!"

"Uh…" said Zephrum.

"There are a lot of questionable things going on in the magical world these days. We can't afford to take chances with our safety. Explain yourself," continued Aunt Gussie. "Put your cards out on the table. No sugar coating things. Just tell me everything that happened."

"Well," said Zephrum. "It first started in Partner Acrobatics class."

"Yes, yes," said Aunt Gussie. "I've already heard about your acrobatic 'Ninja Star' turning into a helicopter. And I heard that you came back and were sent directly to the Healing Dome. Why didn't you listen to Mr. Bender?"

"Aunt Gussie…" said Gai. "It was kind of my fault. I was wondering if she could do it again. Zephrum didn't want to risk going off on her own, so I offered to be her buddy. We didn't know if it would work. It was just a kind of an experiment."

"An experiment?!?" screeched Aunt Gussie. "Are you two kids totally crackers?"

They tried not to smile. They could tell that Aunt Gussie was very upset with them.

"It's sweet of you to try to take responsibility for Zephrum's questionable choices, Gai, but really. At this point, she should know better."

Zephrum felt like she was standing on the edge of a knife.

"Now, I might be a little long in the tooth," Aunt Gussie continued, "but it seems to me that this flight to who knows where…was as practical as whittling dynamite. What happened out there?"

Zephrum said, "Well, we saw something that resembled the vapor of Strasidous Rowpe. I got scared and brought us down to the fire road."

"Finally, something a little more down to earth," interjected Aunt Gussie.

"Once we landed," Zephrum continued, "A strange looking goblin came out of a burned out stump near us. It was Strasidous Rowpe as a goblin. He wanted me to help him find a Sea Monster. When I refused, Gai spoke up for me. That's when Strasidous…or Virgidous or whatever he's calling himself now…blew Gai into the trunk of a nearby tree."

"Sweet Mother of Molasses!" cried Great Aunt Gussie.

"I know," said Zephrum. "It was pretty scary. But after that, he said that he would give me until sundown to agree to help him. He tossed this coin to me and said I should blow on it if I would be willing to help him. And if I didn't, I would lose something near and dear to me."

Aunt Gussie took a closer look at the coin in Zephrum's fingers. "I have only seen a coin like this once before. It was on the day that my dear departed husband passed on from this world."

Gai and Zephrum looked at each other.

"My dear Zephrum. I believe you have been given an Obolus."

"A what?" asked Zephrum.

"It's a death coin," blurted Aunt Gussie.

"What?" cried Gai.

"The deceased of olden times used to be buried with an obolus, placed in the mouth of the corpse," explained Aunt Gussie. "Once a deceased's shade reached the underworld, he or she would be able to pay for passage across the river of life. It's likely that Strasidous has enchanted this coin in his typical malevolent way. Has anyone else touched it besides you?"

"No," said Zephrum. "I just put it in my pocket right after I showed it to Gai."

"Gai…Are you sure you didn't grab for it?" asked Aunt Gussie.

"Yeah," said Gai. "I was still in shock after being thrown up against that tree trunk."

"Zephrum," said Aunt Gussie very seriously. "Keep this out of reach. Don't let anybody else touch it. Meet me at your cabin after you're done with Nurse Asa. I'll go collect some neutralizing herbs and we'll bury it into the ground before sundown. That way, nobody will have to pay the piper."

Zephrum slipped the coin back into her pocket, very carefully.

"I can't believe you picked it up at all," said Aunt Gussie as she turned to leave the Healing Dome. "If I didn't know better, I'd think you might really have a screw loose in that noggin of yours."

She rushed out of the Healing Dome and towards her guest cabin.

It was Zephrum who broke the silence. "Aunt Gussie almost never gets upset with me like that. This death coin must be pretty serious."

Nurse Asa let them know that they were free to go, so they all ran out and rushed towards Zephrum and Daphne's cabin.

Zephrum opened the door to let Nomad out. She wagged her tail in her usual happy way. The wisps of her tail hairs created a soft wind near Zephrum's knees. Nomad looked up at Zephrum with her kind eyes and Zephrum kneeled down to her level to hug her. "Oh, Nomad. I love you sooo much." As she squatted down to hug her pooch, the obolus fell out of her pocket. Nomad followed the trajectory of the coin and touched her nose down to the ground where it fell.

Daphne screamed, "Noooo....!!"

Before Zephrum knew it, her dog's nose had touched the death coin. "Oh, no..." cried Zephrum. She scooped it up as fast as she could, but it was too late.

Nomad looked up at Zephrum in wonder. Her back legs began to buckle.

Zephrum said, "Daphne...Go get her blanket and water bowl!"

Daphne rushed to bring Zephrum the items.

Zephrum put her hands inside the water bowl and tried to wash Nomad's nose off, but it didn't make any difference. The spell on the death coin was so strong that it was already clearly affecting her. Her eyelids became heavy.

Zephrum said, "No…Don't go. Don't leave me. Please."

Just then, Aunt Gussie arrived. "For Heaven's Sake! What's going on now?"

Zephrum looked up with tears in her eyes. "The death coin fell out of my pocket when I bent down to hug Nomad…and she put her nose on it before I could…gr..gr.. grab it."

Daphne put her hand on Zephrum's back. She wasn't able to hold back her tears.

"Oh, goodness gracious," said Aunt Gussie. "I don't know if there's anything we can do to help Nomad's body now."

Zephrum began to sob uncontrollably. Her tears rolled down her face so strongly that it looked like someone had poured a glass of water onto her cheeks.

"Wait a minute," said Gai. "Remember what Virgidous said? He said that if you blow on it, it will be a signal to him that you're willing to help him. Maybe that could help?"

"Help Strasidous Rowpe?" said Zephrum. "Are you crazy?"

Gai shrugged his shoulders. He didn't know what to say. He was just trying to help. "I don't know, Zephrum. I mean…nobody wants to see Nomad go. We ALL love her."

"Of course, we do," said Aunt Gussie. "But agreeing to help Strasidous Rowpe would undoubtedly come at a very heavy price."

Zephrum pulled the death coin out of her pocket and looked at it through tear-filled eyes. "Stupid Coin."

At that moment, one of her tears fell upon the coin and it began to sizzle into a fizzle of ether. It dissipated into the air in front of them.

With that, Nomad's spirit left her body. Her life energy passed right through Zephrum's heart.

A crow started cawing from a nearby tree.

Aunt Gussie placed her hand on Zephrum's shoulder and said, "It's her time, Zephrum. This crow will help carry her to the other side."

"I can't," said Zephrum as she began rocking Nomad's lifeless body in her arms. "I can't let her go. I just can't."

"Nobody escapes death, Zephrum. But if we're lucky, like Nomad is…we'll be surrounded by loved ones and be able to pass on in blissful peace."

Zephrum nodded her head as spots of drizzle began to fall from the overcast sky. She looked up at the crow. "Nomad…if you have to go, fly free like a bird. Fl..fl..fly free… like the wind."

The crow cawed and then, took flight over the trees. A gentle wind followed behind and feathered the hairs of everybody circled there.

"We all go in time," said Aunt Gussie. "We can only hope that we all go as gracefully."

Zephrum was sniffling through her face full of tears as Aunt Gussie said, "Her spirit will live in a better place, a place where hatred has no home…and where she can be truly free."

Zephrum was overwhelmed. Even Gai and Red and Daphne were all full of tears.

Aunt Gussie circled Nomad's body with her neutralizing herbs. "She will always be our spirit familiar now."

The kids were all crying harder than before.

"Get it out, kids," said Aunt Gussie, as tears formed in her own eyes. "Better out than in."

She looked at Zephrum. "Your tears were so powerful that it dissolved that death coin completely. Lots of love was in those tears, so much so that you were able to free Nomad from whatever darkness Strasidous Rowpe had in store for her."

Zephrum's tears flowed more abundantly now.

"Stupid dark magic," said Zephrum as she wiped her eyes.

"Magic is just the higher understanding of nature, Zephrum," said Aunt Gussie. "Dark or light is often a matter of our perspective."

"I tried. I tried to stop it, but I couldn't," sobbed Zephrum.

"We always feel as though we could have done more when somebody goes. We re-play the events in our minds and think of all of the 'could have's' and 'should have's,' but that is just the downward spiral of grief. That kind of loopty loop really goes nowhere." She paused for a moment. "We will bury our special friend in a sacred place and we'll tell stories about her…and keep her alive in our hearts."

"I can't," said Zephrum as she hugged Nomad and looked at her motionless body. "I just can't."

"It's OK if you need to hug her for a time…to talk to her and say your goodbyes."

Zephrum laid on the ground with Nomad, while the other kids took turns petting her quiet body.

"I can never let her go," cried Zephrum. "Never."

Aunt Gussie's face was full of tears now as well. "In time, you will find that a courageous kind of love resides on the other side of grief.

In time."

--Chapter 19--
"Obolus"

The news about Nomad and the death coin spread quickly.

Zephrum stayed in her cabin during dinner, crying into her pillow. Daphne stayed nearby, hoping to be of some help, but there really was nothing she could do. Aunt Gussie brought a cup of chamomile tea over to help Zephrum get to sleep.

Rocko Pounder, Gai, and Red dug a hole over near the beehives, for Nomad's body. Everyone at Fiddlesticks was quite disturbed over the loss of Nomad. Magenta Scorcher even managed to dredge up some kindness inside. She brought a note and a flower over to Zephrum's cabin. It said, "Although I deedn't know your dog for very long, I know I weel miss her."

That night, there was a rainstorm that made it sound as though thunder beings were coming down from the sky.

Zephrum had a dream with Nomad…that she would somehow always be with her. It was just a feeling she could sense in her heart.

Gai came by with a flower for Zephrum in the morning. She hugged him with tears in her eyes. Then, he and Daphne went out to help Zephrum with her morning ritual of attending to the horses. As they shoveled up the horse poo and loaded the hay feeders with alfalfa and dry grass, they began talking about what happened.

"I wish there was something I could have done. I wish I had seen that death coin fall out of my pocket," said Zephrum.

"Do you think you would have blown on it if your tear hadn't dissolved it?" asked Gai.

"I don't know," said Zephrum. "But I sure wish I could have had the choice."

"If it was me," said Daphne. "I'm sure I would have."

"It's probably better that you won't have to help Strasidous Rowpe," said Gai. "But it's all pretty overwhelming."

"Yeah…" agreed Zephrum. "The dream I had with Nomad last night was amazing. It was as though she was still with me. I could even feel her body at the foot of my bed, even though I know she couldn't have really been there."

"Wow!" said Gai. "That's cool."

"Yeah," said Daphne. "Super weird."

"The other thing that's weird," said Zephrum, "is that I felt her in my body somehow. I don't know how to explain it. It's as though some of Nomad's life force was coursing through me."

"Trippy," said Gai.

"Very," said Zephrum. "I know it's going to take me a long time to get over this. I would have never thought that I could feel so weak and powerless. Understanding what happened will definitely take some time."

"For sure," agreed Daphne.

"Totally," said Gai.

They heard the morning cowbell. "Sounds like it's time for breakfast," said Daphne.

"Don't worry," said Gai. "While you're with us, everybody will give you space. We all understand what you're going through."

Zephrum smiled and looked like she was going to cry at the same time. She grabbed Gai's arm as Daphne put her arm around her. Then, the three of them headed in the direction of The Sun Lodge.

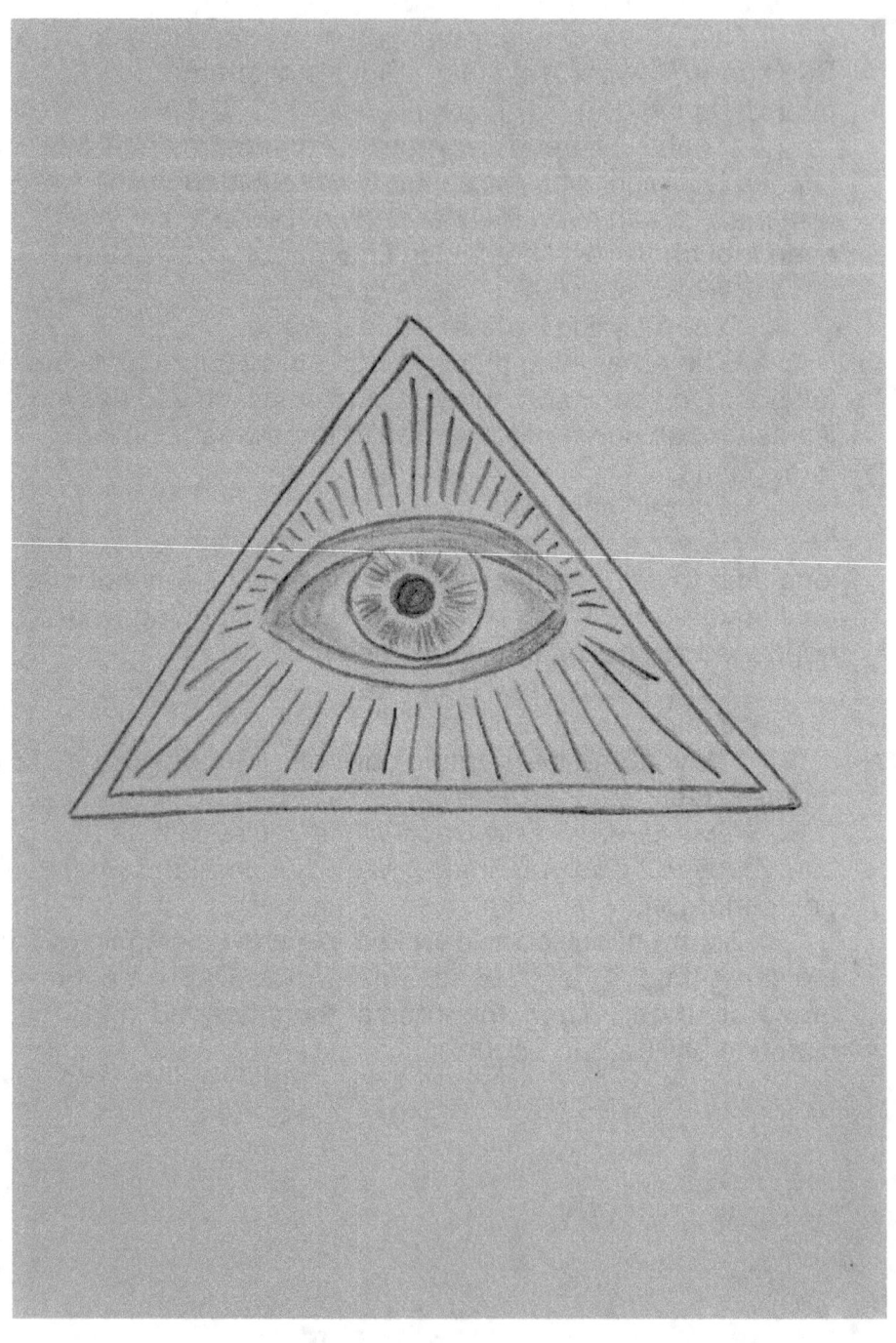

--Chapter 20--

"Grizalda's Warning"

Meanwhile, deep within the Goblin caverns, Virgidous was feeling weaker than ever. Wavering where he stood, he asked, "What has happened? Why am I so unsteady?"

"Sire," said the Virgil voice from within. "Could it have something to do with Zephrum Gates?"

The deeper Strasidous voice responded, "Oh…That little runt of a girl couldn't possibly be affecting me from such a great distance. Maybe we need a different dosage of our potion?"

"Maybe," said the Virgil voice. "But what if it's something else?"

"We'll just have to figure that out, won't we?" said Strasidous.

"Or…" commented the Virgil voice inside. "Maybe we should make another visit to… Grizalda the Great?"

"Mmmm…" said the Strasidous voice. "I would like to know more about the dream I had of her, but let's go to our Goblin Healer first."

He emerged from his sleeping chamber and was greeted by Zultr Zeki, who was standing guard outside of the doorway to his chambers. Zultr Zeki accompanied Virgidous as he wobbled through the goblin tunnels. Finally, they reached the misty cavern of Healer Groikz.

The Healer was stooped over a boiling pot of brew as Virgidous entered his laboratory. Healer Groikz greeted Virgidous with a cross eyed look. "Sire? Be you ill?"

"Something is not right, but I cannot say what it is," responded Virgidous. He staggered closer to the healer.

The healer scampered near to Virgidous. He put his hand above Virgidous' eyebrows, stretched his eyelids open, then took a penetrating look at his pupils. "Mmm… Very interesting."

"What's so interesting?" snapped Virgidous.

"Sire, your lights have gone dim. Your life force is being drained." He scurried over to his healing tincture table and grabbed a small dark bottle. Darting back over to Virgidous, the healer said, "To increase your life force, take a dropper full of these super greens, mixed with frog liver. Take a dropper-full every two hours today. Then, continue taking a dropper-full twice daily for the next week. If your condition does not improve, it may be out of our hands, Sire."

Virgidous looked down at the tincture bottle and then, back to the goblin healer. "Alright, I'll do as you say." He twisted the tincture bottle open, squeezed the dropper, and dripped the contents into his mouth. Immediately, he started to gag. "Blech!! What is that vile taste?"

One of the eyes of Healer Groikz moved so far away from the other that it almost disappeared completely into his eye socket. "Sire, frog liver is one of the most vile tastes in the universe. It secretes a digestive bile that is bug flavored, but the entire organ can be quite life giving to those who ingest it in a tincture."

Virgidous wrinkled his nose. "If you say so. But taking this every two hours today? Have you nothing to make it more palatable?"

"No Sire. The taste will remain with you for many moments after you drop it into your mouth, no matter what you do."

Virgidous looked at Zultr Zeki. "I think a visit to The Bucaneer's Barnacle might be in order."

"Yes Sire," said Zeki. "Let us away."

Zeki helped to stabilize Virgidous as they walked through the dank tunnels to the dirt staircase that led above ground. Then, they made their way to the pub's street.

Entering the darkness of the tavern, they saw only the gray bearded bartender at the bar.

"Seems fairly empty today," said Zeki.

"Yes," wobbled Virgidous. "Just as well. I could not tolerate the noise of pirates right now."

Teetering onto one of the bar stools, Virgidous spoke to the bartender in a low tone. "One of your finest ales, for each of us."

Geezer nodded and placed two frothy mugs of beer in front of them. Then, he continued drying glasses with a clean bar towel.

"Ah…Now, that's more like it," said Virgidous, taking a sip of his beer. "Really, this frog liver tincture is one of the most disgusting tastes I've ever encountered."

"Worse than your ToadFlax potion?" asked Zeki.

Virgidous winced. "Yes, even worse than that."

They sat there, savoring their sudsy lagers until Virgidous finally said, "Zeki, I think I would like to make a journey to Grizalda The Great again."

"Sire, are you sure you're up for it?" asked Zeki.

"I cannot say," said Virgidous. "All I know is that I have lost something. I was full of malcontent and gusto when I last saw Zephrum Gates. Our spell against humanity got a boost right after that as well. The humans' lack of consciousness and stupidity worsened and I was almost giddy with wickedness. But just mere hours later, it is as though the ground left me somehow. Very odd."

"That does seem strange," said Zeki.

"I believe 'Grizalda The Great' will know what has happened," admitted Virgidous.

"Grizalda might have more protection now. If we go to see her, I think we should bring an 'Eyes All Over' amulet with us. It will be like a mirror to those Gathering Squee and it will confound them if feathers do not work to distract them this time."

"Mmm… Very good, Zeki. This is why I value having you as my guard. You are full of cunning thoughts."

"Yes, Sire," agreed Zeki as she touched a hand to her sword's handle.

The two eventually finished drinking their beers. Virgidous left some coins on the bar and nodded at Geezer as they departed.

Stepping precariously as he moved, Virgidous said, "You might need to hold me up as we walk."

"Yes, Sire," said Zeki. She wrapped Virgidous' arm over her shoulders to support his weight. They ambled down to the underground tunnels and stopped to pick up the "Eyes All Over" amulet from Zeki's chambers. Zeki showed him the round marbled amulet with eyes looking in all directions. She threaded a leather tie through a loop attached to the amulet and placed the strange object around Virgidous' neck.

From there, they tottered on their way until they came to an old rickety cart on the rusted tracks of the underground cart system. They got into the wagon, which swerved and curved as they rolled through the serpentine path that led to Creeper Clan Territory. There they got out of the cart and were raised upward as they held onto vines that led to the land up above. Seeing the seaside lighthouse of Grizalda The Great, they trudged forward. Zeki was dragging Virgidous along as they trekked.

As they approached Grizalda's lighthouse, Zeki said, "Just hold the 'Eyes All Over' amulet out as we approach the Gathering Squee. It should make them confused enough to spin in circles."

Virgidous did as Zultr Zeki suggested…and within moments, the pathetic creatures looked up and down in apparent confusion. They spiraled around in place and seemed as though they were not able to see anything before them.

"And now, we are free to enter Grizalda's tower," said Zultr Zeki with a smile.

Virgidous trudged up the narrow stone stairs, with Zultr Zeki supporting him from behind. As they entered Grizalda's lantern room at the top of the lighthouse, they saw Grizalda smoking a long cigar and sitting on her large seaweed cushion at her divining table. She looked up and growled through her yellowing teeth, "You again! What now?"

In labored breaths, Virgidous gasped. "Ahh… But I thought you were all-knowing."

Grizalda's jeweled turban was askew. "Of course, I know all, but you have created such mayhem in such a short amount of time that I don't even know where to start."

Virgidous mustered his strength and slammed a heavy fist down onto Grizalda's divining table, lifting dust into the air. "You do NOT talk to ME in such a manner! Remember, I am the source of all that is evil and I will have your head if I wish. It matters not who you are."

Grizalda took a puff of her cigar and said nothing.

"Now that we are clear who's in charge, I will ask again," continued Virgidous. "Why has my energy waned so? I must know what is going on and what I can do to return to full power."

Grizalda's warty face looked down at her bag of rune stones. She reached a skin-cracked hand into the bag and took out a few stones. Then, as she put the stones onto her table, her eyes flitted.

She looked directly at Virgidous. "Your wish to commission Zephrum Gates has back-fired. The death coin you gave her was sniffed by her greatest love of all, her canine. The rules for death stones are not the same for dogs as they are for humans. When Zephrum realized her dog was going to leave this world, the tears from her eyes rained upon the coin and disintegrated it into nothingness. At that time, with her love so great, her dog became a being of protection that is so strong and loyal that there is almost NO way to break the bond. Zephrum's grief is so strong that it has taken a great deal of your life force from you. She sees you as responsible for this grave tragedy. Since there is nothing you can do to bring her dog back to the known world, you will suffer as long as she."

"I suffer because SHE suffers?" asked Virgidous.

"Yes," continued Grizalda. "For this transgression, the worst of fates awaits you. Aside from the link between human parents and children…and the connection of soul pairs, the love of dogs by their humans is one of the most powerful bonds known to us. In short, you will suffer for your actions, no matter how much power you have amassed."

"What?!?" said Virgidous indignantly. "What can I do to re-claim my power, my rightful birthright?"

"Two paths," said Grizalda. Her eyes flickered.

"One path will lead to your ultimate destruction."

"The other path will lead to a liberation of your spirit from this mortal bondage you are in with your goblin servant, Virgil."

"Tell me more!" demanded Virgidous.

"Although your wish to lure the Leviathan with the Globster was a sound choice at first, your methods have angered this mythical beast. Your spell on humanity that has made humans unconscious and inspired them to throw massive amounts of trash into the ocean has worked against you. There is so much trash in the ocean that the garbage islands have created 'Dead Zones.' There is so little light beneath these masses of garbage that nothing can live beneath them. The Leviathan can no longer feast in his typical way…and he is angered. You will feel the wrath of the Leviathan whenever you do meet, for he now knows it is you that is behind this madness."

"How does he know such things?" asked Virgidous, perplexed.

Grizalda's head shook. "It is because the Leviathan is connected to realms of spirit neither you nor I can understand, his ancestors."

Grizalda continued. "After Zephrum's dog departed from this world, all of Zephrum's feelings…which her dog knew all so well…were transferred into the spirit world, where the Leviathan is a master."

"Stupid Dogs!!" screamed Virgidous.

"You have made a fatal error," said Grizalda. "And now, you will pay a heavy price."

"WHAT can I do to regain my ultimate power?" asked Virgidous. "I must know."

Grizalda's body started to shake and flinch. Finally, she opened her eyes as wide as tea cups. Her face lurched forward. "Your power is doomed! Unless you can KILL the Leviathan and eat its heart, you will live as a mere shadow of yourself for an eternity."

"What?!? This cannot be," protested Virgidous. "How do I kill it?"

"It is almost impossible to kill a Leviathan," said Grizalda. "For its powers are greater than almost any creature."

"There must be a way," screamed Virgidous.

"You must break your spell on humanity, but it appears there is so much momentum behind their folly, they may also be beyond repair."

"Do not tell me what I CAN'T do!" Yelling now, Virgidous continued, "I am Strasidous Rowpe! I can do ANYTHING!"

"Yes," said Grizalda. "You have immense power, but I fear the only way you can gain it back now…is by commissioning the help… of ZEPHRUM GATES."

"Aaarrgh…" growled Virgidous. "Why must it always come back to HER?"

"Because," explained Grizalda. "You are linked to her through your magical misdeeds. When you collected all of the malicious fairies of the Unseelie Court long ago, you created a bond with them. Ever since Miss Gates absorbed their fairy power when they were inadvertently released by her parents at your old dwelling long ago, you and Miss Zephrum Gates have been connected. What she feels affects you. You absorb the energy she cannot contain. This is why the passage of her faithful dog companion has diminished you so deeply."

"That little pipsqueak ruined all of my plans! And now, she stands in the way of my power?!? This, I cannot tolerate!" screamed Virgidous. "What must I do?"

"You must get her to help you kill the Leviathan, but she cannot know she is assisting you. For if she was aware of your plan, she would not kill it. She has no lust for killing. But I will tell you now...it is only with the help of Miss Zephrum Gates that you will regain your power. Then, you will live for a millennium."

And at that, Grizalda fell face forward onto her divining table.

Virgidous pulled Grizalda's head up by her rat's nest hair. "Grizalda? Is that it?"

Grizalda was unresponsive.

"It appears she is done with her reading," commented Zultr Zeki.

"Yes, it does," said Virgidous. He let go of Grizalda's head and it fell back to her table with a thump.

--Chapter 21--

"Mysterious Leaves"

Back at Fiddlesticks, the teachers tried their best to keep the students on track. After morning announcements, the students were sent off to their classes. In Dr. Moot's "Scientific Inventions to Change the World" class, Malvin asked, "What do you all think we can do to absorb oil spills in the ocean? Does anyone have any ideas?"

Sarah Bellum raised her hand. "I've read that hair inside nylon stockings absorbs a lot of oil. Maybe we could create something like that on a large scale?"

"Yes, very good idea," said Dr. Malvin Moot.

Daphne grinned, "We could call the invention 'Hair Today, Gone Tomorrow'."

The students cracked up. Daphne turned a little pink in the cheeks.

"Yes, very innovative," said Dr. Moot. "And what about radiation leaks that seep into our oceans. Does anybody have any ideas of what we could do about that?"

Nobody said anything. Even Sarah Bellum was stumped.

Razebir said, "Maybe we just shouldn't create radiation in the first place."

"Well, yes," said Dr. Malvin Moot. "In an ideal world, damaging radiation would not exist at all. In truth, the scientific community has questions about how to handle radioactive waste. Presently, some of it gets buried in canisters deep beneath the ground, but these canisters will need to be dealt with by future generations because containers won't last for more than 100 years."

"Why would we create energy with a byproduct that we don't know how to recycle?" asked Gai.

"Good question, Gai," said Dr. Moot. "When we can create solar energy or wave energy or wind energy, it is a wonder why we would choose something so dangerous and volatile instead."

"What about free energy?" asked Sarah Bellum.

"Oh yes," said Dr. Moot jumping from one foot to the other. "The future of free energy is very exciting indeed."

"What is free energy?" asked Razebir.

"It is radiant cosmic energy from our Sun," said Dr. Moot. He pulled out some diagrams from one of his books and continued. "You see, the sun emits small particles, each carrying such a small electric charge that they move with great velocity and speed. The cosmic rays ionize the air, setting free many charged ions and electrons. We can actually store this unlimited static electricity obtained from the air and convert it into a usable form."

Gai said, "It sounds like free energy could help us connect to the very wheel-work of nature."

"Yeah! An awesome idea!" said Razebir enthusiastically. "Why don't we use this energy for everything we need?"

"Good question, Razebir. The technology for capturing this cosmic energy has not been widespread, but we could help change that." Dr. Moot ran his fingers through his hair. "This cosmic energy operates the universe and is everywhere present and in unlimited quantities. The central source, for the Earth, is our Sun."

"What about generating energy from the magical world?" asked Misty. "I'll bet nobody's thought of that yet."

"True," said Dr. Moot. "But accessing free energy almost seems like magic to us, doesn't it?"

Head nods and muttered sounds peppered the room.

"Let's get back to the question of solving some of our existing environmental issues," said Dr. Moot. "Being that scientists have not yet thought of an appropriate way to deal with all of our problems, I would like all of you to put your thinking caps on...and have a list of ideas for us to consider in our next class in a couple of days."

The cowbell sounded from the Sun Lodge, signaling that it was time for students to move on to their next class.

Zephrum did her best to pay attention for the rest of the day, but her mind drifted as she tried to make sense of all that had happened. Thankfully, she made it through her classes without any of her teachers calling on her.

By later in the day, the sun was hidden behind a gray afternoon sky. After class, Zephrum was looking at the horses from outside their round pen. Aunt Gussie came up and put her arm around her.

"How was your day today, Zephrum?" asked Aunt Gussie.

Zephrum shrugged her shoulders. "OK…I guess."

"You know," said Aunt Gussie. "What happened with Nomad really made my heart sink like a stone."

"Me too," said Zephrum in a quiet voice.

"I don't mean to rub salt in an open wound," said Aunt Gussie. "But I've found that it's best to talk about our feelings when we are full of so many of them."

Zephrum just gazed upon the horses. She didn't utter a sound.

"When somebody special leaves this world, it often takes time for us to understand. We miss them, naturally, but they are on a miraculous spirit journey that we can't even imagine."

"I hope so," said Zephrum

"It's easy to feel as if our get up and go, got up and went," Aunt Gussie continued.

Spots of rain began to fall from the overcast sky, as a tear formed in Zephrum's eye.

"You know," said Aunt Gussie. "Grief sometimes needs to flow in order to get to the deeper heart beneath."

Zephrum said nothing. She just stood staring into space.

Finally, Aunt Gussie said, "Could you be quieter? I'd like to hear the grass grow."

Zephrum snapped out of her trance. "What? What did you just say?"

"Oh, I just wanted to know whether you were listening or not," commented Gussie.

"You want to hear the grass grow?" asked Zephrum.

Aunt Gussie giggled. "Just trying to get your attention is all."

Zephrum half smiled. "I'm sorry. I just don't know what to say. I feel numb somehow."

"Believe it or not, that's normal," continued Aunt Gussie. "The reality is that you will grieve forever in a way. You won't get over the loss of a loved one, but you'll learn to live with it, in time."

Zephrum nodded.

"You'll heal and re-build yourself around the loss you've suffered. And you might even be able to appreciate how lucky you've been to have had Nomad in your life, even though it was for a shorter time than you had hoped for."

Zephrum sniffed and wiped a tear off of her cheek.

Aunt Gussie squeezed Zephrum's shoulder. "You WILL be whole again, but you'll never be the same…nor should you be."

"Tonight, after dinner in the Sun Lodge, I'm going to tell everybody a story. I think it will help elevate our spirits," said Aunt Gussie.

"What's the story about?" asked Zephrum.

"Oh…That's a surprise," said Gussie. "I just wanted to tell everybody a little lore about Halloween. Did you know that it used to be called, 'Cabbage Night'?"

"No," said Zephrum. "Why?"

"Well," said Aunt Gussie. "It turns out that cabbage leaves used to be used for foretelling the future and predicting information about our potential spouses."

"That's silly," commented Zephrum. "How could a cabbage leaf know anything about that?"

"Well," continued Aunt Gussie. "It's an old wives tale. But it turns out kids used to have to dance for their Halloween treats. Oh…And people wore animal skins and heads during the earliest Halloween celebrations."

"Mmm…" thought Zephrum. "So strange. What else?"

"Oh, I don't want to give it all away now. It's something for you to look forward to." Aunt Gussie squeezed Zephrum around the shoulder. "There's a message behind every one of our strange traditions. One thing I like about fairy tales and folklore stories is that they are a reminder that things can always get better if we just hold onto hope."

Zephrum nodded.

She looked back at the horses. "I had better get in the barn to feed and groom the horses. It will probably be good for me."

"Yes," said Aunt Gussie. "And good for them too."

Zephrum smiled. "Definitely." She waved to Aunt Gussie. "See you later."

In the following days, life at Fiddlesticks moved forward in a fairly typical way. Students were busy constructing parts of their "Trash Collecting Array," learning about sea life, developing their magical skills, and practicing all kinds of circus arts. On some days, Zephrum felt as though it was totally "normal" to be without her canine friend. Some days, she felt kind of 'naked' without her.

Even so, as time moved on, things started to feel slightly better. Zephrum's connection to the horses really helped fill the void that was left in Nomad's wake.

Then, one afternoon after Zephrum was finished with trampoline class in the Circus Tent, she decided to visit Nomad's gravesite near the beehives.

Nomad's grave mound was marked with a special rock that had her name on it. And Gai Holmes had planted some pretty flowers there as well.

"I miss you so much and wish I could see you again. I really do," whispered Zephrum out loud. A subtle wind formed as she spoke. It stirred a pile of leaves. They spiraled up into the air and shifted into a familiar shape.

"This is mind boggling, but it's actually forming into a shape that looks strangely like…a dog." She rubbed her eyes, barely able to believe what she was seeing. When she opened her eyes again, the leaves slowed down. Before they floated back to a pile on the ground near the door, she heard one loud "Woof!"

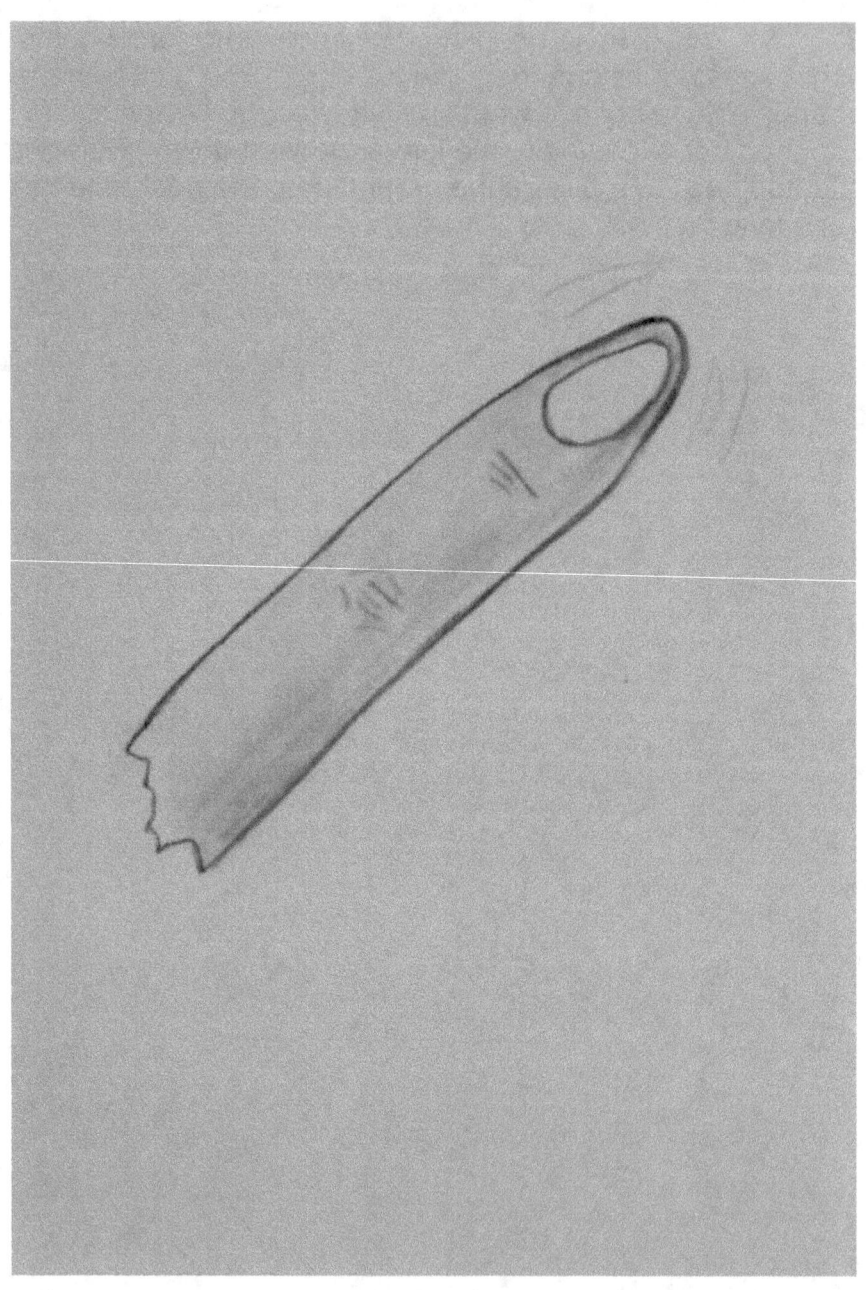

--Chapter 22--

"The Missing Finger"

Meanwhile, beneath the ground, in the tunnels under the town of Haversville, Virgidous' "condition" was showing signs of improvement. "Although the taste of that frog liver tincture is still repulsive to me, I must admit that I am feeling more vital and crooked," he confided in Zultr Zeki. "I am simply more wicked and malevolent and this has me feeling that I must be on the right track."

"Yes, Sire," agreed Zultr Zeki.

"Let us make another journey out to sea."

"We will make the preparations and set sail tomorrow morning," said Zultr Zeki.

"Good," said Virgidous rubbing his hands together. "My renewed strength will serve us well on the journey."

"Yes, Sire," said Zeki. "Without a doubt."

The sunrise of the next morning was coming up pink on the horizon. Captain Muttonchops and his crew were already on the ship when Virgidous and Zultr Zeki arrived at the docks.

"Deckhand! Are you three sheets to the wind?"

"No, Cap'n," said the scraggly pirate. "I have not had a swig of spirits yet this mornin'. It was just a late night is all."

Muttonchops barked, "Well, hoist that mainsail, then. And hop to it…or else we'll have ye walk the plank."

The clumsy pirate hoisted the mainsail up the mast without delay. "Aye aye, Cap'n."

Virgidous and Zultr Zeki stood at the foot of the gangplank. "Well…Fill me boots with barnacles! Ahoy Sailors! Walk over our gangplank and join yer ship's crew."

"Get those lines in order!" bellowed Muttonchops. "Prepare the rigging or else you'll all feel my rope's end."

The pirates on the deck scurried around, picking up stray ropes and securing the sails.

"Ah…Give them the threat of a proper flogging and they speed it up, don't they?" Muttonchops chuckled, "It's all in a day's work, aye?"

"Yes," said Virgidous, not amused.

Muttonchops looked back at his crew and hollered, "Alright ye scallywags. Our VIP's have arrived. Get ready to weigh anchor."

The pirate with the peg leg helped a scraggly pirate to lift the anchor onto the deck of the ship. Then he said, "All hands away!"

Virgidous and Zultr Zeki went below deck as the ship glided away from the docks, into the bay, and out to sea.

Muttonchops stationed himself at the captain's wheel as the rest of the crew adjusted the sails with each tack. After a bit of time, Zultr Zeki peeked up from below deck only to find that they were sailing beneath an overcast sky.

"It looks like it's not too bright out today," she said.

"Mmm…" said Virgidous. He peered into the sky above the deck. "I think I will go and help sail this ship, then."

The two walked up the steps and approached the captain's wheel. The wind was blowing Muttonchop's black beard around so much that it looked like he had rats playing inside it.

"Ahoy Maties!" blustered Muttonchops.

"Ahoy!" responded Zeki. "Our great leader would like to assist with the sail, as the sky is dim today."

"Aye Bucko…Why don't you take charge of the lines from the mainsail?" said Muttonchops. "Just be careful with those ropes. We've got surprise gusts coming up from these here winds."

Virgidous nodded. Then, he went in the direction of the mainsail and took over for the clumsy little pirate who was holding onto the lines there. Virgidous smiled as he held on tight to the sail's lines. "It's true what Muttonchops said. There's quite a bit of wind power going into the sail. I can feel it through the tug on the ropes here."

"Yes, Sire," said Zeki as she stood watch.

An unexpected gust came and Virgidous had to let the lines slack. "Sailing is exciting, Zeki."

"Yes Sire," said Zultr Zeki. "And maybe we will even catch a glimpse of the Leviathan today."

Virgidous' eyes widened. "Oh, I would love to find that sea monster while I am feeling so strong with vigor and malice."

Another big gust of wind blew into the mainsail and then subsided. Virgidous let the sail out and then, pulled it back in after the gust diminished. "I think I will wrap these ropes around my hands, so as to be more ready for the next gust," said Virgidous.

"Sire," said Zultr Zeki. "It is my understanding that the lines must be left free, in order to be ready for whatever might happen next. If you loop them around your hand, is it not dangerous?"

"Are you questioning my judgment, Zeki?"

"No, Sire. Just wondering if it is safe for you to wrap the lines around your hand when we are experiencing so many unpredictable gusts is all," said Zultr Zeki.

In the next moment, a powerful gust pulled on the mainsail and yanked the rope tight around one of Virgidous' hands. He tried to get his hand free of the loops, but as he was doing it, another gust blew in. The lines coiled out of his hand, all but one, which snapped hard upon his fingers. It fixed around his pointer finger so hard that it actually POPPED the end of his finger OFF with unpredictable force. Blood spurted from his finger like water from a hose.

Zultr Zeki leapt to Virgidous' side, grabbed the bandana from around her neck and wrapped it around her master's finger fast. "Sire, hold this cloth around the wound and I will search for your finger."

The little stub of his index finger was rolling around the deck and Zeki was chasing after it. Because of the unpredictable gusts, the ship was rocking about strangely and making it difficult for Zultr Zeki to grab Virgidous' finger. She chased it from one side of the boat to the other…and from bow to stern. Finally, just before she was about to snatch it up, it rolled off the bow of the boat and into the ocean.

"Nooo…" screamed Zeki.

Tricia Riel

She ran over to Captain Muttonchops. "Is there any way we can circle around the area where our leader's finger dropped into the sea?"

Muttonchops spun the wheel around. "Aye!" Then, he barked out orders to his crew. "Coming about! Hard alee!"

Zeki picked up a long pole with a net attached to it. She scooped and scooped, but it seemed that Virgidous' fingertip was officially lost at sea.

With her head bent downward, she walked up to Virgidous. "I'm sorry Sire, but I could not retrieve your fingertip. I came up empty handed."

"Don't make puns, Zeki."

"Sire, forgive me." She bent down on one knee. "I am sworn to protect you and I have failed."

He winced as he held tight to his bleeding finger. "You did try to warn me about safety with the lines and I chose to ignore you."

"Yes, Sire."

"Just tell Muttonchops to get us back to shore and bring me to our goblin healer the moment we arrive at the docks." Virgidous got up and added, "I'll be below deck."

"Yes, Sire," said Zeki. And she rushed over to Muttonchops to relay the message.

Below deck, Virgidous sat on a cot to rest. The stronger Strasidous voice spoke as he held onto his bleeding finger. "This pain is a teacher, Virgil."

"Yes, Master," replied Virgil's voice from within.

"We must not let our frail body get in the way of our ultimate goal to control all things."

"Yes. Whatever you say, Sire," responded Virgil's voice.

"It is a mere fingertip, Virgil. And we are much more than that," said the Strasidous voice.

"Yes, Sire. Much more," added Virgil's voice.

"Once we commission the help of Zephrum Gates and kill the Leviathan, we will have eternal life and power beyond belief."

"Yes sire," said Virgil's voice. "Power beyond belief."

—Chapter 23—

"Freaky Frog Juice"

When the ship reached the docks, Zultr Zeki quickly rushed Virgidous back to the underground tunnels and to the Healer Goblin's steamy laboratory. Healer Groikz's eyes moved as though independent from his cranium when he saw Virgidous' finger injury.

"Sire, without the tip of your finger, I can only help the wound to heal as it is."

"Fine," said Virgidous. "Do what you must, so we can be done with this business."

Healer Groikz shuffled around his laboratory and gathered supplies for Virgidous' finger. With his arms full of bandages and bottles, he returned to Virgidous and started cleaning the wound and wrapping it up. Once finished, he said, "Return to me tomorrow, so I can monitor your progress, Sire."

"Yes, yes," said Virgidous.

He handed Virgidous a dropper bottle. "And take this tincture to help with the pain."

"Fine," said Virgidous, wincing.

Virgidous stood up and Zultr Zeki ushered him back to his sleeping chamber. Once they arrived at his dusty door, she said, "Rest well, Sire."

Virgidous nodded. Then, slid into his chamber for the night.

Even with the help of the pain-killing tincture, Virgidous struggled with incredible pain throughout the evening. His dreams were stranger than strange, even for him. Screams echoed from his chamber and throughout the goblin tunnels.

Bleary-eyed the next morning, he hobbled to the door and opened it when Zultr Zeki arrived.

Zeki ushered Virgidous to the healer goblin's lab, as planned. Once there, Virgidous sat down on a stool and placed his arm on the goblin's treatment table. As Healer Groikz undressed the wound, his head cocked to an odd direction. He peered deeply at the finger. "Sire, it defies all logic, but it appears that your finger is growing back."

Virgidous looked deeply at his finger in surprise. "Yes, I can see a little stump forming."

"Sire, I recommend a special treatment to encourage the growth," said Groikz.

"Yes, yes," said Virgidous. "Do what you must."

Groikz scampered around his laboratory and brought a number of things over to the examination table.

"Firstly, Sire...I would like to submerge your finger in this sodium liquid and then, charge the water."

"Fine," said Virgidous. "Healer...Why do you think this is happening?"

"I can only theorize," said Healer Groikz. "But, I think it may be a side effect of the potions you have been taking."

"A side effect?" asked Virgidous.

"Yes, Sire," said Groikz. "Both of your potions are derived from potent frog parts. In nature, amphibious frogs, salamanders, certain insects, and even some earthworms have unusual regenerative abilities. Tadpoles can re-grow their tails, many insects can re-grow antennas or legs, and worms can often re-grow an entire body."

"So...you think that the frog tinctures have given me regenerative abilities?"

"It is the only explanation, Sire," said the goblin healer. "Our bodies can enlarge organs when needed, but regeneration of whole body parts is something that very few creatures have been able to master."

"Very good," said Virgidous with a sinister smile.

"It is an avalanche of growth that can only be explained by the abundance of frog essence in your system," said Healer Groikz. "You should return to me for treatment each day until your finger has fully grown back, Sire."

"Yes, wise counsel," agreed Virgidous.

"And I would suggest delaying any more sea voyages until we are done with your treatments," said Groikz.

"Whatever you say," said Virgidous.

There was much pain in the days that followed, but Virgidous' finger was, indeed, growing back.

Virgidous grew stranger in other ways as well. His eyes appeared wider, he started to "sleep" while sitting up, and he began developing an appetite for bugs. He'd see a little gnat or mosquito flying about and quickly grab it with his thin green hands. Then he'd gobble it up.

"Sire," asked Zultr Zeki. "Your reflexes appear faster. This is a good sign, I think. But why the sudden interest in flying insects?"

"I know not why," said Virgidous. "All I know ith that I am drawn to the tathte of them."

"The 'taste' of them?" asked Zeki.

"Yeth," replied Virgidous.

Zeki gave Virgidous a sideways look. "And Sire?"

"Yeth," he replied.

"Have you noticed that you are talking with a fairly prominent lisp now?" asked Zeki.

"Am I?" said Virgidous, oblivious. "I hadn't notithed."

"Yes, Sire," said Zeki. "I think we should have Healer Groikz do an examination…to figure out why this is happening."

"If you think tho," said Virgidous. "But I thwear that I feel jutht fine. Very malevolent. Better than ever, actually."

"Yes, Sire," said Zeki. "Whatever you say."

--Chapter 24--

"Dragon Dreams"

Halloween was just around the corner and preparations for the annual Halloween party were well underway.

"Yous all got to get the Halloween decorations up in the Sun Lodge, so wees can create a real spooky haunted house. We all wants to attract the spirits, don't we?" said Rocko Pounder.

"I'm not so sure about that," said Zephrum quietly.

"Oh, it's going to be soooo much fun to dress up in costumes," said Daphne. She knew what her friend was thinking.

"And I'll be teaching everybody how to make festive cookies and ghoulish snacks," commented Mrs. Fliffle.

At bedtime, Daphne and Zephrum were talking about all the Halloween plans before they went to sleep.

"In honor of Nomad's memory, I think I'll dress like a skunk this year," said Zephrum.

Daphne grinned. "Oh yes. That would be great. She looked so cute when you dressed her up as a skunk before."

Zephrum smiled. "She really did, didn't she?"

Remembering the joy that her dog brought her was definitely more fun than being depressed about missing her.

"I think I'll give all three horses a unicorn horn this year," added Zephrum. "And maybe have them each wear a decorative sash.

"Ooo…That's so fun," said Daphne. "I can help you make the sashes if you want. I'm already done with my kangaroo costume, so I have plenty of time to help you with the horses."

Zephrum smiled under her covers. "Yes, that would be great."

That night, Zephrum's dreams were filled with images of flight, similar to how she felt when she was having telepathic dreams with the dragon creature from the previous year. She could almost hear the voice of Waylon the Wyvern, the dragon creature she had gotten to know the previous year.

"Miss Zephrum Gates Creature! I found my mate on a distant mountaintop northward. She was many hills and valleys away. It was long days of coasting upon the thermals to get to her. After we mated in the most glorious union, she laid a clutch of eggs and buried them for safety, as is our way. Unfortunately, the magical world is under attack from a strange purple vapor and most of our dragon babies never hatched."

Zephrum mumbled in her sleep, "Waylon? Is that really you?"

"Yes, Miss Zephrum Gates Creature. It is I."

Zephrum could "hear" the breathy sound of bellows from this dragon's great lungs. He continued, "My mate and I are flying southward and will reside back at my old mountain cave for a time. BUT…we fear the vapor is following us and will infect our offspring. We need your help, Miss Zephrum Gates Creature."

"My help?!?" said Zephrum's voice in her dream.

"Yes! You must shield our three little hatchlings while me and my mate rest and fortify my mountain cave."

"Shield them? Where? How? Why me?" said Zephrum aloud in her sleep.

"Because Miss Zephrum Gates Creature," continued the wyvern's thoughts into her mind. "You are powerful enough to fend off evils beyond evils. We will deliver our hatchlings to you before the sun rises, before the others like you awake."

"Around twilight? In the early morning?" asked Zephrum.

"Yes. In what you call the 'morning.' Be near the dwelling of your flying horses and be ready for our fledglings. All they need is warmth…and maybe some of your raw chicken eggs. They are too young to understand your clever riddles."

"But Waylon…I have never cared for dragon babies before. How will I know what to do?" asked Zephrum in her dream.

"You will know, Miss Zephrum Gates. Just keep them warm. We will leave them with you until the sun rises again. Once we regain our strength from our long journey and once we prepare my mountain cave in our ways, we will retrieve our hatchlings."

An image of a giant dragon's eye blinked within Zephrum's inner sight. Then she woke up.

She rubbed her eyes and thought about the strangeness of her dream.

Daphne rolled around in her bed and faced Zephrum. She mumbled, "Zephrum, you were talking really loudly in your sleep. Hmm…were you having a weird dream?"

"Uh…" said Zephrum. "Actually, yes."

She stared at Daphne until Daphne's eyes opened.

"Daphne," said Zephrum. "I think that Waylon the Wyvern was telepathically communicating with me, like he used to do last year."

"Really?!?" asked Daphne. "Didn't he fly northward to find his mate?

"Yes," said Zephrum. "He found her."

"What did he say?" asked Daphne. "Could you make sense of it?"

"I know it might sound strange, but I think he's going to bring three of his baby hatchlings to the horses' barn just before sunrise."

"Do you mean baby DRAGONS?!?"

"Yes," said Zephrum. "He says that we just need to keep them warm until the sun rises again, while he and his mate regain their strength from their long journey back to his mountain cave."

"He wants you to babysit?!?"

"Yeah," replied Zephrum. "I guess that a mysterious purple vapor is affecting many magical creatures and these are the only of his hatchlings that have survived."

"What are we going to do with baby dragons?" asked Daphne.

"Well, we could put them in one of those old metal cages we have in the barn…and put them in an empty horse stall. Maybe we could plug in the heat lamp that we use for baby chicks?"

"Is this really going to happen, Zephrum?" asked Daphne. She still looked foggy from sleep.

"I don't know, but I think I should get up before sunrise, just in case."

"You had better wake me up," said Daphne. "I don't think this is the kind of thing that you should do alone."

"Agreed," said Zephrum. "Thanks."

"Set your alarm and I'll go with you, ok?"

Zephrum nodded. She set her alarm an hour and a half earlier than she usually rose, then rolled under her covers to get some more sleep.

In what seemed like no time, the alarm sounded. Daphne and Zephrum looked at each other, knowing the whole idea was kind of nuts. They put their headlamps on and walked over to the barn in their pajamas.

Once there, Zephrum brushed off an old metal cage that was stored in the barn. Daphne put some dry hay in the bottom of it, while Zephrum looked for the heat lamp, an extension chord, and an electric outlet to plug it into.

Daphne looked up at some metal hooks hanging from the ceiling of the stall. "Why don't we use one of these high hooks to hang the heat lamp above the cage?"

"Good idea," said Zephrum.

"Miss Zephrum Gates Creature," said Waylon's voice inside of Zephrum's mind. "We are upon you. Are you ready for our fledglings?"

Zephrum looked at Daphne. "We had better go outside the barn. I think they're here."

Daphne and Zephrum went outside and looked up. In the deep dark blue of the twinkling early morning sky, they saw a pair of large shadowed wings approaching.

"Holy Moly! It looks like they're really here!" said Daphne in surprise.

"Yeah," said Zephrum, as stunned as Daphne.

Waylon and his mate veered downward. As they approached the barn, their spiky wings flapped slowly to control their descent to the ground.

Once they got their footing stabilized on the earth, Waylon spoke to Zephrum's mind. "I was not sure you received my message. You are a strange creature, not always trusting your inner knowing as we wyverns do."

"Yes," said Zephrum aloud. "It was hard to know if it was a dream or real."

"You are an odd creature indeed," said Waylon to Zephrum's mind. "All wyverns know that the dream life is part of waking life. They are one and the same."

"Uh…" said Zephrum.

"Will you have a way to keep our hatchlings warm?" asked Waylon.

"Yes," said Zephrum. "We have a thing we call a heat lamp. We've set up a comfy nest for them under the heat. I think they'll be fine."

"Miss Zephrum Gates Creature," said Waylon. "These hatchlings will need the warmth of a real body for portions of each day. Your friends, the ones that helped you in my mountain cave in days past. They will help, yes?"

Zephrum looked at Daphne and then back at Waylon. "Yes, my friends will help."

"Do not tell others besides them, Miss Zephrum Gates Creature," said Waylon. "As you remember, we do not want humans to know we exist. You will have to hide the hatchlings from others of your kind. Can you do this for the length of another sunrise?"

"We will do our best," said Zephrum.

And at that, Waylon and his mate revealed their hatchlings, which had been holding on to scales beneath their wings. The baby dragons jumped to the ground, just beneath their parents. Once their little wings out stretched, the hatchlings started screeching. Waylon and his mate nudged the baby dragons in the direction of Zephrum and Daphne. They clumsily walked towards the girls without fear. Zephrum picked one of them up and Daphne picked up the other two.

"Take care of them well, Miss Zephrum Gates Creature," said Waylon into her mind. "We are only able to produce offspring every thousand years. We will have to wait for quite some time before my mate's eggs are fertile again. These hatchlings are precious. Very special. You understand?"

Zephrum nodded. "Yes. We will keep them safe."

With that, Waylon and his mate turned around, jumped into the air, flapped their wings, and then soared eastward towards Waylon's abandoned mountaintop cave.

—Chapter 25—

"Sneeze Attack"

After Zephrum and Daphne brought the baby dragons to the cage inside the empty stall in the barn, they covered three sides of the enclosure with burlap.

"This burlap covering will hide them, just in case anybody else happens to glance into the stall," said Daphne.

Zephrum put a bowl of water in the corner of the cage and said, "I think we should get some chicken eggs for them too."

"OK," said Daphne.

The girls went down to the chicken coop in the dark of the early morning, scooped up some eggs from one of the chicken's brooding boxes, and brought the eggs to the baby dragons.

Zephrum put the eggs in a metal bowl and gave it to Waylon's hatchlings.

Immediately, the baby dragons poked holes in the eggshells and began to lap up the golden insides. After the eggs were gone, the hatchlings began to snuggle each other and groom one another. They made little screeching sounds. Their eyelids then became heavy with sleep.

"They are sooooo adorable!" said Daphne.

"They really are, aren't they?" said Zephrum. She smiled. "And they're a lot easier to take care of than I had imagined."

Daphne yawned. "Oh, we had better go get ready for our day. By the looks of the brightening sky, it looks like the sun will be coming up pretty soon."

"I think we should tell Gai about the dragon babies," said Zephrum. "But I don't think we should tell anybody else."

"Sounds good," said Daphne. "Maybe Gai will be able to help us with them?"

"That's what I was thinking too," said Zephrum.

"Well," commented Daphne. "This is going to be a pretty unusual Halloween, isn't it?"

The girls smiled at each other as they headed back to their cabin to get ready for their day.

Because it was Halloween Day, everyone was abuzz with excitement. At breakfast, Zephrum and Daphne pulled Gai aside and told him about the baby dragon visitors.

"Whoa!?!" exclaimed Gai. "Really?!?"

The girls just nodded.

Before classes, Zephrum showed Gai the sleeping dragon babies. "Wow! They're surprisingly mellow," said Gai.

"I know," said Zephrum. "That's exactly what I thought, but I guess we'll also have to hold them for part of the day or night."

"Cool," said Gai.

That afternoon, Zephrum brought the dragon babies some more chicken eggs. She watched them eat and waddle around their cage until they all curled up with each other again. Daphne and Misty were busy with the last-minute decorations in the Sun Lodge, while Gai and Red put pretend hanging spiders at the doorways. Mrs. Fliffle was making spooky looking cookies in the shape of fingers and eyeballs.

The students had an early light dinner, so they could have more time to get into costumes for Halloween night. Daphne jumped into her kangaroo costume, Zephrum got dressed in her skunk costume from the previous year, and Gai became a tall tree. He had a hollowed-out hole in the center of his costume that he put a stuffed owl animal into. As the sun slipped below the horizon, the sky darkened. Spooky Halloween haunts were pumped in through the Sun Lodge sound system.

Zephrum, Daphne, and Gai went to check in on the baby dragons before the Halloween party. They gave them more chicken eggs, but the little winged babies kept on crying with screeches.

"They probably need warmth from real bodies," said Daphne. "You know, like what Waylon told you when he dropped them off."

"Yes," said Zephrum. "Let's each pick them up for a few minutes and see if that helps."

Once the baby dragons were being held tight, the screeching stopped. They were content.

"They sure are cute," said Gai.

"Totally," said Daphne.

"Well…it seems like they're ok now. Let's put them back into their cage and go to the party," said Zephrum.

But as soon as the fledglings were back in their nest, they started screeching again. Daphne picked one back up and it got immediately quiet, so Gai picked one up and noticed the same thing. Zephrum finally picked up the last baby and all was quiet.

"OK…Let's try this one more time," said Zephrum. "Let's try to put them down really close to each other this time."

As soon as the little dragons were put down, they started screeching loudly again.

Daphne sighed. "It looks like we'll just have to bring them with us."

"But we have to go to the Halloween party," cried Zephrum.

"Well, I could fit one into my kangaroo pouch," said Daphne.

"And one of them could fit inside the hole in my tree trunk," said Gai.

"OK," said Zephrum. "But you guys had better be careful. We can't let anybody see them."

"Absolutely."

"For sure."

I guess I could get Nomad's old skunk costume from last year…and wrap the other one up inside it, it will look like I'm carrying a baby skunk around with me."

"Great idea," said Daphne. I could take the stuffing out of my baby kangaroo and put it on the dragon I carry around. And Gai could probably do something similar with the stuffed owl inside the hole of his tree trunk."

Zephrum opened the cage and picked up one of the dragon babies. It started to coo as soon as she had it in her hands. She passed it over to Daphne, who gently stashed it inside her kangaroo pouch.

Zephrum picked up another dragon baby and gave it to Gai.

The last one was screeching and trying to spit out smoke until it got re-united with its baby sibling inside of Daphne's kangaroo pouch.

"I think you'll have to hold both of them inside your pouch until we can get Nomad's old skunk costume in our cabin," said Zephrum.

Daphne nodded. "Once we're there, we can use my scissors to cut up the stuffed kangaroo and the stuffed owl. It will be like giving them costumes. Ha! Ha!"

Once they got the dragons properly hidden inside their new "costumes," they headed for the party inside the Sun Lodge.

Mrs. Fliffle was standing at a treat table. "Remember what Great Aunt Gussie told us a couple of weeks ago? If you want a cookie or a treat, you'll have to dance for it."

Zephrum rolled her eyes at the thought, while Daphne enthusiastically created a little choreography on the spot.

It looked like the Halloween party was getting off to a great start. Dexter Droudy wore a pair of dangly googly-eyed glasses over his regular eye glasses, Rocko Pounder dressed himself up in a cardboard box and fashioned it to look like a giant picnic table, Great Aunt Gussie dressed like a flower, and Geezer came dressed as a bumble bee. Nobody seemed to notice the baby dragons, since they were so well hidden inside Zephrum and Daphne and Gai's costumes.

As the sound system's decibel reached a higher level, it was clear that the party was really getting into full swing.

Then, without warning, Aynia flittered into the main area of the Sun Lodge and let out a large sneeze.

The music screeched to a halt.

"With the spirits out and about

Fairies are all a buzz
Strasidous Rowpe has changed
Again, he's different than he was."

Zephrum spun her skunk tail around to look more closely at Aynia. "What do you mean?"

"He's growing new parts
And is acting shifty and strange
Even the way he talks
Is starting to change.

He has become a hybrid
His goblin self more wild
He's becoming part Frog
It is anything but mild."

Daphne said, "A Frog? Like for Halloween?"

"No. It is much more
With Frog Essence within
He's fully confident
That he can only win.

Be warned, dear friends…
He is more frightening than before.
He is growing in ways
Predicted by Fairy Lore."

And then, as quickly as she had appeared, she vanished, followed by a cloud of sparkly fairy dust and another VERY loud sneeze.

"Whoa…" commented Daphne, letting out a little squeak of a sneeze herself. "I wonder why Aynia felt like she had to come to tell us about that."

"I don't know," said Zephrum, blowing a sneeze into her elbow pit. "It does sound pretty strange, though."

"Strange indeed," said Daphne.

The music resumed and people continued as though nothing had interrupted the party, except that the room was peppered with sneezes for quite some time.

"I wonder why nobody seems concerned about Aynia's message?" said Zephrum.

"Or why we're all...ah-chuuu... suddenly sneezing," said Daphne. "I guess that everybody is just extra happy from all the sugary treats they've eaten."

"Maybe," said Gai, sneezing. "Ah...choo..."

And then, without warning, Rocko Pounder let out such a big sneeze that it shook the entire Sun Lodge.

"Ah..ah..ah..Chooooooooooooooooo..."

For some reason, Rocko's enormous sneeze inspired sneezes from everybody. All of the people inside the Sun Lodge started sneezing uncontrollably. Sneezes sprinkled through all the people on the dance floor, those that were playing games in the basement, and even the people lingering near the snack table were sneezing. Autumn Visage (who was being the DJ) had to stop the music and run outside because she feared her sneezes would spray all over the equipment. It seemed like there was no end in sight.

After Geezer's "busy bee" sneezed directly into the flower of Great Aunt Gussie's headdress, Aunt Gussie realized she had to put a stop to this, once and for all.

"Alright already," yelled Aunt Gussie, "This is the last straw. I don't know how Aynia did it, but it seems that her visit has inspired a cascade of never-ending sneezes. We could probably power the entire Sun Lodge with the energy of these sternutations."

"Oh," commented Dr. Malvin Moot beneath a muted sneeze. "That is a most curious idea, especially since sneezes can travel up to 100 miles per hour. We should absolutely explore ways to harness and use 'sneeze power'."

Great Aunt Gussie gave Malvin a stern look, as she sneezed onto one of the flower petals from her costume.

"Uh," said Malvin quietly. "I mean, later. Later, after we've gotten this situation...ah-choo...under control."

Sneezes from the room were still coming out of everyone in unpredictable intervals. Students started cracking up because they JUST couldn't stop sneezing. The baby wyverns that were safely hidden inside Daphne and Gai's costumes started to sneeze and it singed parts of the material.

Daphne jumped when she felt another dragon sneeze char broil a hole in her costume. She looked at Zephrum. "The baby dragons are also having a sneeze attack."

Zephrum's eyes widened, not knowing what to do.

"OK everybody," announced Aunt Gussie. "Squeeze your noses or pinch your upper lip when you feel one of these sneezes coming on. If that doesn't work, you can press your tongue behind your two front teeth, grab the spot between your eye brows, or hold your face about one inch from a table and stick your tongue out."

Soon the room was filled with people trying all of Aunt Gussie's techniques. Aunt Gussie added to the list. "Now, if none of these things work, you can distract yourself with your hands, wiggle your ear lobes, or simply get angry."

"They all look busier than mosquitos in a nudist colony, don't they?" Geezer chuckled, then sneezed.

As Daphne wiggled her ears. "I had no idea that there were so many ways to stop ourselves…ah..choo… from sneezing."

"Oh yes," said Aunt Gussie. "The biggest way people give up power is by not knowing we have it to begin with."

Just then, Zephrum let out a giant sneeze. The power of it propelled her backward into the air and made her body slam up against the wall. Stunned, Zephrum landed in a heap on top of some of the Sun Lodge pillows that littered the floor where she fell. The baby dragon she had been holding onto, scurried away in its little baby skunk costume, its large skunk tail trailing behind it along the floor. Daphne jumped up and ran after it.

It was sneezing char broiled sneezes onto the floor as she ran, leaving little black marks everywhere.

Daphne bent over to scoop up the little dragon. As she bent over, the baby dragon inside her pouch jumped out of her costume and waddled away.

"Oh no," said Daphne. "Now, I've got to catch TWO of them."

They were scurrying every which way and sneezing smoke wherever they went. She ran around trying to herd them together, so she could grab them both at the same time. One almost set fire to the long curtains that bordered the Sun Lodge's French doors.

Meanwhile, Great Aunt Gussie and Geezer ran over to Zephrum, as a crowd of students gathered around her.

"Are you ok, Miss Zephrum?" asked Geezer.

"Wow," exclaimed Razebir. "How did that happen?"

Gai rushed to Zephrum's side, "Zephrum, Are you ok?"

Zephrum nodded.

"Daphne is going after your 'baby skunk," he whispered." So don't worry, ok?

Zephrum started to cry.

She said, "It just seems like it's starting all over again. Strasidous Rowpe threatening all of us and morphing into who knows what? He seems to be gaining power again. I just don't understand how anybody would support him, even goblins."

"Yea," said Gai. "It's pretty weird, no doubt about it."

Zephrum continued, "Strange things keep happening all around us and we don't have any real explanation or know how to stop it."

An uncomfortable quiet spread through the room.

"Now, don't you kids worry," said Great Aunt Gussie. "You're at this school to learn about your inherent talents and that is a very important quest."

"So true," said Geezer. "A smooth sea never made a skilled sailor."

Daphne had finally collected the last baby dragon and hid it inside the kangaroo pouch of her costume. She joined the group surrounding Zephrum, still a little breathless from the chase.

"Fear is a membrane between the known and the unknown," continued Aunt Gussie. "You are all discovering solutions to the world's problems here. This is wonderful, but the REAL problem in the world is that people can no longer recognize their true nature. This whole thing with Strasidous Rowpe and sneeze attacks and all the rest is all simply a symptom of what's wrong. We have to see these challenges as an opportunity to help us grow."

Daphne nodded. "But it's hard to think straight when I'm uncontrollably sneezing… and for no reason."

Aunt Gussie looked at Daphne and said, "You're an Artist, Daphne. Thinking straight is not your line of work."

Daphne smiled. A few kids chuckled.

"It's still just so scary," said Zephrum.

"Oh, sure it is," said Great Aunt Gussie. "But Zephrum, you've seen more darkness than any other girl I know and you never let it dim your soul. This is part of who you are."

"But aren't you scared?" asked Zephrum. "Isn't everybody?"

Mumbling came from the crowd as Aunt Gussie said, "Oh, you bet your sweet bippie I am. But letting fear take a grip of you will not help you move forward. A healthy dose of fear gives you wisdom, but letting fear consume you will never help you plant your garden. You've got to get up with the sun every morning and know that it's a new day."

Dexter cleared his throat. "Speaking of, we should all think about getting to bed now that our party seems to be winding down. We've got classes tomorrow and many plans for all of you."

"Yes," agreed Aunt Gussie. "Time to lean up against the door of sleep. Giddy-up now. Everybody get a move on."

Gai helped Zephrum up from the floor and said, "Let's go back to the barn before our friends start sneezing again, ok?" He gave Zephrum a sideways glance.

Zephrum nodded.

Without warning, the two baby dragons inside of Daphne's costume both sneezed such powerful dragon sneezes that the center of her kangaroo costume burst into a tiny flame. With her tummy ablaze, she jumped. She screamed as she tried to pat out the flames.

Zephrum and Gai immediately extinguished the blaze by patting down the flames.

As the three dragon babysitters left the Sun Lodge, they overheard Geezer talking to Great Aunt Gussie. "Oh, Gussie... You're so good with the kids. Makes me want to squeeze you like a tube of toothpaste."

"Oh Geezer," said Gussie. "You dreamy slice of provolone cheese. You make me feel like I could do anything."

Zephrum rolled her eyes as Gai and Daphne laughed.

Then they ran over to the horse barn before anybody could discover the dragons beneath their costumes.

--Chapter 26--

"Baby Dragons"

"That was a close call," said Daphne. "Your little dragon was running all over the place after you slammed up against the wall. I could barely keep up with it. Then, the baby in my costume slipped out of my pouch when I was bending over. I had to chase both of them all over the Sun Lodge and they were darting in completely different directions."

"Oh my gosh! I can't believe that happened," said Zephrum. "Did anybody see you?"

"I don't know," said Daphne. "It seemed like almost everybody was surrounding you at the time. But the baby dragons were sneezing smoke plumes all over. They almost set the curtains on fire over near the Sun Lodge French doors!"

"Whoa…" said Gai. "I can't believe that you were dealing with all of that. I had no idea."

"I was pretty scared that somebody would see me," replied Daphne. "Now, there are little burn marks all over the Sun Lodge floor from the baby dragon sneezes. Somebody is bound to start asking questions."

"I wonder if we should sleep out in the barn throughout the night, just to make sure the babies don't set their cage on fire?" asked Gai.

"That's a good idea," said Zephrum. "I don't think we should take any more chances. We don't want them to be discovered."

"Yea," said Daphne. "And we don't want the barn to burn down either."

"Agreed," said Gai. "I'll stay in the barn and watch them, while you guys go get your blankets and stuff."

They placed the baby dragons back in their cage. Then Zephrum and Daphne ran off to their cabin. They brushed their teeth in the nearby outhouse bathroom, got their pajamas on, grabbed their head lamps, and brought their sleeping bags and pillows back to the barn.

Gai was waiting for them, but he was beginning to nod off. He shook it off when they entered. "Just in time. I was starting to get really sleepy." He got up and said, "I'll be back soon."

"Wait," said Zephrum. "What are you going to tell Red? He's bound to notice that you're gone for the night."

"Oh yea," said Gai. "I hadn't thought about that."

"Why don't you just tell him that you and Zephrum are going to have a 'romantic evening' in the barn?" Daphne said.

Zephrum's jaw dropped open and Gai's eyes widened. If the barn had been bright enough to see the complexion on their faces, their blushing would have been really obvious.

"Daphne!!" exclaimed Zephrum. She slapped Daphne on the arm.

"I don't know," said Daphne. "It's just the first lie I could think of. I mean, you guys like each other, right?"

Gai was speechless.

Zephrum's eyes narrowed at Daphne. "Well...yes, but no. Uh...I don't know. Daphne!"

Daphne giggled. "Oh Gai, I'm sure you'll think of something. Just come back soon."

He nodded and then darted out.

"Daphne, I can't believe you," said Zephrum the moment he was out of earshot.

"What? It was just an idea," said Daphne innocently.

"Ugh! It's just soooo embarrassing," said Zephrum.

"Only because you loooooove him," said Daphne.

"Oh stop," said Zephrum.

"Ha! Just admit it," said Daphne. "You guys have had the hots for each other for a while."

"Whatever," said Zephrum. "Even if we did like each other, you should never talk about it out loud! What were you thinking?"

Daphne shrugged her shoulders. "Well, it's a believable cover story, right?"

"Whatever. Let's just forget about it and get set up for the night," said Zephrum. She un-packed her sleeping bag.

"OK, Love Bird," said Daphne.

Zephrum glared at Daphne. A wind started forming in the barn.

"Uh Zephrum," said Daphne. "You had better tone it down a bit, or else we'll have a tornado to deal with, on top of all of our other problems."

Zephrum glanced around. She took a deep breath and tried to calm her mind. "OK, but don't embarrass me in front of Gai like that, alright?"

"OK, alright already," said Daphne.

By the time Daphne set up her bedding on the barn floor, Gai had returned.

"Well," said Gai. "I told Red that I was going to be sleeping in the barn with Zephrum and now, I don't think I'll ever hear the end of it."

Zephrum looked away and blushed up to her ears.

"At least, it was believable," said Daphne. "The main thing is that we protect the baby dragons throughout the night and keep the barn from catching on fire, right?"

"Right," said Zephrum and Gai in concert.

Gai set up his sleeping bag on the straw of the barn floor. "Is it ok if we fall asleep? Or does somebody have to stay awake to watch them?"

"I think we'll wake up if anything weird happens," said Zephrum.

"OK," said Gai. "Let's hope you're right."

As they reached deeper into the land of sleep, Zephrum started dreaming about Waylon the Wyvern. First, she felt a floating upon the thermals. Then, more effort with wings and a glide. "Miss Zephrum Gates Creature," said Waylon into her mind. "I trust that our hatchlings are safe, yes?"

"Yes," mumbled Zephrum in her sleep.

"There is more that I must say... about the entire magical world. My mate and I have had to fortify our mountaintop cave with the deepest of fog in order to shield it from the sickness that is growing."

"Sickness?" asked Zephrum inside her mind.

"Yes," replied Waylon. "The darkness that Starsidous Rowpe is invoking is almost palpable. You can taste it in the wind and smell it in the scent of consciousness that permeates. When someone as evil and corrupt as he…is allowed to rise to power, a darkness shrouds all living things."

"Uh…" said Zephrum in her mumbling state. "Are you going to be ok?"

Deep bellows of a dragon laugh came from beneath his lungs. "Ha! Ha! Oh yes, Miss Zephrum Gates Creature. I have lived for an aeon and I will live for many more. I am almost as ancient as the spirit beings who guide me. But you and your kind will need help to prevail over this subterfuge."

"Subterfuge?" asked Zephrum in her sleep. "What do you mean?"

"This Strasidous Rowpe is hiding something, Miss Zephrum Gates Creature," replied Waylon with a growl. "Through mis-information, he will attempt to divide and conquer. He will start to believe his own lies and will conjure dark times."

"What do we do?" asked Zephrum out loud.

"You will have to unify with all of nature and those of your kind… and others who are nothing like you," continued Waylon. "Don't allow darkness to consume or divide us. It is a kind of 'belief storm' that is upon us, but nature will reward the dreamers."

"The whole thing feels so overwhelming and scary," said Zephrum. "And I'm just a kid."

"Grrrr… You are not a mere hatchling, Miss Gates. You have come from realms of unimaginable power and light, like myself. And one day, you will return to those realms. Have courage, Miss Zephrum Gates, for we exist in a time and place of great opportunity," said Waylon's confident thoughts. "We are evolving from a past gone wrong. Out of the chaos can come a new beginning, a new hope."

"Will you be around for a while?" asked Zephrum

"Yes, Miss Zephrum Gates Creature," streamed Waylon's thoughts into her mind. "You can call on me for help in times of need, as I will be nearby, but you will need to muster the strength to keep your course true on your own. There will be many tests ahead and you may face marvelous creatures beyond your present knowing. When in doubt, remember …mind conjures miracles…and can spawn wonders out of time."

Suddenly, Zephrum felt a great whoosh and a swerving movement downward.

"Miss Zephrum Gates," said Waylon inside her head. "We are almost upon you. We look forward to being re-united with our offspring."

At that, Zephrum sat bolt upright. She rattled her head awake, then shook Daphne and Gai by their shoulders. "They're almost here. Wake up! Let's get the baby dragons out of their cage."

Bleary eyed and groggy, Daphne and Gai rolled out of their sleeping bags and stumbled a little to gain their balance as they stood up.

Zephrum opened the cage and handed a little dragon to each of them. The babies screeched and cooed. Then, she picked up the last baby dragon. "Let's go."

The moment they arrived outside of the barn, they saw the shadows of giant dragon wings descend upon them. Within moments, Waylon and his mate landed on the ground and folded their wings to their sides.

"Miss Gates," said Waylon aloud. "We would like to thank you and your friends for shielding our hatchlings during this immense transition. We are in your debt. Know that you can call on us whenever you need be."

Zephrum nodded as Daphne and Gai set the baby dragons free to join their parents. Zephrum brought her baby dragon directly up to Waylon. He touched noses with the hatchling before she set it down to the ground.

"Thankyou, Waylon," said Zephrum as she touched the side of his scaly neck. "Your wisdom is very helpful to me."

"I am glad that you are finally listening to your inner knowing, Miss Zephrum Gates." The dragon babies securely climbed up onto their parents. Then, without delay, Waylon and his mate turned around and soared into the twilight skies above. Waylon looked back and telepathically spoke to Zephrum once more. "We will meet again, Miss Zephrum Gates Creature. We will meet again."

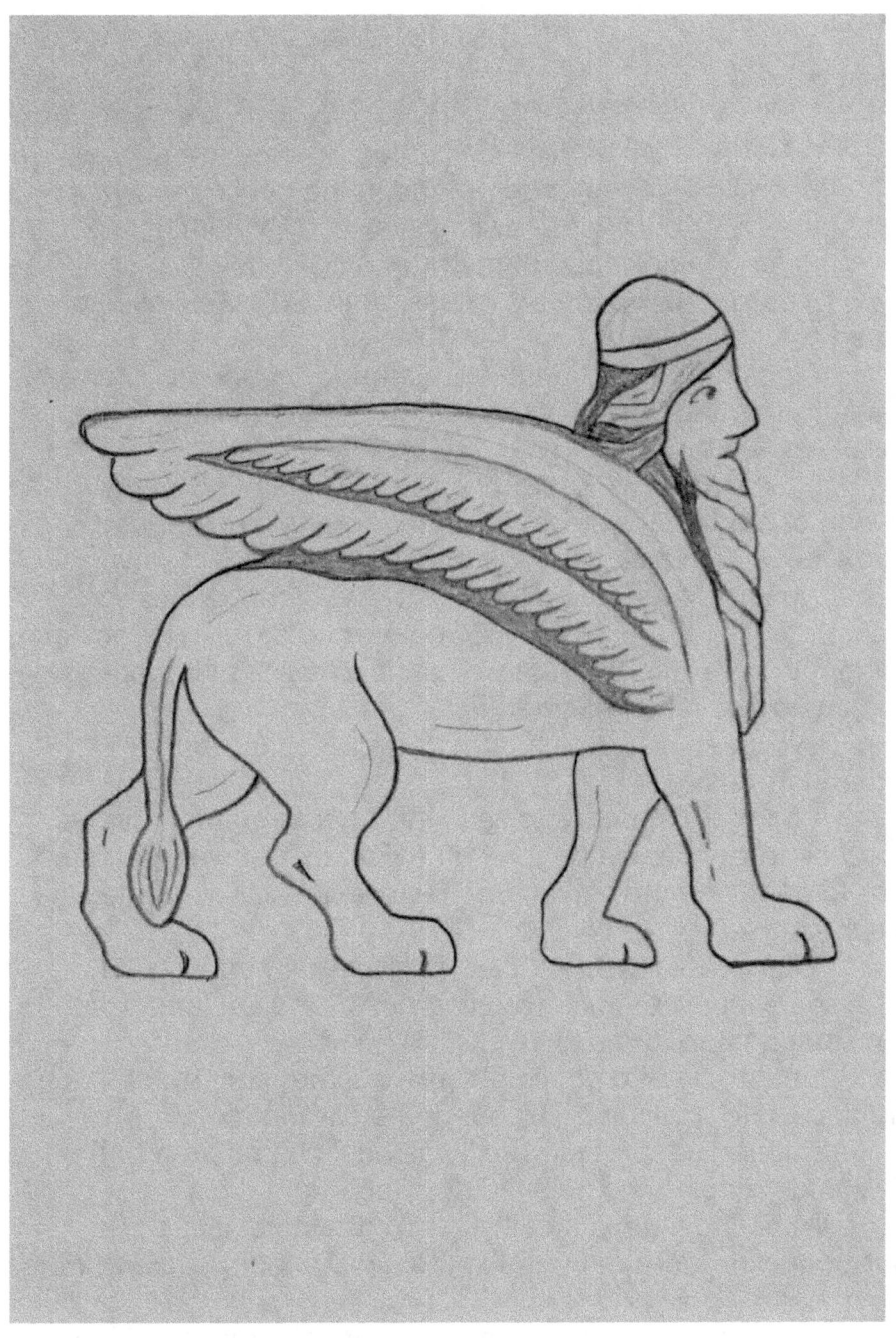

--Chapter 27--
"The Shedu"

Meanwhile, deep underground in the goblin caverns, the finger of Virgidous was healing slowly. "Thith ith taking much too long," exclaimed a frustrated Virgidous.

"Yes sire, it is quite a process," said Zultr Zeki as she bowed.

"Quite a protheth indeed," reiterated Virgidous. "I am feeling fruthtrated. I want to be out there, thearching for the Leviathan and the globthter."

"Yes, sire," said Zultr Zeki. "Couldn't we find a way to get one of our loyal subjects to search for the globster and keep an eye out while you heal up?"

"Mmm…" said Virgidous as he slowly rubbed his jawline. "I think there ith thomething we could do." He took a moment to consider it. "Yes, we can invoke a thpirit protector from our loyal realm of demonths."

"Which spirit? Which demon were you thinking of?" asked Zultr Zeki.

"I think we should invoke… the Shedu," said Virgidous. "It is their instinct to watch for the Leviathan, tho we won't have to quethtion their loyalty. They are already obthethed with the tathk."

"Good thinking," said Zultr Zeki. "A demon who is obsessed with the task of watching out for the Leviathan is the best spirit demon for us to invoke. When do we start?"

"Let uth get the goblin elderth together right away," said Virgidous. He snatched a fly out of the air and ate it.

Zultr Zeki departed from Virgidous' chambers with the mission of bringing the goblin elders together.

Within no time, a small circlet of the most evil and corrupt goblins were gathered in the elder chamber, along with Virgidous.

Virgidous waited until he had their full attention. "Ath you know, I mutht remain nearby our goblin healer until my finger ith better."

"Yes, yes, yes," chimed the crew of green-skinned elders.

"To insure our thucktheth with our plan to control all thingths, we are going to invoke...the Shedu," explained Virgidous.

"But sire," said the craggiest goblin. "Can we not find another path to success? Once we invoke this winged bull spirit, it is free to act on its own instincts."

"Yeth, I am aware of that," said Virgidous.

"We will tether the thpirit to our mission, tho that it will only be in thervith to our cauth," Virgidous further explained.

"But sire," said the eldest goblin. "To get the Shedu spirit to be in service to our cause, we will have to invoke the most ancient of goblin magic. This could involve a sacrifice on our part."

"Are you not WILLING to do what we must do?" asked Virgidous in a growing rage.

Bowing, the grey skin of the eldest goblin shivered. "Of course, we will do what we must, sire. It could come at a cost to us is all."

"I am aware of thith," said Virgidous. "But we mutht do what we mutht."

"Yes," agreed the goblin wearing the jeweled turban. "We must do what we must."

"Let uth begin," commanded Virgidous.

Without delay, the craggiest goblin retrieved a cauldron. The goblin with the largest collection of shiny necklaces added strange herbs to the pewter pot. The wrinkliest goblin started a small fire beneath the cauldron. The goblin in the large satin pants added a vile smelling liquid to the kettle.

Finally, the goblin with the jeweled cowboy hat said, "Sire, the concoction is ready."

The silence in the elder chamber was so potent that you could almost chew on it.

"We will invoke our old ancient wayth by yuthing ancient goblinethe," declared Virgidous. He looked to Zultr Zeki and said, "Becauth of the issue with my thpeach, you will have to lead thith ancient rite."

Zultr Zeki bowed her head. "By the power vested in me, I lead the rite of invocation." She removed her sword from its sheath. "Demons, dwellers of the abyss… we summon you. We call to Lamassu, our ancient Shedu brother."

The circlet of elder goblins repeated the words. "Demons, dwellers of the abyss… we summon you. We call to Lamassu, our ancient Shedu brother."

Zultr Zeki spoke loudly. "We require your watchful protection, the greatness of your demonic spirit. Visible and invisible, we call to you. Lamassu, our ancient Shedu brother."

The elder goblins chimed in. "Visible and invisible, we call to you. Lamassu, our ancient Shedu brother."

Zultr Zeki held her sword up high. "Winged bull, we call to you for the greatest of tasks. By our atcha, our earned honor, we invoke your guul, your strength."

Repeating after Zultr Zeki, the elder goblins said, "By our atcha, our earned honor, we invoke your guul, your strength."

"Above our great ocean, we ask that you show yourself. We ask that you search for the Leviathan that lurks in our great waters," continued Zultr Zeki. "Show yourself! Tuul ogaach! Tuul ogaach! Tuul ogaach."

Everyone standing there repeated the ancient goblinese. "Show yourself! Tuul ogaach! Tuul ogaach! Tuul ogaach."

Zultr Zeki touched her sword to the now bubbling cauldron. In that moment, a glimmer of demonic red light traveled down her sword to the edge of the swelling pot. A wisp of darkness oozed from the blade and plunged into the basin. The elders watched with bulged eyes as the darkness circled within the liquid. Within seconds, a clear dark swirl formed.

The circlet of elder goblins stared with anticipation and horror as the dark swirl separated from the vat and flew out into the open air. In the deep of the night, they all watched in awe as the dark energy shot through the goblin caverns and out in the direction of their great ocean.

Zultr Zeki looked at Virgidous. "It is done, my lord."

"Very good. Very good indeed." Virgidous looked at the entire circlet of elder goblins. "You have performed a great thervice to your kind...and to our cauth."

The elder goblins shivered and bowed low before Virgidous.

"Yes, sire."

"Yes, my lord."

"For you, anything."

"Be gone now," said Virgidous. "Your work here ith done."

With that, the elder goblins all departed without delay.

Virgidous looked at Zultr Zeki. "Nithe work, Zeki. You invoke well."

"Yes, sire," she responded. "For all our sakes, I do hope the invocation of the Shedu works in our favor."

"As do I," said Virgidous. "As to I."

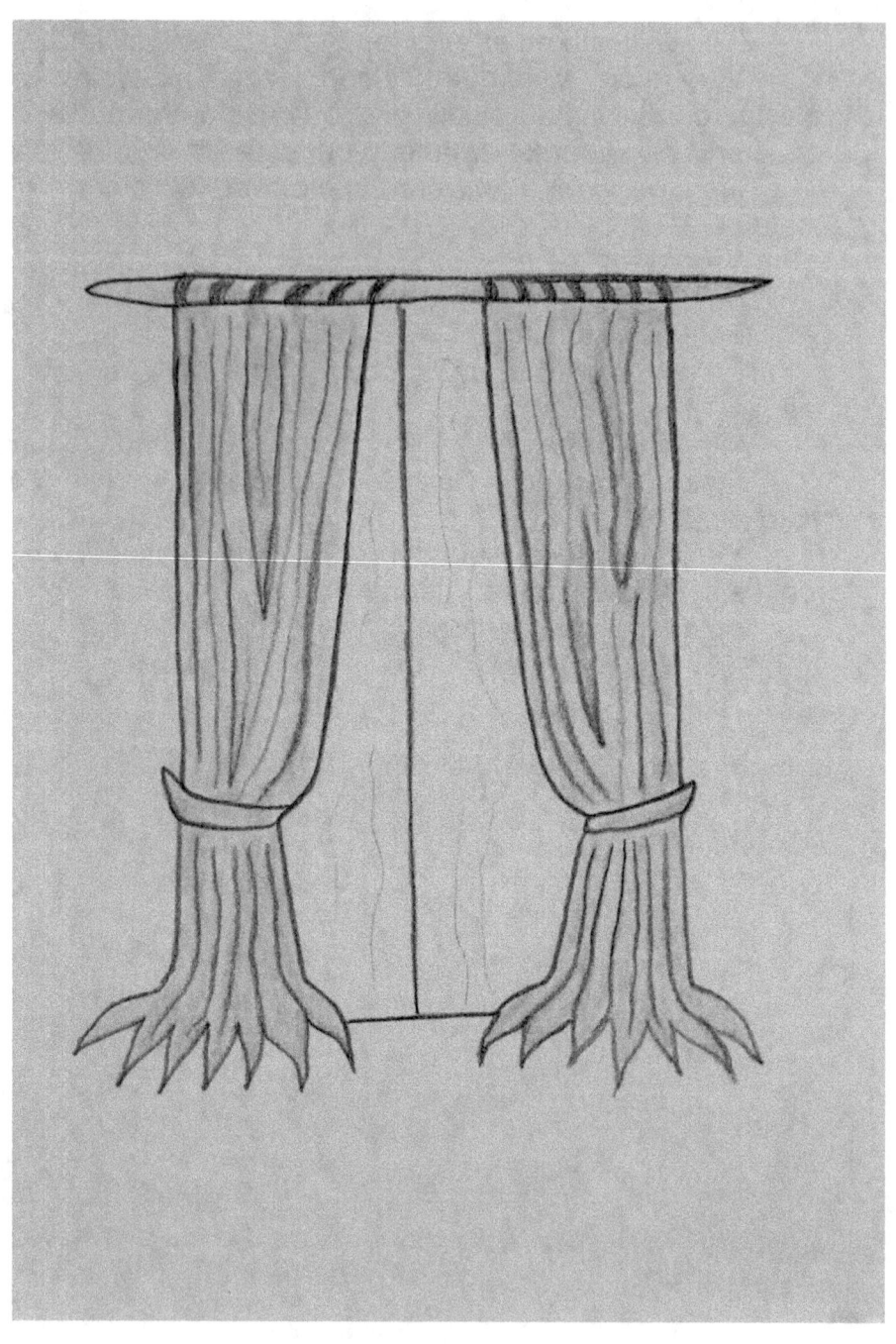

—Chapter 28—

"Scorcher's Lament"

The morning light brightened the skies with pink and blue streaks as the rest of the residents of Fiddlesticks started waking up. Zephrum, Daphne, and Gai went back to their cabins and got ready for the day, doing their best to act as if nothing unusual had happened with the baby dragons the night before.

As students streamed into the Sun Lodge for breakfast and morning announcements, Magenta Scorcher was hissing seething complaints about the condition of the floors and the walls and the char broiled curtains. Magenta swooshed her flaming red hair to one side. "Where has thees damage come from? Who is responseeble for so much burning all over thees place? How did thees happen?"

Zephrum, Daphne, and Gai tried to avert their eyes as they sat down on one of the low dining tables. "I hope she doesn't figure out that it was us."

Daphne said, "Well, it wasn't 'technically' us. I mean… it was the baby dragons that burned things, not us."

Zephrum rolled her eyes. Gai chuckled.

Rocko Pounder then silenced the room with a loud, "Hooo-eeee…"

"Hooo-eeee…" veiled the students in response.

Rocko planted his massive body in the center of the room. "Before wees all get our breakfast, we have some important mornin' announcements for yuz'."

Magenta Scorcher stood up. She began grilling the students about the damage to the Sun Lodge. "I want to know who scorched so much of thees building last night. There are burn marks all over thees place." She pointed to the marks on the floors and the walls. "You see thees spot and thees and thees?" She finally made it over to the curtains hanging from the French doors and raised the dangling fabric up so that everyone could see the frayed and burned material. "Who would set fire to thees lovely curtains?"

The students were silent.

"I know that your Halloween has a heestory of tricks and treats, but thees eez a fire safety issue."

A couple of the students giggled nervously.

"You tsink thees eez funny? You tsink it eez OK to damage property and poot your fellow students at reesk? You tsink you can just set fire to your school?"

The silence in the room was deafening. "It's so quiet in here, I can almost hear myself blink," whispered Aunt Gussie to Dexter.

Magenta's thin body snapped around. She glared at Aunt Gussie, then returned her attention to the students. "You will all be required to re-do your course on fire safety during your regular afternoon circus training time thees afternoon. I will eekspect all of you to attend class and take thees training very seriously."

The students moaned loudly.

"Moaning will not protect you if you are burning to a crisp," responded Magenta.

Her piercing amber eyes daggered at Zephrum. "And I am watching you, Leetle Miss Wind Fairy, as I'm sure you have sometsink to do with thees."

Zephrum's eyes widened in surprise.

"Alright already," interrupted Rocko, revealing a couple of his missing front teeth. "Yuz' all heard Miss Scorcher. Everybody's got to report to the circus tent for fire safety later on this afternoon, during your regular circus class time. Now, take your turns to gets yourselves some breakfast, alright?"

Autumn Visage pointed to the table closest to the kitchen island counter. The students from that table rushed to load up their plates.

Zephrum looked at Daphne and Gai. "Why does Magenta always seem to single me out? Why would she think I have anything to do with the burn marks in the Sun Lodge?"

"I don't know," said Daphne, "but she really does seem to have something against you, doesn't she?"

Gai shrugged. "Well, you do have a way of doing unusual things."

"Oh, we ALL have a way of doing unusual things," retorted Zephrum.

"True," said Gai. "But you're the only one that has flown off by your own wind power. And you have to admit that strange stuff always seems to happen around you."

"I can't help that," said Zephrum.

"I know," said Gai. "But the rest of us have weird skills and talents and we just don't seem to get into as much danger as you."

"You mean, unless you're with ME, right?" said Zephrum.

"Uh.. um.. well, I'm just saying," continued Gai. "It's easy for Miss Scorcher to single you out is all."

"Oh Zephrum," said Daphne. "Stop badgering Gai. Jeez, you seem so stressed out."

Zephrum took a deep breath in and put her head into her hands. "Yeah, I guess this whole thing with the baby dragons was just a lot to deal with, on top of all of the other stuff I'm worried about."

Gai said, "Hey, don't worry. We've always figured out a way to get through stuff before, right?"

Autumn Visage finally motioned to their table to go get their breakfast. Daphne grabbed Zephrum. "Come on. Let's go. We'll all feel a lot better after we've eaten something."

Gai jumped up. "I know I will. I'm so hungry I could eat a horse."

Zephrum scowled at him with narrowed eyes.

"Oh…uh…" said Gai. "I mean…you know what I mean. I'd never eat a horse, Zephrum."

She relaxed her expression and smiled.

Daphne laughed. "Gai, you are really living life on the edge today. Ha! Ha!"

They all three laughed and went up to the morning buffet counter.

Later on in the day, all of the students funneled into the circus tent for their refresher class on fire safety. A number of the other teachers were also present. Magenta Scorcher started out by talking about basic household safety. "As you know, you should always turn off a flame when you are done cooking on a stove. Be sure thee gas eez completely off. If you are cooking wiz propane, you must shut off the propane at thee source. Because eet eez heavier than air and has no scent, eet can fill up a room without you realizing eet. Then, when you light a match, thee whole space goes, as you say, 'Kaboom'!"

Magenta took out some of her fire props and demonstrated proper "shake off" technique. "You must always be sure to shake off excessive fuel from wicks after dipping your fire toys in gas and before lighting up. Always have a damp cloth nearby and always keep your fuel station separate from fire."

Zephrum whispered to Daphne, "How long do you think this is going to go on for?"

"I don't know," said Daphne as she shrugged her shoulders.

Magenta stopped her demonstration. "Oh, Miss Gates! Do you have something to share with thee rest of us?"

Zephrum just shook her head.

"You are just like your mother, Miss Gates," said Magenta. "So full of yourself and your unbelievable stories. I knew your mother and father when I came here for an exchange program in my youth."

Magenta got right up into Zephrum's personal space as she continued. "Your father was a beautiful man, sweet as can be. But your mom, she was quite thee opposite. And you, you are thee spitting image of her. Too bad you deedn't inherit some of your father's qualities."

Magenta glanced back at the other students. "This concludes your fire safety lesson. Be sure to remember all of these things when dealing with fire in the future."

The students quickly dispersed.

"Now we know that Magenta has some reasons for why she's always singling you out," said Gai when they got outside.

"Yea," said Daphne. "I guess you just remind her too much of your mom."

"I suppose," said Zephrum. "But it seems deeper than that."

"I'm just glad we didn't get in trouble or get blamed for what those baby dragons did," said Gai.

"Totally," agreed Daphne.

--Chapter 29--

"Flying Horses"

In the weeks that followed, preparations for Fall break were underway. Daphne was going to go home to be with her parents, as were a lot of the other students. Gai Holmes was planning to stay at Fiddlesticks and be part of the harvest festivities that happened while school was on break.

"This is going to be soooo much fun," exclaimed Gai. "Getting to eat food that we've grown is really the best part of gardening."

Zephrum said, "And we'll have more time to play with the horses too."

Ever since doggie Nomad left her body, Zephrum had become even more connected to the horses, especially Majestic. Majestic's beautiful black body looked much shinier from all of the extra grooming and attention he was getting from Zephrum. All of the horses were clearly more comfortable with the wings they grew the previous year as well.

"During break we should definitely take the horses out for some rides," said Gai.

"For sure," said Zephrum.

"As long as we bring our magical rowen branch with us, we'll be safe," said Gai.

"Good plan," nodded Zephrum.

Since most of the students were shuttled off to their parents' homes for Fall break, the harvest was brought in from the garden by those who remained. Gai, Aunt Gussie, and Rocko Pounder were busy collecting all of the squash off the vines and digging potatoes up from under their withering brown leaves. Zephrum and Misty Falls helped gather the remaining apples from the trees. Mrs. Fliffle washed everything as it came in from the yard and started to prepare a few of the ripest tubers and squash for immediate eating. Dexter and music teacher Mr. Adolfo Hemming helped carry everything else down into the Fiddlesticks root cellar, for safe storage. Zephrum also helped by taking the imperfect apples over to the horses. She cut them up so that the horses could eat them easily.

Before Aunt Gussie left for her cabin down river, she brought a few cardboard boxes over to the gardens. "Be sure to keep the tops of the plants that have seed pods on them, so we'll be able to plant them again in the spring. I've got to go do this same process over at my property," she said. "Oh…a gardener's job is never done."

After the seedpods were cut from the remaining dried plants, Gai and Rocko Pounder tore up the rest of the plant matter. Zephrum brought horse manure over to the garden beds so that Rocko and Gai could till it into the dirt in the gardens. Misty Falls helped rake up a bunch of dry leaves to add to the top of the mulch.

Zephrum delivered another load of horse manure in a wheel barrel. "Harvesting and preparing garden beds for winter is a lot of work."

"Absolutely!!" exclaimed Gai. He flashed her one of his charismatic smiles. He lugged a whole basket full of potatoes over to The Sun Lodge for Mrs. Fliffle to wash.

After a few days of this rigor, they finally had time to take the horses for a proper horseback ride on the surrounding trails. Misty Falls joined Gai and Zephrum on the adventure.

"Remember," said Zephrum. "If we encounter any danger, we'll all need to find a way to be in physical contact with each other so that the rowen branch can help us."

"Yeah," said Gai. "And we have to be really specific with our words too."

"Oh, I remember," responded Misty. "Last year, when Zephrum got separated from us in those goblin tunnels under the park in the center of Haversville, the only way we got her back is because I was able to gush water down into their tunnels through my eyes."

"That was pretty amazing," said Zephrum.

"Totally," agreed Gai. "Let's just hope that we won't have to deal with anything else like that again."

They put a saddle blanket on each horse, then saddled them up with new girth straps that fit better with their wings. Then they put the horse's bridles on.

Gai rode Star Struck, a stocky chestnut colored horse. Misty got onto Bandit, who was deep brown with black on its main and tail. Finally, Zephrum put on her Fiddlesticks sweater and got onto Majestic. They walked the horses down to the fire road and headed east. They went to a trot and cantered up hills. The horses loped easily as they traveled. "This is great!" exclaimed Misty.

"Absolutely!" said Gai.

Zephrum just smiled. She felt so at home in her skin while riding.

They got almost as far as Donald Snodgrass's corn farm when Zephrum had an idea. "You know what would be cool?" she said. "If we could get the horses to fly over the garbage island nearby in the ocean, we could get a better idea of how big It is. We could think of it as research for our school project with Dr. Malvin Moot."

Gai and Misty stopped their horses in their tracks.

"Are you serious?" asked Gai.

"Aren't you a little afraid of what we'll find out there after the weird oceanography field trips we've already had?" asked Misty.

Zephrum brought Majestic to a halt and said, "Well, the horses haven't had a chance to fly since last year and I think it might be good for them. Plus, it would be so much fun."

"It's true," said Gai. "Flying on a horse is amazing."

"It does sound cool," said Misty. "Do you think it will be safe?"

Zephrum shrugged her shoulders. "Well, there's only one way to find out."

Gai took the rowen branch out of his side bag and handed one end to Zephrum. Misty walked her horse close to Majestic and touched Zephrum on the arm. "Well, I'm ready if you guys are."

Zephrum touched the rowen branch in Gai's hand. "Let's get these horses flying over to the ocean to check out the garbage island, and then, we can return to Fiddlesticks."

A bright light traveled down the rowen branch between Zephrum and Gai. It surrounded all of the horses and Misty. Within moments, the horses started to ruffle their feathers. They flapped their wings and shifted to a trot. The horses then all levitated off of the ground and flew into the sky in the direction of the ocean.

"Wow! This is amazing!" shouted Misty.

Zephrum and Gai smiled widely.

The wind was blowing in their hair. The horses galloped through the air, flapping their wings. Eventually they saw the ocean in the distance and smelled the sea air on the wind.

"I can finally smell the ocean," cried Zephrum.

Misty pointed down to the Haversville River. "Hey, it looks like there's some dark stuff dumping into the ocean from the river. I wonder what that is?"

"Oh yes," said Gai. "I've heard of this. It's called non-point source pollution. It can be a combination of fuel run-off, waste from septic tanks, pesticides from farms, or top soil or silt from construction sites. Once that stuff gets into our waterways, it can harm fish and wildlife habitats."

"Wow!" said Zephrum. "It's worse than I thought."

"Yeah," said Misty. "I just thought we had to clean up the trash, but it looks like we have to prevent other forms of waste from getting into our rivers too."

"It's pretty wild," said Gai. "I've heard that eighty percent of pollution to the marine environment comes from land."

"It looks like cleaning up the ocean will mean that humans will have to keep our rivers clear as well," said Zephrum.

"Totally," said Gai. "Maybe we can get Dexter to help us print some newspaper articles about it in the Diurnal Journal? People will have to know about this stuff so they can prevent it."

Just then, a strange flying bull came into their field of vision. It was barreling towards the horses, flying towards them really fast.

"Zephrum! Gai! What is that?" Misty shouted.

"I don't know," shouted Gai.

"I've never seen anything like that before," said Zephrum.

"It doesn't look very friendly," hollered Misty.

Zephrum took a better look at the bull as it got closer and closer. "Whoa...it looks like it has a man's face and a beard. That can't be normal."

Gai looked at Zephrum sideways. "And a flying bull IS normal?"

"You know what I mean," shouted Zephrum. "It's definitely super weird. I think we should abandon the mission to the garbage island."

"Agreed," screamed Gai and Misty in concert.

But every time the kids tried to shift their course, the horses kept turning back towards the ocean.

"Oh no!" yelled Zephrum. "Our magical request with the rowen branch makes the horses want to make it to the garbage island no matter what."

Gai bellowed, "We'll have to get close enough to each other to touch, so we can use the rowen branch to get them to adjust and start flying back to Fiddlesticks."

"We had better do it fast," said Misty. "It looks like that flying bull means business."

Misty got Bandit to fly close to Gai's horse, but as Zephrum turned Majestic around to do the same thing, the flying bull charged at them. It banged into Majestic and pushed Zephrum off course. It took all of Zephrum's strength to remain on top of Majestic's back.

The air surged inside of Zephrum's lungs. Her heart started racing.

The flying bull smashed into Zephrum and Majestic again. This time, the massive force of the bull banged directly onto one of Zephrum's legs.

She felt a shooting pain just below her knee. That side of her body went numb and weak. Majestic lost altitude.

Zephrum heard Gai and Misty screaming from up above. "Zephrum! Zephrum!"

The flying bull was coming around for another pass. Her hands trembled. "Come on, Majestic. You can do this," Zephrum begged, holding tightly to Majestic's reins.

Majestic's ears turned back at the sound of Zephrum's voice. Just before the flying bull barreled into Zephrum for a third time, he flapped his powerful wings. They zoomed directly upward.

Zephrum's stomach lurched at the quick upward pulse.

Misty and Gai galloped their flying horses over to Zephrum as fast as they could. Gai already had his hand on the rowen branch and Misty had already grabbed one of the reins from Gai's horse.

"Zephrum! Reach for it!" cried Gai.

Zephrum was feeling really nauseous from getting smashed around and injured. She summoned one of her trembling arms and grabbed for the rowen branch.

"Go back to Fiddlesticks as fast as we can!" cried Gai.

A feint blue light traveled down the rowen branch to Zephrum, Gai, Misty, and all three horses. Suddenly, the horses turned eastward and zoomed in the direction of Fiddlesticks.

The horses flew so fast that the children could barely breathe. The air blew their cheeks up like balloons. They buried their faces into the manes of the horses. They had to squint their eyes to protect themselves from the intensity of the wind's speed.

Finally, they descended down to the fire road closest to Fiddlesticks. As the horses landed on the ground, they folded their wings to their sides. They were still running unbelievably fast.

"Whoa…" screamed Zephrum as she pulled Majestic's reins back.

Gai and Misty tried to pull back on the reins as well, but the horses kept running at a lightning speed.

They galloped up to the barn, kicking up dirt with their hooves. Finally, they trotted to a stop.

Zephrum, Gai, and Misty all just looked at each other, stunned.

"What was that?" asked Misty.

"I don't know," said Zephrum.

"Me neither," said Gai.

"But I sure am glad we got away from it when we did," added Zephrum.

"For sure," said Gai. "Zephrum, are you alright?"

Zephrum looked down at her limp leg and shaking body. "I don't know. I really don't know."

--Chapter 30--

"Muckerhouse Returns"

Gai helped Zephrum down from Majestic as Misty collected the horses. "I'll take all of their saddle pads off and stuff, so you can bring Zephrum over to Nurse Asa in the Healing Dome," said Misty.

Zephrum nodded and said, "But what are we going to tell them when they ask what happened?"

"I know you won't want to lie," said Gai. "Just tell them it was an incident with the horses."

"Yeah, but they're going to ask me questions about it," Zephrum winced.

"You could just tell them that you really don't want to talk about it right now. I mean, you do seem pretty shaken up over it, right?" said Misty.

Zephrum nodded.

Gai looked at Zephrum. "Hey… Misty is almost as good as Daphne at thinking up great excuses, huh?"

Zephrum eeked out the suggestion of a smile behind her discomfort and nodded.

"You know you won't have to worry about them getting water, right?" said Misty.

Zephrum tried to smile again, but she really was in too much pain.

"We'll see you later, Misty," said Gai. "I'm going to get Zephrum over to Nurse Asa right away."

Zephrum wrapped her arm around Gai. He helped her hop on one leg towards the Healing Dome.

"You know," said Gai, when they were about halfway there. "This would be easier if you just let me carry you."

Zephrum was too weak to protest. She nodded and whispered, "OK."

Gai carried Zephrum the rest of the way to the Healing Dome. He placed her on one of the waiting room cots and went looking for Nurse Asa. "Nurse Asa! Nurse Asa! Are you here?"

Magenta Scorcher peaked her brilliant red head out of Nurse Asa's office and said, "No, Nurse Asa ees away for fall break. I'm here to fill een for her today."

"Uh..um... you?" asked Gai.

"Yes, Meester Holmes," said Magenta. "I have training een first aid and can be very helpful. What eez the matter with you?"

"It's not me," said Gai. "It's Zephrum!"

"Oh..." hissed Magenta. "What is it now?"

"Well, uh..." said Gai. "It was incident with the horses. Her leg seems to be hurt pretty bad."

Magenta's eyes narrowed. "I weel take a look at eet."

When Zephrum saw Magenta Scorcher, she recoiled. "Where is Nurse Asa?"

"She's gone for fall break," said Gai.

"Don't you worry about a theeng," said Miss Scorcher. "I can take a look at you. What seems to be the problem?"

Zephrum grimaced. "It's my leg. It might be broken."

Magenta wrinkled her nose as she looked at Zephrum's leg. "Alright, I'll have to touch eet to diagnose thee situation."

Magenta touched her leg.

"Ow..ow..ow!" screamed Zephrum.

"Oh, does that hurt?" asked Magenta without concern.

"Yes," said Zephrum. She began to cry.

"Oh, please," said Magenta. "Spare me thee water works. What happened?"

"It was a situation with the horses," said Zephrum in a well-rehearsed manner.

"Yes, yes," said Magenta. "Meester Gai Holmes already told me thees. Did you get kicked? Did you fall? What happened?"

"Uh...I don't really want to talk about it," said Zephrum.

"Oh, no elaborate story?" asked Magenta. "What are you trying to hide?"

Zephrum and Gai both looked at each other.

"Miss Scorcher," said Gai. "I think that Zephrum might be in a little bit of a shock. Should we take her to the hospital? Or ask Great Aunt Gussie what to do?"

"Great Aunt Gussie has gone to her cabin to play een her garden, so she cannot help you thees time, Mees Gates. I weel give you a removable splint for now and a pain killer, but eet does look like you'll need an x-ray."

Magenta left the examination area to retrieve the splint and painkillers.

"What are we going to do?" whispered Zephrum as soon as Magenta was out of earshot. "They are bound to start asking questions if I have to be brought to a regular hospital. How are we ever going to explain what happened?"

"I don't know," said Gai.

"Eet is taking me a while to find theengs, but I weel be there as soon as I find what I am looking for," Magenta called from the supply area.

A dense dark moment passed.

Gai frowned, deep in thought. "Wait a minute. I have an idea," he said at last. "Maybe I can use some of the same healing skills that your Aunt Gusssie has with growing things? You know, with the help of the rowen branch?"

Zephrum looked up at him and shrugged. "Well, it's worth a try."

Gai took the rowen branch out from the inside of his vest and touched it to Zephrum's leg. "Heal this leg, heal it so that it's as healthy as it was before it got hurt."

Almost instantly, a feint blue light traveled down the rowen branch to Zephrum's leg. She felt an intense tingling in her limb.

"Whoa…it's sooo itchy. And so tingly all over too," said Zephrum.

"Is it helping?" asked Gai.

"I don't know. Maybe? I think so. I have no idea," said Zephrum.

The blue light absorbed into her body and disappeared into the deep core of her leg just as Magenta Scorcher returned. "OK, Mees Gates." She offered Zephrum a glass of water. "Take thees painkillers and I weel wrap your leg up in thees temporary splint."

Zephrum swallowed the painkillers with the help of the water.

"You are not cringing, Mees Gates," said Magenta as she wrapped the leg. "Did you fake all of thees to get more attention?"

"No!" said Zephrum.

"You must just be really good at this," said Gai quickly. "Thankyou so much for getting Zephrum a splint. I'm sure she'll feel much better tomorrow."

Magenta raised her nose higher. "Mmm…alright then." She looked at Zephrum. "At least your boyfriend has thee good sense to thank me."

"He's not my boyfriend," said Zephrum defensively.

Gai put his hand on Zephrum's shoulder. "It's ok, Zephrum." He looked at Miss Scorcher. "She's just shy about our connection."

Zephrum turned a very dark shade of pink.

Magenta looked them both up and down. "I see."

She turned to Zephrum. "Will you need crutches? Or will your boyfriend carry you out of here?"

Zephrum tried to stand up. She put a little weight on the leg with the splint. It didn't actually hurt. "I think it will be ok with the splint," said Zephrum.

"Oh…that's probably thee drugs talking," said Magenta. She looked at the bottle. "It does say theez are fast acting. I weel get you some crutches from the back. Don't go anywhere."

As soon as Magenta left the room, Gai asked, "Did it work? Did the rowen branch help heal you?"

Zephrum wiggled her toes. "I definitely feel better, but it's hard to tell with this splint on. Let's just get the crutches and leave. We can see if my leg will support my weight when I take the splint off in my cabin later."

"Sounds good," said Gai.

Just then, Magenta Scorcher brought a pair of crutches into the examination area. "I theenk I weel have to adjust the height of these for you. You are a leetle beet short, afterall."

Zephrum rolled her eyes and pressed her lips together.

"You'll have to stand up, so that I can get eet just right," said Magenta. "Maybe your boyfriend can help hold you up while I do thees."

Zephrum did her best to keep quiet while Gai helped stabilize her. Miss Scorcher adjusted the screws to the right height for Zephrum. "I theenk this weel do it. You must check in with me tomorrow. I want to know how the leg is."

"OK," said Zephrum.

"Thanks, Miss Scorcher," said Gai.

Back at her cabin, Zephrum took off the splint to test her leg. "The pain that I felt is not there, but I don't know if I can trust it."

"Maybe just keep the splint on for now," said Gai. "We can try to do a second healing with the rowen branch tomorrow."

"OK," said Zephrum. "Since Misty will be staying in the cabin with me tonight, she'll be able to help me if I need it. I'll see you tomorrow."

Gai gave Zephrum a hug and jetted out of the cabin door.

Zephrum's heart fluttered as Gai left the cabin. She wondered, "Was it the experience with the flying bull? Or the hug with Gai?"

She was still lost in thought when Misty came in a few minutes later.

"I just saw Gai outside and he told me what happened. Do you think the rowen branch actually helped heal your leg?"

"I think so," said Zephrum. She started slurring her words a bit. "It's a little hard to know what I'm feeling right now, though."

"Zephrum, are you ok?" asked Misty.

"Oh…it must be the painkillers that Miss Magenta Scorcher gave me," said Zephrum in a very unarticulated way.

"Maybe I should help you get into bed," said Misty.

"Ohh…Kay," said Zephrum, happily.

"Mmay..bee…gr..grr..slp..shd..hlpr.." said Zephrum the moment her head hit the pillow. Then, she passed out.

Morning seemed to arrive in almost no time. As the dawning sun beamed in through the windows, Misty groggily asked, "How are you feeling? Any better?"

Zephrum shook the fog out of her head. "Yes, I feel a lot better than yesterday. Wow! What a day!"

"I know," said Misty. "What do you think that flying bull thing was?"

"I don't know, but I know I don't want to see it again." Zephrum paused a moment. "How was Majestic? Did he seem ok when you un-tacked the horses last night?"

"Yeah," said Misty. "It seems like that flying bull only really hurt YOU."

"That's lucky," said Zephrum. She stood up. The splint was still on. "I think my leg is actually ok."

"You and Gai might want to try to do a deeper healing with the rowen branch today, so you can ditch the splint," said Misty.

"Totally," agreed Zephrum. "We don't want people asking any questions."

A few minutes later, Gai came by Zephrum's cabin with the rowen branch. "How's your leg this morning?" he asked.

"It feels like I can support my weight pretty good, but Misty thinks we should try to do a deeper healing with the rowen branch so that I can ditch the splint."

"Totally," said Gai. "I've got it right here."

He sat down next to Zephrum on her bed. Zephrum pulled the Velcro away from the splint straps and exposed her leg.

Gai placed the rowen branch onto the skin of Zephrum's leg. "Heal Zephrum's leg on the deepest of levels." A feint blue light emanated from the rowen branch and disappeared into Zephrum's leg. Within moments, it absorbed into her core.

"How does it feel?" asked Gai.

Zephrum rotated her ankle and moved her leg from the knee joint. "I think it's ok." She used Gai's shoulder to help her stabilize and then, she stood up. "I think it worked."

"This is such a great relief," said Gai.

"Totally," agreed Misty.

"You guys are both so awesome," said Zephrum. "Thanks so much for all the help."

"You'd do the same for us," said Gai.

The morning cowbell rang.

"Sounds like it's breakfast time," said Misty. "Do you think you can walk to breakfast on your own, without the help of the splint?"

"I think so," said Zephrum in surprise.

The three of them walked into the Sun Lodge and got plates of food from the kitchen island counter. They sat down at one of the low dining tables.

Magenta Scorcher watched Zephrum walk across the room. As soon as they were seated, she rushed up to their table and looked at Zephrum's leg, "What?! No crutches? And no splint? What are you thinking, Mees Gates?"

"Well, it seems like my leg is a lot better today," responded Zephrum.

"All of that whining and you're just fine overnight?" asked Magenta.

Zephrum shrugged her shoulders. "It seems so."

"You lead a charmed life, Mees Gates," said Magenta. Then, she swooshed towards the kitchen island counter to get some breakfast for herself.

Zephrum, Gai, and Misty all looked at one another with relief.

Preparations for their fall feast continued over the next couple of days. Everyone was getting excited about the many foods they were going to eat.

Great Aunt Gussie returned to Fiddlesticks. She planned to give a talk about gratitude before their big harvest dinner.

Without the splint and crutches, Zephrum avoided having to answer questions from Aunt Gussie about the incident. She was able to take care of the horses in her usual way. It seemed like she was really going to be able to put the whole "flying bull incident" behind her.

BUT… when Daphne returned to Fiddlesticks after the Fall break, she had a very strange drawing to share. She showed Zephrum her sketch. "I passed out after I drew this. Do you have any idea what this could be about?"

Zephrum looked down at Daphne's sketch pad. There was a clear image of herself flying on Majestic and getting slammed by a flying bull with a bearded man's face. Even though Zephrum had seen Daphne draw these "psychic sketches" so many times before, she was still shocked at the detail of it all. At the bottom of the sketch, the word "Shedu" was spelled out.

Zephrum's jaw dropped. "Daphne, you won't believe what happened while you were away."

Zephrum recounted the entire story about taking the horses on a flying journey and seeing the brown gunk empty into the ocean from the Haversville River. She told Daphne all about the flying bull and her injured leg and everything.

"Wow!" exclaimed Daphne. "That's wild. I wonder if the flying bull is a Shedu? We should look it up in our Mythical Creatures in Literature book to see."

"Absolutely," Zephrum agreed.

On their first day back on schedule after all the other students returned, there was an unexpected visit from Inspector Muckerhouse, from the Educational Board of Alternative Schools. It put Dexter Droudy in a bit of a panic.

Unannounced, Inspector Muckerhouse arrived at the Sun Lodge during breakfast and before morning announcements. His round frame entered through the French doors, carrying a clipboard and a briefcase. He looked almost exactly the same as he did when Zephrum had seen him last year. His well-manicured mustache curled at its ends and his goatee sat upon his chin like a mistake from a meal that missed going into his mouth. As he entered the Sun Lodge, he tipped his bowler hat to Mrs. Fliffle and then, walked directly up to Dexter Droudy.

"Mr. Droudy!"

Dexter jumped about a kilometer. "Oh…Inspector Muckerhouse! What brings you here…and so…uh… unexpectedly?"

"Mr. Droudy…there have been reports of flying horses in the skies above the Haversville River. AND a flying bull! Apparently, there was a fight between one of the flying horses and the flying bull." He showed Dexter a photo from his clipboard. "One of our citizens even captured this on camera."

Zephrum and Daphne could barely believe their ears.

Dexter was dumbfounded. He started stumbling over his words. "Uh, um, well, I wouldn't know anything about this. And it does seem strange indeed. Very odd. Unusual, to be sure."

"This is very bad, Mr. Droudy," continued Inspector Muckerhouse. "If any one of your students was involved in this incident, we may need to consider shutting this school down. We can't have the public seeing this kind of thing. It will incite fear. And you know people, Mr. Droudy. They will wreak havoc if they allow fear to run them. We do NOT want to provoke mayhem in the general community."

"Oh, um, um, yes, of course," sputtered Dexter. "We would not want that."

"We would have too many questions to answer and too many public statements to make. It will just be too much controversy if we have to explain the nature of 'some' of our 'alternative' institutions," said Muckerhouse.

"Oh, ah, ah, yes, of course," stuttered Dexter. "We..we..w..w..wouldn't want that."

"If people are made fully aware of the unusual nature of your students, they will get scared and want to lock them up," continued Muckerhouse. "We don't want to imprison the children, do we?"

"No, no, of course not," said Dexter. "Uh…but why do you think that it might have been one of our students?"

Muckerhouse pulled out a blown up photo of the flying horse that had been captured in the original photo. "Well, it's interesting that you should ask. Our staff photographer did a pretty good job of enlarging this original photo, so we have a fairly clear picture of the person riding on the flying horse."

"Oh no," whispered Zephrum.

Dexter examined the photo. "Uh..uh… I see. Uh…it does look like the person is wearing one of the Fiddlesticks sweaters, but that doesn't mean that it was one of our students."

Inspector Muckerhouse gave Dexter a sideways glance. "It does, however, suggest that someone associated with Fiddlesticks was riding that flying horse. Would you have any idea who it might have been?"

Zephrum whispered to Daphne, "Even if they can't prove it was me, they'll see that it was Majestic. I mean, is there another horse with wings around that's all black?"

Daphne didn't even know what to say.

Just then, Great Aunt Gussie entered the Sun Lodge. She saw Inspector Muckerhouse at once. "Oh…look what the cat dragged in."

"Hello, Mrs. Gooler," said the inspector.

"What brings you to our school?" asked Gussie.

Dexter pointed to the photos that Inspector Muckerhouse had on his clip board. He started to frantically explain, "Well, uh, um, you see, the inspector believes that one of our students might have been r..r..r..riding this flying horse above the Haversville River…b..be..because it looks like the person is wearing a Fiddlesticks sweater."

Aunt Gussie eyed the photo and calmly. "I see."

"A..a..a..of course, I was just about to assure the inspector that we don't know anything about it, as h..h..he claims he'd have to consider shutting down our school if our students are doing unusual things in and around the community."

"That's right," said Inspector Muckerhouse. "We cannot have your kind wreaking havoc in the skies or elsewhere. It's just too much to explain to the general populace."

"Well," said Aunt Gussie. "I'm sure we can handle it from here. If it was one of our students, we will get to the bottom of it. Can we hold onto these photos in order to help us uncover this mystery?"

Inspector Muckerhouse reluctantly handed the photos to Great Aunt Gussie. "Well, I'd rather interrogate your students myself, but if you think you can adequately deal with the situation, I will let it go this ONE time. But ONLY this once."

"Understood," said Aunt Gussie. "Thankyou for bringing this to our attention. Would you like to join us for breakfast?"

Dexter's eyes darted in every direction.

"No, no," said Inspector Muckerhouse. "I have a number of other important matters to attend to today. I would, however, like to know what you discover from your students, as we will want to create a file of the disciplinary action you will be imposing upon this student."

"Of course," said Aunt Gussie. "If we discover anything, you'll be the first to know."

Inspector Muckerhouse tipped his bowler hat to Great Aunt Gussie, gave Dexter a shrewd gaze, and let himself out of the Sun Lodge.

Aunt Gussie took the photos and walked directly up to Zephrum.

"Oh no," whispered Zephrum. "I'm never going to hear the end of this now."

Daphne moved aside as Great Aunt Gussie approached.

Aunt Gussie waved the photo in front of Zephrum's nose. "What is the meaning of this?"

Zephrum had nothing to say.

"What?" asked Aunt Gussie. "Are you afraid of whistling with crackers in your mouth? Explain."

"Well, it's a little complicated," Zephrum finally uttered.

"Complicated?!?!" exclaimed Aunt Gussie at a higher decibel.

The students in the Sun Lodge all started to look at Aunt Gussie and Zephrum.

"You seem like you're up a creek without a paddle. We should step outside and I'll tell you what's complicated," said Aunt Gussie as she grabbed Zephrum by the arm.

The two of them left the Sun Lodge through the kitchen side door. Once outside, Aunt Gussie started in on Zephrum more loudly. "Haven't we already discussed how dangerous it is for you to be flying around in plain sight of the regular community? Do you not understand how dangerous it is out there, now that Strasidous Rowpe has returned? What were you thinking?"

"Well...uh..." said Zephrum.

"This stunt was about as sharp as a marshmallow sandwich. Explain yourself."

"Well, we thought it would be good for the horses to get some experience flying since they hadn't flown since last spring," explained Zephrum. "And we thought we could do some research from the air, about the garbage island. You know, for our oceanography project?"

"Yes, I am quite aware of your oceanography project," snapped Aunt Gussie.

"We didn't know that we would encounter that weird flying bull on our way out there. I didn't plan to fly so low, but the flying bull was trying to attack me," explained Zephrum.

"For Heaven's Sake!" exclaimed Aunt Gussie. "This is like jumping out of an airplane and knitting your parachute on the way down. After all of the things you've experienced during your oceanography field trips, didn't you have an inkling that danger might be lurking near the ocean?"

"We did consider it," said Zephrum sheepishly.

"Obviously, you didn't consider it very seriously," continued Aunt Gussie.

"I know it seems like I'm flying off the handle here, but you put yourself in real danger. I think that Dexter and I will have to put that rowen branch in a safe location and OUT of your reach."

"But Aunt Gussie," pleaded Zephrum.

"No. I've made up my mind. It's simply too dangerous for you to have access to it."

"Aunt Gussie," implored Zephrum.

"No," said Aunt Gussie. "I've hit a wall. I don't know any other way to get through to you. There are consequences to your actions and you simply have to understand that."

"But I dooooo," wined Zephrum.

Aunt Gussie stared Zephrum squarely in the face. "Do you know WHAT this flying bull creature is?"

"Uh, um…?"

"This is a Shedu!" yelled Aunt Gussie. "This is one of the most dangerous creatures known to the magical world. It will kill to protect whatever it is watching over. You were lucky to get out of this situation alive!"

"Uh, um…" responded Zephrum.

"I'm surprised you weren't hurt," continued Aunt Gussie. "These Shedu are ruthless and strong, normally killing whatever is in their path. What are we supposed to do to get through to your cauliflower brain?"

Zephrum was speechless.

Aunt Gussie warned, "Now that we know it's out there, we are ALL going to have to be VERY VERY careful!"

—Chapter 31—

"Dream Stream"

After the incident with the flying bull, Dexter Droudy decided that Zephrum should be prevented from going on field trips for the remainder of the semester. The weather was beginning to get a little colder, so there weren't a lot of special outings scheduled in any case.

He also took the rowen branch from its hiding place near the bee hives and locked it in a secure location that Zephrum and Gai could not access in his office.

After hearing the news, Gai said, "Not being able to bring the rowen branch with us on field trips and stuff... is going to make it a lot harder for us to stay safe."

"I know," said Zephrum, dejected.

"Well," Gai half-smiled. "I guess we'll just have to stay out of trouble then."

Zephrum grinned at his sarcasm and said, "Sure, cuz' we never find ourselves in dangerous situations, right?"

The colder weather limited the sailing journeys of the pirates and Virgidous too. Goblins were not accustomed to such cold brisk winds. Captain Muttonchops was also sure that the search for the mythical Leviathan would turn out to be fruitless. More than once, he grumbled. "We'd rather warm ourselves by drinking fine rum."

It was taking some time for Virgidous' finger to grow back, so he was doing his best to busy himself in the underground goblin caverns as well. He oversaw the creation of a great throne in the Elder Chamber and he worked hard to overcome his very large lisp problem. With his extra long tongue, he practiced saying "s" words on flash cards. "Snake," universal," "books," etc... He was doing pretty well, but would often slip up when there was an "s" in the middle of the word. "So much work still to be done," he whispered to himself.

While sitting idle, Virgidous considered putting an even stronger curse on humanity. "We must escalate humanity's drive to destroy themselves. If they increase their pollution into the air, it will create such an imbalance that they will be overwhelmed with the consequences."

"Good idea, sire," agreed Zultr Zeki.

"Yes," continued Virgidous. "They will feel daunted by the enormity of their problems. Their power to change things will elude them as they slumber awake. Those who try to awaken from our spell will be consumed with fear."

"A devious plan, to be sure," affirmed Zultr Zeki.

"We will send out a vibrational force to feed off their fear, so that our spell will gain power with each negative frightened thought they have," added Virgidous.

"Brilliant," confirmed Zeki.

"Bring the elder goblins to the throne room at once," commanded Virgidous.

"As you wish." Zeki bowed as she left the chamber.

Virgidous paced within the elder chamber as he considered his grand plan. "If Zephrum Gates had knowledge of this spell, I could make her come to my aid to stop it. Mmm… yes. I will give her the choice of helping me find the Leviathan…or the choice of being an agent of destruction for all of humanity. I believe that little pipsqueak will wisely choose to assist me in my quest."

Zeki ushered the senior goblins into the elder chamber, she said, "Our illustrious leader, Virgidous, has an idea he wants to share with all of you…and a potent spell for us to cast."

Virgidous cleared his throat. "Humanity must speed up the pace of their destruction."

"Yes sire," said the craggiest goblin as he lit a candle.

"But first," said Virgidous. "I need to enter into the dreams of Zephrum Gates and deliver a methage to her. You must all hold space around me as I focus my thoughts into her dream stream."

"A message?" asked Zeki.

"Yes," said an annoyed Virgiodous. "That's what I said."

"Yes, sire," said the craggiest goblin.

"Whatever you want," said the one with the long necklaces hanging from his neck.

"Your wish is our wish," said the one with a jeweled cowboy hat.

"Let us begin," commanded Virgidous.

At that, the circlet of goblins surrounded Virgidous. He mumbled his thoughts into the dusty bowels of the elder chamber.

Cackles from the elder goblins erupted with glee when they heard the words that he spoke.

"Planning the downfall of humanity can only mean more riches for goblins," cried the craggiest goblin.

"Silence!" ordered Virgidous. "I need assistance penetrating into Zephrum's dreams, so that she can know the terms of my demands."

The circlet of goblins quieted themselves and bowed.

"Of course, sire."

"It is our honor to serve you."

"For you, anything"

The elders huddled around Virgidous more closely. They stretched out their arms until their long gangly fingers touched. They created an electric blue current that flowed between them as Virgidous focused.

Virgidous reached into Zephrum's dreams to offer her a deal. He sent his telepathic message deeply into her mind with mumbles.

Eventually, his mumbles became clearer. "Miss Zephrum Gatse!" he yelled. Help me find the Leviathan OR be an agent of destruction for all of humanity. Your choice!"

Virgidous finally put his hands together. "And now, my friends. We wait."

--Chapter 32--

"The Paintings"

Zephrum awoke from her dream with Virgidous, visibly shaken.

Daphne looked over at her, wondering if she was fully awake. "What's wrong? Did you have a bad dream?"

"Yeah," said Zephrum. "But it felt like more than a dream. It felt like a real visitation."

"From who?" asked Daphne. "Is Waylon the Wyvern bringing his baby dragons back to Fiddlesticks again?"

"No," said Zephrum. "It was Strasidous Rowpe. Or Virgidous or whatever he's calling himself these days."

"What did he say? Does he want something from you again?" asked Daphne.

"Yes," said Zephrum. "It's the same thing. He wants me to help him find this mythical Leviathan. He says I have two choices. Either help him find the Leviathan...or watch as humanity destroys themselves and our habitat."

"What?!?" asked Daphne. "Those aren't reasonable choices."

"He says that if I don't help him, then I will be...uh...'an agent of destruction' for all of humanity," responded Zephrum.

"How?" asked Daphne.

"I don't know," said Zephrum. "But it felt pretty serious."

"Are you sure it wasn't just a bad dream?" asked Daphne.

"He does do his darndest to come through on the threats he makes," said Zephrum.

"What are we going to do?" asked Daphne. "I mean, we have school and so many tests coming up. How are we supposed to make time for this crazy idea?"

"I don't know," said Zephrum. "But he said he would appear when the time was right. And that I will have to make my choice then."

"I wonder when that will be," said Daphne.

Zephrum shrugged her shoulders and dragged herself out of bed.

The girls got their day clothes on, and brushed their teeth in their nearby outhouse bathroom. Zephrum went to tend to the horses and then got on with the rest of her school day.

Because it was only a few weeks before winter break, the teachers were heaping an unbelievable amount of schoolwork onto the students. They had upcoming tests in every subject and had to spend a lot of time studying. Zephrum was a little distracted because of the Strasidous Rowpe dream, but she did her best to focus on school, none-the-less. Thankfully, they still had their morning circus workouts and their special trainings in the circus tent in the afternoons. Having these regular physical outlets was really the only reason that Zephrum was still able to keep her mind clear.

In the last couple of weeks leading up to their end of term tests, students gathered together in the Sun Lodge and sat on beanbag chairs while quizzing each other. Others spent time in the Lunar Mansion's library, with their faces glued to their books.

Zephrum was especially fretting about their tests in Waldo Vestor's class on Forecasting the Future with Mathematical Trends. Mr. Vestor had the students accessing so many tables and charts that it was almost staggering. He even wanted them to make parallels between planetary cycles and economic trends. "Who has ever heard of such a thing?" complained Zephrum.

"Obviously, Mr. Vestor has," commented Daphne.

Gai Holms was really getting into their Writing the Truth class with Dexter Droudy. Gai was writing an article about protecting our rivers and waterways. He said, "I want people to know about pollution going into our rivers. If my writing is good enough, Mr. Droudy could choose to share it as a letter to the editor in The Diurnal Journal."

Of course, Zephrum was especially interested in reading more about the Leviathan in their Mythical Sea Creatures in Literature class, but there were also so many other mythical sea creatures to learn about that it was a little overwhelming to memorize ALL of them.

There was quite a lot of information to remember for Dr. Malvin Moot's oceanography class too. Sarah Bellum was probably one of the only students who was actually enjoying the intense rigor of having to study so much.

Lots of students were getting excited about the winter holidays and the end of their semester as well. Most of the kids would be returning home to see their parents over winter break, but some of the students and teachers would be meeting up for a very special adventure at New Years.

Daphne's parents, Steve and Tiffany Gumption, decided to host a small group of students for a sailing adventure down to Cape Larboard at the southern coast on a large yacht.

Zephrum, Daphne, Gai, Misty, Sarah Bellum, Great Aunt Gussie, Geezer, and Dr. Malvin Moot were all planning to go on the journey.

After Winter Solstice and before New Year's Eve, The Fiddlesticks Shuttle brought this northern crew far south, to Gumption Manor outside of the city of Freeman. It took many hours to get there, but it was definitely worth the drive. Daphne's butler, Edward, greeted the group at the entryway to the mansion's foyer after the van made it though the secure gates at the driveway's entrance. The manor was quite opulent, with balconies outside of each bedroom upstairs and a marble floor at the main entrance. The Gumption's chef had prepared a luncheon for the people arriving from Fiddlesticks. It was all set up on their long dining table inside.

Mr. Gumption was visibly excited to see everybody. Smiling widely, he said, "Welcome. Welcome. We've been looking forward to your arrival."

"Yes," Mrs. Gumption chimed in. "We've got a sushi snack ready for you in our dining room." When she spotted Zephrum, she gave her an enthusiastic hug. "Oh, my dear Zephrum…it's so lovely to see you. We really missed you this Christmas. Shopping just wasn't the same without you."

Daphne rolled her eyes. "She couldn't stop talking about how much she wished you were here with us."

"It's true," said Mr. Gumption. He squeezed Zephrum with a side hug. "Our kids have heard all of our stories and philosophies about life, so it's always refreshing to share our ideas with somebody new. We are very much looking forward to our sailing adventure with you and the rest of your friends."

Sarah Bellum and Misty Falls had never seen Gumption Manor before, so their jaws dropped in disbelief.

"It's so…big," said Sarah.

"And you have a swimming pool INSIDE?!?!" exclaimed Misty.

"Oh yes," said Mr. Gumption nonchalantly. "We've done well for ourselves."

"Let's go to the dining room, so we can tell you more about the plans for our adventure on our friend's yacht," said Mrs. Gumption.

"This is quite the palace, isn't it?" said Geezer to Aunt Gussie.

Great Aunt Gussie agreed. "It's so big that we could get lost in every room."

Geezer raised his eyebrows. "That almost sounds like an invitation."

Aunt Gussie batted her eyelashes and coyly said, "Oh Geezer."

At the dining table, there was a lot of talk about the boat they'd be traveling on, as well as some description about their southern destination. "You will just LOVE it," affirmed Mrs. Gumption. "It's so warm and the beaches are simply divine."

After everyone ate their sushi snack, they made visits to the bathrooms to freshen up, and then, they squeezed back into the Fiddlesticks shuttle. From there, they drove to the bay where their yacht was docked.

Once everybody piled out of the van at Freeman's Wharf, they collected their bags and followed the Gumptions down the wooden dock to the yacht they had heard so much about. The name of the boat, Discovery, was printed in a fancy typeface at the stern's far end.

Mr. Gumption stretched his arms wide to present the large vessel to everyone. "One of my clients was so exhilarated after my inspirational speech at his company that he's offered his yacht to us for as long as we'd like to use it. His captain and staff will take us to our great southern reef. There, we'll be able to enjoy the tropical weather, sunbathe, play on the white sand beaches, and go snorkeling in the warm sea. I've even arranged for us to have scuba diving gear, for deeper exploration."

"Oh, the kids will learn sooo much," said Mrs. Gumption. She tweaked Mr. Gumption's nose. "This is SUCH a good idea, my schnookums."

Mr. and Mrs. Gumption rubbed noses and gave each other a little kissy kissy.

Zephrum whispered to Misty, "I forgot how affectionate Daphne's parents are with each other. It's a lot to get used to."

"I've never seen adults act so lovey-dovey in public," agreed Misty.

The boat was such a big yacht that there were crew quarters for everybody inside. The kids found more things as they explored.

"Look at all this," said Zephrum. "There's a dining room and a swimming pool?!?"

"Wow! And there's a bar and a movie room too!" said Gai.

Daphne's older brother Niko was on winter break from his prep school, so he joined their expedition as well. He was super fit, blonde, and he looked a little taller than last year.

"I didn't think it would be possible, but Niko looks even cooler than he did the last time I saw him," Zephrum whispered to Misty.

When Niko saw Gai, he slapped him on the back and flashed him a charismatic smile. "Alright, my singing partner is joining us."

Gai cracked up. "Ha! I can't believe you remember me as your 'singing partner' from those silly New Year's songs we sang at your parent's party last year."

Niko gave Gai a cool handshake that ended with a finger snap. "Hey, I thought we could have gone on the road as a band with all of that talent."

"Ha!" Gai was obviously excited to be able to hang out with Niko again.

As Zephrum surveyed the interior of the yacht, she noticed a bunch of old photos in picture frames peppered throughout the boat. "Who are all of these people?" she asked Mr. Gumption.

Mr. Gumption said, "Oh, those are the many ancestors of the owner of the yacht. He apparently comes from a long line of sailors and entrepreneurs."

"Just my kind of people," said Geezer.

Once everybody was settled on board the yacht, they motored out of the bay and out to sea. When they reached the open ocean, some very large sails were hoisted up and the mammoth yacht picked up speed.

Geezer announced, "The journey southward will have the advantage of a North to South tidal push. We'll get to our southern coast in no time."

Mr. Gumption said, "Yes. It will take much longer to journey back up north. This is why we'll all be flying back. We have a friend with a small private airplane who will be picking us up down south in Cape Larboard in a couple of weeks."

Zephrum's eyes widened. "Wow! ALL of us?"

"Yes," said Mrs. Gumption. "It will be the easiest way to make sure we get you back to school in time for classes once school starts up again."

"Our journey south will take a few days of constant sailing before we reach our destination, so we'd like to give scuba lessons on our boat to help pass the time," said Mr. Gumption.

"Yes," said Mrs. Gumption. "We'll start tomorrow morning at the yacht's pool."

That night, Zephrum, Daphne, Misty, and Sarah were walking in the narrow hallways of the yacht, just looking at everything and checking out the starry night over the sleepless ocean.

Out of the corner of her eye, Zephrum could have sworn that she saw an impenetrable fog emanating from one of the framed pictures on the wall.

Moments after the dense mist appeared, a human figure arose from one of the frames. The shape looked exactly like the old sea captain from the largest painting hanging on the wall there. He wore a formal blue captain's uniform and had a thick gray mustache that met his sculpted beard below. He looked in the direction of the girls and pointed directly at Zephrum. "You, with the braids! The wild one!"

Zephrum brought her hand to her chest. "Me? Are you talking to me?"

"Yes, it is only someone on the furthest edge of this world that could summon me from my canvas," said the ghostly sea captain.

"I didn't summon you," said Zephrum. "We were just walking by and looking is all."

"Tell yourself this if you must," responded the ethereal captain. "But it is only someone who is living on an edge between worlds that can arouse my spirit from this portrait. You are troubled. I can see this from the other side."

Daphne, Misty, and Sarah watched the captain, dumbfounded.

The captain continued, "There is not much time, as these portals are rare. Although you may feel tempted by an evil greater than you have ever known, my message to you is paramount."

"You have a message for me?" asked Zephrum.

"Yes," confirmed the apparition. "You cannot help this world if you sacrifice your own true north. Whatever you do, do not fall victim to the traps of the dark side."

"The dark side?" asked Zephrum. "What do you mean?"

"Fathom my weighty words. Stay on the starboard side of your conscience."

With that, the sea captain dissipated into the haze in front of his portrait.

Zephrum looked at her friends in disbelief. "Whoa… "

"Where did he go?" asked Misty.

"Have any of you ever seen anything like this before?" asked Sarah.

Everyone shook their heads.

"What do you think he was talking about?" asked Daphne.

Zephrum said, "I think it has to do with the choice that Strasidous Rowpe gave me in my dream when we were back at Fiddlesticks before our break. Either help him find the Leviathan…or be an agent of destruction for all of humanity."

Sarah said, "Those are not choices. Those are two very bad options."

"Exactly," said Zephrum.

"What are you going to do?" asked Misty.

"Well…" responded Zeprhum. "If I take the advice of this sea captain, I think I should do nothing."

"Let's hope that will be possible," said Daphne.

"For sure," agreed Zephrum.

The girls all stood looking at the empty space in front of the picture frame for a while.

"I wonder if he'll come back," said Misty.

"It seems like he's really gone now," said Sarah, inspecting the painting, hoping to locate some kind of technology that could have made his presence possible.

"Yeah," added Daphne. "I guess he felt like he said what he needed to say."

"I guess so," said Zephrum. "But that sure was weird."

--Chapter 33--

"Leviathan's Journey"

Meanwhile, the Leviathan was arrowing through the deep cold waters in the ocean on the northern coast near Haversville. He was beginning to tire of his constant quest for food. "My inner sense tells me it is time to journey southward, to warmer waters."

Aiming his large ancient nose in a southern direction, the Leviathan headed away from the rocky coast of the north. He dove through the waters like a warm knife in melted butter, his thoughts quickened. "It has been some time since I have fed off of tropical fish." Just pondering the possibilities lit his inner fire chambers. Glimmers of fire light emanated from his chest as he moved.

"So many feasting varieties are swimming within the corals southward, ready to be consumed. I am hankering for greater ease. I am guided by my longing, but also by my wish to thrive as I once did in aeon's past."

He flew through the water using the great power from the strength of his spiny wings. His momentum moved him through the currents at an unbelievable speed. "Now that I have a goal, I am renewed. I will feast with vengeance. I will gorge myself, then rest in an ancient underwater cave that I have rested in before. Once my hunger is satisfied, I will return to the northern currents, as my blood desires the cooler waters most."

"Ahh yes, but to rest in warm waters and to sleep undisturbed for a time is just what I need. This distant cave is the one place I have never been bothered. It is one sanctuary that has always given me peace beyond peace, a secret place where I can let my ancient guard down. I can curl up and slumber there for as long as it takes my body to enjoy my feasting. Yes. Going to the southern waters will reinvigorate me beyond measure. And being in the inner sanctum of my deepest dreams will be a welcome relief from the never ending toil of this mysteriously darkened ocean."

"Curious times are these." He swerved and bent his body with the waves of the open waters. "I will find my way, as always, but I do wonder if this toil will be my new normal. Mmm... ??"

He directed himself with purpose and thought, "No matter. These concerns of mine are trivial in the larger scheme of things, as this body is just a vehicle for my ever growing inner strength and wisdom."

With that, he veered with the currents to coast upon the natural pathways of the ocean's circuits.

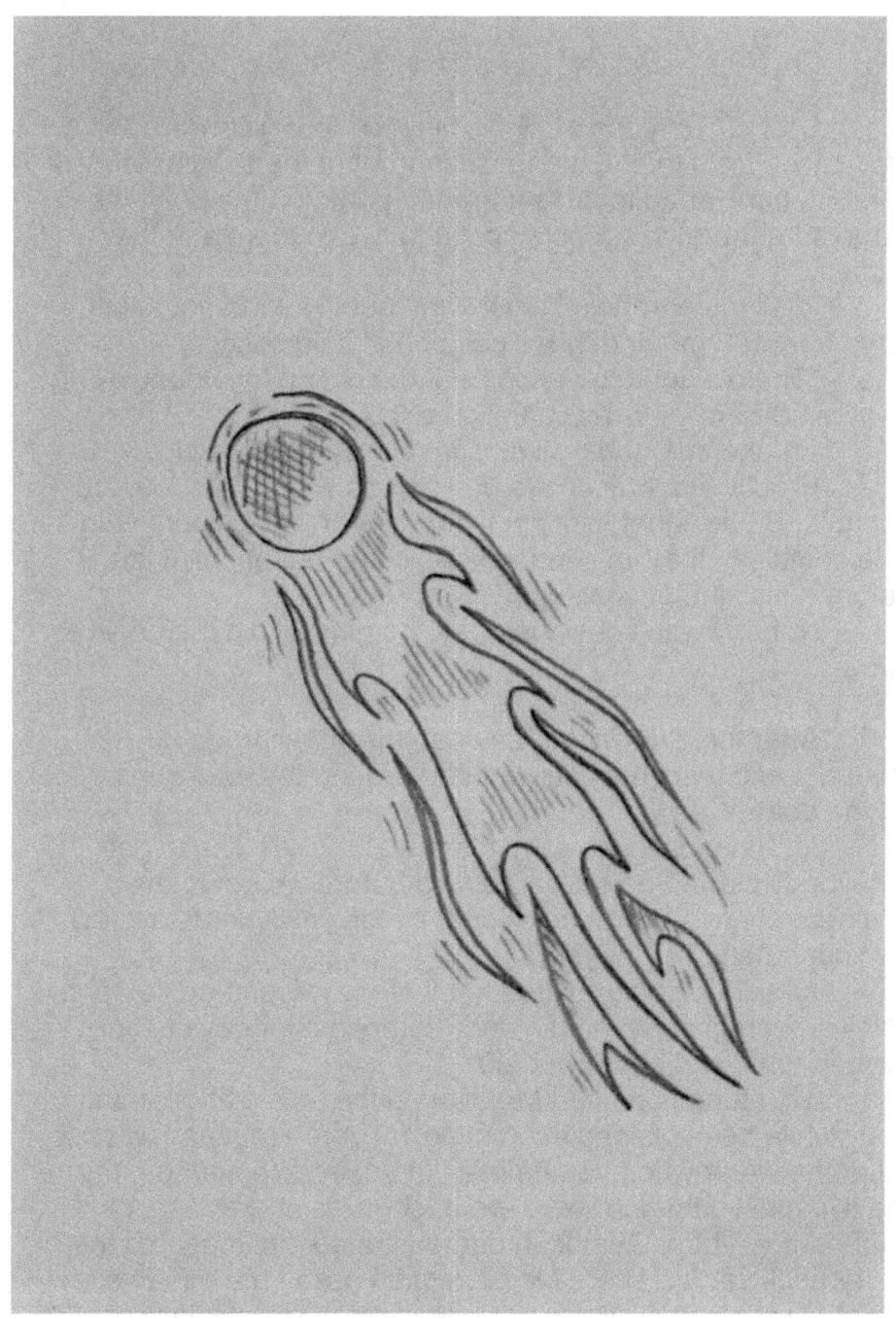

--Chapter 34--

"Underwater Cave"

On the yacht the next morning, all four girls were still a little rattled from their experience in front of the sea captain's portrait. If they had to pass a framed photo on the boat, they made sure there was ample space between them and the frames.

"Call me paranoid if you want, but I want to put a lot of room between me and those paintings," said Misty.

"There's got to be a logical explanation for what we saw," said Sarah. "But I can't figure it out."

An uncomfortable silence lay between them.

Finally, Daphne spoke up. "It was weird. No doubt about it. But let's not let it spoil our adventure. I mean, who else could say they've seen images come out of paintings before? It's kind of cool, right?"

Nobody was convinced, but the girls all did their best to agree.

After their morning breakfast, the small group of students and teachers congregated around the swimming pool on the boat.

Mr. Gumption welcomed them all. "We'd like to get everybody started on scuba training before we get to the southern shore. There are a lot of things you'll need to know, for your safety."

Mrs. Gumption pointed to all of the needed equipment. "We've each got fins, a buoyancy compensator device, our oxygen tank, and a weight belt."

Mr. Gumption used Mrs. Gumption as a demonstration body while he explained everything. "There are many ways to enter the water when you have all of your equipment on, but the two most common ways are backwards or with a giant stride entry." Mrs. Gumption demonstrated a plunge into the water backwards. Then, Mr. Gumption asked his wife to show a giant stride entry. "We'd like everybody to try doing these techniques in our yacht's pool."

Everyone got geared up and took turns trying the different methods for getting into the water.

Mr. Gumption continued talking to his dripping wet students, who were now all bobbing up and down inside the swimming pool, "Now, the first thing you need to remember with scuba diving is to never hold your breath. You'll be doing normal breathing through your mouth the whole time."

Mrs. Gumption put the breathing tube into her mouth to demonstrate. "When you don't have the regulator in your mouth, blow a fairly constant stream of bubbles," said Mrs. Gumption.

Everyone tried to blow bubbles in the water.

"The other thing to remember is to equalize early and often. You do this by blocking your nose and pushing a little bit of air into your head. You'll feel the tubes in your ears making little pops as you adjust to different depths under the water. This helps to neutralize your buoyancy as you explore."

Mrs. Gumption held her nose to show what to do.

"The other thing you need to do is know how to clear your mask if it gets fogged," said Mr. Gumption. "Just allow a small amount of water into the mask and swish it around. "

"For your underwater navigation, you will inhale to rise and exhale to sink. Take your time coming back to the surface. Avoid rapid ascents."

Great Aunt Gussie sighed, "I suppose I'll have to take the curlers out of my hair for this experience."

Zephrum and Daphne giggled.

For the next few days, the group of travelers practiced putting all of their equipment on, using hand signals to communicate, and submerging under the water in the yacht's pool.

Everyone was excited when they finally arrived at the southern harbor where they would remain docked during their adventure. When Zephrum finally set foot onto dry land, she still felt like she was swaying and moving with the waves. "Is that normal?" she asked Geezer.

"Well, for those who are not old sea dogs like myself, you could feel a bit wobbly for a while," Geezer replied.

"As long as you don't throw up, you should be fine," added Daphne.

Zephrum tried her hardest to regain her balance and ignore the nausea. "I kind of feel like I should hold onto the ground to stop the world from moving."

Gai nodded in agreement.

A visit to the beach helped to distract her from the weird feeling of being on a boat when she wasn't.

During the first day, they played on the beach and did some basic snorkeling. A coral reef that was accessible from the shore was really fun to explore. Zephrum's eyes widened under her snorkeling goggles. She saw green and rust colored coral outcroppings, unique forests of seaweed, and schools of tropical fish. "Wow! I've never seen anything like this in real life before."

At dinner on the yacht that night, there was lively discussion about what everyone had seen and how fun it was to swim in such warm waters.

Mr. Gumption said, "Tomorrow, we'll take our scuba equipment with us, with our small commuter boat. You'll be able to explore even more once you can check out the reef at deeper depths."

The next morning, they motored out to where they would take their first deep ocean plunge. Each person had a buddy to scuba dive with. Zephrum and Daphne took their giant stride entry together and slowly swam down to the reefs below. There were so many varieties and species of coral under the surface. Some looked like the petals of a flower, some looked like reaching fingers, other corals had branching patterns, and some were just large massive plates. The reef provided safe hiding places for all kinds of creatures. Turtles and fish of all shapes and sizes swam by Zephrum and Daphne as they explored. In some of the gardens of coral, they saw sea otters, stingrays, and sea dragons that were about 1 foot long. They also noticed that some of the coral looked white, kind of like a dead skeleton.

"It feels like time slows down when you're in the water," said Zephrum when they reached the surface.

"Totally," agreed Daphne. "It's pretty cool."

"I saw **cloud fish,** puffers, eels, and a whole bunch of different kinds of fluorescent fish too," said Gai when they all met back up at the commuter boat. "What about you?"

Zephrum said, "Yeah, there was so much life in and around the coral. It was so cool."

Aunt Gussie had been waiting on the commuter boat while everyone was below the water. When the kids all returned, she said, "Dr. Malvin Moot has been burning the midnight oil and staying up at all hours to prepare a presentation about the reefs. He plans to share it with us one evening at the end of this week. That will really be the icing on the cake, won't it?"

Zephrum, Daphne, and Gai all nodded. Daphne's brother Niko stood perplexed.

Zephrum smiled. "Don't worry, Niko. You'll eventually start to understand the way Aunt Gussie talks."

"That's right," commented Great Aunt Gussie. "Time is a great thickener of things."

Niko smiled politely. He still wondered what the heck Aunt Gussie really said.

As their vacation days went on, Zephrum and Daphne started to feel more comfortable in deeper waters, so they explored some of the coral reefs that were a little further away from their commuter boat. They actually discovered an underwater cave and motioned to each other to go inside. They turned on their waterproof headlamps in order to see better. The entrance to the cave was a long wide tunnel. It seemed to go under the shelf of the land for an eternity. This cave was so massive that it looked like a large horizontal building could fit inside it.

They hadn't swum into it for long when Zephrum and Daphne came across a spiky rounded wall inside the underwater cave. The spikes were as hard as stone and looked like rows of shields. When they touched it, they discovered that this weirdly shaped wall was actually slightly warm. Suddenly, the wall MOVED!! There was a churning roll that revealed a very large pointy wing. The wing looked like it was connected to a relative of a giant prehistoric bird. Their eyes widened in disbelief. The spikes continued to roll before them, revealing more and more of an enormous body. It was camouflaged so well within the rock walls of the cave that it was hard to tell where this gigantic creature ended and where the cave began. Zephrum panicked. She motioned to Daphne that they should swim out of the deep underwater cavern.

With an abrupt jerk, the massive creature stirred awake and blew a large plume of fire through the water and in their direction. Zephrum and Daphne swam as fast as they could. The entrance to the cave was far ahead. They swerved just in time for the fire blast to speed past them, zooming into the ocean beyond their position.

Zephrum sensed another fire plume coming. She dodged it at the last moment. Her heart pounded inside her chest as she glanced behind her, only to see the ancient mouth of this giant creature open wide. The creature shot one last fire blast at her and Daphne. Zephrum heard a massive roar as it spit a massive fireball out of its mouth. The gigantic flames jetted directly at them. There was no escape. Just then, Zephrum had an idea. She grabbed Daphne and held her tight.

Zephrum created an underwater swirl of wind to pierce through the water like a high speed jet.

They zoomed out of the tunnel and escaped as the fire blast roared through empty water. They made their way to the surface of the ocean outside of the cave, took their breathing tubes out of their mouths, and gasped for air.

"What was that thing?" asked Daphne.

"I don't know," cried Zephrum. "But we got out of that tunnel just in the nick of time."

"Totally," said Daphne breathlessly. "I can't believe how fast you got us out of there."

"Me neither," agreed Zephrum. "I guess my instincts took over."

"That was a pretty large creature," said Daphne. "We must have disturbed its resting place. Are you thinking what I'm thinking?"

"Yeah," said Zephrum. "I have an idea that it could be the creature that Strasidous Rowpe is so obsessed with."

"Yeah," agreed Daphne.

And then, at the same moment, they both said, "The Leviathan."

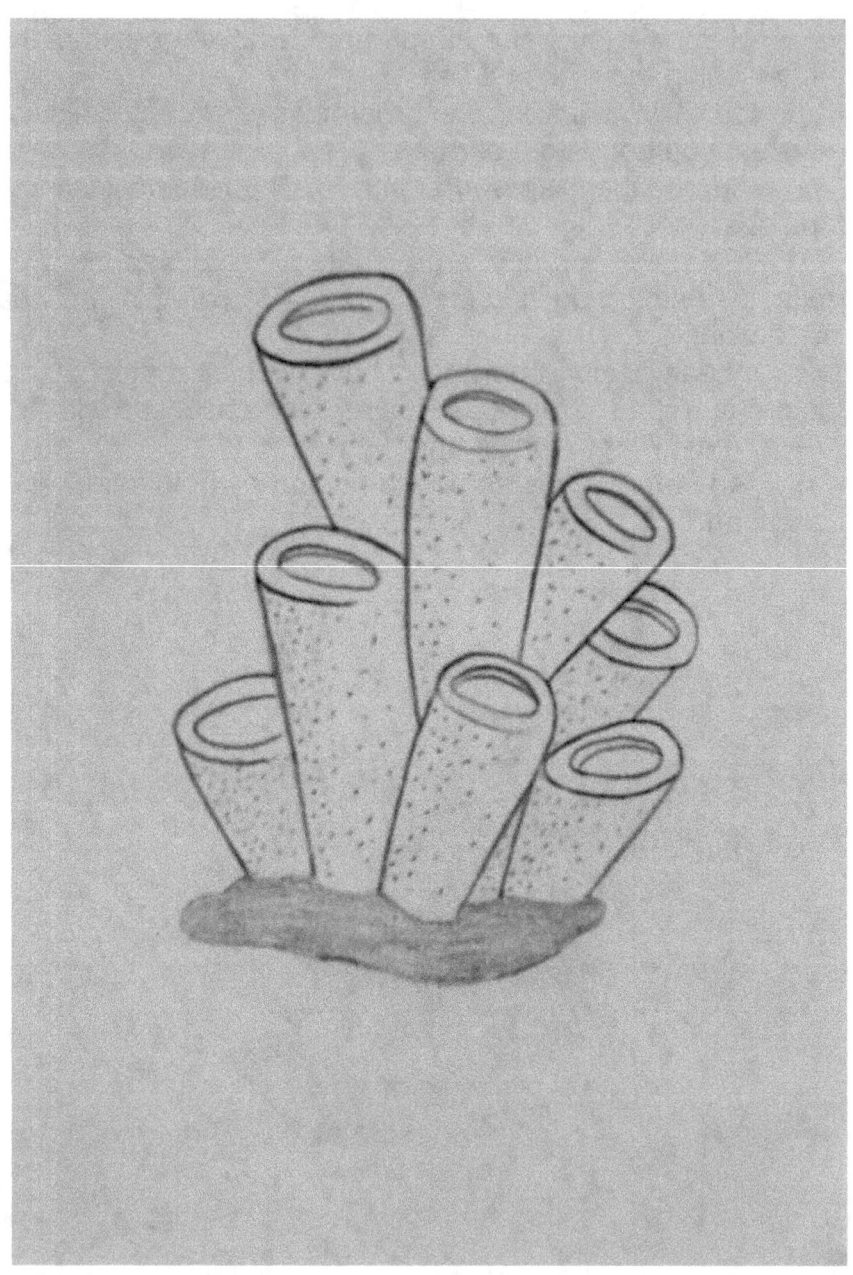

—Chapter 35—
"The Corals"

The Leviathan was fully awake. "Who dares to stir me from my feasting slumber? What kind of creatures can move so fast so as to escape my flaming breaths? I must sniff out these creatures. I will track their scent and I will find them. Once I discover their lair, I will bust them to bits with my jagged teeth. I will pummel their bodies with my massive tail and I will turn them into soft morsels. I will use my fire to make them crispy. Then, I will devour them."

His piercing yellow eyes looked out of his private underwater cave. From there, he sniffed the water with his great snout. Within moments, he was swimming in the direction that Zephrum and Daphne went.

Gai and Niko were waiting for the girls on the commuter boat. Once they reached the commuter boat, they quickly heaved themselves back on board.

"We found an underwater cave over there," said Daphne, pointing in the direction of the cave. "You won't believe what we saw inside."

"What did you find?" asked Gai.

Zephrum could barely find the words. "Spikes on giant wall. An ancient wing. So huge. Big Creature. Fires plumes."

Niko and Gai just stared.

"What she's trying to say," explained Daphne, "is that we think we just escaped getting scorched by an ancient Leviathan in a giant underwater cave. It was soooo frightening. I think Zephrum is in shock."

"A Leviathan?" said Niko. "You realize that's a mythical creature, right?"

"Yes, yes, we know that," said Daphne. "But one still lives. And it's right over there."

"We want to go see it," said Niko.

"Oh no you don't," said Daphne. "We were lucky to escape with our lives. If Zephrum hadn't jetted us out of there, we would have been burned to a crisp by the fireballs it was spitting at us."

"Fire balls?!?!" exclaimed Gai.

"Yeah," said Zephrum finally. "Massive plumes of fire in the water, directed right at us."

Zephrum looked at the ocean in the direction of the cave, still barely believing it herself.

"We think we should warn everyone in our group, but we don't know how to explain what we saw," said Daphne.

"Fiddlesticks School must be teaching you guys to be a little koo-koo," said Niko. "It's great that they're encouraging your imagination and all, but don't take it so seriously. You're likely to end up in the nut house."

Zephrum looked at him without smiling. "Niko, you saw some of my abilities when I pummeled you with a whirlwind of snow balls last year at your parents house…and when you watched us take off on that magic carpet ride too. You've also seen your sister foretell the future with her art since she was little. You know that our magical abilities are real. But we're not the only magical beings around. What we just saw was a REAL Sea Monster."

"We have to tell everyone to stay away from that cave over there," said Daphne.

"I think we may have disturbed its resting place," added Zephrum.

"Yeah," continued Daphne. "And it was really mad about it."

"You both seem really freaked out over it, whatever it was," said Niko.

"We should ask Geezer and Mr. and Mrs. Gumption about it," said Gai. "Or maybe some of the local people know what kind of creature it is? Maybe it was something else?"

Gai could sense that Zephrum was really overwhelmed.

He went up to her, put his arm around her and said, "It's ok, Zephrum. You're safe now."

She put her face into Gai's chest and hugged him.

Zephrum wiped the water from her face. "It was pretty scary, whatever it was."

Eventually, Mr. and Mrs. Gumption emerged from the water and made it back onto the commuter boat, along with Sarah and Misty.

"Well," said Mr. Gumption as he hoisted himself onto the boat. "How was it out there today? Did you all have another great day of adventure?"

Zephrum and Daphne sat speechless, while the others described the tropical fish they had seen.

Finally, Daphne pointed in the direction of the underwater cave and said, "Zephrum and I discovered a fairly large sea monster in a cave we found over there."

"That's fascinating," said Mr. Gumption enthusiastically. "You'll have to tell us all about it when we get back to the yacht."

He turned on the commuter boat's engine and motored everybody back to the large vessel. There was no use trying to talk over the noise of the boat's engine.

Once they were back at the yacht, they all showered, got into their night clothes, and met in the galley for some dinner.

Zephrum and Daphne told Geezer about the creature in the underwater cave. They warned everyone to stay far away from the cave that they had found.

Geezer said, "Well, that is quite a tale, my friends. I've heard tell of Sea Monsters over the years, but have never heard a story with so much detail. Locals here in the southern shore around Cape Larboard have a name for their sea monster. They call it, 'el Leviatan'."

"What?!?" cried Zephrum.

"Well," continued Geezer. "I guess that they think that their local sea monster is a relative of a Leviathan."

"That's the creature that we've been warned about. And it blew flames right at us!" exclaimed Zephrum.

Aunt Gussie put her hand on Zephrum's shoulder. "It seems like that creature scared the living daylights out of you."

"No kidding," said Zephrum.

"You do find a way to get yourself into a real kettle of fish, don't you?" said Aunt Gussie.

"I guess so," said Zephrum. "But now that we know this creature really exists, what are we going to do about it? You know that Strasidous Rowpe is looking for it."

"Well," said Aunt Gussie. "If this creature is as dangerous as you say, it sounds like it might be good if he finds it. Maybe Strasidous will finally bite the dust."

"You think the creature will destroy him?" asked Zephrum.

"It sounds like you almost met your maker, so yes. Why not?" said Aunt Gussie.

"Strasidous Rowpe has a lot of power," said Zephrum. "Maybe he's figured out a way to defeat him."

"Maybe," said Aunt Gussie. "But every dog has his day. It's possible that the Leviathan would be too great a match for Strasidous Rowpe or Virgidous or whatever he's calling himself. It's also possible that all of this worrying is for nothing. All wretch and no vomit, as they say."

"Eeeuuww…" said Daphne.

"On that note, it looks like it's time for us to break bread together," said Aunt Gussie. "A little dinner will take your mind off of all of this, for sure."

The girls weren't too convinced, but they went along to the galley with Aunt Gussie and Geezer.

The dinner in the galley was a buffet style, like most nights on the yacht. They had steamed veggies, local fish in a yummy sauce, black bean burritos for the vegetarians, and a tropical fruit dessert.

Once they were all done with their dinner, Dr. Moot began showing some slide show photos to start his highly anticipated presentation. "Our ocean is a fascinating place, isn't it?"

There were many sounds of agreement. Zephrum and Daphne just eyed each other, still frightened by their encounter with the Leviathan.

Dr. Malvin Moot continued, "You may not know this, but our oceans control our weather and the oxygen we breathe too. Did you know that our ocean provides more oxygen to our planet than the surface plants and forests?"

"Wild."

"Really?!?"

"Cool."

"Now that you've seen coral reefs up close and personal, you can understand more about them. They are where sea life begins. Coral can build their own environments and create habitats for many creatures. They deposit their calcium skeleton beneath and grow on top of that bony structure. You probably noticed how they can even create 'high rises' in the sea. The more complex the system, the more bio-diversity can live there."

Gai sat up taller. "Me and Niko noticed that there even seems to be 'fish traffic'... with so many creatures going from here to there."

"Yeah," added Niko, "I could have sworn that I heard a kind of a chorus, with purring sounds and fish grunting too."

Zephrum thought of the roar she heard from the Leviathan. She plugged her ears for a moment to stop herself from re-hearing it inside her head.

Oblivious, Dr. Moot continued. "It is quite a fascinating world in the sea, isn't it?"

Again, there were a lot of head nods and sounds of agreement from their small group.

Dr. Malvin Moot continued, "Coral are a foundation species. They provide habitat and food for many organisms and different forms of sea life. Corals create breakwater, protecting the land, so its existence helps us on land as well. Some reefs can even be seen from space." He showed a photo of the earth from the point of view of space and pointed out some larger reefs.

"Wow!" "Cool." "I had no idea."

He continued, "Coral is an animal with many polyps. These polyps have a circular mouth and are surrounded by tentacles. The tentacles come out at night. It is simple, yet sophisticated."

Then, he showed a microscopic photo of algae. He said, "Inside the tissue of coral are micro-algae. These are very tiny plants that synthesize inside the coral during the day, feeding the coral all the food it needs."

Showing a photo of dead white coral, he said, "You may have noticed how the reef was turning white in some places. This is called 'bleaching' and is a threat across the planet. You see, normally, corals live on indefinitely. Dying is NOT part of their natural cycle."

Sarah Bellum raised her hand. "Well, if dying is not part of their natural cycle, why is it happening?"

"Good question, Sarah," said Dr. Moot. "You see, due to excess heat in the ocean, the micro-algae can't do their work, so the coral tries to eliminate the defective micro-algae. Then, the coral starves to death and turns white."

"Where is all of this heat coming from?" asked Misty.

Dr. Moot messed up his hair as he explained, "It's a complicated answer, Misty. As you know, burning fossil fuel creates carbon dioxide, which traps heat inside our atmosphere. The heat bounces off our atmosphere and back to the earth. The oceans absorb about 93% of that trapped heat. This has raised the temperature of the ocean by about two degrees."

"That doesn't seem like much," said Misty.

"No, it doesn't seem like two degrees is very much warmer, does it?" said Dr. Moot. "But it's similar to what happens when our body raises its temperature by two degrees. It's like having a fever. This 'fever' gets the coral to expel the defective micro-algae to cleanse itself and then, the coral starves to death."

So many silent jaws dropped when they heard this information.

Dr. Moot continued, "The coral reef is a casualty of climate change. These changes are catastrophic really. Coral reefs are a fundamental part of a quarter of ocean life, so their death is a serious ecological issue. It will affect little fish, which will affect big fish, which will affect humans. Everything on the planet is connected."

"It's true," commented Geezer. "Melting glacial ice and dying reefs are part of the same problem."

Without thinking, Zephrum blurted out, "I believe that Strasidous Rowpe is responsible for this."

"Strasidous Rowpe?" asked Mr. Gumption.

"Who's that?" asked Mrs. Gumption.

Zephrum didn't know how to explain this very complicated topic, so she sat frozen in her seat.

Sarah saved the moment. "So, how can we help to cool the ocean?"

"Well," said Dr. Moot. "The best way is to stop putting fossil fuels into our atmosphere. But there are some other ideas that have been thrown around in scientific circles too. One very popular idea is fertilization of the ocean. Basically, we'd use iron to stimulate the growth of phytoplankton. This is a good idea because phytoplankton can absorb huge amounts of carbon dioxide."

"Great," said Daphne. "Why don't we start doing this right away?"

"Well," said Dr. Moot. "It's a bit of a complicated subject. Firstly, we would need international agreement to really make this work. And this form of ocean fertilization could have some unintended consequences. It could affect rainfall, giving us more rain in some places and less in others."

"Mmm…" said Sarah. "Aren't there any other ideas?"

"Yes," said Dr. Moot. "But ocean fertilization seems like the most practical idea so far."

"Maybe we could do a small experiment as a project for our class," said Sarah.

"Good idea," said Dr. Moot. "The truth is, we really don't know how to solve some of these bigger problems. For now, the best course of action is to stop polluting the atmosphere. Then we will be able to have a healthy eco-system and enjoy our glorious ocean in perpetuity. Uh, for a long time."

Sarah had another question. "Francine Muller is the community organizer in Haversville. She drives on a vehicle fueled by vegetable oil. Why doesn't everybody just switch to something like that?"

"Well, that would be wonderful," said Dr. Moot. "But everyone would have to have diesel powered engines in order to use vegetable oil as a fuel. There's another promising possibility, though. And that is to use algae fuel. This kind of alternative could be used in most engines and it would not add any harmful pollutants into our atmosphere."

"Why don't we just do that then?" asked Sarah.

"Well, it will take time," said Dr. Moot. "But it is possible."

Aunt Gussie added, "Don't you worry, kids. The long arc of history bends inevitably towards justice. Something will work out, no matter how bleak things look right now."

Suddenly, the yacht rocked wildly. Everyone jumped up from their seats and ran outside to the deck. They held on to the railings of the boat as they looked around. It was a clear starry night. There were no other boats nearby.

"That's strange," said Mr. Gumption. "There's no storm, no clouds, no wind, and no large waves. I wonder what could have bumped into the boat to make it rock like that."

At that moment, the yacht lurched again. This time, they saw a massive spikey tail swoop up into the air from the ocean waters just as the yacht rocked.

"It looks like some kind of massive animal just banged into us," cried Mrs. Gumption.

In the water, the Leviathan spoke to his inner mind, "This creature's lair is protected by a hard outer shell. Mmm... I will try to reach it from above the water."

The Leviathan shot a large fireball up from the water. The fire ball flew into the air, missing the boat by mere millimeters.

"Oh my!"

"Holy Moly!"

"Where did that blast of fire come from?"

Seconds later, the Leviathan spit out another fire blast, this time with better aim. It was a direct hit. It blasted through the ceiling of the captain's viewing room, right onto the helm's steering wheel.

Mr. Gumption ran up the stairs to the captain's helm. He grabbed a fire extinguisher and doused the flames. Then he turned on the yacht's floodlights and sounded a loud alarm. The sound was so deafening that the Leviathan quickly streamed off into deeper waters.

"Grrr...," growled the Leviathan as he swam away. "This creature's screams are thunderous. Too loud of a sound for my ancient ears to be so near. Quite an ingenious defense."

He arrowed through the waters and pondered, "No matter. I am sure I have given it a fright. It will think twice before disturbing me in my slumber again."

"Mmm..." he continued thinking. "But I will never forget the scent of the creatures that awoke me. If I smell the creature again, I will not hesitate. I will bust them to bits and chew them up, whether I hunger or not. Grrr...."

—Chapter 36—

"Invoking the Storm"

Meanwhile, deep within the goblin caverns under the city center of Haversville, Virgidous was growing more and more impatient. "It is taking much too long for Zephrum Gates to assist me. I need to find that Leviathan at once. I need to look at its glowing eye and carve out its heart, so I may possess eternal life."

"But sire," said Zultr Zeki, "Grizalda The Great was fairly clear that you will fail without the help of Zephrum Gates."

"Yes. Yes. I know this," snapped Virgidous. "I just want to quicken the pace of things. This waiting is torturous. I must do something with my frustration. I must not waste all of my angst on trifles and worries. I must harness this irritation and do something with it."

"Yes, Sire," agreed Zultr Zeki. "But what?"

Virgidous paced on the dirt floor of the elder chamber for a moment. Then, paused in one spot. "I know. I will create such a massive storm that the Leviathan will be forced out of deep waters and closer to our shore. It will be such a glorious storm that even the hu-mans will be impressed."

"Sire, I have never created a weather spell before," said Zultr Zeki. "Is it even possible?"

"Oh Zeki," said Virgidous knowingly, "The stories we tell ourselves have everything to do with what is or isn't possible. Of course, it's possible!"

"How shall we proceed?" asked Zeki.

"Spells which control the weather and elements can take a lot of concentration and devotion to cast," said Virgidous. "This is mostly due to the fact that we will be controlling elements over a wide space with many varying effects."

"How do we begin, Sire?"

"We will have to go to Healer Groikz to see if he has the plant of Scotch Broom in stock. It is a gorse type plant with prickly yellow flowers. Then, we will need rice, salt, water, and a red candle."

"What then, my lord?" asked Zeki.

"The water will symbolize the rains of time," said Virgidous. "We will stir the water to imagine a huge storm cell forming. The Scotch Broom will bring the winds, tearing through every limb of a tree. When we add the rice, we will invoke a downpour."

"And just imagine a massive storm in our usual way of imagining, yes?" asked Zeki.

"Exactly," said Virgidous. "Salt seals the mixture. We'll bring it outside and throw it into the wind."

"Of course, we will want to cast a separate spell to protect the goblin caverns," added Zultr Zeki.

"Of course," agreed Virgidous. "I say we do the protection spell first. Then, we can revel in the madness of our incoming storm."

"Yes, Sire," said Zeki. "In this way, we will be most aligned with nature's evolutionary genius in the most powerful way possible."

They rubbed their hands together, grinning at one another with sinister smiles.

"But will it work without a purity of intention?" asked Zultr Zeki. "My ancient studies have taught me that intention is a powerful element in all spells."

"True," said Virgidous. "If our plan does not pan out due to this 'intention problem,' we will find another way. However we do it, we will have our storm, my friend. And we'll have it exactly where we want it."

"Sire, you are most wise and corrupt," said Zultr Zeki.

"Yes, I am," said Virgidous smiling. "Let us go to Healer Groikz immediately."

"Yes, Sire," said Zultr Zeki. She stood up and opened the elder chamber door. "Right away, Sire."

As they walked through the caverns to see Healer Groikz, Zultr Zeki said, "It is quite a dream you have picked, Sire. Quite a dream indeed."

"Oh Zeki," said Virgidous. "Our dreams pick us, not the other way around."

—Chapter 37—

"The Tornicane"

Back at the yacht, Zephrum and all of the other kids ran up to the captain's viewing room to look at the wreckage from the fireball.

"Wow!" said Niko. "What kind of a thing could make so much damage?"

Zephrum shook her head. "I'm sure it was the Leviathan that me and Daphne saw."

"He was probably seeking us out," said Daphne.

"Whatever it was, at least we know that it doesn't like loud alarm sounds and bright lights," said Gai.

Mr. Gumption was doing his best to clean up the mess from the char broiled roof. "Tiffany, could you go get us one of those hefty tarps from down below? I think we'll need to cover this gaping hole in the ceiling."

"Of course, honeybun," said Mrs. Gumption. She headed in the direction of the lower levels of the yacht.

"Well," said Mr. Gumption. "Whatever that creature was, it sure did pack a wallop." He looked at the damage and sighed. "Explaining THIS isn't going to be easy. I mean, who has ever heard of fireballs jetting out from the water?" He looked at the kids who were clearly still stunned. "It's a good thing that we'll be flying back home, right?"

The kids simply nodded.

"Whatever it was, it sure swam away like a bat out of hell," said Great Aunt Gussie.

Geezer said, "In all of my time out at sea, I've never seen anything like it before."

"Well," said Aunt Gussie. "I guess we're all in the same boat, then, huh?"

Geezer smiled and winked at her.

"Aren't you worried it might come back?" asked Zephrum.

"Being that it swam off in such a fright, the chances of it returning are slim," said Aunt Gussie. "Most creatures have strong self-preservation instincts. If it did come back, though, we'd be up a creek without a paddle, wouldn't we?"

"Don't you worry, kids," said Geezer. "We'll keep the yacht's floodlights on and that will surely keep the creature from returning."

"OK…Chop Chop," interrupted Great Aunt Gussie. "There's nothing more to see here. You kids best hit the sack. Tomorrow is a big packing day…and a cleaning up day too. After we've left the yacht all spick and span, we'll be ready for our flight northward on the private airplane that Mr. Gumption arranged for us."

"It's one adventure after another, isn't it?" said Mr. Gumption. He gave Daphne a little squeeze.

"I guess so," she said half heartedly.

Later on, when Daphne and Zephrum were in their beds in their yacht's cabin, they talked more about the excitement with the Leviathan.

"Can you believe that sea monster found us? I mean, HOW?" said Daphne.

"I don't know," said Zephrum. "But it's totally freaking me out."

"Maybe he has a super sense of smell or something?" said Daphne.

"Maybe," replied Zephrum. "I'm just glad we'll be getting a lot of distance from him."

"Totally."

After everybody got up the next morning, the entire crew got busy with scrubbing and cleaning. They cleaned the bathrooms, the galley, and all of the other common spaces of the yacht. Even though they had only been staying on the large boat for a short time, there was a lot to clean up. They managed to make it back to the beach for one last swim and a little basking in the sun. By nighttime, everybody was very hungry for their last meal on their very special vessel.

"Tomorrow morning," said Mr. Gumption, "we'll finish packing up our things and we'll have breakfast at a little place in town. Then, we'll fly back up north to Freeman. We've had an amazing vacation, wouldn't you say?"

"Totally!"

"Really amazing!"

"Wonderful!"

Zephrum sat deep in thought.

As the morning light turned the sky a subtle tinge of pink, Zephrum began to stir under her sleeping bag. She and Daphne slowly rose out of their beds, changed into their day clothes, brushed their teeth, and packed their pajamas with the rest of their things. Then they met the rest of their group on the main deck of the yacht.

Before long, the group was picked up by a few taxis and brought to a little breakfast café in town, named "Casa Verde." Zephrum noticed that the roads were pretty rustic in Cape Larboard. "Look Daphne, the buildings look like they're constructed from a plaster stucko."

"Yeah," said Daphne, "And farm animals seem to roam free here too."

Their eyes widened as they entered "Casa Verde." It felt like walking into somebody's living room. The staff had prepared a large group meal, which was served family style.

Their morning breakfast at the café included tropical fruits of papaya and mango, as well as some very yummy egg and bean tortillas with slices of avocado and local spices.

"I think this might be the tastiest tortilla I've ever eaten," said Gai.

With mouths full, Zephrum, Daphne, and Niko had to agree by nodding their heads. After finishing their breakfast, the kids thanked all of the smiling staff as they left the restaurant.

The taxis were waiting to bring the entire group to a local landing strip on the outside edge of Cape Larboard. There, they all entered a small commuter plane to fly back up north.

Zephrum's ears popped as they rose higher in the air. It was the first time she had ever flown in an airplane. As she looked out of the airplane window, she discovered that the homes looked like little dollhouses and the people looked as small as ants. The airplane dipped up and down a bit as it adjusted to higher altitudes. Although it was exciting, it was a little unsettling. "I think I prefer flying by my own power," she said to Gai with a smile.

"Totally," he smirked.

After a little over an hour up in the air, the airplane started its descent. Eventually, their small aircraft landed on an airstrip at Freeman's Airport. Although it had taken them a number of days to get down to the southern shore, they had returned by plane in what seemed like no time.

After they landed, they piled into the Fiddlesticks shuttle, which was driven by the Gumption's butler, Edward.

Edward asked how their trip went and everyone started talking all at once. Obviously, there was a lot to share.

During a lull in the conversation, Edward informed them that a large storm was on the way. "You'd better not linger too long here in Freeman, as you should stay ahead of the storm. That way, you can all reach Fiddlesticks safely before dark."

The sky was gloomy and overcast when they finally arrived at Gumption Manor, but the air was warm and balmy.

Aunt Gussie said, "You can really feel that a storm is on its way, can't you?"

Inside the manor, the Gumption's chef had prepared a special light miso soup for everyone. After they finished eating the soup and freshening up, the whole crew headed for the Fiddlesticks commuter van, which would bring them on the long journey back up to Haversville.

Mr. and Mrs. Gumption hugged Daphne and Zephrum together. "Oh, we'll miss you," said Mrs. Gumption.

Mr. Gumption looked directly at Zephrum. "We'll expect a visit from you again before too long."

All of the kids were so full of gratitude and thanks, especially Zephrum. "It was a really eye-opening experience. Thankyou so much for bringing us on such a special adventure."

"Oh, you're going to make me blush," said Mrs. Gumption.

"We'll see you all again soon," said Mr. Gumption.

Then, they all waived goodbye as the shuttle pulled out of the gated driveway of Gumption Manor.

It was a long day of travel with gloomy gray skies looming overhead. Although they played road games to pass the time on their journey northward, everybody was really exhausted by the time they reached the winding dirt road to Fiddlesticks. "I'm going to sleep good tonight," said Daphne.

"Yeah," agreed Zephrum. "Me too. I'm so relieved we're so far away from that sea monster now."

"For sure," said Daphne. "FOR SURE."

As they drifted off to dreamland in their cabin beds at Fiddlesticks, bits of rain began falling from the sky. At first, the rain was just a drizzle that they could barely hear outside, but as the night grew darker, the rain increased. Zephrum and Daphne heard a relentless stream of water on their cabin's roof throughout the night.

The wind howled and the storm seemed to be gaining in strength. Leaves fluttered by the windows and the trees creaked. Branches broke off of trees, falling onto the roofs of the cabins. By morning, the grounds around Fiddlesticks were sopping wet. Puddles peppered the walking paths. Tree matter from the surrounding forest was strewn all over the place, littering the whole area with forest duff and branches. Meanwhile, the rain continued to pour down in sheets.

When Zephrum and Daphne got up to tend to the horses, all of their four-legged friends were clearly spooked by the creaking screams of the trees. Their manes shivered every time they heard a new creaking sound.

Geezer and Aunt Gussie ran over to the Sun Lodge and took their rain gear off as soon as they entered. Inside, they joined Rocko Pounder, who was listening to a news report on the radio.

The radio announcer spoke with urgency. "Roads are closed and the center of Haversville is flooding. The eye of this storm has not even hit our coastal area yet and we are already at an extreme saturation point. Because of the severe winds, weather experts are calling this storm a 'Tornicane'... part tornado and part hurricane."

"We had better batten down the hatches," said Aunt Gussie.

"Yeah," said Rocko. "It looks like we'll have to ride this storm out right here."

After finishing up with the horses, Zephrum and Daphne ran over to the Sun Lodge. They took their rain parkas off as they entered the back door. Dr. Malvin Moot, Mr. Dexter Droudy, Gai, Red, Misty, and Sarah Bellum squeezed in the door just behind them. They all removed their boots and rain gear just in time to hear the final bits of the news flash on the radio.

"Because roads north and south of us are closed, people traveling back into the area after their holiday vacations have no way back into town. Some climate scientists are saying that much of the flooding around Haversville could have been avoided if city planners had never allowed developers to pave over our wetlands. More on this later. For now, here's a list of all of the schools and businesses that will be closed until further notice."

Rocko turned the radio volume down. "Can you believe it? They say that this storm is probably the most intense downpour we've had in over 500 years."

Dr. Moot chimed in. "Scientists have been warning the public about more extreme weather for a while now. The value of wetlands in helping us to cope with flooding is immeasurable. As well as providing a habitat for numerous creatures, wetlands filter water down into the ground."

"I've heard that wetlands offer an essential cleansing process to fresh water too," said Sarah Bellum.

"Absolutely," replied Dr. Moot. "Water held in wetlands can drip down below to our water table, but because wetlands can also remove carbon dioxide and store it in the form of soil, wetlands are an affective carbon sink, helping us to remove pollution from our environment, naturally."

"You wouldn't think that people would pave over wetlands or build on top of them when they're so important," said Gai.

"No, you wouldn't think so," commented Dr. Moot. "97% of earth's water is salty and 2% is locked in snow and ice, so that leaves less than 1% of fresh accessible water for us. To preserve what we've got, we can create roads that seep and allow wetland plants to grow near vernal pools. Wetland plants can help aerate the ground, so that water can drain more easily where it tends to build up. It's all very logical."

"I've heard that wetlands are a safe breeding ground for salamanders and frogs too," said Gai.

"Yes, it's true," said Dr. Moot. "Frogs living in marshes and swamps also really help with mosquito control because they eat the bugs."

"It seems like bugs are the least of our problems right now," said Geezer.

"So true," said Aunt Gussie. "We've got to keep ourselves on our toes here. An argument about bugs just doesn't hold any water right now."

Zephrum and Daphne smiled at each other and tried to hold back their giggles.

"What I meant to say," said Aunt Gussie. "Is that we should focus on protecting the grounds around Fiddlesticks."

"It's true," said Rocko Pounder. "If water damages any of the structures around here, it will really twang on my last good nerve."

The kids didn't even know what to say.

"Rocko, did you just swear?" asked Misty.

"No, no," said Rocko. "I only swear when I'm driving, doing carpentry, working on cars, watching sports, or stubbing my toe. Why don't we start talking about wetlands again?"

Everybody giggled.

"Seriously, though," said Rocko. "Yuz' should all set up hay barriers around the structures and raise anything off the ground that might be in danger if we get more flooding around the property."

"Yes, we should get to it while we still can," commented Geezer. "With all of this rain, it looks like we're either going to sail together or sink together."

"Well, let's gear up and go out to the barn to create the hay barriers we need," said Rocko.

"We can wrap the hay into long narrow barricades, so we can control where the water seeps to," said Geezer.

They all got their rain gear and boots back on. Then, they ran through the raindrops to the dry barn structure. Leaves were fluttering around in the air outside, as the wind howled.

The sound of the wind was deafening and the rain kept pouring down. "I wonder how intense this storm is going to get," said Zephrum.

"It is a wonder, isn't it?" said Great Aunt Gussie. "A real wonder."

—Chapter 38—
"Go With The Wind"

At the edge of the sea, the storm was bashing large ocean waves up against Grizalda the Great's lighthouse. She looked out upon the large whitecaps with narrowed eyes. "This stormy upsurge is clearly the work of that Strasidous Rowpe. He is really starting to scratch my jewels. The squall is growing in such strength that it might even wash away some of my Gathering Squee. They're not all that pretty to look at, but I admit, I do like having them around."

She took another puff of her cigar. "It looks like I'm going to need to take matters into my own hands. I may need to get the whole of my Creeper Clan to rebel against this madness."

She took a puff from her cigar and said, "If we live through this tempest, we will set traps to impede Strasidous Rowpe's progress."

She rubbed the "all seeing eye" at the center of her turban and said, "Yes, I believe that this is war now. A war he cannot possibly win."

She closed her eyes, scratched at one of the green warts on her face, and picked a partially eaten grub out of her teeth. "He is not the only goblin with tricks up his sleeve."

Grizalda eeked out a crooked smile and took yet another puff of her cigar. "Yes, we in the Creeper Clan have tricks of our own." Then, she guffawed an ear-splitting cackle that echoed through her entire lighthouse. "Ha..ha..ha..ha..haaaa…"

Captain Muttonchops and his tango of pirates were also getting fairly antsy. His pirate underlings were drinking more rum than usual and brawling with each other.

"We have been confined indoors for too long now," said the one with the peg leg.

"When will we be free to seek treasure and adventure on our great ship?" asked the one with the longest beard.

"This foul weather is making me want to force a landlubber to walk the gangplank," said the tiniest pirate.

"Have we been hornswaggled?" asked the one with the most missing teeth.

Captain Muttonchops stroked his beard. "Ah…If we were being cheated, I would be the first to know. No, no hornswaggling here. Just bad weather is all."

"Are you sure we've not been marooned?" asked the littlest pirate.

"Me mateys," said Captain Muttonchops. "We will pillage and plunder soon enough. We'll have more swag and treasure than we can imagine."

"More loot than we can cram into our pockets?" asked the littlest pirate.

"Aye," confirmed Muttonchops. "More booty than we can fit in our ship's hull."

"Are you sure this Virgidous is not some kind of 'weevil'?"

"I tell ya' strait, he's a son of a biscuit eater, but he needs us, so he will surely give us our just deserves…or get the pox," cried Muttonchops.

All the pirates busted out in raucous laughter.

From the safety of the goblin caverns, Virgidous was listening to the giant storm. "The tumult and furor of this mammoth 'tornicane' will deliver the Leviathan to our shores, for sure! It was a brilliant scheme, if I don't say so myself."

With his newfound levity, he practically floated through the underground caverns to the narrow stone steps that led above ground to downtown Haversville. He looked at the center plaza and all of the closed shops. "Ahh…it brings such satisfaction to feast my eyes upon this storm. It is a guilty indulgence to see the achievement of destruction that I have forged." Virgidous grinned at the strength of the downpour. "To see my power in full force is exhilarating. This upheaval and mayhem fills me with an invigorating malice. I have needed this, Virgil."

"Yes, Sire," responded the Virgil voice from within. "We both rejoice in the chaos of this squall."

"Ah," said the stronger Strasidous voice. "But there is an order to this chaos."

"Yes, Sire… a method to the madness."

"Exactly," said Strasidous. "We see as one now, don't we Virgil?"

"Yes, Sire," said Virgil. "A great honor it is, to share this view with the likes of your greatness."

"Yes, Virgil," said Strasidous. "You are a very fortunate goblin, indeed."

"Indeed, Sire."

Virgidous smirked a pestilent grin and continued to watch the dark clouds heap buckets of rain upon Haversville.

Back at Fiddlesticks, the staff and students had finished setting up the last of the hay barriers around all of the structures of the property. Great Aunt Gussie said, "It sure is raining cats and dogs, isn't it?" Zephrum, Gai, and Daphne all nodded as they hung up their raincoats at the back entrance of the Sun Lodge. They took off their rain boots and got cups of warm cocoa from the kitchen. The trio huddled around the main fireplace with their warm cocoa mugs, sitting cross-legged on large pillows close to the hearth.

"How long do you think the storm will last?" asked Daphne.

"Not sure," said Gai.

"I've had the weirdest feeling about this storm all day," said Zephrum.

"Me too," said Daphne.

"I think we've all been a little freaked out about it," added Gai.

"No," said Zephrum. "It's more than that. I feel connected to the storm somehow."

"What do you mean?" asked Daphne.

"It's not as though I created it from my wind powers or anything, so it doesn't make any real sense," admitted Zephrum. "It's just... I feel a strange kind of power on the edge of it. I don't know how to explain it."

"Well, the weather report on the radio said that it was the most potent storm this area has experienced in over 500 years. It's probably going to make a huge amount of damage." said Gai.

"I know," said Zephrum. "But it's something else. There's some thread of a connection that I feel to this storm."

Daphne's right eyebrow lifted up, "Zephrum, what are you saying exactly? Do you think you could stop this storm?"

Zephrum shrugged. "Uh...I don't see how."

They all three sat in silence for a moment, staring at the flames in the fireplace.

Daphne broke their trance with an idea. "Maybe I should try to make a sketch, to see if we can get any messages about the storm?"

"That's a cool idea," said Gai. He lept up from his seat and said, "I'll get your sketchpad and be right back."

Within moments, Gai returned with Daphne's medium-sized sketch pad and some drawing charcoal.

She put the sketchpad on her lap and started to draw. At first, she sketched swirls of wind and rain on the page. Then, the weird eye in a triangle appeared in one corner of the sketchpad. At the bottom of the sketch, Daphne wrote "Wind, Wrong Way." Then, she sat back and looked at it.

"What does it mean?" asked Gai.

"I don't know," said Daphne.

They all sat there for a long weighty moment.

Zephrum finally asked, "Would changing the wind's direction be able to stop the storm in some way? I wonder if our oceanography book would have any information on how wind affects weather patterns?"

Gai lept up from his seat. "I saw one of our oceanography books over near the kitchen counter. I'll go get it."

In no time, Gai returned with the book, then flipped to the back index to see if there were any pages devoted to weather.

Gai said, "There's a whole chapter on ocean currents that talks about how warmer ocean waters contribute to larger hurricanes and there's a chart of wind speeds for a variety of large storms throughout history too."

Daphne peaked into the book. "It looks like there's some information on air currents and air pressure as well. Listen. The dominant air currents that affect climate are known as 'prevailing winds'. Prevailing winds are winds that blow in one direction more often than any other. Prevailing winds bring air from one type of climate to another."

Zephrum was following along. She read, "Warm winds that travel over water tend to collect moisture as they travel."

She looked up from the book. "Well, that makes sense. Maybe the storm could shift if the prevailing winds changed?"

"Rain causes storms to dissipate," said Gai. "Hurricanes rely on a constant source of moisture from warm ocean water to maintain themselves. If a storm moves over land, it loses strength."

"Maybe it's a good thing that we're getting such a strong storm over Fiddlesticks and Haversville? Maybe it will all die out soon," said Daphne.

Zephrum's face scrunched up. "Maybe?"

Gai continued reading. "Other ways that large storms dissipate is by encountering a mass of dry air. If a hurricane encounters strong wind shear, it can essentially be ripped apart."

"That's it!" said Daphne. She looked at Zephrum. "All you need to do it send a mass of dry air towards the storm!"

Zephrum's mouth opened, but no words came out.

Finally, Zephrum said, "I don't know how I'd ever do that. My wind powers aren't that developed. They kind of just happen whenever I get emotional over something."

"True," said Gai. "But they are growing and you're able to do a lot more than you could do last year. Plus, you're the one that said you felt connected to this storm. Maybe you could change its trajectory or get it to rip itself apart somehow?"

"That would be cool," said Zephrum. "But I really don't see how."

For a long moment that seemed to stretch beyond real time, all three of them sat in silence again. The glow of the fire light from the fireplace cast warm shadows upon their faces as little crackles of wood burned before them.

"I know," said Daphne, perking up. "We could use the rowen branch to help you."

"The rowen branch?!" exclaimed Zephrum. "We'd have to find where Dexter has hidden it and we'd need to be super specific and I'm not sure if we really know what we're doing. I don't know, Daphne. It seems too risky."

Again, silence filled the air between them.

"Well," said Gai at long last. "If we break it down logically, we can be clear on what we need to do." He grabbed Daphne's sketch book and turned to a blank page. "Let's just figure out what we know."

Gai started to make a list. "Winds, Wrong Way (from Daphne's sketch)… Prevailing Winds… and a Mass of Dry Air rips a storm apart." He looked up at the girls. "These seem like the most essential things we need to know."

"So," said Zephrum, thinking aloud. "We use the prevailing winds to send a mass of dry air in the direction of the storm and the strong wind shear should rip it apart?"

"Exactly," said Gai. "You're brilliant!"

Zephrum smiled, "I only just said what you said."

"Yeah, but you put it all together in a way that makes sense," said Gai.

Daphne took the sketch pad and wrote, "Use prevailing winds to send a mass of dry air in the direction of the storm…to rip it apart. That's it. Those are the specific words we need to use."

"What do you say, Zephrum?" asked Daphne.

"Well," said Zephrum thoughtfully. "IF we can find the rowen branch, it could work. But if we get caught using it, we could get in a huge amount of trouble."

"Yea," said Daphne. "But we'd stop the storm and prevent a lot of destruction. It might be worth the risk."

Gai finally weighed in. "What do you think, Zephrum? Can we do this?"

She thought for a moment and nodded. "Yeah. I think we can."

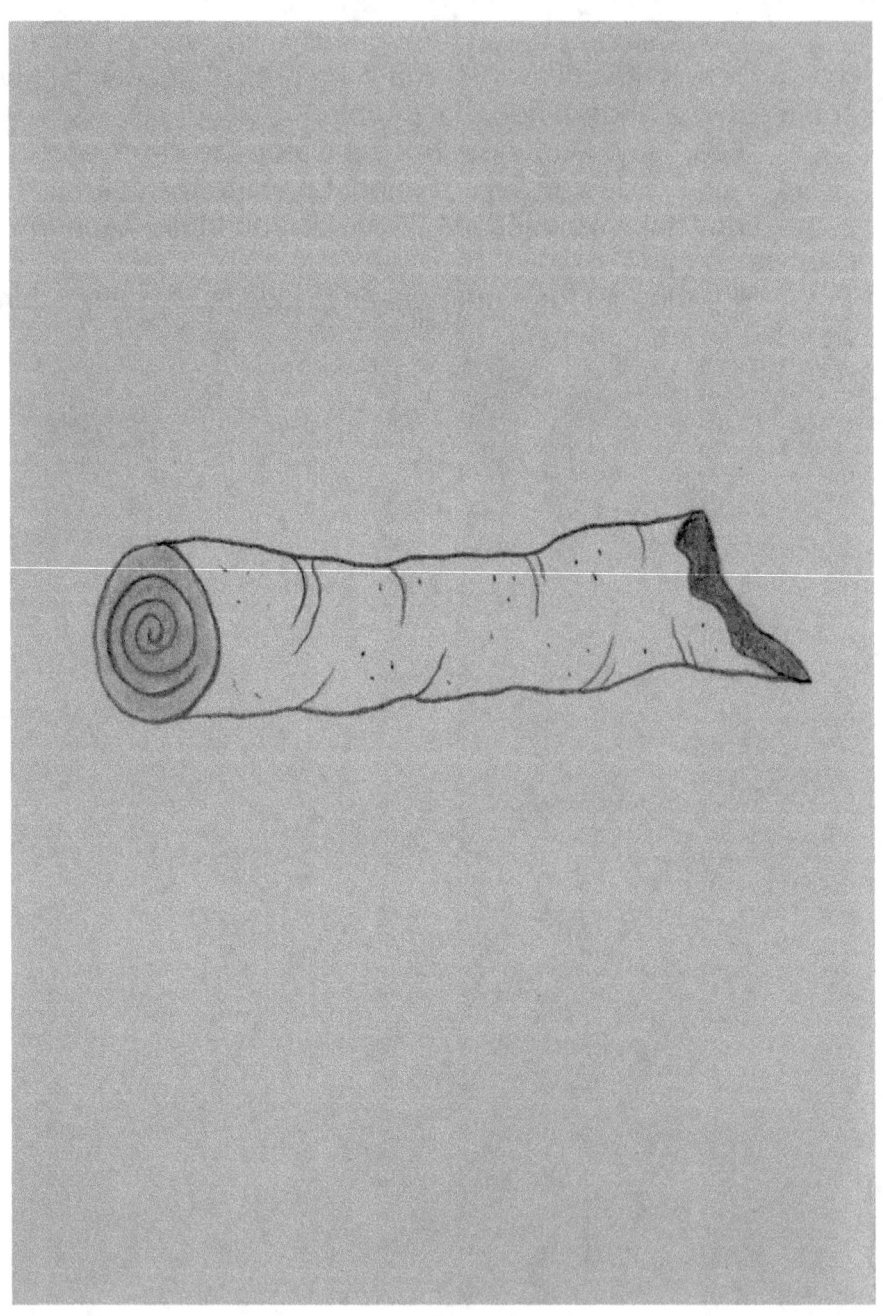

—Chapter 39—

"Possession"

Zephrum tore Daphne's sketch from the sketchbook, folded it up, and put it in her pants pocket, along with the piece of charcoal. They brought their cocoa cups over to the kitchen and they geared up to go outside.

"What are you kids doing now?" asked Great Aunt Gussie.

"Oh, we just have to go do one more thing," explained Zephrum as she slipped her boots on.

"OK, whatever floats your boat," said Aunt Gussie. "But don't stay out there too long. It's getting biblical out there."

The trio nodded and zoomed out of the Sun Lodge. They ran to the Lunar Mansion to search for the rowen branch. Once inside the Lunar Mansion, they tore off their rain gear and quickly dashed into Dexter's office.

They closed the office door quietly and started looking in all the most likely hiding places.

Zephrum opened his closet door and looked inside of boxes, Daphne opened up every one of the drawers of Dexter's desk, and Gai funneled through the file cabinets.

After many minutes of fruitless searching, Zephrum said, "I don't know. I'm not seeing it anywhere in here."

Daphne echoed the same sentiment. "Same here. There are a ton of other things, but no rowen branch."

Gai looked inside the last filing cabinet drawer. "Yeah. Nothing here either."

They all stood motionless for a moment, thinking.

"It was such a good idea, looking for the rowen branch in here," said Zephrum.

"I wonder if Dexter stored it somewhere else?" asked Daphne.

"This would be the most likely place, don't you think?" asked Gai.

"Yeah," said Zephrum in a quiet voice.

They all stood in silence for a moment.

Finally, Zephrum sighed. "It just feels like there's something really bad about this storm. Something beyond real nature."

"Totally," agreed Gai.

Zephrum turned around to look inside Dexter's closet one more time and said, "I wish we could find the rowen branch in here."

Gai came up to her, placed his arm around her shoulder, and encouragingly said, "If it's in here, we'll find it."

In that moment, a strange blue light emanated from a small shoe box on an upper shelf inside the closet.

Daphne was the first one to see it. She said, "Hey, check that out."

Gai reached for the glowing box and looked inside.

Wrapped within some old newspaper was the glowing rowen branch.

"Wow! Here it is," exclaimed Gai. "It's like it found US."

Daphne said, "Has that ever happened before?"

"No," said Zephrum. "We've never had to go looking for it before…cuz' we always stored it over near the bee hives and we always knew where it was."

"Zephrum… Did you notice how the branch started to glow the moment that Gai put his arm around your shoulder?" said Daphne.

"Hmm…" thought Zephrum. "I hadn't noticed, but that's pretty cool."

Gai put the shoebox back on the shelf, pocketed the branch safely inside his vest pocket. "Well, now that we have it, let's continue on with our plan."

They swooshed out of Dexter's office and quickly put their rain gear back on at the doorway of the Lunar Mansion. Then they sprinted through the raindrops towards the Circus Tent on the sopping wet grounds.

Once they squeezed through a seam in the Circus Tent flaps, they shook the dripping water off of their rain gear and came together in the center of the tent.

"OK," said Daphne. "So, how's this going to go?"

"Well," said Gai. "Like usual, we all need to be in physical contact with each other when we use the rowen branch, but we also really need to be specific with our words."

"Yeah," said Daphne. "We know that, but will we all remain here? Or will the rowen branch take us into the storm? What's going to happen?"

"I think we should try to influence the storm from here," said Zephrum. "I don't want to go inter-dimensionally traveling into a giant storm. That just sounds crazy."

"Agreed," said Gai.

"OK," said Daphne. "So, we just need to be super specific with our words…and be open to what happens after that. Where's that piece of paper from the sketch book with our list of specific stuff to say?"

Zephrum pulled it out from the back pocket of her pants and said, "Here it is."

They all eyed the page while Daphne read their wording out loud. "Use prevailing winds to send a mass of dry air in the direction of the storm…to rip it apart."

Zephrum added, "Can we skip the 'rip it apart' section? Why don't we say 'Use the prevailing winds to send a mass of dry air in the direction of the storm…and stop the storm."

"OK, fine," said Daphne. "I mean, it basically has the same end result, right?"

"Yeah," said Gai. "Basically."

"OK… Let's do this," said Zephrum. She haphazardly stashed the sketch under a gymnastic block on the floor of the Circus Tent.

Gai took the rowen branch out from under his raincoat and Zephrum and Daphne both touched it.

Zephrum cleared her throat. "Use the prevailing winds to send a mass of dry air in the direction of the storm…and stop the storm."

A feint blue light emanated from the rowen branch and connected to all three of them.

They sensed a balmy wind surrounding their bodies inside the Circus Tent. The wind picked up and circled into a spiral around them. They grabbed each other and held on tightly. Their hairs were flying around wildly. Suddenly, the warm balmy air that was swirling inside the Circus Tent scooped them up off the ground, pushed them outside of the Circus Tent, and DIRECTLY towards the storm.

All three of them were flying through the squall at an incredible speed… and surrounded by warm dry air.

"What the heck is going on?" said Daphne.

Zephrum and Gai just shrugged and held on tight.

As they flew closer and closer to the coast, the winds and rains from the tornicane intensified with increasing voracity.

Suddenly, Daphne's eyes rolled back into her head.

"Daphne! Daphne!" screamed Gai and Zephrum in concert.

Then, Daphne's eyes opened up VERY wide. An odd gravely voice came out of her mouth. "Listen to my foretellings and be forewarned! My advice to you is to prevent sea water from evaporating up into the eye wall of this tornicane."

Zephrum said, "Daphne, why are you talking like that?"

Daphne spoke with the gravely voice again. "I am not Daphne! I am 'Grizalda The Great,' the most feared and revered goblin fortune teller of all time."

Gai looked into Daphne's eyes. "Daphne? Come on, stop messing with us. We've got to stay focused here."

The torrent of wind was spiraling and picking up more speed as they traveled through the air.

Grizalda's voice came out of Daphne one more time. "Let us not waste time on the minutia of who's who. I am connected to this Daphne through her strange artwork. I live in a lighthouse at the edge of the sea, protected by my gathering Squee."

Zephrum and Gai looked at each other, perplexed and concerned, as the wind whistled all around them.

Grizalda's voice continued coming out of Daphne, "Now that this Daphne is closer to my lighthouse, I am able to speak through her."

"Whoa," said Gai.

Grizalda's voice went on. "I know that goblins have not done much to assist you in these past days, but I am your ally in your quest to stop this storm...and to stop Strasidous Rowpe."

Zephrum and Gai stared at Daphne with open-mouths. The spiral of wind flapped their rain gear and haphazardly blew their hair around.

Grizalda's voice continued. "In the center of the storm, over the ocean, the water goes from bubbles to air full of spray, with a smooth transition between the two. This fuels the rain clouds of the tornicane's tempest. The storm will continue to grow in strength until it gets ripped apart by a blast of warm air from prevailing winds going in the opposite direction. You must bring your balmy dry air with you to the walls of the CENTER of the storm."

"Holy Moly!" said Gai. "Daphne, come back to us!"

Grizalda's voice gave one last message. "Do not trouble yourself about my way of speaking. It is time to fight back. Strasidous Rowpe is not as 'all powerful' as he would lead you to believe. The Leviathan will deal him the worst of fates, in time...IF you do as I say."

Daphne's eyes fluttered back into her head and she shook herself awake. "Whoa..."

"Daphne?" asked Zephrum, looking into her eyes as they all three spun in swirls of wind in the air.

"Yeah..." she said, in her normal voice. "Zephrum, are you alright? You look like you just saw a ghost or something."

Daphne looked around at the swirling windstorm that they had clearly become a part of. "Whoa...it looks like we're traveling closer to the center of the tornicane. Are we sure we want to do that?"

Zephrum and Gai looked at each other in disbelief.

"Yeah, it looks like our blast of warm air really needs to make it all the way to the center of the storm if we want to stop it," said Gai at last.

As the trio blew closer and closer to the eye wall of the ever-growing cyclone, they had to work much harder to hold onto each other. The strength of the winds were so intense that it felt like they could all be torn apart by the fury.

"Hold on!" screamed Gai.

"Ahhhh…." "Ahhhh…." "Ahhhh…"

All three of them screamed as they plummeted into a twister of wind. It spun them so fast that the outside world looked like a blur.

With a final windy blast, all three of them and their blast of dry balmy air met with the eye wall of the storm. They spun in the center of a strange quiet as everything outside them whirled around.

"Now what?" asked Daphne.

"Yeah," said Gai. "It seems like the tornicane is as strong as it was before. What do we do now?"

Zephrum's eyes widened as she had a new idea. "I think our balmy dry air needs to be bigger and stronger than it is. I think we'll need to expand upon our original request."

"OK," said Daphne. "But we had better do it quick. All this spinning around me is starting to make me feel really nauseous."

"Agreed," said Gai.

Zephrum said, "Gai, hold the rowen branch out and I will direct it to help more."

Daphne squeezed Zephrum's arm harder and said, "Zephrum, are you SURE you know what you're doing?"

"No," said Zephrum. "But we have to try."

Gai held the rowen branch out and Zephrum spoke directly to it. "Rowen Branch… expand our mass of balmy dry air at the eye wall. The dry air must reduce the intensity of this tornicane, so that it can STOP the storm!"

Another blue flash of light flickered and emanated from the rowen branch, connecting Gai, Zephrum, and Daphne together.

In the next instant, the balmy air around them ballooned in size and filled the eye wall completely. It became such a massive force of warm dryness that the storm started to slow.

The winds lost their fuel and the ocean water got re-deposited back into the sea below.

Zephrum, Gai, and Daphne floated in the air within the eye of the storm, surprised beyond measure.

Back in the center of Haversville, Virgidous noticed that the storm was easing up. "How can this be?" he demanded.

He rushed out of the goblin tunnels and felt the downpour of rain turn to a light mist. "What is the meaning of this? Why isn't our plan working?"

He looked in the direction of the ocean and saw the dark clouds dissipating. "The gales from this massive storm were supposed to be the talk of the century. They were meant to bring destruction beyond repair...and troubles beyond troubles."

He was growing into an intensely foul mood as he considered his failure. "And what of the Leviathan? How will I lure it out of hiding now?"

"Sire," said the Virgil voice.

"What is it now?" snapped the stronger Strasidous voice.

"Is it possible that this tornicane has stopped BECAUSE the Leviathan has finally surfaced?"

"Oh Virgil," snarled Strasidous. "Must I explain EVERYthing to you?" He grabbed himself roughly by the jowels. "YOU were present for our storm invocation. You know what we conjured."

"Yes, Sire," said Virgil. "It's just a thought I had is all."

"Stop having thoughts, Virgil," said the Strasidous voice. "That's MY job."

"Yes, sire," said Virgil. "I forget my place."

Virgidous then spun around. The cape he was wearing snapped in the air before he slinked back into the goblin caverns.

Back at what was left of the eye of the storm, Zephrum, Gai, and Daphne watched in awe as the skies continued to clear before them.

"Wow!" exclaimed Zephrum. "It really worked!"

"Wow is right!" said Gai.

"I can't believe it," added Daphne, looking at Zephrum. "How did you know we had to make it all the way to the center of the storm? That was brilliant."

Zephrum and Gai just looked at each other.

"Uh… it's a long story, Daphne," said Gai finally. "Let's make our way back to Fiddlesticks and we can talk about it there."

He looked at Zephrum. "Do you think we're done here yet?"

Zephrum looked around at the slowing winds, the rain turned to mist, and the clearer skies on the distant western horizon. "Yes, I think we've done what we set out to do. Pretty wild, huh?"

"Indeed," agreed Gai.

He held out the rowen branch one more time and Zephrum spoke as she also touched it. "And now, we go back to Fiddlesticks, swiftly and safely."

In that moment, their bodies zoomed through the stratosphere, in the direction of Fiddlesticks.

--Chapter 40--

"Hissy Fit"

In the depths of the goblin caverns, Virgidous stomped on the ground and grabbed roughly at his long pointy ears. He was beginning to stammer into a large hissy fit. "Why didn't my plan work? Why did my giant tempest fizzle into nothing?"

He started to break bony torches off of the goblin's cavern walls as he passed them, unconcerned with the flames that fell to the ground in his wake. "I was finally feeling on the edge of my most malevolent power. The storm was bringing utter destruction and annihilation, just as I had invoked. It had so much momentum! HOW could it have petered out to a mere mist? How could it have become so WEAK?"

He said "weak" as though it was the dirtiest word in the underworld.

He raced through the goblin caverns with his fists clenched. When he got to the elder chamber, he took all of his anger out on his mammoth throne. He grabbed at the jewels and ornate decorations that he had painstakingly added to the royal seat months earlier. He yanked them off the structure and threw them to the ground.

Inside, he was burning with a white hot fury. He kicked at one of the wooden armrests from the throne, then ripped it off with his bare hands. He hammered the chair with the broken piece of wood, beating it into a crumbled mess on one side.

Zultr Zeki heard the ruckus. She poked her head into the doorway of the elder chamber. "Sire?"

Virgidous abruptly turned around, ferocious red eyes in a rage. In his madness, he threw part of the wooden chair in the direction of Warrior Zeki.

She snapped it from the air as it flung at her. She was ready for battle, but stood strong, awaiting Virgidous' next move.

Seeing her standing there, ready to fight, something snapped inside of Virgidous. He started laughing maniacally. "Bwa..ha..ha..ha..haa…"

Zultr Zeki remained in her solid stance.

"Ahhh…" exhaled Virgidous as his body breathed longer breaths. "That was exactly the kind of rampage I needed." He kicked some of his wrecked throne about on the floor a bit and breathed out a heavy wry smile, "Yes… That was vital to my mood, Zeki."

"Stand down, Warrior. I just had to express my frustration is all."

"Sire?" inquired Zeki.

"The storm, Zeki… It has failed."

"Failed?" asked Zeki.

"Yes. Fizzled to nothing."

"But sire! How?"

"I know not," admitted Virgidous.

Just then, the in-house goblin fortune teller (that Virgidous had met when he first arrived at the Goblin Grotto tunnels months ago) announced himself at the elder chamber doorway.

"Sire," said the teller courageously. "I have news."

"What news?" said Virgidous. He narrowed his eyes in the direction of the little goblin.

"Sire," said the teller, revealing a small crystal ball. "It's about your storm."

"What about the storm?" asked Virgidous with an agitated leer. "Haven't you seen? There IS no storm!"

"Sire," boldly continued the little goblin teller. "The storm has ceased due to the workings of Grizalda The Great AND Zephrum Gates and her friends."

"WHAT?!?!" screeched Virgidous.

"It's true," continued the teller. "They stopped it via old fairy magic. And they were assisted with possessed messages from Grizalda."

"Explain!!!" demanded Virgidous. He edged his body uncomfortably close to the teller. "Why would Grizalda assist that pipqueak, Zephrum Gates? Why?"

"Sire," said the teller, slightly averting his eyes. "Grizalda is opposed to your methods. The storm was putting her Gathering Squee in peril. Her lighthouse was on the edge of destruction, being so close to your tempest."

"Grrrr..." growled Virgidous.

In a teeny tiny voice, the small goblin fortune teller said, "Grizalda is working against you now, Sire."

Virgidous looked up and screamed upward to nowhere. "Ahrrrr...."

He grabbed for the teller's crystal ball. "Give me that fortune telling ball. I want to see it for myself." He looked into the images still lingering within the sphere. He could see Zephrum and her friends swirling as Grizalda's ugly face guided them.

A long uncomfortable moment went by, while Virgidous composed himself. With a sinister smirk, he announced, "Frankly, this only fuels my quest, Teller." He kicked at the other side of his throne until he heard the wood crack. Then, he looked up at Zeki and the in-house goblin fortuneteller and bellowed, "This is WAR!"

Back in the eye of the storm, Zephrum, Gai, and Daphne felt a strong blast of warm balmy air spin around them as it scooped them in the direction of Fiddlesticks. They zoomed through the air in what seemed like no time. They swirled under the flaps of the Circus Tent and drifted to a stop. Once they were solidly back where they started, they let go of one another and exhaled sighs of relief.

"Wow! That was a trippy experience," said Daphne. "Have you guys ever done something like that before? You know, while traveling by rowen branch?"

"No, not at all," said Gai.

Zephrum looked Daphne squarely in the eyes. "Daphne, while we were traveling to the eye of the storm, you started channeling a goblin fortune teller that called herself, Grizalda The Great."

"What?!" said Daphne. "What do you mean?"

"You spoke in her voice and had messages for us and everything," said Zephrum.

"What?! Really?!? That's totally weird," said Daphne. "I don't have any memory of doing that. Are you messing with me?"

"No," said Gai. "It kind of freaked us out, but I guess you're connected to her through your artwork somehow."

"Yeah," added Zephrum. "And she said that our proximity to her lighthouse was making it easier for you to channel her."

"Whoa..." Daphne's eyes bugged out.

"You really don't remember anything about it?" asked Zephrum.

"No," said Daphne.

Daphne bent down and picked up the sketch book from beneath the gymnastic block on the floor. She turned the page to look at the sketch she had drawn when they were sitting in front of the Sun Lodge fireplace. She pointed to the eyeball in the triangle. "This. This eyeball I've been drawing all year... It's hers, isn't it?" she asked.

Gai and Zephrum nodded.

"I'm seeing an image in my head," said Daphne. Once we get near another sketchbook, I can draw it out."

Zephrum said, "Well, I have a piece of charcoal in my pocket."

Gai ran towards the stacked milk crates that teachers used to store class rosters and stuff. He found a couple of clipboards. There was some blank paper on one of them. Holding up the clipboard with the paper on it, Gai asked, "Will this paper work?"

Daphne nodded. Zephrum gave her the small piece of charcoal from her pocket. They crouched down on one of the gymnastic mats on the floor as Daphne started drawing. Gai and Zephrum watched in awe as Daphne sketched an entire turban with the eye in a triangle in the center of it. Skeleton bones were attached to the sides of the turban. Below the headdress, Daphne drew a cracked face, bordered by wild hair. The mouth was half-open and revealed a number of oddly disfigured teeth. Finally, she drew a long cigar. Then, she looked up and said, "That's her. That's Grizalda The Great, isn't it?"

Gai and Zephrum really didn't know, but they had an eerie feeling that it was.

"Are you alright?" asked Zephrum.

"Yeah," said Daphne. "It's all a bit weird is all."

"Totally," agreed Gai.

Zephrum added, "I know that this whole thing is the kind of thing that Dexter wants to know about, but I don't think we should tell any of the teachers about what we did."

"Yeah," agreed Daphne. "Your Aunt Gussie will totally give us a lecture about how dangerous it was to take matters into our own hands."

"I know they'll be glad we don't have to worry about that storm any longer," added Gai. "But I'm sure they'll freak out about us stopping it the way we did. I'm not really up for hearing a lecture from anybody."

"Me neither," said Daphne.

"What about the rowen branch?" asked Gai. "Should we put it back in Dexter's office?"

"Well," said Daphne finally, "if we put it back now, nobody will ever know we used it."

"True," said Zephrum. "But I feel a lot safer knowing where it is."

They all stood looking at each other for a moment.

Zephrum finally said, "Well, we definitely don't want to get caught, so let's bring it back to Dexter's office."

Gai put his arm around Zephrum and said, "It looks like we'll be able to find it again, as long as we do it together."

The rowen branch glowed slightly.

"Ok, let's go put it back now, before anything else weird happens," Daphne agreed at last.

Zephrum and Gai separated and the rowen branch went back to looking like a regular branch.

The three of them slipped under the flaps of the Circus Tent and out into the misty air. They jetted over to the Lunar Mansion and put the rowen branch back in the shoebox inside of Dexter's closet, just as they had originally found it. Then they all made their way back to the Sun Lodge. As they took off their rain gear, they heard a radio announcer blaring the unlikely news about the tornicane dissipating. "In honor of this wonderfully surprising news, we've got a special song for all of our listeners."

In the next moment, they heard a woman's jazzy song blast from the radio's speakers. "Blue skies... smiling at me... Nothing but blue skies...do I see..."

A peachy color from the sky beamed through the Sun Lodge windows and all of the teachers and kids inside brightened as well. Soon, everyone in the Sun Lodge was dancing together in celebration of the great news.

Zephrum, Gai, and Daphne smiled as they looked upon the scene. Daphne said, "Aww... they look so happy. We did good, guys."

"We sure did," said Gai, grabbing Zephrum by the hand and pulling her into the open area of the Sun Lodge. Gai twirled Zephrum around and started dancing amongst the others. Zephrum didn't really know how to dance, but she was having fun, all the same.

Daphne watched the scene, thinking how sweet it was. Suddenly, Grizalda's voice came out of her just loud enough for only her to hear, "Yeah, they're almost as cute as my Gathering Squee, aren't they?"

Daphne put her hand over her mouth as her eyes opened as big as saucers. In her regular voice, she said, "Whoa... I can't believe I heard that. It sure is pretty weird."

--Chapter 41--

"The Kiss"

After the storm, spring classes at Fiddlesticks resumed in earnest. Zephrum was super busy with all of her school work and responsibilities. She had tons of studying to do and it took a lot of time to take care of the horses too. She thought out loud about everything. "I know that Strasidous Rowpe is still out there, but our success in quelling the giant tornicane gave me a kind of unexpected confidence."

One morning as they were dressing, Daphne grabbed Zephrum by the shoulder. "What's different about you? Does it have something to do with Gai?"

Zephrum blushed. "Noooooo…. Gosh, Daphne."

"Well, we know you like each other," said Daphne. "Heck, even the rowen branch responds when you guys touch each other. I mean, that can't be normal."

"Nothing about that branch is normal," said Zephrum.

"True," agreed Daphne. "But don't you feel something?"

Zephrum fell face first onto her bed and burrowed her head under her pillow.

"Well, I guess that's a yes," said Daphne.

"Alright, already. Yes."

"OK… so what are you going to do about it?" Zephrum rolled herself into a lump. "I don't know. I like him so much. I mean, me and Gai really have a lot of fun together. And it's so easy to talk to him too."

"So," said Daphne. "Everything's great. You should tell him how you feel."

Zephrum's eyes rolled. "Oh, he already knows how I feel."

"Does he?" asked Daphne.

"Yeah, of course," said Zephrum. "How could he not?"

"I don't know," said Daphne. "Most guys are pretty dense. You might need to clue him in a little."

"How do you know so much about guys?" asked Zephrum.

"Oh…it's just common knowledge that girls mature faster than boys," said Daphne. "My Mom says that most men don't get emotionally integrated until they're in their mid-30's."

"What?!?" said Zephrum. "What's that supposed to mean?"

"Well," said Daphne. "My mom says not to expect too much of them. That way, when they seem to have ANY sense at all, we're impressed."

Zephrum giggled. "That's not really fair. What about cool sensitive smart boys like Gai?"

Daphne raised her eyebrows. "What about those boys, Zephrum?"

Zephrum blushed. She picked up her backpack full of books. "I don't know. How am I supposed to know?"

Daphne cracked up. "You know that I'm messing with you, right?"

"Yeah," admitted Zephrum. "I guess I'm just not sure what to do with all of the fluttery feelings I feel in my stomach when I see him. I wonder if Nurse Asa has anything for it. Maybe it's a weird kind of indigestion that is only caused by being around certain people?"

Daphne laughed out loud. "Yeah, why don't you go ask Nurse Asa if she has a remedy for you. Ha! Ha!"

"Very Funny," said Zephrum. She sat down and pulled on her shoes.

"Why don't you just enjoy it?" asked Daphne. "I mean, it's kind of fun, isn't it?"

"Yeah," said Zephrum. "It really is."

After classes were over for the day, Zephrum was busy taking care of the horses in their barn when she heard a weird scuffling sound coming from the garden shed.

She darted outside the horse barn. "Get your grubby little hands off me!"

Zephrum sprinted over to the garden shed. A goblin's bony fingers were wrapped around Gai's arm. "Oh good. Miss Gates is here." It sneered. "This gift will be for The Great One, our Virgidous. He wanted us to bring him something that YOU care about. You WILL help Virgidous, Miss Gates. Whether you want to or not."

"Let him go," screamed Zephrum.

"Oh, I'll let him go," said the goblin. "I'll let him go WITH ME."

With a snap of his fingers, Gai and the goblin disappeared.

Zephrum raced over to where Gai and the goblin just stood, but there was no trace of either of them.

She bolted over to the Sun Lodge and found Aunt Gussie in the kitchen with Mrs. Fliffle.

"Aunt Gussie… Aunt Gussie!! A goblin just took Gai away with a snap of its fingers. He said that Virgidous wanted something that I cared about. What are we going to do? How are we going to get Gai back?"

"Oh my!" exclaimed Aunt Gussie. "That Strasidous Rowpe is really ticking me off. Where did this goblin say he was taking him?"

"He just said it was for The Great One, for Virgidous."

"Mmmm…" thought Aunt Gussie. "I think we should meet up with the teachers to get the ball rolling on this one."

"OK…you do that and I'll go find Daphne."

Zephrum tore over to the Lunar Mansion and rushed into the Art Studio. Daphne was in there by herself. She blurted out, "Daphne! Gai got taken by a goblin just now!"

"What?!? When? How?" asked Daphne.

"Just now," said Zephrum. "The goblin said that he was a gift for Virgidous. That he wanted something that I really cared about. Then, he snapped of his fingers and they both disappeared."

"Whoa…What are we going to do? How are we going to get him back?"

"I don't know," said Zephrum. A subtle wind feathered art papers around on the tables. Zephrum's emotions were on the rise. "I was hoping YOU might be able to help us figure out a clue."

Daphne walked over to a large sketchpad on an easel and closed her eyes for a moment. When she opened her eyes, Daphne started to draw the familiar eyeball in a triangle. Then came a number of vines, all running vertically along some kind of textured surface. At the bottom of the page, she wrote, "Creeper Clan."

Zephrum urgently asked, "What does that mean, Daphne?"

Daphne closed her eyes and then opened them wide. She spoke in the voice of Grizalda The Great. "Don't you worry about a thing, Miss Gates. I...Grizalda The Great... will get your friend back for you. This is a clash of the clans. Goblin business. Give me the length of one day and your Gai will be returned to you."

Daphne's eyes rolled back inside her bobbling head. She blinked. That was Grizalda, wasn't it?" she said in her normal voice.

Zephrum nodded.

"What did she say?" asked Daphne.

"She said it was goblin business, a clash of the clans, and that she'd get Gai back to us in the length of one day."

"Whoa..." said Daphne. "I wonder where he went."

Zephrum pointed to Daphne's sketch. "Maybe to the Creeper Clan? Wherever that is."

Meanwhile, Gai had been transported to the deep darkness within the bowels of the goblin tunnels beneath Haversville. His arms were bound behind his back with a twine and his mouth was silenced with a magical goblin clothe stuffed into his mouth.

The tiny goblin that had brought him to the underground caverns poked him above the ear. "First, I will read your mind to find out the plans you have with Miss Zephrum Gates. This is our main reason for collecting you." The goblin climbed onto Gai's body and put his long gray fingers around Gai's head. He looked deep into Gai's eyes to see inside his thoughts.

"Hmmm…" said the goblin. "So you do have plans, I see."

Gai couldn't respond.

"We will want to question you further about your ocean invention, but I must drag you into our fathomless chambers for such interrogation." The goblin tried to drag Gai through the short tunnels, but Gai was much taller than the tunnels. He had to stoop over and simply couldn't be dragged too fast that way.

"Why must you be so TALL?" complained the goblin. "We will need to shrink your body, so that you will fit into our tunnels better. I need the help of my artifacts of power. You will stay here for a while, towering stick."

Gai stood silent. He couldn't say anything.

"I will go get my satchel of magical stones and artifacts. With those tools, I will be able to cast a spell that will transform you into any size I like. First, I will put a binding spell upon you." The goblin waved his hands in one big swoosh. "Kaalkac Maagaan! Remain here."

The goblin walked in the direction of his personal chamber to get his satchel of magical stones.

Gai wanted to run from the dark dank tunnels, but he couldn't move his legs. What was he going to do now?

Suddenly, a strange looking goblin slunk around the corner of the tunnel. "Shhhh…" hushed the goblin as she put one finger up to her lips. "I am here from Grizalda's Creeper Clan. I will rescue you!"

"Akec Mel. Unbind him," whispered the goblin. The twine that tied Gai's wrists together began to unravel.

When his hands were free, Gai removed the goblin cloth from his mouth.

"Dhaan men kaac! Free his Legs!" commanded the Creeper Clan goblin.

Gai was suddenly able to move his legs again.

"Very good," said the rescuing goblin. "Now, come with me."

The tiny goblin who had originally captured him returned with his satchel of stones. "Stop! Thief! This human is MINE."

Suddenly, energy balls were flying past him. Gai ducked and the Creeper Clan goblin warded them off the best she could.

Gai decided to help his rescuer by putting his hand in the way of two energy blasts. In that instant, the goblin that brought Gai to the underground caverns was knocked unconscious. Gai unfortunately got whammied with the same vibe. He buckled at his knees. The Creeper Clan goblin caught him just before he hit the ground.

Although she was a fairly small goblin, the rescuing goblin possessed a goblin's super strength. She hoisted Gai up around her shoulders in a kind of fireman's carry until she came across an underground trolley. Once inside the rusty old trolley, they swerved through the musty darkness until they reached the Creeper Vines that led to Grizalda's infamous lighthouse. The goblin hoisted Gai out of the water well at the top of the Creeper Clan's Vines. She carried Gai over the sand and to the entrance of Grizalda's lighthouse, where Grizalda stood at the doorway. She puffed on a cigar and waved her hand in a way that lulled her Gathering Squee into a dreamy surrender of snoozing. The matted hair under her turban looked as though it had been living under a rock for a thousand years.

Grizalda gazed at the rescuing goblin. "Fine job, goblin. For now, Virgidous will not be able to proceed with his twisted plans."

Grizalda took a closer look at Gai. "Pity he's gone unconscious. I would like him to feast his eyes on my glorious form." She took another puff of her cigar and re-positioned her turban on top of her head. "Oh, it's probably better this way, for he's unlikely to be able to resist my charms."

She picked a bit of grit from her teeth and spit it onto the ground. Grizalda and the rescuing goblin then flashed toothy grins at each other. Grizalda said, "Before we return him to whence he came, I would like to implant a message in his head."

She stood in front of Gai's body. "Tell Miss Gates that she must begin truly trusting her feelings about all things. Tell her that she must act on her instincts, even when faced with new and unfamiliar circumstances. It is then that her true heart will guide her best."

Grizalda placed her gnarled and cracked hands out in front of her as she commanded her ancient goblin magic. "Kaakhor den molkac duun men tuuch! Return this human to his school." A zoom of ultra-bright light surrounded Gai as he was then transported back to Fiddlesticks.

Gai's unconscious form instantly appeared laying on the grass in front of the Healing Dome. Nurse Asa almost tripped right over him as she was leaving for dinner. She checked Gai's pulse and breathing, then she ran over to the Sun Lodge to find somebody who could help her move Gai's body into the Healing Dome.

Rocko Pounder and Dexter used a portable stretcher to move Gai's limp body onto one of the Healing Dome cots. Nurse Asa set him up with some intravenous drip hydration tubes and she hooked him up to a few monitors, so she could track his vitals. Aside from being completely comatose, Gai's body appeared to be functioning fine. Even so, Gai laid unconscious.

News of Gai's condition spread rapidly through the Fiddlesticks Community. Zephrum and Daphne were especially worried.

"I wonder what happened to him after that goblin took him away?" said Daphne.

"I don't know," said Zephrum. "The whole thing is super weird."

The next morning, Zephrum found it very difficult to focus on being in class, knowing that Gai was laying unconscious in the Healing Dome. She made it through oceanography class in the morning, but was so pre-occupied that it's as though she wasn't really there. Her thoughts wandered. "All I can think about is Gai. I want him to wake up and I want us to be able to have fun together, like we usually do. I feel so weak inside, like something has taken over every cell inside my body. It feels like some weird sickness has gotten into me, and from every crack in my skin. What the heck is that?"

When Dr. Malvin Moot's class was over, Zephrum whispered to Daphne. "I'm going to skip my classes for the rest of the day. I have to go see Gai. I can't think of anything else."

Daphne nodded. She understood.

Zephrum ran to the Healing Dome. "Has there been any change?" she asked Nurse Asa.

"No dear, but his vitals are stable, so I'm hopeful he'll come around."

Zephrum pulled a chair up close to Gai's cot. She wrapped her hands around his forearm. She knew he couldn't respond, but she started to babble even so. "I've heard that people recover from head injuries a lot more quickly if they hear music or if loved ones talk to them, so I'm just going to talk to you."

She looked up and rolled her eyes. "Oh man, I feel as nutters as Aunt Gussie right now, but here it goes." She took a deep breath in and whispered, "I was so worried when I saw that goblin take you away. And totally freaked out about how he did it too. I mean, with the snap of his fingers? How are we supposed to protect ourselves from that kind of magic?"

She shrugged and bit her lip. "I really want to know what happened to you. I want to hear what you experienced. I want to know how you got back here. I want to know how it all made you feel."

A tear rolled down Zephrum's cheek. "Oh no, now my eyes are leaking." She wiped the tear away, but more started forming. "OK…so I admit it. I really like you, Gai. It's all really new to me, but I feel so open to you and my stomach gets all fluttery when I'm around you and it's all so embarrassing."

She pulled a tissue from the tissue box near Gai's cot and blew her nose. "Now, look at me. I'm a mess." She smiled awkwardly, then continued. "So, anyway… I feel too shy to tell you how I feel. I'm afraid how you'll respond if I expose my true feelings. I don't want to ruin our friendship with strong emotions I don't really even understand in myself. I just really like you a lot and I've never felt like this before, so I don't know. I guess it just freaks me out a little and that's why I act so awkward and stupid sometimes."

She blew her nose one more time. "I don't know what I'm doing here. I mean, you're unconscious. Why couldn't I tell you these kinds of things when you could actually understand me?"

Her chin trembled. "I guess I just get scared, ya' know? Like, what if you don't feel the same way and I freak you out and mess up our friendship? I would never want that." She wiped the tears running from her eyes. "I definitely don't want to think about that. That would be the worst, not having you as my friend."

She sniffled. "Obviously, sharing my feelings is not helping matters here. I'll just tell you about things at Fiddlesticks."

"OK, so after you were taken by that goblin, Daphne created a sketch that had vines on it…and a mention of the Creeper Clan, whatever that is. Then, she spoke in the voice of Grizalda the Great for a moment. It was pretty weird. This Grizalda said she would return you to us and that all of this was goblin business." Zephrum got more animated. "I know, right? We didn't know what we were supposed to do. And it's not like I could use the rowen branch without you, so all we did was wait. Aunt Gussie got the teachers together for a private meeting, but I have no idea if they came up with any brilliant theories. Anyway, when you showed up here, I was so relieved. But also freaked out that you showed up unconscious and unable to talk or move or anything." She brought her face super close to his. "Gai…what's going on inside you right now? Come back to us."

Gai's still form remained motionless.

She rested her head on his arm. "OK, so I'm just going to tell you all about my super boring day so far." She proceeded to tell him all about mucking out the horse stalls in the morning, about the same old breakfast ritual they had in the Sun Lodge every morning. Then, she blabbered on about how she couldn't pay ANY attention in Dr. Malvin Moot's class.

"It's true," she said. "I couldn't think of anything else. All I could think about is how I could have helped you if I got to you sooner. Or how I could help you if I was near you now. I don't know. I just feel so much more alive when I'm around you. I feel whole and at home somehow. I don't know how to explain it."

She blew her nose again. "I don't know what's wrong with me. It's not as though you're dead or anything. Come on Gai, please wake up."

Gai made a weak groan.

"Gai? Can you hear me?"

"Uh, huh…" Gaid responded.

"Are you ok? Can you talk? Do you understand me?"

"Uh…huh…"

"Oh… I'll get Nurse Asa," said Zephrum.

"No," said Gai. His eyes flickered open. "I want to talk to you."

"OK," whispered Zephrum.

"I have this weird message for you. Not sure why it's so important."

"OK...What is it?" asked Zephrum in a soft voice.

"Zephrum, you must begin to truly trust your feelings about all things. You must act on your instincts, even when faced with new and unfamiliar circumstances. It is then, that your true heart will guide you best."

Zephrum then leaned forward and kissed Gai right on the lips. It was a soft lingering kiss. She sat back in her chair.

Gai's eyes opened more. He smiled and said, "I must be Sleeping Beauty."

Zephrum grinned. "Yes, you definitely are."

Gai lifted his free forearm up and grabbed for Zephrum's hand. He looked her in the eyes. "I heard all the stuff you said to me earlier. It must have taken a lot of guts to say all those things."

"You could hear everything I was saying?" asked Zephrum.

"Yeah, but I couldn't respond. I got caught in the crossfire of these two goblins that were duking it out with energy blasts in their underground caverns. Ever since that happened, I've been able to sense what's going on around me, but my body couldn't respond or do anything."

"You got caught in between a couple of energy blasts?" asked Zephrum.

"Yeah," said Gai. "Long story."

Gai's eyes became heavy again.

"You don't have to talk about it right now," said Zephrum. "Just get better and get your strength back. We can talk about it later."

"Yeah," said Gai. "But I want to tell you, Zephrum. I really like you too. More than I should, I think."

--Chapter 42--

"Strategy"

Zephrum jumped up and called for Nurse Asa. "Nurse Asa! Nurse Asa! He woke up! Now, he's back asleep again, but he woke up!"

Nurse Asa went over to Gai's cot. She took his pulse and checked the monitors around him. "He seems stable. Did he say anything when he woke up?"

Zephrum blushed a little. "Uh, yeah. He said lots of things."

"Did he have any explanation for what happened to him?" asked Nurse Asa.

"Ah," said Zephrum. "Well, he said he got whammied by a couple of energy blasts, but he didn't get totally into it."

"What else did he have to say?"

"Well, it's a little hard to explain. He was mostly responding to stuff I had said to him while he was unconscious. And he had a message for me."

"What was that?" asked the nurse.

"Well," explained Zephrum. "It had to do with me trusting my instincts and stuff." Zephrum shrugged. "It was, well, it was... personal stuff."

"It's a good sign, either way," said Nurse Asa. "We'll try to wake him every two hours from now on, so that he won't slip into a permanent coma."

"Can I stay longer? I'd really like to be near him right now if that's okay."

Nurse Asa nodded. "OK, fine. Just let me know if he wakes up again, okay?"

Zephrum nodded her head and went right back to Gai's side. She just rested her head on his arm while he slept.

A couple of hours went by, with Zephrum snoozing alongside Gai. Daphne eventually brought a plate of food over to the Healing Dome. She woke Zephrum up and said, "How's he doing? I brought you something to eat."

Zephrum shook herself awake. "Oh, he woke up, Daphne. He can understand everything we say. He just can't totally respond right now. Nurse Asa thinks he'll be okay, though."

"What did he say when he woke up? Does he know what happened to him?" asked Daphne.

Zephrum started blushing again. "It was all kinds of stuff. But yeah, he only just started to tell me about what happened when he drifted off again."

Zephrum grabbed Daphne by the arm and pulled her to a spot outside of Gai's hearing range. She whispered to Daphne, "I told him how I feel and now I feel totally exposed," she whispered. "I thought that expressing myself was supposed to help, but now I'm not sure."

"Did he respond? Or was he too unconscious to talk?"

"He said he likes me too," said Zephrum.

"That's great," exclaimed Daphne. "So, what's wrong then?"

"I don't know," said Zephrum. "It changes things. That's scary."

"Oh Zephrum, Stop freaking out over nothing."

Nurse Asa saw the girls talking. "OK, girls. Visiting hours are over now. You can come back and see Gai again tomorrow."

The girls gathered their things and then, left the Healing Dome.

The next day, Zephrum made it to two classes before going over to visit with Gai. She stopped by her cabin to grab a few things first. When she entered the Healing Dome, Gai was sitting on his cot with all kinds of pillows propping him up.

"Hey…You're ok!" said Zephrum.

"Well, I can talk now, but my legs still won't move. I can feel them, but I'm still kind of stuck here until they start working again."

"Wow!" exclaimed Zephrum. "Those goblins really whammied you, didn't they?"

"Yeah, it seems so," said Gai. "What's in the bag?"

Zephrum brightened. "Well, I brought us some games to play." She pulled a couple of games out. "I brought checkers and chess and playing cards too."

"Great! Let's play!"

Gai watched Zephrum set up the checker board. "I used to play checkers with my cousins. They're younger than me, so of course, I would always win."

Zephrum smiled. "Well, I don't think you'll be winning today, Mister."

"Oh yeah? Is that a challenge?"

She nodded. "Black or Red?"

"Black, for sure," said Gai. "Black goes first, right?"

"Yup," said Zephrum smiling. "Starts firsts and loses first."

They played a couple of quick games of checkers. After each of them had won a round, Gai said, "Checkers is too easy. Let's play chess."

"Are your sure you're up for it?" asked Zephrum.

"For sure," said Gai.

Chess was a lot more challenging.

Zephrum captured three of Gai's pawns in a row.

"Not fair. You're taking advantage of my weak condition."

"That's right," said Zephrum smiling. "You'd better get better quick, or else you'll definitely lose."

"Oh, man…" moaned Gai.

Zephrum finally said, "So, about all the things we said yesterday…"

"Yesterday?" asked Gai.

"Yeah, You know when I told you how I felt and you said you felt the same way."

"I don't know," said Gai. "I don't remember anything that happened yesterday. What did we talk about?"

Zephrum's jaw dropped. It was her first real kiss and it felt so amazing to finally connect with Gai in such a close way. She was so happy about how mutual it felt…and how deep and real and alive her body felt too. She just couldn't believe that he had no memory of it. It's like it never happened for him. But for her, it opened up a cascade of feelings that were rushing through her like an unstoppable river. She sat in front of Gai, stunned.

"Zephrum?" asked Gai. "Are you ok?"

Zephrum sat like a stone. "Oh, uh… never mind. It's not important."

"Well, you brought it up for some reason," said Gai looking beyond the chess pieces to her face. "What did we say?"

Zephrum froze. "Really, it's nothing."

"What did we say?" asked Gai, more insistently.

"Uh…" Zephrum looked away from Gai.

"Come on, Zephrum. What did we talk about?"

"I was just wondering what you remembered is all," she finally said.

"I don't remember much, but I'm sure glad it's all over."

Zephrum felt a big lump in her throat. She fumbled with her backpack. "Oh, I forgot. I've got so much homework to do. I really can't stay."

"What about our chess game?" asked Gai.

"We'll just have to finish it another time."

"Are you afraid you'll lose?" asked Gai, a grin on his face.

Zephrum cracked half of a grin. "Nooo… I just have to go is all."

"Uh, ok. Well, when will you come back?"

"I don't know," said Zephrum. "Just rest and get better, ok?"

She slung her bag over her shoulder, leaving the chess board behind. She ran out of the healing dome, all the way to the horse barn. She wrapped her arms around Majestic's long neck and started to cry. Wind feathered his mane as Zephrum's tears ran down her checks. "What is wrong with me? Why am I so sensitive? Why does it matter anyway?"

The stream of tears continued. "I feel so stupid, crying over the loss of something that never got to be. Crying over something that never even happened for him. Why do I care so much anyway? Why do I feel like I have to hide myself away in this dusty barn?"

She wiped her tears away from her face and sniffled. "It's just, I feel so exposed and weak all of the sudden. And all over nothing. My emotions feel like a roller coaster and I want off the ride. What is wrong with me? Why can't I be cool? If I was Daphne, I'd be able to pretend better. I'd be able to be confident, no matter what Gai does or doesn't do. Being a girl sucks!"

Meanwhile, deep within the goblin caverns under Haversville, Virgidous was strategizing with Zultr Zeki and the elder goblins.

"What did we learn from our probe into the mind of Zephrum's tall friend?" asked Virgidous.

The goblin with the jewel-studded cowboy hat grinned. "It appears that Zephrum and her people are creating an invention to surround your garbage island in the ocean."

"Is that so?" said Virgidous.

"Yes, sire," continued the goblin. "And it appears that they will complete this project by the end of this spring. Very soon."

"Very good," said Virgidous.

"We also learned that the Leviathan despises Zephrum Gates, for she disturbed his slumber in warmer shores this past winter," said the goblin with the longest necklaces.

Virgidous rolled his hands together. "So, the Leviathan is looking to destroy Zephrum Gates for us? This is grand news. Better than if I had planned it myself."

"We will be ready for them when they set out to contain our garbage island, sire. Our pirate ship will be lurking. There is no way that Zephrum Gates will be able to escape," said the goblin with the most ornate robes.

"Yes, sire," said the goblin with the satin pants. "Either we will capture her...or the Leviathan will destroy her. In any case, we win."

Virgidous smiled a sinister smirk. "We will plan to surround her. We'll let the Leviathan crush her to bits. Then, we will kill the Leviathan."

Virgidous looked at Zultr Zeki. "You have a special bow and arrow that can pierce the scales of this fierce creature, yes?"

"Yes, sire," said Zeki. "Most definitely."

Virgidous smirked another sinister smile. "I can almost taste our victory now."

Back at Fiddlesticks, the spring semester was really moving into full swing. Gai got all of the movement back in his legs, so he was able to get back to classes again. He and Zephrum didn't talk about their kiss or the stuff he didn't remember. She felt closer to him somehow, but guarded too.

Thinking about playing games with Gai while he was stuck in bed was fun. "I'll just have to focus on what works, not on what could have been," said Zephrum to herself. "I still don't know what to do with all of the fluttery feelings in my body when I see him. And the nausea I feel when I'm away from him. It's all pretty weird. I will have to make a promise to myself that I'll just stay focused on school things."

In their "Scientific Inventions to Change the World" class, Dr. Malvin Moot was getting the students to step up their production of all of the parts they would need for their array.

It seemed like all of Fiddlesticks was obsessed with the completion of their giant science project. Students attached small solar panels to each one of the large filters and they made sure that the inner parts were put together just right. They took a lot of time to plan how they'd be containing the garbage island out at sea…and how they'd put the filters together once they were out there.

Day turned into night…and night bled into day.

Their other classes were demanding a lot of attention as well, but the invention to rid the oceans of trash was at the forefront of everybody's minds, more than anything else.

The weekend before they were scheduled to get their array into the water was beautiful. The skies were clear and the weather was great.

Dr. Malvin Moot said, "Looks like we'll be ready any day now. And it looks like it will be perfect weather for us this week as well. I am soooo very excited."

The night before their big field trip to the ocean, Gai approached Zephrum. "Hey, do you want to go hang out near the barn and look at the night sky? You know, so we can talk about tomorrow and stuff. The skies are so clear that I'm sure we'll be able to see tons of stars."

"Sure," she said. "Let's meet over near the barn after the sun goes down."

Once at the barn, they sat leaning against a couple of hay bales. They looked up. The sky was a blackening canvas, dotted with specks of sparkling white diamonds.

A cool night breeze sent goosebumps across Zephrum's forearms. Gai pointed out certain constellations that he knew until he noticed that Zephrum was shivering a little.

"Hey," said Gai. "It looks like you could use my jacket."

He took his jacket off and wrapped it around her shoulders.

She felt a chill running down her spine, but it wasn't really due to the cool air. "Why does Gai have to be so dreamy?" thought Zephrum in her mind.

Gai leaned his body back onto the hay bales and pointed at a quick streak of light. "Hey, look! It's a falling star."

Zephrum took in an extra big breath. "Wow!" She smiled as she felt the moonlight shining on her face.

A long quiet moment stretched between them as they looked up at the glistening.

Finally, Gai asked, "So, are you worried about going back to the ocean tomorrow? You know...cuz' of all of the weird things that happened all of the other times we went out there?"

Zephrum looked up into the twinkling sky. "I don't know. Seeing a globster has got to be a pretty rare thing. I mean, what are the chances of seeing one of those again?"

"True," said Gai. "But what about the Leviathan?"

"Well," said Zephrum. "Since we saw it when we were down in the southern shore, I doubt we'll see it again. We're so far north that we're probably far away from its territory up here."

"I'm thinking that we should bring the rowen branch on the field trip with us, just in case," said Gai.

"Good idea," agreed Zephrum. "So long as we can get it from Dexter's office closet tomorrow morning before we all leave. I think he locks his office door at night."

"Yeah," said Gai. "I'll sneak in there before we all load up in the commuter van tomorrow."

"Having it with us is a smart idea," said Zephrum.

"You're probably right about the Leviathan living in southern waters and all," added Gai. "It's going to be so cool to see our array in action, huh?"

"For sure," said Zephrum. "It's going to be a great day."

"Totally," agreed Gai. He looked into the distant eternity of the night sky. "A great day, for sure."

Deep within the goblin caverns, Virgidous was gazing into the crystal ball he had taken from the in-house goblin fortune teller months ago. He could see Zephrum and Gai talking about their upcoming visit to the ocean. He sprung up and said, "Tomorrow is our day, Virgil. We must inform the elder goblins, so they can finalize all the necessary preparations."

"Yes, sire," said the Virgil voice. "But what if we do not succeed, my Lord?"

"Oh, we will succeed, Virgil," said the confident Strasidous voice. "We have been defeated in all of our other attempts, but those attempts were mere child's play compared to what we have in store for Zephrum Gates tomorrow."

"True, sire," said the Virgil voice. "We have planned this out well."

Strasidous continued with his pep talk. "We will capture Zephrum Gates and use her as bait to lure the Leviathan to us. As you see, Virgil. Defeat fades, but regret is a lingering question mark that can haunt forever."

"We do not live a life of regret, sire," said the Virgil voice.

"No, we don't," agreed the Strasidous voice. "For all we have endured to reach this grand precipice, we will prevail. Once Zephrum Gates has helped us lure the Leviathan from the depths of the ocean, I will eat its heart and finally be able to embrace the power that is rightfully mine. And once the Leviathan has been killed by our piercing arrows, my power will grow to an unlimited potential."

"Yes, sire," agreed the Virgil voice. "All of our plans will unfold just as we have imagined."

"Yes, Virgil. Our success is assured."

—Chapter 43—

"Crisp"

Finally, the last week of school arrived. The students had finished taking all of their final tests and Malvin Moot's oceanography class got ready for their last field trip on Geezer's boat. Gai managed to grab the rowen branch from Dexter's office closet before they all got into the commuter vans. Students and teachers shuttled down to the docks and boarded Geezer's sailing vessel. They loaded up the equipment they would need, put on life preservers, and set sail into the open waters.

The skies were a beautiful clear blue and the winds were warm and steady. Once Geezer's boat reached the nearby garbage island out at sea, the Fiddlesticks students set to work putting the array around a large mass of trash out there. Some students worked from the deck of the boat, while others wore wet suits and got into the water. Students worked in teams. Zephrum and Daphne were among the handful of students who volunteered to wear wet suits and get into the water to help secure booms to the filters. They used scuba gear so that they could check on the filters from under the water as well. After installing the last boom and making sure that each one of the parts was ready, the filters whooshed to life, powered by wave energy and small solar panels.

"It looks like it's really working!" screamed Gai enthusiastically.

"Well, I'll be," said Aunt Gussie. "Your whose-a-ma-jobbies are really doing the trick."

The trash was soon moving towards the filters.

As the students on Geezers boat watched their invention get into action and remove trash from the water, Gai looked in the direction of a large wake approaching. "Hey, the ocean waves are getting really big over there on that side of the array."

The infamous globster suddenly surfaced and opened its mouth to feed on salps and ick at the surface of the water there.

Gai yelled out. "Zephrum! Daphne! Move out of the way! Quick!"

Daphne saw the globster. She ducked under one of the booms to get out of the way.

"Zephrum, watch out!" screamed Gai.

In that moment, Gai's memory flashed back to when Zephrum sat at his bedside as he recovered in the Healing Dome earlier in the Spring. He suddenly remembered kissing with Zephrum and a rush of feelings overcame him. Seeing Zephrum in real danger in the water cleared the cobwebs out of Gai's mind in a flash.

Zephrum spun around in the water just in time to see the large open mouth of the globster yawning above her.

Gai's heart pounded as he watched helplessly from the deck of Geezer's boat.

So many thoughts raced through his mind as he remembered Zephrum telling him about how she felt. He thought, "Oh no, what if she dies before I get to tell her how I remember us talking about our love for each other?"

Meanwhile, Zephrum tried to swim out of the way of the globster. She even dunked under the water again, but the globster sensed her movement and veered its mouth directly toward her. Before she had any time to think, the globster actually swallowed her WHOLE.

Gai screamed out loud. "Nooooo....!!!"

From that point on, nobody could see Zephrum's body.

She had managed to place her air regulator into her mouth before she went underwater. She somehow even missed getting chomped by any of the globster's teeth.

Zephrum was caught in a massive current going in the direction of the globster's stomach. She could not swim against the flow of the intense momentum. Her body swept down through the velvet darkness of the esophagus of the globster's throat. She landed inside the belly of the beast. She turned on her headlamp and saw the anatomy of his stomach from an inside perspective.

"Whoa…" said Zephrum, as she watched liquid and partially digested fish parts float by her. "How the heck am I ever supposed to get out of here?"

Shaking, she took a deep breath of air from her scuba tank. She looked all around and up towards the opening of the mammoth stomach. "Oh… I wish I knew how to get out of here. Who could possibly help me now?"

She closed her eyes for a moment. In her mind's eye, she saw her doggie Nomad. "Nomad? Is that really you?"

The spirt of her dog wagged its tail in the affirmative.

"Why am I seeing you here? Am I about to die?"

Just then, the image of Nomad blew a bunch of bubbles out of its nose. The doggie spirit blew more bubbles and looked up towards the globster's esophagus.

One last soulful glance and doggie Nomad disappeared.

Zephrum shook her head and then, looked up towards the globster's feeding tube. "Oh… I get it. Bubbles! I'll send bubbles up toward the globster's esophagus and it will feel so full of air that it will burp me out."

Zephrum took air in from her breathing tube and blew it out in the direction of the globster's throat. More and more air was filling the globster's stomach, but there was no sign of burping.

The meter on her tank was dropping quickly towards empty. She continued to blow bubbles into the globster's stomach, despite her doubts.

"I know. I'll try to swim up to the sphincter muscles at the opening of the stomach." She pushed on the creature's pyloric opening while she continued to blow bubbles.

A small groan vibrated from within, but nothing more.

Zephrum kept on trying to activate the globster's burping reflex. The creature finally made a deep loud echoing burp. In that moment, there was a great heave from within the globster and Zephrum got jettisoned OUT of his whole body.

Zephrum swam for her life. She was putting as much distance between her and the globster as she could. Just up ahead of her, an unfamiliar ship loomed into view. It wasn't Geezer's ship, but she didn't care.

Zephrum waved her hands above her body. "Help! Help! I'm right over here!" she screamed.

The vessel sailed closer and closer. A rope with a floatation device was thrown out to her. She grabbed it and pulled herself close to the boat. As she got to edge of the sailing ship, she saw a black bearded man with a hook for one hand. The man motioned for her to come aboard. Reluctantly, Zephrum hoisted herself up onto the upper edge of the boat on a rope ladder. The black bearded man helped her on board.

"Well, well, well...," said Captain Muttonchops. "What have we here?"

"I'm one of the students from Fiddlestick's School. We were installing our science project in the water around the nearby garbage island and I ended up getting eaten by a GLOBSTER!" Zephrum explained. She pointed towards the ocean for emphasis.

"I JUST got him to burp me out and was swimming away from him as fast as I could. I'm so glad you were here to pick me up."

"I see," said Muttonchops. "Fiddlesticks School, eh?"

"Yes," said Zephrum breathlessly. "Have you heard of it?"

"Oh yes," confirmed Muttonchops. "We've also heard of Zephrum Gates."

"Zephrum Gates?!?" exclaimed Zephrum. "That's me!"

"Oh, is it now?" said Muttonchops. His right eyebrow raised.

"Tales of your exploits among pirates are legendary," said Muttonchops. He ushered her to the center of the boat.

"Let us take you down below, to make sure you're safe."

Zephrum walked down a short flight of stairs to the cabin below deck. "Do you think you can help me find the boat with the other Fiddlesticks students on it?"

"Oh, sure," said Muttonchops. He brought her to a wooden seat in a room. "You just rest here for a bit and we'll make sure you get back to where you belong."

Then, Muttonchops swiftly shut the gated door to this room. Zephrum heard the lock falling into place. She jumped up and said, "Wait! What's going on?"

"Oh," said Muttonchops with a wry smile. "You are our first real prisoner. I'm sure we will reap a pretty penny from you. Just sit tight, little missy. Sit tight."

Muttonchops climbed the stairs that led above deck.

"Oh no. This is horrible!" She took off her weight belt and oxygen tank and tried to squeeze through the bars. Her skinny body could almost fit. She was struggling to pretzel her body through when she heard heavy footsteps coming back down the stairs.

She expected to see the pirate, but it turned out that it was something much worse.

The frame of Virgidous emerged and stared directly at her. "Ahhh... My dream come true. I finally have you exactly where I want you."

"Strasidous?" asked Zephrum. "Is that really you?"

"It's Virgidous to you, Little Miss Wind Fairy."

"Why am I all locked up? What do you plan to do with me?" Zephrum demanded.

"Oh… in all good time," said Virgidous. "In all good time."

He peered deep into her eyes. "So, it seems you WILL be helping me with my quest afterall. Doesn't it?" Bwa..ha..ha..ha..ha…

His laughter was interrupted by a large amount of scuffling and commotion coming from above deck. "Sire," screamed the pirate with the peg leg. "You had better come up here. We've got a strange situation on our hands."

"Grrr…" growled Virgidous. "A leader's work is never done."

He made his way up the stairs to the main deck.

"Virgidous," cried Muttonchops. "We believe that we've caught sight of your mythic Leviathan."

Muttonchops pointed to one side of the ship. "It showed itself in the waters just over there, to the starboard side of the boat."

Virgidous peered over the whitecaps until he saw a spikey tail rise up from the waters and sink back down below the waves. "Zeki, Did you see that?" he asked his trusty swordswoman.

"Yes Indeed, Sire," responded Zeki.

"Get the special bow and arrow we have prepared. We must aim for this creature's heart. Oh, we are so close to our wish now that I can almost taste it." Virgidous rubbed his hands together with glee.

Zeki grabbed her special bow and arrow. She saw the spikey tail swoop above the water one more time and aimed ahead of it to where she thought the chest of this great sea monster might be. She kept a watchful eye out for it. She was completely focused on her task.

The Leviathan continued circling the pirate ship.

Inside its tremendous mind, it spoke to itself as it sensed a familiar smell with its great nose through the water. "I have tracked this scent before. It is the smell of that same creature that disturbed me from my slumber in the tropical cave of my ancestors. I will pummel this creature. I will burn it to a crisp."

With that, the Leviathan sent a large fire ball above the water, aiming to hit the main deck of the pirate chip.

The blast hit with a large slam. Fire broke out at the bow of the ship, burning the jib sail there.

Immediately, the Leviathan sent another fire ball in the direction of the vessel. The second explosion shook the boat's structure to its very core.

"What's going on up there?" cried Zephrum. She held tight to the jail bars. "It sounds like we're under attack. How can I get out of here?"

She looked all around the cell and into the dark dank underbelly of the ship. She closed her eyes and wondered, "There's got to be someone who can help me, but who? Who?"

"Miss Gates?" said a gruff voice inside her mind.

Zephrum cocked her head to one side. She didn't see anybody when she opened her eyes, so she closed her eyes one more time and said, "Yes. It's me."

"Miss Zephrum Gates Creature... Are you alright?"

Recognizing the voice finally, she said, "Waylon...Is that you?"

"Yes, Miss Gates," replied Waylon into her mind. "Were you expecting another dragon? Or a different wyvern?"

"Waylon!" cried Zephrum. "I'm in trouble. I've been captured on a boat in the nearby ocean and it's under attack. I'm stuck in a jail cell below deck and Strasidous Rowpe is here and I don't know what to do. I'm scared. Can you help me?"

"Miss Zephrum Gates Creature," said Waylon inside her head. "Keep me at the forefront of your mind and I will find you. Have no fear. You will prevail."

"OK," replied Zephrum. "But hurry."

At that moment, another fire ball hit the top of the ship. A large crash shook the walls around Zephrum as she heard screams from overhead. Little streams of water started seeping into the lower deck from up above.

Far beneath the water, the Leviathan smirked. "I feel my barrage is weakening this protective shell. It is only a matter of time before the creature that stirred me from my slumber will be a charcoal treat."

Virgidous was pacing the deck. "Pierce the Leviathan with our special arrows, Zeki."

Zeki sent many volleys into the sea, but nothing met its mark.

The Shedu suddenly came barreling through the sky. Its bullish body was aiming directly for the pirate ship.

"Abandon Ship!" screamed the pirate with the peg leg.

The life rafts on the starboard side hit the water with a splash.

The pirate with the longest beard sliced the lines that were holding life rafts on the port side. All of the pirates jumped into the life rafts as fast as they could. All except Captain Muttonchops, of course.

"Hold on for your lives," cried Muttonchops as the bearded man's face on the Shedu's bullish body came fully into view.

The Shedu slammed into the boat, narrowly missing Virgidous, but hitting Zultr Zeki at full speed. Virgidous looked upon the mess. Zeki was flattened into pieces and the Shedu's body parts were broken into bits all along the deck of the ship.

"Ohhh…" muttered Virgidous. "That Shedu was protecting the Leviathan. We must be getting close."

Showing no remorse for his dead swordwoman, he scrambled to the side of Zeki's lifeless flat body and retrieved the bow and arrow she had been using. "Now, I will be the one that pierces this Leviathan into submission."

Another giant fireball jetted onto the ship from the water. The fireball crashed a large gaping hole into the center of the boat. More water leaked below deck.

"I will Captain this ship until it goes down," cried Muttonchops bravely to no one in particular.

Suddenly, off in the distance, he saw a number of very large winged creatures approaching. There were two VERY big ones and three smaller ones. "If these creatures become part of this onslaught, I'm afeard we'll be left adrift."

Back on Geezer's boat, everyone witnessed the large fireballs pummeling the pirate ship, but they were also still searching for Zephrum.

Daphne urgently ran up to Great Aunt Gussie. "I know this might sound strange, but those fireballs look a lot like the ones we saw when we went on our vacation to the southern shore this past winter. I think the fire balls could be from the Leviathan."

She pointed towards the pirate ship. "If Zephrum is anywhere, I'll bet you she's over there."

Gai overheard Daphne and hopefully said, "You think she could really be there?"

Daphne nodded her head vigorously.

Great Aunt Gussie ran up to Geezer. "Change course, you hunk of love. Go over to that pirate ship."

"What about Zephrum?" asked Geezer.

"Don't you worry. We'll find her over there," replied Gussie.

"OK…" said Geezer. "Whatever you say. You're wearing the pants on any ship I captain, my sweet. I trust you to the depth of my rain boots."

Great Aunt Gussie gave Geezer a passionate kiss on the lips. Then, he started barking out orders to get their boat to sail in the direction of the ship being pummeled by fireballs.

From the air, Waylon and his mate and hatchlings swerved down towards the pirate ship.

The Leviathan sent one more fire blast to the side of the ship and then slammed the same side of the vessel with his mighty tail.

Virgidous stumbled and slipped into the water, holding onto a large chunk of the ship with one hand and Zeki's bow and arrow in the other. He floated in the water on the large piece of wood that had become detached from the boat in the onslaught.

Waylon opened an ancient "creature-to-creature" channel within the depths of the Leviathan's mind. "Sea Creature… I beseech you. Terminate your onslaught. Cease your fire pummeling."

From the watery depths, the Leviathan responded. "Why? And why should I listen to YOU?"

"You are endangering the wrong creature," said Waylon.

"What do you know of my plight?" demanded the Leviathan. "I am defending my honor. I can smell the scent of a creature who disturbed my slumber in my southern cave. That cave has been a sanctuary of peace that I have enjoyed for Aeons."

"She is a mere child, Sea Creature," said Waylon. "Just exploring the shore like a pup."

"Grrr...." Growled the Leviathan into Waylon's mind.

"She is pure of heart and is not your enemy," said Waylon's telepathic mind. "I am indebted to her, for she helped me find my mate of all mates, who I had been searching for...for a millennium."

"And why should I care?" asked the Leviathan in his way.

"This pup," explained Waylon, "is Miss Zephrum Gates. The evil that seeks to destroy her...also wants to destroy YOU. Do not do the dirty work for this evil... and leave yourself open to more torment."

"What do YOU know of torment?" asked the agitated Leviathan.

"More than you can know, Sea Creature," said Waylon as he circled the ocean water above the Leviathan. "The evil that I speak of, deceived me for the better part of a year, as a disembodied voice in a vat of sludge. It simmered within my lair and lied to me day after day, until the real truth was revealed."

"To lie has no honor," screeched the Leviathan into Waylon's mind.

"Tis true," said Waylon's inner mind. "You must end this evil while you can. You must resist the temptation to lash out towards the innocent."

"Grrr..." growled the Sea Creature.

"Use your strength and wisdom to see clearly," said Waylon's voice.

"And what do you suggest, Winged Voice?" asked the Leviathan from beneath the water.

"Do not mis-direct your anger onto the innocent. Instead, work towards a more lasting change," said Waylon into the Leviathan's mind.

"How so?" asked the Leviathan. "I am enjoying this pummel."

"First, let my hatchlings release Miss Gates from her confines in the bowels of this ship. It will be a good exercise for them… for their developing strength. Then, zero in on your true enemy, the being that wants to steal all of your power for himself."

"Riddles! You dragon types are forever speaking in riddles!" growled the Leviathan.

"Sea Creature," said Waylon plainly. "I speak no riddle. Scan the surface of the water to find the being that is floating upon a piece of drift wood with a weapon that flings pointy sticks. You will see that he carries the piercing sticks. He has been trying to puncture your ancient scales. He is your true enemy. He is the enemy of all life as we know it, for he has put a spell on humanity. The spell has made humans destroy our earthly habitat. They have thrown mountains of ick into our great ocean here. This enemy…he does not care about the balance of all things. He only cares about ultimate power for himself. And as you and I know, power without balance is no power at all. It is a corruption that threatens all of life and must be stopped."

"Grrr…" growled the Leviathan.

"I know that you do not want to live in the ashes of a dead ocean," said Waylon's inner wisdom.

The Leviathan bowed his inner mind to Waylon and said, "Alright, I will pause my onslaught long enough for your hatchlings to retrieve the creature you are sworn to protect. Then, I will exact my vengeance upon the creature that is responsible for the darkening of my ocean home."

Waylon looked toward his mate with a knowing nod.

He spoke to Zephrum's inner mind, "Miss Zephrum Gates Creature… My hatchlings are about to liberate you. Stay alert."

Zephrum looked up. The pirate ship was rocking around and the ocean was seeping into her jail cell. Already, she was standing in ankle deep water.

Waylon's mate directed their hatchlings to the sinking ship. She circled above the ship as the young dragons descended upon the vessel. Muttonchops stood embracing the main central mast, holding on for dear life. His eyes bugged out of his head as he saw the winged creatures land upon what was left of his deck.

The three young dragons landed on the deck and tore apart the floor above Zephrum's jail cell.

Zephrum covered her head to protect it from rubble that was coming down. Dust and sharp pieces of lumber splintered down upon her until she saw the light of day.

The jaws and fangs of Waylon's hatchlings had grown to quite a large size since she last saw them. She shrunk away from their chomping and talons as they tore a bigger opening in the ceiling of her jail cell. As soon as the opening was large enough, all three hatchling heads bent to peer inside her cell. These ferocious creatures gazed upon a frightened Zephrum and they all began to coo.

"Miss Gates," said Waylon's voice into her mind. "You must trust my hatchlings to retrieve you. They cannot speak to you as I can, but they are here to assist."

Zephrum bravely pulled herself out of the rubble and climbed up above her jail cell, to what was left of the main deck of the pirate ship. The three hatchlings nuzzled at Zephrum's body. Their nostrils spit out tiny streams of smoke. They had all grown to be twice the size of Zephrum. She could barely believe her eyes.

"Miss Gates," said Waylon's voice. "You will need to let my offspring carry you to my mate."

Zephrum looked above her head and saw Waylon's mate circling above the ship.

She remembered the message that Gai brought back to her after he came back from the goblin caverns. "You must begin to truly trust your feelings about all things. You must act on your instincts, even when faced with new and unfamiliar circumstances. It is then, that your true heart will guide you best."

"OK," Zephrum looked up at the dragon's lethal spiky wings. "I trust you."

Waylon nodded to his mate, who then directed their children. Two of the hatchlings nudged Zephrum onto the back of the largest sibling. Then, with a jump upward and a massive flap of its strong wings, Waylon's largest baby dragon flew upward toward its mother. All three hatchlings followed Waylon's circling mate.

"Miss Gates," said Waylon's voice into her mind. "You will need to move onto my mate's back, as my offspring are new to carrying weight upon them."

"Uh…" said a frightened Zephrum. "How do I get onto her back from here?"

"One of my free hatchlings will grab you with their talons and deposit you onto my mate of all mates," said Waylon's inner voice. "You must release your grip and allow them to transfer you."

"OK," said Zephrum, shaking.

"Have no fear," said Waylon's voice. "Fear is nothing but a construct of your senses. It is simply a riddle that our ancestors have left us with. You are among your kin now. All is well."

Zephrum felt one of Waylon's siblings grab at her wet suit with their talons. Then, she bravely let go of the young dragon she was holding on to. The young dragon lifted her into the air and lightly placed her onto the back of Waylon's mate. Zephrum grabbed onto the scales of this "she-dragon" the moment she landed on her back. Then, they all flew high in the sky.

"Watch from above, Miss Gates," said Waylon's voice. "You are about to see quite a show."

Meanwhile, Virgidous was doing his best to figure out a secure position for himself on the drifting wood he was floating upon. He had been slipping and sliding all over it.

"Oh, Virgil," said the stronger Strasidous voice. "My hatred for this Zephrum Gates has grown to a fever pitch." He looked around at the destruction before him. "You see how this little imp of a child has foiled our plans. She...like most of her kind... are full of disrespect and chaos. It is up to us to destroy her and to take charge of all things."

"Yes, Sire," said the Virgil voice.

Strasidous continued, "Children like her are just sacks of stupidity. Toxic vermin, I tell you. Noxious pests. Miniature gaseous meat sacks. They are inherently limited, Virgil. We cannot let their sickness take over. Zephrum Gates and her little friends are just little 'germ factories' waiting to infect us. Why can't they see the world as WE see it? Why must they be such a nuisance?"

"I know not why," said Virgil.

"I will not rest until she and all of her kind are eliminated. I will kneel upon the remains of the hull of our great ship here," said Strasidous.

Valiantly, he steadied himself upon the floating piece of wood, lifted his special bow and arrow, and pointed it to where he last saw the Leviathan.

"This is madness," said Virgil's voice.

"Not now, Virgil," said the stronger Strasidous voice, doing his best to remain focused. "We are at the edge of all we have ever wanted."

"Yes, sire," said Virgil's voice. "But we are so small and these creatures are so large. How do you expect to prevail?"

"With cunning, Virgil," said the Strasidous voice. "We will wait until we have the clearest shot and then, we will pierce our arrow into the heart of the Leviathan with exacting skill."

"As you say, sire," agreed Virgil's voice.

Now that Zephrum was safely flying above the pirate ship with Waylon's mate of all mates, Waylon gave the Leviathan one final psychic message, "Proceed."

The Leviathan sent one more fireball at the great ship and then, slammed its tail upon the deck with deathly force. Captain Muttonchops climbed higher upon the central mast of the boat, trembling as he went.

"Begad!!" Muttonchops exclaimed. "This be no child's play. Me hearties have left me marooned here, to defend our vessel til' the very end." He looked around calmly. "Ah… it was a good life…filled with riches to plunder. If this be the day that I leave this world, I welcome it. I have lived a full life on my own terms. I will face death like the warrior that I am. I will sail to the vast beyond as though it's the greatest adventure yet."

He looked down upon the rubble beneath him. "She was a fine ship, she was." He gazed upon the smoldering flames and spied Virgidous as he readied himself to shoot at the Leviathan. "Ah… What a scoundrel. He is determined to the very last, isn't he?"

Virgidous aimed towards the Leviathan's body beneath the water and shot his final arrow. The pointy stick narrowly missed the Leviathan. He swerved slightly, and watched it arrow past him. Inside his mind, the Leviathan said, "Now, I know exactly where my enemy is."

As he raised the whole of his head out of the water, a swirl of wind formed from the ocean's turmoil. The Leviathan's emerald green eyes penetrated into Strasidous like jewels from beyond time. His great snout chuffed heavy hot air. Glaring, he then sent one poignant psychic message to Strasidous. "And now, you dieeeeee! Raaarrrr!" The Leviathan roared such a large stinky roar that even the people on Geezer's boat could hear it from a distance.

An enormous fire bloom blew out of the Leviathan's great mouth and singed Virgidous to a crisp, leaving only mere fragments of his body to sizzle on the floating wood.

Then, as mysteriously as the Leviathan appeared, he vanished deep beneath the waters.

Zephrum couldn't believe her eyes. She had never seen anyone burned alive before. It was a truly frightening sight. The remains of Virgidous' body were still bubbling, as they fused themselves to the slab of wood from his ship.

"Miss Zephrum Gates Creature," said Waylon into her mind.

"I see your people approaching via another sailing vessel. My mate will bring you close to the boat and one of my hatchlings will drop you upon it."

Zephrum nodded. "Thankyou Waylon. Thank you for coming to my rescue when I really needed you."

"Of course, Miss Gates," said Waylon into her mind. "We are deep friends, so we will always assist one another when we are most in need. This is simply the way of things. In this fashion, we always act in accordance with our heart's dictates. It is an honor for me to know you, Miss Zephrum Gates Creature."

Zephrum nodded. "I really didn't know what was possible or how you could ever help me. Nobody in the world would have ever thought I could be helped in all the ways you helped me today."

"Oh, Miss Zephrum Gates Creature," said Waylon. "Do not let the world define what you're capable of."

"It was just my instinct to reach out to you," said Zephrum.

"Yes," growled Waylon's wisdom into her mind. "As it was mine." He breathed deeply from his bellows and said, "A moment of piercing clarity comes only rarely."

There was silence between them for a palpable moment.

Then, Waylon said, "Get ready, Miss Gates. One of my hatchlings is upon you."

One of Waylon's baby dragons grabbed at Zephrum's wet suit from the back of Wayon's mate of all mates. The hatchling flew her above the main deck of Geezer's ship.

Gai watched in awe and anticipation. He knew that this was not the time to talk about his memory returning, but he really wanted Zephrum to know how he felt. He thought, "I really want to kiss her again." He shook his head and rolled his eyes, "How could I have forgotten something like that? It felt so right."

Gai's attention snapped back into the present moment as he watched Waylon's hatchling gracefully dropped Zephrum in a safe spot. She landed more softly on the deck than she expected.

Great Aunt Gussie ran up and hugged her. "Oh, Zephrum. You scared the dickens out of me. You really gave us such a fright! Are you alright?"

Zephrum looked at Waylon's family as they flew off in the distance. "Yes. I'm sure that I'll always be alright, somehow."

A tear formed in her eye as Daphne and Gai and a bunch of the other kids ran up to hug her.

Zephrum mustered the strength to speak out loud. "Strasidous Rowpe is really gone this time. I saw him get burned to a crisp by that mammoth Leviathan. His remains were bubbling on a piece of floating wood from his ship. He really is no longer. We're all going to be alright now. Really."

Geezer adjusted the sails of his boat and said, "Ready about." Kids shouted, "Hard-a-lee." The large sailing boom of his boat transitioned from one side of the boat to the other. The boat was now sailing home, in the direction of Fiddlesticks.

Captain Muttonchops watched the whole scene in disbelief. He climbed down from his boat's mast and landed on what was left of the deck of his ship! "Blimey! I'm ALIVE!!! This is the stuff of legend! Oh, the songs we will sing about this great tale!"

He looked out at the slab of wood where Virgidous had been scorched to a crisp. He spoke out loud as the remains floated by him, still strangely bubbling. "Well, I guess this ship is all mine. There really is no way that scoundrel could need it now."

Muttonchops gave one last look at the bubbling slab of wood and said, "You are truly gone! Really! Ha! Ha! Ha! Ha! Ha!"

----The End----

Zephrum Gates & The Belly of The Beast

About the Author:

Tricia Riel (a.k.a. "Trish The Dish") is the author of "Zephrum Gates & The Mysterious Purple Haze," Zephrum Gates & The Strange Magical Treasure," and the full series of Zephrum Gates books. She writes magical fiction that tickles your funny bone. Her memorable characters discover wondrous solutions to insurmountable problems as they change the world, one page at a time.

Trish has been involved in creative pursuits of all kinds since her first big role as a snowflake at age 5. She has a Bachelor's degree from the Visual & Performing Arts School at Syracuse University in NY, training in Dell Arte', and a Master's Degree in Acting and Theatre Arts Production from Humboldt State University in CA.

Trish has written numerous stage plays, countless journalistic articles, & has some of her early poems published. She was involved with the performance art scene in San Francisco for many years & has also performed numerous educational plays for kids throughout the SF Bay Area. For years, she has worked as a drama teacher at "Kids on Camera" (a TV Acting School in San Francisco, CA). She has been a physical coach at "Circus Smirkus" in Vermont, at "Camp WinnaRainbow" in Northern California, "Swivel Arts" in San Francisco, at "Island Gymnastics" on Martha's Vineyard, at "Arcata Playhouse" in CA.

In addition, she has headed numerous theatrically based school programs in many other parts of California, in Rhode Island, & in many other locations. She's a yogi, a contact improvisor, & a partner-acro person.

For many years, she has been one of the main organizers for "The Humboldt Juggling Festival." Trish is a voice-over actor and has done all of the narration & voiced almost ALL of the characters for her Zephrum Gates Audio Books. She has a trapeze in her living room and she loves to work on films and travel internationally. She has the most amazing cat & a performing dog. She writes most of her books while hiking in the woods. She can also write while she sleeps.

Brandy Whisenant (Cover Artist)

Brandy Whisenant (pronounced "Wizz-nant") has been a professional artist for 25 years and was a very competent scribbler as a child. She currently resides in Las Vegas, Nevada, where she continues to paint and build wonderlands, to both the delight and apprehension of her family.

Graphic Artist, Kelly Karaba
(a.k.a. "Kelly Compost," Hugh Johnson)

Daughter of a screen printer, Kelly has been an artist and graphic designer since she was very young. She grew up separating colors, cleaning up artwork, and making art "print ready" on the computer for her dad. She also printed her own designs. In school, she pursued science and the arts. She got a degree in natural resources, graphic interpretation, studio art, and environmental science. Kelly is a graphic designer and helps her friends and clients make logos, brochures, newsletters, interpretative signs, book covers, and more! And she still loves to help her dad in the print shop!

www.ingramcontent.com/pod-product-compliance
Lightning Source LLC
Chambersburg PA
CBHW070201260626
47160CB00002B/411